THE
WATER
THIEF

THE WATER THIEF

BEN PASTOR

THOMAS DUNNE BOOKS
ST. MARTIN'S MINOTAUR ❧ NEW YORK

This is a work of fiction. All of the characters, organizations, and events portrayed in this novel are either products of the author's imagination or are used fictitiously.

THOMAS DUNNE BOOKS.
An imprint of St. Martin's Press.

www.thomasdunnebooks.com
www.minotaurbooks.com

Book design by Gregory P. Collins

Water texture copyright © Mayang Murni Adnin, 2001–2006

ISBN-13: 978-0-312-35390-2
ISBN-10: 0-312-35390-1

First Edition: February 2007

10   9   8   7   6   5   4   3   2   1

To the innumerable creatures, wild and tame,
killed for sport throughout history, and to this day

ACKNOWLEDGMENTS

As most writers, I owe much to many people, too numerous to thank individually. Because of the love for antiquity they kindled in me, in this case I would like to express my gratitude to the internationally renown scholars I was fortunate to have as my teachers at the Università degli Studi La Sapienza of Rome, especially Achille Adriani, Giovanni Becatti, Ferdinando Castagnoli, Margherita Guarducci, Massimo Pallottino, and Romolo Augusto Staccioli. *Gratias vobis ago.* To my literary agent Piergiorgio Nicolazzini and to the staff of St. Martin's Press: thank you. Also, a debt of affection to Hadrian, Marguerite, Federico, Yukio, and the Boy.

AUTHOR'S NOTE

"To Diocletian Augustus, his Aelius Spartianus, greeting." In the introduction to *The Lives of the Later Caesars,* classical scholar Anthony Birley thus quotes one of the authors of the Historia Augusta. This IV century CE compendium of imperial biographies, translated and richly annotated by Birley, derives in turn from previous historical works. Of Aelius Spartianus, we know close to nothing. With Sir Ronald Syme, I like to think he might have been a soldier, an erudite, and a collector. The story of this investigation is fictional, but the historical characters and the incidents of their lives are based on biographical truth.

Antinous was from Bithynium, a town in Bithynia, also known as Claudiopolis. He had been the emperor's favorite and died in Egypt, either by accidentally falling into the Nile, as Hadrian writes, or—which is the truth—by being offered up as a sacrifice.

—Cassius Dio,
Epitome of Roman History, Book LXIX

All these things, in truth, never happened. Yet they will exist forever.

—Sallust

THE
WATER
THIEF

PROLOGUE

Y ou may call me Spartianus. I was born during the reign of Aurelian, restitutor exerciti at Castra Martis, in Moesia Prima, then called Moesia Superior or Dacia Malvensis. I grew up at Ulcisia Castra in Valeria, then called Pannonia Inferior, where my father served with the Legion II Adiutrix, and rose from the ranks to attain the position of tribune, that is colonel, of the Schola Gentilium Seniorum, Crack Regiment of the Senior Confederates. My aunt Mansueta, having through warfare become a widow, was taken as a wife by the dead man's brother, and this is how, through her second marriage, she is to me aunt and mother, and I am—as it were—my half-sisters' and my own first cousin. We are of Pannonian stock, but— as my name Aelius suggests—ever since the reign of the deified Hadrian my family has had ties with Rome, first as slaves, then as freedmen, and finally as free men. My paternal great-grandfather Aelius Spartus be-came a citizen under the rule of the deified Antoninus Caracalla, when citizenship was extended throughout the empire.

As expected of one of my birth, I was trained as a cavalry soldier. Thanks to my father's good name and accomplishments I was directly commissioned with the rank of protector domesticus, officer of the

Guard, at the age of nineteen, and saw action against the Saracens during the Syrian campaign. Before the age of twenty-two, given my disposition naturally inclined toward study and an inherited attitude for the res militaris, I had already been promoted to praepositus Vexillationis Primae Pannonicae, commander of the First Pannonian Regiment, in which position I served under our Lord Diocletian Augustus in Egypt, when the rebellious Domitius Domitianus and Achilleus were defeated. This was nearly eight years ago, and between then and now I also served with our Lord Galerius Maximianus in the victorious second Persian campaign (which we began by traversing Armenia), as praefectus alae Ursicianae, colonel commanding the Bear-Standard Cavalry Regiment.

My latest assignment has been as commander of a thousand-man cavalry wing attached to our Lord Diocletian Augustus at his headquarters and capital of Nicomedia. Presently, having all along continued my studies, I am being afforded for a time the opportunity to lay down the sword for the pen, in order that I may take up a narrative of the lives of those who were called by the name of caesar, princeps, or augustus. As tribunus vacans, colonel on special duty and imperial envoy, it is with gratitude to our Lord Diocletian Augustus that I prepare myself to follow this new course in my life.

PART I

The Emperor and the Boy

FIRST CHAPTER

Aspalatum, Dalmatia,
15 May (Ides), Monday, a.d. 304

The pounding of mattocks and mallets followed Aelius Spartianus as he entered the compound, so much like a military camp that he wondered whether all of them, from the emperor to the last recruit, were so shaped by their duties as to think exclusively in those terms. The foursquare shape, secure and solid, to be multiturreted in the end no doubt, enclosed him with the old safety that held in without dwarfing, although its perimeter must be a mile and half at least. At once the impeccable seaside sky was locked into a rectangle of sun-filled brightness above, run by swallows and quarrelsome gulls.

"Your credentials, Commander." A noncommissioned officer held out his hand, and when Aelius obliged, he saluted and let him pass.

Against the massive perimeter walls, some of the apartments in the imperial compound had been built already, and from what it seemed, a series of arched courtyards would dissect the floor plan soon. Freshly hewn limestone cornices, pedestals, and steps lay orderly according to their kind, numbered and ready to be fitted.

"Commander, may I see your credentials?" Same uniform, another face, another proffered hand.

"Here."

Aelius was curious to see that every square piece of land not specifically taken up by the workers or their tools, was carefully tended and watered, and even without much familiarity with gardening, he could tell it was cabbage that grew in neat, pale green rows.

"Soldier, who put these here?"

"His Divinity."

"The cabbage, I mean."

"His Divinity planted it."

Having presented his credentials to a third guardsman, Aelius walked past the vegetables and between heaps of ground pumice stone, lime, and sand, smelling cement being mixed. Columns lay side by side just ahead, more stacked stone. For the past twenty miles—that is, from the turnoff from the main road, where a path led to the quarries—he'd overtaken ox carts laden with squared and dressed blocks, local tufa, and a cream-colored stone meant perhaps to highlight the facings of the court. Bricks were arriving, too, by the thousands, and Aelius had asked the soldiers escorting the mule pack how far they'd come. "Aquileia," they'd answered, though of course they must have picked up the loads at the harbor of Salonae up the road, if not immediately across from the building site.

In what would likely become the second courtyard, a matter-of-fact, balding secretary halted his progress. His Divinity was inside, he said, overseeing the laying of pipes in the baths, so he should wait here. "Just get in line." He handed him a chalk disk with a number. "When I call your number, follow me inside."

Aelius looked at the number, which read a discouraging 36. "Very well. Is there a place where I can spend the night?" he asked.

"You can check with the barbers outside the gate. They rent cots on the side."

It was common knowledge that Diocletian did not care for curls and bangs, so that barbers within the environs of whatever imperial residence he happened to be in, made a small fortune by promptly shearing off the locks of those who arrived fashionable, but had to enter the precinct dismally traditional. Even here, one could tell by the pale swatches of skin on their necks, how the fair Batavians and Swabians serving on this or that general's staff had had to submit to shearing. As in Aelius's case, they were here for official business, and waited their turn in the courtyard alone or in small groups, talking under their breath in their native language, or the army Latin familiar to all. The round felt army cap, dark red, common to all ranks but for the quality of its knit, stood planted like a cork on the head of some, pushed back from the forehead on others, slightly cocked to the side on most, as the song went:

> *You'll know us by our jaunty caps*
> *Tipped to the side, eià eià*
> *You'll know us by the steely swords*
> *Hung at our side, eià eià!*

Spotted dogs—they were the emperor's own, bred at Nicomedia—ran freely on the grounds, sniffing and playing, collar-free and friendly. The story was that Diocletian had trained them to smell perfume on his visitors (another of the things he did not abide), but even though Aelius knew it to be a tale, still there were those officers who stopped by the closest facility before walking in, and washed their faces and necks to remove the reek of scent and bath oil.

Aelius was about to retrace his steps to inquire about lodgings when, by the way the men in the courtyard turned and stood at attention, he could tell the imperial retinue was in sight. Indeed, Diocletian himself was looking out from an unfinished doorway to the side. "Ha!" He called out. "My historian—come, come! Let him through, boys; he's my historian, just in from Nicomedia. Aelius, how are you coming along with the drowning of the Boy?"

The words were shouted, which created an effect. Aelius knew what Diocletian meant, but was surprised that he should recall the subject of their last correspondence. The death of an imperial favorite nearly two centuries earlier was hardly of interest to anyone but a researcher. He said apologetically, passing between the rows of frowning officers who'd have to wait even longer now, "It's the least clear episode in the life of the deified Hadrian, Your Divinity."

"Well, you'll have to say something about it. If it was an accident, you have to say that. If it was murder, then you have to say that, too."

"The sources are ambiguous, Your Divinity." Having come within a few steps of the emperor, Aelius greeted him showing the palms of his hands, slightly cupped, resting his forehead against the fingertips.

"The sources might be, but the Nile is not." Diocletian laughed at his own joke, waving him closer. "It happened there, so you'd be well advised in traveling to Egypt, all the more since there are things I want you to look immediately into."

This was altogether news.

Within moments they were walking toward the other end of the compound, far from the waiting visitors. Diocletian looked well, carrying his bull-necked and tanned sixty years on a solid pair of legs. "Well, I figured it was high time for me to have a house," he was saying. "After all, a house I have never really had. A palace is not a house, and as for Rome, the whole damn thing is a palace! You may quote me, for all this calling me *domine,* a 'lord of the house' I have not in fact become until now. And as you can see, bad habits die hard. The military camp follows me in my own house; I had to design it in a way that was comfortable for me." That this was the same man in the presence of whom one *adored the Sacred Purple* was difficult to believe. Diocletian had an old tunic on, threadbare at the elbows and stained here and there. On his head, as in his old military days, hair stood short and straight, an enlisted man's haircut. Even his boots were army boots, scuffed and worn, and the left leg of his trousers hung out while the other was tucked in. "Palaces are not efficient. In the army, it's all square angles: no fumbling about, no wondering where it's at. It's either here, or there. So, as the imperial pensioner I aim to be eventually, I get to have my own kind of quarters at last. They tell me diplomats and such will look down on the vegetable patch, but if I want to grow cabbages by the window, by God, I will."

Aelius agreed promptly. "There's a lot to be said for growing one's own."

"That what *I* think. Have you seen the north gate? You have to see it. I'm showing it to everyone who comes. All the gates are going to be beautiful, but the north gate is special, my *golden gate*. I'm going to have four statues on top of it—me and the three others—and cornices and consoles and plinths and niches and all that. It all looks big but it isn't, you know. You could fit it six times or so inside a full-sized legionary camp."

The sightseeing continued, and as he listened to the emperor, Aelius Spartianus discovered that traveling here held its own melancholy for him. He'd gone around with the army so much, he, too, hungered for a place to call home, though he had no clear idea of what "home" might be, since army camps and officers quarters were really all he'd known. In that sense, being requested to start his book with a biography of the deified Hadrian intrigued him, because that ruler had done nothing but travel for years on end. And, having come to the only place that—as far as Aelius's readings to date showed—he could call "home," he'd named its many buildings after the many places he'd visited. As if, even at home, he needed to feel that he traveled. Which of course might also mean that, everywhere Hadrian had journeyed to, he'd been thinking of his Tiburtine home. It was this disquietude and this longing that allowed him to discern Hadrian's nature, which in every other sense—its cruelty, its fickleness, its obsessive love for the Boy who'd drowned during a pleasure trip along the Nile—was so different from his own. Ever the soldier, he made ready for the travel as soon as he left the emperor's palace.

Antinoe, also known as Antinoopolis,
Heptanomia Province, Egypt (Aegyptus Herculia),
6 Payni (1 June, Thursday), 304

In the eight years of his absence, Egypt had changed the way a mountain changes when a grain of dust is removed from it. Since landing at Canopus on the Nile Delta, all the way through the temple-dwarfed, tourist-ridden, named-after-animals cities of Leontopolis, Crocodilopolis, Oxyrhynchus, Cynopolis, he arrived in the city named for the dead Boy nearly eight generations ago. The river was already in flood at the First Cataract, they told him, and was expected to break through it and other such dams before reaching Antinoopolis in a couple of weeks, at the healthy level of eighteen cubits. So as not to contravene local superstitions, for the last forty miles Aelius had foregone traveling by water, leaving the well-rigged navy launch that battled the current like a shuttle through a rebellious weave.

Everything along the river was old, old, old. The world itself seemed to have started here.

It was the weight of the ages that he most remembered about Egypt. All was overshadowed by it, so that for all its being a land so dry and sun-drenched, still the past cast across it a long shadow of incomprehensible or only half-understood antiquity. His campaign days here had been like serving anywhere else: an objective to be reached, the means to do so, and going at it as by training and temperament. He had been busy meanwhile, and put them out of his head. Yet, then as now, place names haunted him, the slow procession of riverside villages enormously ancient, choked by sand at the back, with their outlying measly oases where shade was as precious as water. Crocodiles still sunned themselves openmouthed, and the murkiness of the river itself remained—today as it was eight years ago—more treacherous and unnerving than the seas one had to cross to get here. He remembered the swiftness underwater of the reptiles that moved like hideous living driftwood, and bore the name of gods, their lumbering advance on the ground, divested of the means that gave them speed in water and made them conquer; their sleeping in the sun looking for the world like this country, grizzled and hard-skinned, immensely powerful if only one let one's guard down, not to be trusted, intriguing, and divine.

At the command post none of the recruits knew him, but rank and uniform—not his being here to study history and the mysterious death of an imperial lover more than a century earlier—ensured that all appropriate deference was shown to him. The head of the unit was away, so Aelius deposited his credentials with his adjutant and headed for his quarters; these, he had already picked out across from the city mall, a vast ground-floor flat with everything in it, including private baths. And it so happened that as he prepared to leave the command post, the officer of the day should meet him at the entrance. "Aelius Spartianus?" he half-shouted in recognition, staring him in the face. "It's Gavius, old man! Why, it's good to see you! What are you doing in this neck of the—and what's happened to your hair, for crying out loud? How do you mean, 'gone gray'? You're younger than I am!"

They embraced, clumsily, in the crowded space of the street. "Well, it's gray." Aelius smirked. "At first I thought it was just bleached from the sun, but there's no fooling myself."

Gavius Tralles led him back inside by the arm, and preceded him down the hallway. A brother officer from the days of the Egyptian campaign, he was, like himself, an army brat of Pannonian descent. Light-haired, yellow-eyed, with the build of a wrestler, he looked much as he'd looked years earlier, good-natured, perennially in need of a shave, ready to laugh. "Welcome to Tau country." He glanced back, using the army slang that described Egypt by the T-shape of the Nile and its delta. "You're here on official business, no doubt."

"Partly, yes."

"A-ha! It's the Christians, isn't it?" From his friend's silence, Tralles seemed to recognize the inopportune nature of his question, and corrected himself. "Well, you're not here to sightsee."

"That, too." Aelius kept his eyes to the brightness of the window at the end of the hallway, that made the command post look dark even at this hour. Politely, he mentioned his history project, and neutrality returned to the conversation.

"Really?" Tralles sneered a comment. "And you start the list of emperors with a faggot-lover first class? But then they mostly were, those old crowned heads. So you did not joke in the old days when you said you wanted to be a historian."

Together, they walked out to the inner court, and across it to the regimental chapel, for the little ceremony of sacrifice to the gods and the unit standards. "It isn't exactly what I said." Aelius faced the altar, gathered a pinch of incense, and tossed it on the brazier. "What I said is that I meant to write about history. What's the *difference*? Claim to greatness, for one."

For all the perfunctory nature of their visit to the chapel, they were both religious men, and a few moments of devout prayer followed. Then, "Let's go get a beer," Tralles spoke up.

They did, and as at the officers' club there was scarcely anyone given the midmorning hour, Tralles secured plenty of drink and snacks for their table. After catching up with one another on acquaintances and assignments, the conversation widened to gossip.

"Do you remember Serenus Dio?"

"No."

"Yes, you do. Used to run provisions to the post. From Zeugma."

"I don't remember him."

"Tall, Aelius—hatchet-faced, a slight stoop—used to sell books on the side."

"Ah, yes, yes. What about him?"

"He died." Tralles chewed on nut meats, having called for more barley drink. "Was coming upriver from some property of his, in the neighborhood of Ptolemais. The story has been all over town for the last two days. The crew became curious when he didn't emerge from under his tent in the morning, and they checked on him. Serenus wasn't there. No one had seen him after he'd retired, and it was about twelve more hours before they found him on the shore a bit down river, by a potter's shed. The crocodiles must not have been hungry, because they left most of him intact."

"I see." Aelius cracked two walnuts against each other in his palm. "He could have fallen off."

"Nah. He was killed."

"What makes you say that?"

Tralles took a swig, and rinsed his mouth with it. "You really do not recall him, then. He was terrified of drowning while on travel, seeing that he couldn't swim. His personal boat had high railings on all sides, to make sure he wouldn't accidentally lean too far over."

Now that he heard the details, Aelius remembered the merchant with the acidulous voice, a man who'd moved mountains of food-stuff and fodder and provisions of all kinds during the campaign against the rebels. He dealt in rare books as an avocation, and Aelius had ordered from him copies and originals, spending half of his yearly bonus on them. Twice he'd had Serenus bring him volumes from war-torn Alexandria, where the dealer knew all the little copyist shops attached to the library, from which obscure historical tracts not in circulation could be commissioned. Serenus's boat—whenever he traveled by river, which wasn't often, but still remained the fastest way to go up and down Egypt—had such high bulwarks as to resem-ble a box with oars and sails.

"So," Aelius thought he should ask, "who would gain from his murder?"

"That's the oddest part. To all appearances, no one. His finances were in order, but I heard that a stipulation in the will—since he had no heirs—states that in case of suspicious death, all assets will be frozen indefinitely. Folks who're afraid of water shouldn't be sailing, you'll say. But doesn't the will sound as if he was afraid of being done in?"

Aelius was still thinking of the legal aspects of the inheritance. "Unclaimed real estate and cash would eventually end up in the Roman fisc."

"But it could take years for the tax men to hunt down his invest-ments, and he surely had plenty of undeclared revenue. Of course his lover, friends, and business partners are rushing to point out that they couldn't possibly have anything to gain from doing him in. They're weeping and pulling their hair even as we speak, and not only because they lost a dear associate."

"Money isn't the only thing one may gain from disposing of somebody."

Tralles finished his drink, and craned his neck to look into his friend's glass. "Right you are. That'll be for the authorities to figure out. Are you going to finish that?"

Aelius was not fond of Egyptian beer, and pushed the glass over. "Go ahead."

"Thanks. What about Anubina—did you go to see her?"

Mention of his great physical passion of a few years back made him ache a little. "No," Aelius hastened to say, "but I inquired. Married. Has children. What about you and Cosma?"

"Oh, it's been long over. Likes being a widow, so there wasn't much of a chance of her asking me to marry her. I got along with her son well enough, so it isn't as though we couldn't have made it work for us. I was ready to settle down, so I married someone else. And you?"

"I came close, a couple of times, but no."

"Last time I saw you, you were bedding Constantius's put-away concubine."

"Helena? It's long over."

"I bet. Subemperors' girlfriends are trouble."

"Yes, especially when they have ambitious and obnoxious sons."

After leaving the officers' club, Tralles insisted on accompanying him to his quarters. Beyond the roofs, to the south, the mirror-bright sky had grown slightly flushed, and the wind had picked up enough to cause awnings to vibrate and door curtains to make snapping sounds. "Sandstorm coming," Tralles muttered. "Must have been waiting for you."

In the street, Aelius overheard Serenus Dio's name, fragments and snippets of conversations in Greek as he and his friend walked past vendor stalls and doorways. ". . . he'd been to court not too long ago, on account of some local dispute. I heard it at the baths, but to tell you the truth I didn't pay attention," and, "I had dinner with Serenus the week before. Who'd have thought?"

"I told you it's on everyone's lips," Tralles said. "Historian that you are, if you're interested I can put you in touch with the best gossips in town."

Around women's ankles, the wind caused their gauzy green and blue skirts to whip and flag, and Aelius glanced at those passing flashes of color. "No, no. I'm not interested in the least, thanks, I have other things to do. It seems at any rate a matter of getting the truth out of the boat's crew. Clearly it is in its midst that Serenus's killer is to be found."

"That's what I think. Thanks to the laws of the deified Hadrian, the sailors—all slaves of his—haven't been automatically strung up by the neck, as they probably deserve. As late as yesterday they were still vouching for one another. A little roughing up in jail ought to effect results before long."

Not so leisurely—as both men were still in the habit of walking at a good pace, and keeping step besides—they reached the end of the mall, and crossed the street to the entrance of Aelius's flat. Extending from the cornice on the façade, awnings stretched like a cool piece of evening, although it was close to midday. The wind abated as they stepped under the shade and took leave from one another in the doorway.

"Don't be a stranger while you're here," Tralles recommended in good humor. "You know where to find me."

In his flat, provident servants had readied the small plunging pools in the baths. Aelius decided to take advantage of a quick scrub in lukewarm water, and relax while reviewing the paperwork pertaining to his official duties.

The province-wide crackdown against the Christians, long expected, was to start in earnest: Tralles had seen through his assignment well enough. Along with Diocletian's letter, spelling out his orders, copies of two lengthy imperial subscripts, penned at the foot of requests for clarification and advice by local authorities, formed the basis of the information on which, as Caesar's envoy, Aelius was to act. Reading them seated at the poolside, with his feet in the water, he managed to cull from the bureaucratic padding of sentences what the petitioners (the commander of the garrison and the city mayor) were actually saying. Outward signs of unrest were still infrequent but violent; political graffiti were appearing here and there, and there was increased need for police patrols throughout the city. Arrests of recalcitrant clergy and sympathizers had begun in the countryside, several detentions might follow, and although collaborators seemed scarcer than during the last crackdown, it was too early to tell.

What were officials expected to do? The imperial replies, redacted in the recognizable official jargon of palatine secretaries, acknowledged the complex nature of religious ideology, but confirmed the need to err on the side of clemency in the proceedings, even allowing for priests and bishops "to sacrifice to the gods and be freed, to the discretion of my envoy, as was granted in occasion of the twentieth imperial anniversary in November."

Aelius read on, then put away the letters and slipped into the pool. The Christians would call it persecution, and make a big deal of it, never mind that all care was being taken to abide by every accepted courthouse rule. Still, he was to oversee a few of the trials himself, and report in writing. Submerging himself entirely in the tepid water, ever so briefly he shut the world out. Clemency was well and good, and fully in keeping with a time Diocletian himself termed *tranquillitas nostra*. Unless the armed fundamentalist branch of the Egyptian Church had changed its methods in the last seven years, personal risk in Antinoopolis would be within hours very much a factor again.

Egypt wanted to exact a price from him, again. He'd fought and won here, but the accounts between them had clearly not been settled, even though as a young officer he'd learned all he could about Egyptian history and ways before coming. From Herodotus's travel notes and the accounts of Caesar's permanence, he'd devoured the texts, down to the encomiastic, perhaps unreliable narratives of Hadrian's visit in the seven hundred and eighty-ninth year of Rome, and more. Egypt's antiquity was cumbersome and incomprehensible. He'd felt as one stepping into the footprint of a giant, measuring oneself—one's comparably poor and limited claim to culture and importance—with enormous steps taken hundreds and thousands of years before.

At the end of the Rebellion, guides had pointed out to him the relief portraits of Cleopatra, looking exactly like any other Egyptian queen on a temple wall, with her half-Roman son resembling any other young prince of the land. Aelius sat in the water, rubbing his neck, thinking how he was both attracted and troubled by the way this country made one look like anyone else, as though—smoothed out, carved into the unforgiving medium of porphyry or basalt—the human faces of power were in the end always the same, immutable because they were endowed with the same traits of native or acquired greatness. He'd considered, unlikely as it was for a cavalryman just out of a civil war, and a barbarian at that, how superior Rome was in its portraits, whose stone or bronze or clay became another self to the person they represented. Even the imperfect likeness of his father on the sandstone stela resembled the man in life more than any of these ten-cubit high figures of Egyptian rulers and scribes, alike as cats are alike. Egyptian cats at that, mummified in aromatic packets like new-born babies, a practice he'd attributed to local piety and love of animals until he'd seen the priests break the necks of the creatures to sacrifice them.

So he had now come back to cruel Egypt, in whose long existence his having been away meant nothing. Out of the water, Aelius began to dry himself methodically. *He* had changed. Disquiet—it was hard to give another name to his unease—accompanied him here, a need to find out about things, turn stones over to see what lurked below, or part the weeds and peer into the brushwood, whatever metaphor indicated his need to have answers. Surely, he was here on official duty and to pursue history, and Serenus Dio's death meant nothing to him, but there was a personal dimension to this trip as well. He had heard once that in the end the traveler is always looking for himself, and if he's fortunate he discovers parts of his own nature wherever he goes; even as Odysseus did, who had confronted his vices and virtues and desires and gone beyond all those to go home again. If not, his travels served him nothing.

Elsewhere in the well-appointed flat, Aelius heard the servants rush about and begin to close shutters and doors. There might be meaning in the fact that he had, as Tralles joked, arrived at Antinoopolis on the day of a sandstorm.

8 PAYNI (3 JUNE, SATURDAY), 304

The sand blew all evening, and all night, and the day after. On the third day, the sky was clear once more, and the Nile flood two days closer. Brooms were clearing doorsteps all over town when Aelius met the local commander—just back after a holiday in the Delta—and handed him sealed imperial orders from Aspalatum.

With more gossip to report, Gavius Tralles met him in the command post's courtyard. Two of Serenus's sailors had hanged themselves in jail, whether because they had something to hide or because the *roughing up* had been too much for them. "I was in the courthouse on account of the Christian trials starting up," he said in a knowing way, but received no encouragement on the subject from Aelius. "Well, anyhow, it was there that I heard the news about the merchant's sailors, and met his friend—his *pal,* you know—in the lobby. He told me that Serenus had something for you. I don't know what, he didn't say. If you want to, send for him, or you can go and ask him directly. Goes by Harpocratio, though his Egyptian name is Petesuchus. They still live at the fourth mile of Hadrian's Way, by the linen manufacture—the *nice villa.*"

It was just like Tralles to emphasize names of places and people he assumed others should know and remember. Aelius had not even known Serenus had a male lover. "Why would Serenus have something for me?" he asked. "I hadn't seen him in years."

"Search me. Maybe it's a book."

The possibility was intriguing. Having declined a morning beer, he left Tralles in his office and headed for the mall bookstores and antiquarian market, seeking—to no avail—rare or noncirculated material on the deified Hadrian. He then stopped by the priests' house in the annex of the temple to the deified Antinous. Here, he set up appointments for the research visits he intended to pay to the various shrines, their libraries and collections.

It was close to midday when he decided to follow up on Tralles's piece of information. He left town by the monumental east gate, and having climbed the cliff called the Antinoan ledge past the hippodrome, he rode without haste along the lonely, handsome road Hadrian had built to link Antinoopolis to the Arabian Gulf. Burials of Roman soldiers, a couple of them in the shape of small pyramids on high plinths, flanked the road, and there was a wayside miniature shrine to the Boy as well, paid for, as the inscription read, "by the piety of the officers of the Alexandrian Fleet."

Shortly before and to the left of the fourth mile marker, a lush, walled jubilation of cultivated trees, and the manufacturing plant beyond, identified Serenus's property at the end of a shady graveled path. Out of what he'd selectively tried to forget about this place and these days, Aelius noticed he recalled minute visual details about corners, walls, gates, as if in his recollection the small things were more important and more revealing than the large ones.

He'd actually come here to see Serenus Dio a couple of times, when the books set aside for him had been too rare or too many to take to the army post, or he'd wanted to take a look at them in private. He recognized the garden gate with a blue tile threshold, the way dust from the road, desert dust, and small pebbles made it gritty under one's feet when one entered.

Serenus's *pal,* as Tralles had called him (Tralles had no patience for homosexuals, as he had little patience for anything that did not fall within the parameters of what he knew, which was the army, army posts, horseflesh, and women) met him in the garden, under an elaborate barrel vault of cane-work heavy with vines. He stood to greet him, a middle-aged fellow with a paunch, green eyes, and dyed hair, and a countenance of politely contained grief. All niceties and expressions of condolence disposed of, he did say something to the effect that a letter addressed to Aelius Spartianus at his most recent assignment, which was Nicomedia, had been deposited by Serenus Dio across the river, at the army post exchange of Hermopolis.

"It was to leave early next week with the army mail, but since you are here—we did not expect you, Commander, but it's nice to see an acquaintance of Serenus's, it really is, especially at this time—you might want to pick it up there. No, he did not tell me what it contains, but probably it has to do with books. He was more and more into books and less into army provisions, we were hoping to retire from that business altogether by next year. Now it's all up in the air, and I assure you I'm here barely holding on, like a crazy woman. It's hard, it's hard."

Aelius had learned not to say much when people began to reveal things. He was himself private about his inner workings, and acutely sensitive to the possibility of being pried into. So he kept quiet out of courtesy, but also because—it was a side benefit—silence often produced more information than a set of questions. Through the cane-work, slices and droplets and squares of sunlight created patterns on patterns out of the shade, and the white hands of Serenus's *pal* moved under them like fish under a veil of water, such as Aelius had seen in garden ponds. He was saying, his unlikely golden head bobbing a little, how hard it was to have lost Serenus, and how dreadful it was for him to have died in water when he was so afraid of it. "He avoided it all he could, you know, traveling by water. This time he could hardly do something else, since he was pressed for time. But he'd picked a most favorable day and started way before the flood, so there was no sacrilege on his part. No sacrilege."

The details came out a bit at a time, and in the end the gist of the story was that Serenus Dio had fallen overboard in the dead of night between Panopolis and a spot named Tanais-by-the-River, while traveling back from his caravan road site offices at Tentyra, Phoenicum, and Ptolemais. The crew, as Tralles had mentioned, swore no one had seen him go down, his money and things were all on board where he'd left them, including his slippers. "Can you imagine? He never went about barefooted, his feet were so delicate. He wore socks in bed, even. When his body was recovered, they found him with his legs eaten by crocodiles to the knee. I can't reconcile myself to it, I can't. It's too awful."

Aelius could not think of a time when the description of a civilian's loss had not troubled him; irritated him at times, saddened him at others, made him uncomfortable always. By the time he left the *nice villa,* he was ready for the anonymous atmosphere of the army post. There, one knew that everyone came and went, and some folks got killed in the meantime, and then one mentioned them in passing, as Tralles had just brought him up to date with the deaths the regiment had suffered for one reason or other during the last few years.

I n the afternoon, having secured a slim book of poems on Antinous's death at one of those general stores called *pantopoleion,* he set off for the army post exchange across the river. With a little luck, Serenus's letter would be easy to find among the packs of outgoing mail.

Hermopolis Magna, crowded with shrines, baboons, ape- and ibis-headed imagery and whatever else related to the veneration of Thoth-Hermes, lay on the opposite bank from Antinoopolis, and was at this time of year fairly overrun by pilgrims and tourists. The bridge leading to the venerable district capital had been built by Hadrian in the last year of his life, and spanned the Nile on both sides of a leafy island, with piers high and powerful enough to withstand the flood about to reach it. Crossing over on horseback, Aelius observed Hadrian's inscriptions to Antinous, after whom the bridge was named. The inscriptions were covered with graffiti, pious or obscene, depending on the writer's opinion of the Boy. Below, unrolling between high banks, the current raced still green, but the depth of its color already had muted from yesterday, and soon would shade into the floodborne mud yellow.

From the highest point of the bridge, the old Serapis Avenue, now Antinous Boulevard, could be seen parting downtown Hermopolis, with Central Mall Avenue intersecting it. Crowded with government buildings, shopping centers, Greek and Roman temples, the thoroughfares were still reasonably free of traffic at this early time of day, but Harpocratio had warned that by midmorning ceremonies involving veterans would begin at the sanctuary of Serapis-Nile, some sports award had been scheduled on the stairs of Antinous's temple, and the Main Shrine would be "a regular circus of fortune tellers and baboon embalmers this week, and for the next month or so."

Seven years ago, Aelius's dismounted unit had fought house-to-house in the neighborhood of the Shrine's massive wall, and the losses incurred to secure the garrison inside it had been disastrous. To this day, approaching its gate, he found the seventy-some feet of the wall looming to the right of the avenue oppressive and sad, as did the monstrous complex of the city shrine to Thoth-Hermes facing him from the threshold. Secondary chapels, priest houses, and a labyrinth of offices flanked it, the whole of Diocletian's palace would fit into this walled square twice at least, and his men had bloodied the width and length of it to overtake other Roman soldiers. Today live baboons, once more, had the run of the place. They squatted and called out, stole, argued, and urinated among their stone counterparts when Aelius left his horse with an attendant before entering the garrison command.

Inside, local recruits busied themselves with paperwork and the details of bureaucracy, looking alive for the benefit of the high-ranking visitor no doubt. The letter was found and duly handed to him, and a small office placed at his disposal for undisturbed reading. Written in Serenus's crab-lettered Greek, the message began in a tone so mundane that Aelius had to wonder why he'd taken the time to come here and read it when he had better things to do. The latter part of the narrative, however, awoke the old curiosity and an edgy, newer unease, in view of what had befallen the writer.

To Aelius Flavius Spartianus, esteemed scholar, erstwhile commander of the First Cavalry Crack Regiment of the Pannonians, good health and greetings. Having heard through the booksellers' grapevine that you were entrusted by His Divinity to draft new lives of the Caesars, and might be traveling our way soon in order to gather information on the deified Hadrian, I make so bold as to acquaint you with a find that might intrigue you. Now four weeks ago, Commander, returning by land from Cyrenae, I was approached by Berber merchants trying to make a fast sale out of a saddlebag they'd found in the Western Wilderness, along the caravan road that leads from Lake Moeris to the Oasis of Ammoneum.

I should premise the rest by acknowledging that I was always interested, as my father before me, in pursuing the fabulous remains of Cambyses's army, given the utter disaster encountered by that Persian king's blasphemous expedition to plunder the temple of Zeus Ammon and its wealthy oasis. The merchants insisted the saddlebag was Persian, but I could see at once that—though of a type unlike the present one—it was definitely a Roman army saddlebag, with papers in it. Sight unseen, I bought it for a small amount, and of all that was in it, one sealed packet attracted my interest. It was, as it turns out, a private autographed letter by the deified Hadrian, hence of remarkable antiquarian value in and of itself.

The text, addressed to a not otherwise identified Caesernius, is undated, but mentions grave matters concerning the safety of the Empire, salus imperii, *adding that a record of them has been deposited, and I quote:* "in memoria Antinoi nostri" *or* "in the funeral monument of one Antinous." *Should I hazard a date, I would suggest it was sent sometime during the months that followed the Boy's death in the early*

*part of the fifteenth year of the deified Hadrian's reign, while
he was still traveling through Egypt. As there is also an injunc-
tion to the recipient to consign this information to silence, it is
possible that loss of the letter before delivery might not have
been noticed by the emperor.*

*There is no certain answer for this, but recalling your in-
terest in things antique during the Rebellion, I thought you
might wish to see this unique piece, and perhaps decide to acquire it. If the document as described holds some curiosity for
you, please let me know at once. Ever since it has been in my
possession, one month to the day, such unusual things have
befallen me, that I am fearful for my safety. No more than this
will I commit to paper, but know that on my way back from
Libya I stopped by the oasis temple of the blessed and ever-
powerful Ammon, and the oracle confirmed my anxiety. None
of this have I told anyone until now, not even my dear friend
Harpocratio. But I have entrusted the original of the letter to
my freedman Pammychios, also known as Loretus, who lives
outside the Moon Gate at Hermopolis, on the way to Cusae,
at the second mile of the country lane that goes by the name
of Dovecotes Alley. I beg you, Commander, to let me know
promptly whether you are interested in this artifact, as I do not
wish to keep it in my possession longer than necessary. Written
at his estate in Antinoe by Serenus Dio, also known as Sara-
pion, the eighteenth day of Pachon, in the ninth and eighth
year respectively of Our Lords Diocletian's and Maximian's
consulship.*

Aelius would have followed through on the matter at once, out of curiosity if nothing else, but there was no escaping the Hermopolis
military compound without having lunch with staff officers desperate for news from outside Egypt. All were bored beyond their ability
to conceal it. One of them, afterward, led him into his paper-stuffed
cubicle and handed him a petition to Diocletian. "It would help if

you added a couple of words in my favor, Commander. If I don't get out of this assignment I will lose my mind—I can't take another year of these people and this town and this climate."

Aelius glanced at the letter. "Where are you from, originally?"

"Lambaesis."

"That's not what it says here."

"I thought that indicating a more northern birthplace I'd stand a better chance for reassignment."

"Here." Aelius gave the petition back. "You had better tell the truth, or come up with something less ludicrous than saying 'the Rhine' when you mean Africa."

The officer looked crestfallen. "As you say. I'll send the new draft to your residence for your perusal, along with some good local Chios."

It might have been only courtesy, offering to accompany the request for a favor with wine, but it smacked of provincial intrigue all the same. Specifically instructed to accept no petitions, Aelius found a polite way to refuse gift and request, knowing full well that the bribery wine would be delivered at his doorstep in any case.

By the end of the fifth hour, with the sun reaching nearly the zenith, he was finally on his way out of Moon Gate.

When he arrived—Serenus's freedman's house was a small one, recessed from the road, and this a narrow lane off the main track, which neither the noise nor the smell of the town reached—all he could hear was the clucking of chickens in the backyard. Lizards squatted on a low mud wall, brownish against the sun-baked brownish surface. From the dirt path leading to it, the house, built on a knoll that might become an island in a few days, resembled every other local dwelling: whitewashed, plain, with faded awnings shielding the windows from the pitiless light of day. For a moment, but enough to startle him, the impression was of having seen this place before, and Aelius wondered whether he'd dreamed it or seen it during the Rebellion, but the impression was gone already.

The soldier's habit was not to make noise, not to call. Although he should make himself known to the man inside, he caught himself walking so as not to be heard, wondering perhaps why there were no human sounds, no serfs around, curious that no sign of life came from inside.

He had to come as close as the swing-beam well, with its motionless bucket at one end, and a harnessed stone as counterweight at the other end, before perceiving what he thought at first to be a dog's yelping. Behind the dark blue drape hung by the door frame, the door was open, and Aelius stepped into a peasant's square room. A woman, or more than one woman, could be heard sobbing in a back room, and Aelius smelled blood in advance of walking into that second space. Less than eight years ago, on patrol not far from here, he'd taken the same careful steps, smelled the same stench. Crouching in a corner, a black-dressed, greasy-haired old woman cradled the head of a recumbent man in her lap, weeping over it. Blood and brain fragments filled the fly-ridden room with stench, and having stepped into the mess that trickled from her lap to the threshold, Aelius looked at his feet, and recognized that through this death, Egypt was violently taking him back.

I t took me some time to get any information out of the women. The old one is the freedman's decrepit nursemaid, the other two, slave girls who don't have enough sense to get out of the rain. None of them speaks Greek, much less Latin. I finally managed to dispatch one of them to fetch the owner of the farm down the road, whom I sent to call the river patrol. But aside from the fact that there was nothing to do for Pammychios, it's clear to me he surprised thieves in his house, and was done in by them."

"Well," Tralles spoke as he helped himself to roast duck, "timing is everything, even in misfortune." They were having dinner at the officers' club, where vessels and odors and people were so much like everywhere else cavalry officers congregated, Aelius felt both at home and removed from reality, as though there were a dimension of common, communal life for men like himself, and no matter where destiny led them individually, they were all bound to meet in this One Place sooner or later. Tralles tore meat from the duck's breast and put it in his mouth. "What were you doing there, anyway?"

The diplomatic untruth came out of him before Aelius thought about a motive for lying. "Serenus had left a box of books for me at Pammychios's place."

Tralles did not insist. "Well, a freedman more or less makes no difference. What's it to us?"

"It's nothing to us, but it does come less than a week after his former master's death."

"I don't see the connection. One drowned by fair means or foul on a business trip, the other was killed by robbers."

Aelius had been eating without an appetite, and now pushed the plate aside. "I know." The coincidence bothered him, that was all. No, not quite *all*, since the ancient letter Aelius had come to claim was nowhere to be found in the freedman's house, and no witnesses for a murder that seemed senseless enough. From what he could judge, Pammychios had no money to speak of. His three slaves—the two girls, spending every morning in the fields, and a boy he'd apprenticed out—were not in the house at the time of the killing. As for the toothless nursemaid, she came daily to cook his meals, and had stumbled into the blood even as he had. The farm down the road was far enough so that its owner wouldn't hear a scuffle, or cries for help. "Do assaults in private homes happen often, around here?" he chose to ask.

"No more now than they ever did. What was stolen, do you know?"

"They tell me a small silver cup the master had given him, loose change, a box where he kept deeds and documents. The usual small household items easy to remove and resell."

"I see." Tralles cleaned the meat off the duck's rib cage, looking beyond Aelius to greet someone with a nod. "There you have it. What's there to add?"

"It's not as simple as that, Gavius. The matter was planned. Pammychios had been called off urgently on the false pretense that his pregnant daughter was dying. His son-in-law, who arrived shortly after my coming, showed me the note, scratched in Greek on a piece of pottery. He said that, contrary to the news, his wife and new-born child are perfectly fine. But Pammychios had rushed off from home in a panic, and was one third of the way to Cusae before he met with the girl's husband, who happened to be coming in the opposite direction. Being at once reassured that all was well, without waiting for the young man to accompany him, Pammychios hurried back."

"So, they wanted him out of the house to rob him. Pretty smart, I'd say."

Pammychios's small property had been easy to search from one end to the other. Aelius had done it while waiting for the river police, and concluded that Hadrian's letter had been in the locked box of documents, stolen in hopes it might contain worthwhile objects. This, too, he did not tell his friend. With the flood coming, any items the thieves might discard were as good as lost forever.

Tralles saw him troubled, or else wanted to give him a lesson on the realities of Egypt. "Look, Aelius, it probably was someone the victim knew, who killed him not to be turned in. If not, there's thieves up and down the river. Water thieves, they call them. For three hundred years we've taxed these people until they squeak, and what may seem slim pickings to us—a silver cup worth less than a pair of boots—is very inviting for the average local yokel. His Divinity may have capped the price of everything, but folks' savings aren't buying shit these days." One fingertip at a time, Tralles licked the last of the duck sauce from his right hand. "How is it that you're traveling alone, anyway? I'll give you a couple of recruits, if you want them."

From the flat bread on the plate between them, Aelius tore a wedge-shaped piece, and bit into it.

"Why? Do I need an escort?"

"When you start dealing with the Christians, you will."

The first letter from Aelius Spartianus to Diocletian Caesar:

To Emperor Caesar Gaius Aurelius Valerius Diocletian Pius Felix Invictus Augustus, his Aelius Spartianus, greetings. In obedience to Your Divinity's commands, I have delivered letters and sealed orders to Epidius Censorinus, commander of the garrison of Antinoopolis, and to Rabirius Saxa, epistrategos of the Heptanomia and representative of Clodius Culcianus, praefectus Aegypti. As it is Your Divinity's wish that I report regularly in writing, what follows is the first of my communications.

We landed at Pelusium after an astonishingly brief and successful trip of barely ten days aboard the Fortuna Isiaca, *sister ship to the* Tyche *that took us to Egypt during the Rebellion and was then wrecked off the shore of Antiphrae with its million pounds of grain. Traveling by river to Cynopolis, I then continued by land to my destination. Here, as you directed, I secured quarters outside the military compound, in the Hellenium quarter of Antinoopolis. My escort, I elected to leave at Cynopolis for the moment, as I believe my work to be best accomplished without the obvious trappings of an envoy.*

Indeed, I am mindful of the dual nature of the duties with which Your Divinity entrusted me in the Heptanomia. Tomorrow I will begin a review of the measures taken to purge the army ranks of Christian officers and noncommissioned, originally scheduled to be accomplished as of the last day of last month, but still ongoing. I heard troubling reports of high-profile incidents in the Delta, where Phileas, bishop of Thmuis, just appeared for the fourth time before Culcianus. Of the latter, general opinion is that his rigor is tempered by common sense, though his patience with recalcitrant clerics may be wearing thin. Because Thmuis is what they call a titular see, its events hold importance for the Christians of Pelusium and Alexandria, so everyone will be watching how it goes with Phileas.

Ever since arriving, I have also been zealously adding to my draft of the biography of the deified Hadrian, especially with an eye to your recommendation that the truth about the death of the blessed Antinous (as they refer to him here) be ascertained, along with the circumstances that led to the rise of such discordant accounts. The priests at his temple have promised to show me artifacts connected with the incident, recovered from the riverbanks near what used to be a village or rural shrine sacred to Bes, now grown into the city of Antinoopolis.

Coincidentally, only yesterday I came close to acquiring a letter to Caesernius (perhaps Caesernius Quinctianus, governor in the East, the deified Hadrian's comes per orientem*), purported to be authored by the emperor himself, but for reasons I will detail below in the postscript to this brief, I was prevented from doing so. Your Divinity's advice as to the matter will be eagerly awaited. I am entrusting this letter to Julius Agrabanis, skipper of the* Felicitas Augustorum Nostrorum, *and veteran of the victorious British campaign, during which he served under my father's command. He is to deliver it personally.*

Ever grateful for the chance afforded me to travel, research, and write of men and things pertaining to the glory of Rome, I write this in Antinoopolis, on Monday, the fifth day (Nonae) of June, in the twenty-first year of Our Lord Caesar Diocletian's imperial acclamation, the seventh year of the consulship of Maximianus Augustus, and the eighth year of the consulship of M. Aurelius Valerius Maximianus Augustus, also the year 1057 since the foundation of the City of Rome.

SECOND CHAPTER

They were not expecting him here at all, so any gossip that—informally or not—an envoy from Caesar was in the province, had not reached the old garrison town lying only a couple of hours southeast of Antinoopolis, set at that uneasy edge between the green strip of cultivated land and the desert.

Around the garrison fort, where everything happened (from tax collecting to organization of corvees to the administration of law by soldiers—expressly forbidden—to extortion), the place was like a hundred such. A struggling community with a mixture of styles and patterns, low houses with a bright wash over plaster, the occasional upper story with narrow windows, women doing their wash in wooden pails, with goats and children trampling in the squishy mud nearby. The rare Roman-style house also looked on the street, gate, and courtyard, imported bright tiles fading in the strong sun. Not at all like the metropolis, where the *colonial patterns of being* were carefully replicated in the crowded malls, baths, book stalls carrying the newest titles, all of them with third- and fourth-generation Greeks or soldiers and officers patronizing and maintaining the economy. Here, as in the big cities, beyond the edge of sand stood the bulwarks of

ancient temples and palaces, whose walls seemed to tremble with the
heat like fabulous mountains. Tourists crawled on them antlike, risking their necks.

No hide nor hair of Christians these days. Yet the prosecution
was on.

Across from the lazy, third-rate marketplace, the courtroom had
that odor of public offices that one could never mistake. An odor of ink
made from lampblack, and of pews and chairs where too many had sat
too long in weather far too hot, filled the space. Flies must have lived in
it for generations. The presiding judge—bearing like all of them the
title of *strategos*, but being as removed from a soldier as one could—had
an ominous, hollow cough. Flustered by Aelius's coming, he emerged
from his office in a dither, and Aelius had the strong impression he'd
just pinched his cheeks hard to make them look less sickly pale.

"Why, *legatos*," he greeted him in Greek, "it's an honor, and no
mistake."

More likely, it was the most stress he'd faced in months. Under
his feverish instructions, dockets were pulled out, minutes of hear-
ings displayed without Aelius's asking. It was clear that he went about
the business of prosecution with the dogged, weary energy of an official who'd probably come here for his health, and was now all too
aware that not even the climate could save him. Punctiliously he
walked Aelius through the court records, painstakingly kept, of the
trials concluded thus far. In some cases the sentencing was referred
to Rabirius Saxa, *epistrategos* of the Heptanomia, although on one
occasion—a Christian cleric who had set the recruiting office on
fire—the trial had been moved to Alexandria, for the prefect himself
to oversee. In every case Aelius chose at random, old-fashioned and
deliberate Roman fairness had been observed, and common sense
had occasionally prevailed with no need of sentencing. Capital execution seemed rarely but evenly applied, invariably carried out *ad
locum solitum,* a given place on the road to the town dump.

"What about the military?" Aelius asked. "How much do they
interfere?"

Now that blood had drained from his cheeks, the consumptive judge looked like his own death mask. It was a loaded question, so, trying not to sound suspicious, he said, "It depends on what you mean by that." Which meant, "Why do you ask? *You* hold military rank."

Aelius caught the meaning. *But I'm not on the take,* he thought. "Well," he went on, "we're a bit out of the way, here. Does the local commander—no, let me rephrase that. Do local commanders hold court?"

The answer came reluctantly, as expected. "Now and then."

"Now and then, or often?"

"Quite often."

"What do you do about it?"

The judge averted his face to cough in his sleeve. "I?" he replied then. "To tell you the truth, nothing. Whatever time I have left, I intend to live it out. Now, as for the last six or seven generations, the military runs the show in town, here and elsewhere."

It was nothing Aelius didn't know already, but tolerance of excesses varied from place to place. In the outposts, commanders had always ruled like princelings, and soldiers were more often than not on both sides of the law. The Rebellion had succeeded for a good reason in this province. "What about the trials of Christians in the army?"

"Oh, that." The judge wiped his mouth with a crumpled and stained cloth. "The army mostly takes care of its own trials."

Aelius looked away from the traces of pink spittle on the cloth. "Must I pull each sentence out of you, *strategos,* or will you volunteer some specific information?"

"I don't see why you take it out on me, *legatos.* Why don't you go across the street to the fort, and see for yourself what's going on? There are trials scheduled for today."

"Be sure, I will. What about murders—are they frequent? I'm not speaking of random acts, or honor killings, but rather of theft-related ones. Do you sit in judgment of those?"

The judge spoke with his nose in the handkerchief. "We have a bigger territory than it seems, so—yes, there are killings, especially now that money's tight everywhere. I sit in judgment of civilian cases. For the rest—"

"—the army takes care of its own, I understand."

By the time Aelius left, the judge was in a paroxysm of coughing. Down the street, only a scattering of soldiers were on hand in the fort, a typical round-cornered small enceinte of stone and masonry, with walkways built on the roofs of some twenty quarters and service rooms. The administrative building was arranged around a dinky chapel to the genius of the cohort, *genius Turris Parvae,* to which Aelius dutifully stopped to pay his respects. Because he wore civilian clothes, the soldiers—none of them understood Latin, and their Greek was not much better—felt no compulsion to show an interest, and he was able to walk into the trial presently being held next to the chapel.

Notes taken by Aelius Spartianus during the trial of Syrion Antonius, private in the X cohort of the Heptanomian border guards stationed at Turris Parva:

PRINCEPS KARANUS, *acting as judge: Is your name Syrion Antonius?*

ACCUSED: *You know it is.*

K.: *Do you serve in this unit?*

S.: *You know I do.*

K.: *Are you a Christian?*

S.: *You know I am.*

K.: *Did you refuse time and again to sacrifice to the genius of the cohort?*

S.: *You know I did.*

K.: *Do you realize what the punishment is if you persist?"*

S.: *You know I understand.*

And so on. One of the most abysmally dull exchanges I ever heard. It ended with K.'s ascertaining how much retirement

*pay and other assets S. has. S. seems reasonably well off, and
the sentencing (illegal, as the* princeps *has no jurisdiction whatever) has been suspended. Upon promise of sending him a
good physician from Antinoopolis, I managed to pull out of
the* strategos *that moneyed soldiers get away with their Christian superstition, unless they're hell-bent on dying for the
faith. Poor recruits are out of luck, and for every one who re-
cants, two play stupid, and one goes to his death.*

*I have confronted Captain K. on the illegality of his sitting
in judgment, and he gave me a song and dance about the military being the sole guardian of virtue at Turris Parva, though
the few merchants I succeeded in approaching showed me re-
ceipts where extortion in K.'s name tops the list of their monthly
expenses.*

*Reminder to myself: Send a full report to Prefect Cul-
cianus, with triplicate copy to the imperial court. Further note
to myself: Murders are disgracefully frequent along caravan
roads, and as a result of disputes between neighbors. That's
probably how Serenus's freedman Pammychios ended up.*

On his way back, the road to Antinoopolis passed by a settlement of
artisans and small retailers not far from the metropolis' walls and
sturdy south gate. The settlement's glorious name was Philadelphia,
but apart from a badly kept chapel dedicated by the deified Trajan to
his sisters, there was no other sign of *brotherly love* that Aelius had
ever been able to find. Except, of course, that his former lover lived in
the settlement. It was here that upon arriving in Egypt he had meant
to stop first, and look her up, but—having asked around, as he'd told
Tralles—he had decided against it.

Anubina was half-Greek and half-Egyptian, a soldier's orphan.
They didn't know exactly, but she was around twenty-six now. She'd
been seventeen or eighteen when Aelius Spartianus had met her, and
for his stay in Egypt had hired her out as his own. They'd liked one
another a great deal. He had set her up in a little house, painted blue

in and out, bought her things, had even written to her afterward five or six times. She had never answered. Not because she was illiterate (she was, but there were scribes who could do the job for her), but because, as she had told him from the start, "There is no point, and we both have other things to do."

The acacia trees were still shading this side of the street, and he remembered them in bloom, yellow and dusty-scented, with their graceful ragged shade topping the roof.

She came to open the door barefooted and with her hair pinned up, holding in one hand the brush she'd been using to scrub around the house. She saw him there, and for a moment looked transfixed, but it was just a moment and immediately she was lifting the scarf she had on her shoulders to her face, turning away a little, but stepping back to invite him in. It was surprising how there was no need of words between them, how the changes in them spoke for themselves, and had a bearing on how they would behave toward one another.

"Come in, I have food ready." This had been so much like Anubina, he felt both moved and comforted and did not question whether he should accept. The wide room received light from the door only, and the chalky blue of the walls resembled it like a square pool; a copper jar catching the sun by the wall was like a fire in the water. "Welcome," Anubina said.

Beyond the blue room, another room painted blue, which he remembered so well. It was where their bed had been, and that room had a small window on the alley behind, just enough to make one know whether it was night or daytime (the daytime, always regretted in those days). Aelius looked away from that door, and toward her. The scarf had been lowered again as she tasted food in the steaming pot.

She'd put on weight in these eight years. Her feet were still dainty, scrawled and dotted with henna, but she'd grown plump in her linen dress, and her face had filled out under the black waves of well-combed, crispy hair. Aelius looked at her only because she did not look at him, but went about putting food in the bowl, and wine on the table, as if he'd gone out this morning, and were coming back to be fed.

"Your husband?" he asked.

"In the fields." Her hands sprinkled spices, broke bread, poured wine. "How did you know?"

"I asked."

"Sit down, will you?"

It was fennel-flavored meat wrapped in vine leaves, brightened with turmeric: food he'd only had here, and longed for many times. As Aelius took his place by the table—he'd bought it for her, a Roman import solid and well-made—two children came tramping in from the street, and were at once checked on the threshold by the presence of the stranger. They stood there like restive young goats, a tall little girl with hair plaited all over her head, big-eyed, and a younger boy who wore the Egyptian braid on one side of his head, and the rest of his head shaven and bluish. The boy covered his face, laughing.

"Is he my uncle?" the little girl asked.

"Shush," Anubina said, handing them round cakes. "Go outside and play."

The children did. Having set the food in front of her guest with a half-turn of the plate, so that the meat rolls were at a graceful angle, Anubina sat down across from him. Despite her weight gain, she still had a beautiful face, and her eyes especially had lost none of the charm they'd held for him.

He said, "Have you been doing well?"

"I have. What about yourself?"

"Well." Aelius began eating slowly, without asking himself if he was hungry. Her cooking had always been exceptional, like her love-making. Food and love were so inextricably linked in his recollection of Anubina, memories of his few leisure days in Egypt were always about those two things. He was not an empty-headed young officer in those days, either, but the simplicity of that feeding of the body in two different but somehow sweetly connected ways had meant so much to him.

"Will you stay long?"

"Not very."

While he ate, for a short time Anubina's daughter came back in to munch on her cake; she sat on a stool with her legs crossed, staring at him. Then she skipped to the door and looked outside; when the noise of a mule pack clacked down the road, "Hello, uncles!" she called out, and waved to the drovers.

Aelius tasted the wine. "She's tall," he observed.

"Not that tall, Aelius."

"And what color are her eyes?"

"Like mine."

Anubina's hands clasped slackly on the table, her round forearms were still smooth. Copper and silver bracelets bound the flesh tightly; all so similar, he could not recognize those he'd given her. She absentmindedly—no, not absentmindedly, self-consciously—gathered a wisp of lustrous hair from the side of her face and pinned it back. He'd seen her indulge in that neat grooming gesture many times.

Looking at the girl leave the doorway for the street, he asked, "What is her name?"

"Thaësis, but we call her Thea."

Thaësis was Anubina's Egyptian name, too. There were constraints like veils between them, subtle and resilient, allowing them to see each other but not to slip into desire. He thought with a little shame that he'd *bought* her—that the procuress had asked him if he wanted a virgin and he'd said no, but not because of the cost. Anubina had been dancing at men's parties for six months already when they'd first met.

So now they exchanged a few sentences, as former lovers do, in the tidy space of her house, but Aelius's mind was also conversing with itself, without answers for his questions. Where did he keep his tools, this husband who was out in the fields? His cloaks? Was this the plate from which he ate? The benign talk of people they had both known, the bland statements about life in general, those were exchanged effortlessly. Her eyes rested on him with immense heifer-like calm, as though she had come to terms with everything in her life.

"How old is she, Anubina?"

"Seven."

The image of the poor judge coughing in his cloth came to him, because reticence seemed to be a part of this country as much as the acacias with their bright yellow flowers, or the old temples at the desert's edge. Within days of his coming he, too, was falling into this habit of indirect speech, and had to remind himself that historians and soldiers can never be vague. He said, forcing himself to look her in the eyes, "Anubina, are you going to tell me before I leave?"

"No."

"Why not?"

"Because it's none of your business."

Aelius looked into his plate once more. He was unsure of why he'd want to know whether the girl was his; it would only complicate things, and he had no great interest in starting to see himself as a fa-ther, albeit of a prostitute's child. "Well, it's somewhat my business," he spoke back.

"I don't see it."

"Come, tell me."

"No."

He finished his meal in silence, with Anubina watching him and saying nothing either. She was comfortably off, he could tell, and per-haps it was because of this that she wanted nothing from him—if the girl was his. She looked like her mother entirely, so there was no telling who had fathered her. As it seemed, she called all men "uncle," and was lovingly taken care of. Through the corner of his eye, Aelius could see that the sun-fire in the copper vase had been extinguished, and now it was a dull pottery jar that took in the light from the door-way, dimming it without reflection.

"Is she going into the profession?"

"No. She's learning her letters. I mean for her to do something else."

He stood up from the chair, and Anubina with him, but slowly. "The boy?"

She smoothed her dress on her belly, and he couldn't tell whether it was a fleshy midriff or she was pregnant again. "He'll do whatever. His father can figure that out."

"What about *her* father?"

"Aelius, you're not going to get me to tell you anything, so stop it."

"You have to tell me, Anubina."

"No, I don't."

"I'll be back, and ask you again."

She led him to the door, firmly, because the moment he should step out he'd be *legatos* and historian and Caesar's envoy again. "You do that."

ANTINOOPOLIS, 13 PAYNI (8 JUNE, THURSDAY)

An obsequious note from the head of the Hermopolis river patrol awaited Aelius on Thursday, as he returned to his quarters for a break from reading at the city library, in preparation for his visit to the temple of the blessed Antinous the following day. The message informed him that a box "with papers in it" had been found alongside the bank, tangled in a lotus clump at the edge of the freedman Pammychios's property. Having been identified by the victim's family, as by the esteemed commander's request he was now sharing the intelligence, et cetera. The box had been deposited for his viewing at the Moon Gate police district.

Aelius decided to see for himself at once, and before noon he was across the river and at the police station. Three soaked, drying, yet still legible papyri were inside the unpainted, four-footed wooden box: Pammychios's manumission document, a will, and a lease paper. In the head patrolman's opinion, the box had never even been opened by the thieves. "They just took it along and then, by shaking it, they realized it contained only documents, and thought there was nothing to gain from hanging on to those. So they tossed the whole thing. I suspect they were fleeing north, because the box was found downriver. But come to think of it they could have thrown it down from the other direction as well, and it'd have ended up the same way. As you can see, it's the kind of box that locks shut when the lid is lowered, so you need a key. Here, we got this from the dead man's son-in-law."

Aelius glanced at the key. It was an average, toothed little key such as one could buy or have made anywhere, so he didn't bother to ask whether it was a spare, or the only one. It was just as likely for the thieves to have taken other items from the box, then slammed it shut and tossed it.

"Has the son-in-law identified the documents, and was everything there?"

The head patrolman—he wore a faded surplus army tunic from the times of the Rebellion, and was as local, as the saying went, *as the arse of the Sphinx*—said no. "But that's only because he didn't know what was in it. It seems the victim wasn't one to tell his business, not even to his relatives."

Which was why, Aelius thought, the slave women had not been able to answer him whether Pammychios had recently met his former master Serenus or received from him anything for caretaking. "Was anything else found along the river or in the neighborhood?" he asked.

"Yes, sir. As you ordered, we set everything aside for you. Please follow me."

How had he not thought of what might be pushed ahead of the Nile in flood? The zealous patrolmen had filled a small courtyard with piles of flotsam and refuse, including the carcasses of drowned farm animals. He had the men dispose of these immediately, and then spent time alone examining the rest of the refuse heap. He was of course looking for the saddlebag Serenus Dio had spoken of, but—hoping against hope—also for Hadrian's letter itself, presumably written on papyrus, perhaps rolled inside a wooden cylinder or otherwise protected. From the door of the messhall, patrolmen crowded to gawk at him at first, but their leader whisked them away soon enough.

With a researcher's alacrity, Aelius handled rags, woven sandals, cracked wooden bowls, broken pallets, the occasional bottomless reed basket that reminded him of his old enemy ben Matthias, telling him the story of Moses found in the Nile. From the dry land, gathered in a radius of three miles all around Pammychios's house on its knoll, came another set of disparate objects, broken farm implements mostly, shards, two solitary copper coins, even a catapult projectile from the Rebellion days, with Achilleus's name on it.

"Should we keep looking, Commander?" asked the head patrolman afterward, handing him a wash basin and towel to cleanse himself. Aelius said no, but had a mind to ask others to keep an eye on the antiquarian market, perhaps through Harpocratio, for historical letters to appear, specifically concerning the reign of the deified Hadrian.

14 Payni (9 June, Friday)

The priests at the temple of Antinous sized him up, like fastidious cats sniffing a new animal to know what he's about, and whether a threat or an ally. Truly, Aelius was neither, and so neutral was his position here, officially at least, that the priests couldn't do much more than circle him and smile, half-fawning and half-annoyed, assessing him then only for usefulness, as he was Caesar's friend.

Aelius took precautions not to mention that his interest in the funerary temple had deepened since reading Serenus's dramatic last message to him. Clearly, as no official tradition of documents stored in Antinous's tomb existed, the priests kept mum for reasons of their own, or else knew nothing about it. He resolved not to inquire directly unless he ran out of oblique means of finding out. Hadn't Egyptian priests satisfied Herodotus's historical queries, some seven hundred years earlier, with colossal half-truths?

So he played the cultivated tourist, official to the core, with letters from the Imperial Court and a dash of awestruck respect for the antiquities, which could only help his cause.

For all that this was a Greek city, having been founded as such by the deified Hadrian, most everything around this temple, clergy included, seemed Egyptian. The priest house and annexes stood squarish and compact, flat-roofed, nearly windowless, with thick walls, the ever-present awnings protecting doorways and courtyards. The temple itself, at the center of an enclosed colonnade kept as a garden of shade trees and fastidious potted plants, reminded him of the island sanctuary at Philae, complete with twin obelisks. In a country where even the rich boasted, at most, of ashlar lintels and steps in their homes of fired brick, the entire construction—including the rampartlike pylons by its entrance—was of black and white marble, cut and transported from the Greek islands at God knows what expense.

"Feel free to look around, *legatos*." The priests, a fat and a spare one, addressed him in Greek, leading the way. Polite, but surely seeing him as the complete outsider that he was, ready to show him what they wished, and no more—which Aelius planned not to accept, though he was not yet sure of how to get around it. Everything pointed to the wealth and power of this priesthood: the temple had large Antinous-related revenues, from the incubation room where one waited for healing dreams to the hospital, the souvenir shops, and mummification facilities, drawing a percentage even from the sale of mummy-shaped anise and honey cakes, called *kuroi*, sickeningly sweet. The priests would tell him what they wanted about Hadrian's visit and its results for Egypt (the end of a five-year drought) and the emperor (a lover's death). They would not be easy to circumvent. As Aelius stood there, a young baboon came to sit and pick lice off his belly at his feet, and looked up at him with his dull half-dog, half-ape face.

"This way, *legatos*."

Throughout the oasislike sacred area, Antinuous's image was charmingly but obsessively inescapable. Aelius—whose only close-up view of the Boy had been one portrait during the Rebellion, and he'd paid scant attention then—had the odd feeling of seeing double, and in multiples. Boy-headed sphinxes flanked the entrance to the colonnade, and one then walked through a bodyguard of pillarlike representations of Antinous as the god Min, with a tall double-feathered headdress and an erected penis painted black. Past these, on a row of identical pedestals among blooming shrubs, copies of ancient statues made to resemble Antinous stood witness to the expensive piety of local officials.

So, in turn, the Boy held grapes, bow, spear, libation cup, as Antinous-Hermes and Antinous-Apollo, with the attributes of Mars and those of Dionysus, naked, dressed, half-clothed, standing, sitting, and striding and staring back at Aelius from glass paste and marble eyes. Not even Egyptian art could make the brooding young face less distinctive. Still, following the priests, Aelius thought how little the real person had to do with this place—and this cult. He doubted Antinous had asked for any of it, or would prefer artistic eternity to running the natural course of his life. But he was dead, long dead, and enshrined, so that—willing or not—forever this face should be familiar to those who had not known him in life.

On a windless midmorning, with the undulating crest of the Antinoan ledge so sharp against the sky as to seem a cut marring the blue, he came here to pursue history, as was his assignment. Learning about the deified Hadrian, and Antinous's death, was a tall order already. Yet, Aelius's duty already took on a different personal meaning, if Serenus had told the truth about the imperial letter. The thought that unknown papers about the safety of the State—Hadrian's State at least—rested within these walls made him desirous to possess what no historian had spoken of. It might not be true, for all that. Serenus might have been sold a forged document, or even have tried a hoax himself. On the other hand, true or not, the merchant had been frightened by something or someone, and was now dead.

After showing him through the sacred area, and requesting that he wash his hands and face in the water of a small fountain in the antechamber, Aelius was invited inside the temple itself. There, out of the reddish dark swimming before his sun-dazzled eyes, the sudden rise of the immense striding god startled him, nearly perpendicular sunlight pouring like molten metal from an overhead oculus down the sides of a massive black figure of Antinous as Osiris. The cell was dwarfed by it, made oppressively narrow despite its large size, and the heady smoke of incense wafting past really did resemble it like a forge out of which a monster had come to life. On second thought, and at a second look, it all regained a commonsensical reality, and it was nothing but a temple with an oversized basalt cult image in it. The priests had likely noticed his start and were satisfied.

The Boy's anthropomorphic coffin only vaguely resembled a mummified corpse. It was a massive, porphyry boxlike sarcophagus the size of two army supply carts stacked on one another, set at the foot of the cult statue; garlanded with blue lotus, roses, heaps of fresh flowers; wherever in that congeries of petals the light from above succeeded in trickling down, the petals seemed to incandesce out of the dark.

Having offered a sacrifice and expressed appropriate sentiments of respect, Aelius asked general questions, among which he placed the one he really wanted answered. "Has the body been here since the beginning?"

The fat priest nodded. "It has. The deified Hadrian oversaw the ceremony himself, on the sixth day of the month of Tybi."

A rapid calculation on Aelius's part gave him the day before the Ides of January following the drowning on 24 October, which would allow for the seventy days needed to mummify the body. So, these one hundred seventy-four years, Antinous had slept in this aromatic eternity. *Undisturbed,* as the spare priest added, *and gloriously watching over the metropolis.*

Which meant that Hadrian's documents—if they existed—were still inside. Aelius took notes, and followed the priests.

The hall adjacent to, and immediately behind, the temple was with some good claim termed the "collection," as in it were gathered

relics from that fateful river journey. The imperial barge itself, perfectly preserved and majestically set in the dry dock of a wooden cra-
dle painted blue, took the best part of the long, rectangular space.
The walls around had frescoes with scenes of fishing and hunting on
the Nile, and a series of armoires, open to reveal rich boxes stacked
inside, lined the room's perimeter. Aelius kept jotting down details in
shorthand, and committed much more to memory, for his field
notes. On the floor, mosaic scenes showed the edge of the desert with
its wild creatures, and a fanciful bird's-eye view of the mysteries of
the deep south, the Nubian wilds past which no one had ever gone,
searching for the sources of the Nile. The priests poured water from a
dainty ewer on the tessellated floor, to make the colors come alive.

Tralles had the good sense not to say anything when it became
obvious on that afternoon that his former colleague would sit
in on the proceedings against two jailed Christian noncommissioned
officers. Both veterans of the Rebellion, they belonged to the cohort
based at Apollinopolis, in the Thebais, but had been transferred here
for trial because they were registered in the metropolis. Busy writing,
Aelius said nothing during the trials, and after the sentencing (one
recanted, the other persisted, and was led off following the judge's
terse *caput tuum amputabo*), was not in a talkative mood. Beheading
was merciful, after all. The difference between the temple's contained,
venerable space and the efficient summariness of legal procedures
was jarring to him, having stepped from where time seemed suspended, bound by ritual, to a public room where prosecution drove
change, and order was turned upside down as rank mattered little
under investigation and interrogation.

Tralles must have followed him here, because Aelius saw him
pop his head into the door of the archives, where he'd retired to examine recent civil law dockets.

"Do you need a hand?" he volunteered.

Undoubtedly his former colleague had other things to do, but he was curious, and there was no shaking him without whipping up more interest. Distractedly looking up from the roll he was deciphering by the window, Aelius said, "You can help me look for any legally resolved dispute involving Serenus Dio."

"Are you still thinking about that? How does *that* fit in with your research?"

"It doesn't."

It took them some time. The court clerks fastidiously put everything back on the shelves as soon as Aelius signaled that he was done with them. No document bore Serenus's name per se, but he was cited in two instances. Tralles handed over the extract from a hearing dated Phamenoth 5, the beginning of March of that year. The minutes referred to a border dispute between neighbors over the illegal diversion of irrigation canals—"water stealing," as the plaintiff put it—from his property outside the north gate of Antinoopolis. Serenus Dio, who owned a wheat field adjacent to the defendant, had apparently also gained from the surplus of water.

"It doesn't seem enough to justify going after Serenus on his boat and throwing him to the crocodiles," Tralles commented.

"No, but this one is interesting." Aelius read out loud, " 'Pionius son of Alexander, presbyter of the Catholic Church, versus Eutropius, accountant in the mercantile company of Serenus Dio, the Syrian.' "

"Well, what happened, and when?"

"It's dated between the first and second edict against the Christians, and is now superseded by time and circumstances. But it seems the accountant took the rap for Serenus, unless accountants decide on their own for their employers. Presbyter Pionius's accusation is that the mercantile company acquired from the authorities the buildings and lots confiscated from his community, and 'so modified them by erecting new structures and adapting to commercial use the existing ones,' that they could never be reclaimed."

Tralles snickered. "Right! As if they ever will."

"One lot was used as a cemetery by the sect, so there's a whole piece on violation of burials and sacrilege, appealing to the law.

Eutropius claimed it was his idea, and his employer knew nothing about it."

"So, how did it end?"

"The case was dismissed, but Eutropius got a stern dressing-down from the judge."

"Ooh, I bet that scared him. Meanwhile his master Serenus got to keep Church land and buildings."

After leaving the courthouse, Aelius took the long way home, and once he began walking, he kept on until he reached the edge of town, and from there to a spot he'd known during the Rebellion. It was a green, shady field where once a small inn had existed: *At the Repose of Anthony and Cleopatra*, it was called. Destroyed during the fighting, its ruined walls had been a great place to go and kiss the girls, and he'd sat there with Anubina once until nightfall. Since then, the walls had been taken down, and grass now covered the whole swatch of land as if no inn, no Rebellion, and no kissing couples had ever existed. There was still a tall willow tree close to the bank of the Nile, and a bench under it, where Aelius went to sit.

The sluggish river water was like a green broth, with the pale strands of the willow branches coming down to it and submerging their tips, a few yellowed spear-shaped leaves eddying about ever so slowly. The silt and centuries of debris, and for all he knew, crocodiles asleep with their jaws open only a few feet below him, the sky like a burnished mirror above everything, seemed to him a perfect image of what eternity might be like. Untouched, intangible, set forever like carnelian in gold, etched like the distant mountains at the end of Hadrian's Way, where the granite for the obelisks is quarried and begins its journey to the rest of the world.

Anubina had asked him, "Why has your hair gone gray?" and he had no good answer for it. He could have asked, in return, "Why have you grown heavy?" or "What happened to your beauty?" Still, eight years are eight years in a man's or woman's life, and what happens to them, though concealed, is often worn outwardly, all the more if they do not admit within. It made him think—yes, it made him wonder, and he sat with the question a long time—whether the deified Hadrian, too, had been worn out by his duties and travels, loveless marriage, superstition, fear of incumbent doom; whether Antinous had been a young copy of himself, a portrait never aging, kept everywhere as a gently mendacious mirror, whose own aging threatened to destroy that imperial parallel existence as an eternal youth. It came to him then that perhaps Antinous had to die young, and preserve the mirror for all times.

Hadrian's own words, spare as they were, gave hints to the possibility, and what of the coins he'd minted late in his reign, spelling out *Hadrianus renatus*? What had made him be born again? The Mysteries of Greece? A cure effected in this or that temple of the merciful gods? Or the commission to eternity of his alter ego, his little soul to remain forever untouched by time, set like the silt under the river, like the mountains at the end of Hadrian's Way, where granite for the obelisks is quarried and stands up to the ages?

I t was well into the early evening when he returned to his quarters. The old housekeeper who ran the flats was a midwife by trade, and her sign, showing a woman being delivered who rather resembled a water jug, was cemented on a side entrance of the building. At this hour the warmth of day had wearied, and flights of pigeons from the marketplace glittered like silver against a muting sky. Once in his bedroom, Aelius checked the corners and under the bed for scorpions. Whatever the maids said about their sacredness, he didn't want them in the room. He found two, and after considering stepping on them, he lifted them up with a cloth, and put them out of the window.

What the short, fat priest had said (that odious singsong way of talk getting in the way of the value of the remarks) stayed with him. Among his many other charges, Antinous was the protector against water thieves. Whatever for? Because he'd died in the Nile? Because he'd turned into a water sprite? According to Tralles, Pammychios had been killed by water thieves, and one didn't know who'd done in Serenus Dio, but he had recently been involved in a court battle over an irrigation canal. None of it outwardly matched. There was no connection except for the terms "water," and "stealing." Yet Aelius felt there was a link to the mystery in those words; he smelled it as he could smell the dusty evening, and the aromatic scent of the cedar trunk where his clothes were kept.

He kept thinking of the priests this morning: how neither of them could read the ancient stones, he could see that. They singled out sets of signs and images, which at Philae or Coptos had been explained to him to mean one thing, and here at Antinoopolis appeared to mean something else entirely. He of course had no way to tell. Though the drawing of a mosquito or a phallus or a standard seemed easy enough to read, there was no imagining what a crooked line or semicircle or a square stood for. All else was in Greek, or in the half-Greek alphabet that no more resembled the sacred writing of millennia past.

Egyptian gods and temples still unnerved him, there was no two ways about it, whether it was the stuffy half-coolness of the interior compared to the scorching sun of the outside, or the darkness pierced by sunbeams here and there as by flaming spears that should burrow the floor and those passing into their trajectory. It might be, too, the statues of the beast-headed, beast-bodied gods themselves, scented like the sycamore and cypress wood of which they were made, not human or superhuman or whatever it is that magic animals are, less than man in so many ways and yet wiser, or endowed with skills men do not have.

Tonight, all the commonplaces of traveling to Egypt came to him. The prejudice of the old Romans, who saw it as a land of whores and cunning thieves, the grudging admiration of the Greek philosophers, who'd sat in these cities and spoken to the ancestors of these half-smiling priests, surely half-smiling even then. Now, as eight years before, he thought the women beautiful, especially those who had Greek blood—like the girl Anubina, whose father was a dead soldier. The girl who burned like a brazier and who'd married since, and had grown heavy and kept a shop.

17 PAYNI (12 JUNE, VIGIL OF THE IDES, MONDAY)
A religious show trial in the city courthouse was scheduled for Monday. Aelius decided to attend, and took along a minutes-taker this time, in order to concentrate on the proceedings. He also had in mind to see Harpocratio again, and sent him word that he'd be coming for a visit. Killing time before the trial, he stopped by the mall's antiquarian stalls to peruse through copies and originals of old documents and correspondence. They showed him interesting material, unrelated to his present research, but useful for future reference—namely sectarian tracts dating from the conflict between Serverus Caesar and Albinus. He also managed to pick up a booklet of riddles, purported to have been written by the deified Hadrian ("What has no arms but many elbows, and the more elbows, the better for Rome?" Answer: the Nile, whose flood, producing grain for the City, is measured in cubits; or, "What companion's departure always brings death?" Answer: the human soul; or, "What is more silent than the grave?" Answer: a grave that has been rifled, for its hidden secrets are dispersed).

The trial was a painful affair. In attendance were numbers of anti-Christian zealots, ready to create a commotion outside of the courthouse; others threateningly stationed around the building. Aelius, who had fought extremists in Egypt during the Rebellion, knew how volatile tempers became at times like this. The accused—an engineer who had designed the waterworks for the annex of the Serapeum in the old Alexandrine district of Rhakotis—had converted to Christianity as late as the beginning of the prosecution. An elderly widower by the name of Sakkeas, he now went by Pudens. His second wife and children, already dressed in mourning, over and again begged him to reconsider, and became so disruptive in their anguish that they had to be removed from the courtroom. Military escort had been provided for them (they happened to be Tralles's men), so that the mob would not attack them once out from under the magistrates' protection.

Aelius was learning the intricacies of prosecuting in a country like Egypt. The judge was a special referee sent by Culcianus, who excused himself because of his old friendship with the defendant; someone in the audience made the comment that he was actually related to the prefect of Egypt by his previous marriage. This being the third time the old man appeared before the magistrate, it was undeniable that great pressure had been exerted on him. Despite, or because of, his family connections, he had been manhandled and bruised, and spoke with some difficulty.

Thankfully, he used none of the by-now trite religious diatribes: disparaging remarks against the Caesars and Augusti, blasphemies against the gods (which always elicited an expected groan in the audience), declarations of hate for life and preference for martyrdom. Pudens stood his ground in an uncompromising but sedate way, and it was obvious that Culcianus's referee struggled to keep up with the debate, which might account for a certain impatience on his part. There was only one instance in which a witness's zeal took the old man's hand enough to make him step over the line of coolness.

He said, slurring a little, "Take the youth whom we are told the gods accepted among themselves. Was he not a common boy from Asia, who had lain in the emperor's bed, and committed suicide when his master no longer cared for him? Is that someone whom we should look up to and pray to? But he heals the sick and makes the lame walk, you will say, in this very metropolis. And I tell you, his temple is an abode of demons, and his incubation room is nothing but a place where evil spirits come in dreams to trick and corrupt. Why, we don't even know that his body is in the temple! He might have been swallowed and digested by crocodiles nearly two hundred years ago!" The last comment—rather than the stomping and hissing of the angry public—made Aelius sit up with renewed interest, so that he paid little attention to the interesting and no less controversial exchange that followed, regarding what the referee called "a similar lack of evidence for Christ's resurrection."

A fourth reprieve, clearly indicated as the last stay of execution unless compliance was obtained, brought the trial to an end for the time being. Three days hence, the court would reconvene to hear the defendant's last word and act accordingly. Under heavy escort, Pudens was returned to the metropolitan prison, and a bonfire of religious books (many his own, found at his summer home in the resort town of Karanis) was planned within the hour at the horse track outside the walls. Undesirous to follow the court to the book burning, Aelius had a mind to head for Serenus's *nice villa* again, to see if by any chance the saddlebag and Hadrian's letter had found their way back there, or perhaps had never left in the first place.

Much to his embarrassment, as he walked out of the courtroom, Pudens's wife left the safety of armed escort and threw herself in his path. Sincerely no doubt, but with a southern sense of drama as well, she embraced his booted right ankle and placed her forehead against his foot.

"Eminent Spartianus, we are told that you are Caesar's envoy— please save my husband. His mind is affected by too much reading, he had a fever last season that nearly took his life!"

"My dear lady," Aelius said helping her to her feet, "to begin with I am not entitled to the address of 'eminent.' I am only a soldier. Secondly, the prefect himself has chosen to let the law take its course. What makes you think that I should or could interfere in the process of justice?"

The lady hung heavily from his arm, a constriction Aelius would have never suffered from a man, and that in a man he'd been trained to regard as a possible prelude to a stabbing in the ribs. In fact, a courtroom guard stepped in to ask if help was needed, but Aelius said no.

"He is not himself, sir. Ever since his illness, he has been suffering from violent migraines, and is in the habit of taking strong prescriptions. Who in his right mind would join the Christians when laws are declared against them?" She was one of those big-eyed, dark women with fine black fuzz on her upper lip, whom northern soldiers humorously nicknamed "the whiskered beauties" but often found attractive in their swarthiness.

Aelius felt her nails dig into his wrist, and firmly freed himself. "I suggest then that you secure the presence of your husband's physician, who may vouch for his disease and for the treatment as well." "But I beg you to put in a good word. This is why I waited to talk to you. As Caesar's envoy, you have the ear of Caesar: Your word will be listened to."

It was the first time that Aelius considered the possibility that in fact, Diocletian Caesar was listening to his words—indeed, that as a historian, he had been asked by the emperor to speak to all of those who had preceded him on the throne. Still, "Three days' time is not enough for any message to reach His Divinity," he said, unwilling to deceive. "The best course of action is for you to call for your husband's physician and try to make a case for his insanity." Summoning one of Tralles's men in the hallway, he bade him regroup his unit and escort the lady to her house. "I urge you foremost to consider your safety, dear lady, and that of your children." As she left, all but dragged out by the soldier, with the nurse in tow holding the small boys by the hand, Aelius thought that his own ancestors, uncouth as they might have been, had been dragged off to imprisonment and slavery, and no friends of Caesar's had been there to appeal to.

What the engineer had said—that for all anyone knew Antinous might not even be buried in his coffin—intrigued him enough to make him add "collect more specific information on the Boy's burial" to his list of things to do. As for his visit to Harpocratio's house, Aelius actually ran into him at the mall across from his quarters, flat-footed, impossibly blond, and fanning himself as one who has been rushing about until that moment. So he decided to invite him over for lunch at his place, where a comfortable dining area opened on a fountain court.

Harpocratio seemed glad of the chance meeting. He was in town to denounce a crime, he said breathlessly, and "had been sent from pillar to post all morning like a mad woman," without being able to secure the attention of a magistrate high enough to make a difference.

"They're all at the horse track to watch Christian books being burned," Aelius said. Though he was dying to hear what crime he was referring to, he let Harpocratio come to it by degrees, over good food and apricot juice, which Aelius sent for at the mall, since his guest drank no wine.

The story started with a touching reminiscence of "how hard, how hard" it was to come to the metropolis without Serenus, and on a couple of occasions Harpocratio had to stop and sip convulsively from his cup of *serent* to keep from weeping. By the time fruit was brought to the table, he'd come so close to telling the truth that Aelius fairly sat at the edge of his dining couch.

"We didn't speak much about it, Commander, but Serenus had— let us say—other sources of income and other interests aside from supplying the army and collecting old books. One interest in partic- ular he kept practically from everyone." As he reclined there on his el- bow, breathing deeply to steady himself, the embroidered squares of capering infant boys on his tunic came alive as though the stitched babies were about to jump out of the cloth. "Ever since his first years in this country, he'd been acquiring property in the hills, in places so barren that everyone thought he might be after long-exhausted mines, or else gone daft with the heat. But in fact he knew what he was doing, and how. He was one of the last few who could decipher the inscriptions of the ancients, and could read this country like a map. A treasure map, at that."

Here Harpocratio paused to see if the revelation had made an effect on his host, but Aelius said nothing, seated on his couch with legs crossed, looking across the room at a copper vase that reflected the light as did the one in Anubina's house. "Well, Commander," he went on, "I shouldn't tell a historian, since it is common knowledge that from the beginnings of Egypt, kings and queens have been buried and reburied by priests there where thieves would not suspect. Suffice to say that Serenus had gotten hold of texts that gave him clues. He'd go off for a couple of weeks or a month, with a pack of donkeys and mules, and not show up until friends (including myself) started giving him up for gone or dead. Mercy, I stayed awake nights, worrying about him. Then he'd show up again, scuffed and unkempt, saying that he'd been to this outlying village or that lost sanctuary, looking for books. That was all. But," Harpocratio lowered his voice, and though they were alone in the dining room, he forced Aelius to strain to hear what was being said. "I have seen what he was seeking. He'd found the graves of kings, and one by one, like a burrowing insect, he managed to open them and get into them, with no help, no witnesses, breaking seals and smashing plastered doorways, crawling into holes. He told me this himself. Told me how he had to do all this alone, as he could trust no one else in those wilds—oh, he was brave, don't let his fear of the water make you think him cowardly. He'd show me his beautiful hands, and say, 'These hands have carried gold collars and chest pieces of the god kings.' Imagine that. Heart in his mouth, my poor Serenus, alert to the smallest extraneous noise, getting nightmares from fear of being sacrilegious and cursed by the dead."

Aelius had heard tales about hidden gold ever since landing in the Delta with the First Cavalry Crack Regiment, and had not fully believed the accounts. All he'd seen was a small cache of gold coins minted by the rebels in Alexandria, which his unit had spent to build an altar to the Genius of the Roman People. "Well," he said now, "what about these treasures?"

"Oh." Harpocratio reached for a handful of pitted dates, and munched on them. "Much was broken up, melted or sold, or paid in bribes and protection."

Aelius stared at him this time. "Bribes and protection out in the hills or in the city?"

"How can you ask, Commander? Both. It's a way of living with us. Doesn't the saying go, 'The tax man gets the leftovers of the extortioner'?"

"The gold must have yielded noticeable gain even as scrap metal. What about the rest?"

Seemingly no closer to revealing the nature of the crime that brought him to town, Harpocratio was in fact coming to it. "If my Serenus hadn't died—and that's what matters to me most—I'd say this is the worst part. Early this morning, marauders broke in while the household was attending a memorial service at the grave site on Hadrian's Way. Killed the watchdogs, forced the door open, and helped themselves. How true it is that 'A rich man's death alerts the world to his riches'! You should have seen the house. It was in shambles—I will show you if you want. They went through everything we had, busted the armoires to get at the tableware, stole carpets and hangings, broke the kitchen pots, even made holes in the walls. Found some, of course, but not all. Still, I calculate the loss to be around two hundred thousand drachmae. Had Serenus survived this, he'd be a ruined man. As it is there will be barely enough to pay creditors for the last shipment of goods."

Somehow Aelius doubted this. The edge in Harpocratio's voice was crisp and controlled now that he spoke of money, worlds away from the trembling ragged fringe of a few days ago, when he'd spoken of his lover's death. He'd been sincere then—and was lying now. It mattered little what portion of the ancient grave goods had been squirreled away somewhere else. Probably the rest was kept in different places: corporation strong boxes, temple vaults, or what have you. Perhaps abroad, safe from further incursions. The fact remained that Serenus Dio had unexpectedly, perhaps suspiciously, died and his house had now been rifled by thieves.

"No idea of who it could have been?"

"No idea, no idea." Harpocratio had the odd habit of repeating a word or a brief sentence, echoing himself. Of course he had no idea. No one seemed to know why anything happened in Antinoopolis, and silence was applied on crime like salve on wounds, packing it tight.

"Well, let us suppose it was not an accident that befell him. Any idea of who might have wanted him dead?"

"Wanted him dead? No, no. None at all."

"They tell me that he'd incurred the anger of some Christian groups." (It wasn't exactly true; Aelius had made the logical leap after reading the case of Pionius the Catholic presbyter against Serenus's accountant.)

Harpocratio hardly seemed surprised. "And who doesn't at one time or another, I'd like to know? If the laws go against them they become belligerent, and for all their preaching meekness there are gangs of them who go around hitting people over the head in dark alleys and doing all kinds of mischief! Why, that's no clue at all. No clue at all."

It was true, what Tralles said: This was not the Egypt he remembered—maybe because war always brings things out in the open, and the enemy is declared. Inflation and poverty had taken their toll, and now it was all back into the complacent arms of long silence, millenarian tight-lipped watchfulness, and if there were scorpions, they were not only hiding under rocks, they were being fed dainties by those they might sting at any time.

Aelius had never cared much for apricots, but wine made one thirsty in the heat, so now he poured himself a healthy dose of *serent*. "What about the death of the freedman Pammychios at Dovecotes Alley?"

"Yes, I heard. A sad little piece of news. The old man had served Serenus well and deserved to die in his bed."

"Just out of curiosity, do you happen to know whether Serenus had called him in recently or gone to see him?"

"Not that I know of. I can't imagine why he'd have occasion to do so. We have more servants than we can shake a stick at."

Aelius debated whether saying that Serenus's letter had directed him to the freedman's house. Whether or not Harpocratio read his mind or simply thought about the matter that had brought them together the last time, he said, "By the way, did you ever find the letter deposited for you at the post exchange?"

"I did. It mentions an antique saddlebag that Serenus thought would intrigue me. I would love to take a look at it if you still have it."

Harpocratio wagged his head. "A saddlebag? He never said anything about a saddlebag, old or new. I don't recall seeing one around, but we have such a large house, and my poor Serenus was forever bringing objects in and out." He stopped, slamming the table with his ring-heavy hand. "And on top of it, the accursed thieves have gone through everything! You're welcome to come and take a look as soon as we clean things up a bit." He motioned to stand. "Which reminds me, I have to try my luck again at the courtroom. I wonder if they have finished burning the books, which you will allow me, much as I don't like the Christians, goes against my grain as a collector."

Aelius walked to the door to summon the housekeeper. "I have access to a third story study, and you can see the horse track from there. Let's see if there's smoke rising from it."

The midwife-housekeeper led the way up the stairs with a key to the studio. She said, as if it were a cause for entertainment, "There are riots down by the Eastern Gate. The army has just ridden over in full gear. You'll see people looking from every rooftop."

Actually the street riots were not visible, being much too far away and concealed by tall buildings. The flag-bearing rim of the perimeter wall of the horse track, however, could easily be made out at the foot of the Antionan ledge. Against the clear sky, smoke was not clearly distinguishable, but it drew enough of a white spittle on the blue as to betray the bonfire still going below.

Drawing back from the latticed window Harpocratio said gloomily, "Well, I reckon I'll have to wait until they're done."

"Yes," the housekeeper pitched in unbidden, "especially as the crowd tore to shreds the wife of the man they tried today. It's true," she spoke up when Aelius seemed to her troubled or incredulous. "They followed her from the courthouse and didn't even let her get as far as her doorstep, and the soldiers who were escorting her just took to their heels. I wouldn't go into the streets right now, no sir."

Aelius fairly flew down the narrow stairs.

The First Letter from Diocletian Caesar to Aelius Spartianus:

Diocletian to Spartianus:
We are pleased, our Aelius, that your arrival in Egypt was without incident. It did not escape our attention that you did not make use of the imperial post to send your letter, but we assume you have done so for good reasons. In our continuing concern for the well-being of the army, we are particularly anxious to receive detailed information, preferably in the form of court transcripts, of the legal actions brought against members of the Roman armed forces who persist in the Christian superstition, risking their honor and their lives. Likewise, it is our wish that you keep us abreast, in the Heptanomia and elsewhere, of any instances of unconscionable greed and avarice (the vices that prompted us to intervene three years past with our edict on maximum prices, followed at Antinoopolis by our imperial order of the Ides of April in our sixteenth year), by keeping accurate reckoning during your travels of the quality and price of bread, wine, and the items of general consumption listed below. Whenever you see gross disregard of the remedies we put forth, it must be your care to inform the local authorities, and to send a copy in triplicate to our attention.

You do well, Aelius, in pursuing the details of the life of our ancient predecessor, the deified Hadrian Caesar, in the locations he visited, founded, restored, or built up during his permanence in Egypt. We expect the life of this capable prince to be recounted succinctly but with attention to the details of his private as well as public character, omitting nothing from publication unless decency commands.

Within the confines of legality, but with full empowerment on our part, you may also seek the truth concerning any documents concealed within the grave of the Bithynian, even to the extent of requiring opening of the burial chamber. This should be done in utmost privacy to avoid scandal and unrest in that volatile province, but in the presence of selected members of the appropriate religious body to ensure that ceremonies of reparation be performed forthwith. Should you not be satisfied with the results of your research in the Heptanomia, you are to take the investigation wherever it leads you. As for your political endeavors to date, you must have ruffled feathers already, for we received, with speedy delivery, requests that you be recalled to Salonae or Nicomedia. These, we have denied.

We also noticed the impassioned nature of your narrative around the death of the army supplier Serenus Dio, and of his freedman; we advise that you follow your impulse and pursue both cases with all the prudence and zeal that have recommended you to us since your first serving under our command. Lastly, we desire that you address us simply with the title of Domine, *which in the days of our predecessor, the deified Trajan Caesar, sufficed that excellent prince in his correspondence.*

Written at Aspalatum, the seventeenth day of June, fifteenth day of the Kalendae of July, in the twenty-first year of our imperial acclamation, the seventh year of the consulship of Maximianus Augustus, and the eighth year of the consulship of M. Aurelius Valerius Maximianus Augustus.

Items to be checked against our edict's maximum prices include: wheat, rice, wine (Picene, Tiburtine, Sabine), pork, pork mincemeat, army boots (without hobnails), and notary fees for writing a petition.

THIRD CHAPTER

Aelius had learned to recognize the gawky attempts to conceal evidence by soldiers who had turned Christian in the past, and who had brashly gotten religious symbols tattooed on their forearms or biceps. Certain units of the army (he knew of those stationed in Armenia and at Thebes—the *II Diocletiana Thebaea* in particular), were more fractious than others, but generally these days one saw the oddest combinations of tattoo adaptations. Fish pictographs of Christ multiplied until there was a whole submarine scene complete with clams and squid; anchors and doves became catapults and eagles, crosses turned into radiant suns. The pictograph on the hairy forearm of the squad leader was just such a dubious one, but there was no law against odd-looking tattoos. Aelius found himself irked, though, at the idea that a noncommissioned officer might have betrayed his duty as an escort in order to avert suspicion from himself.

On the day after Pudens's trial he walked out of the confrontation with the soldier in a cold rage, and meeting Tralles in the next room of the command post did nothing to soothe his temper. "He and his men have contravened their orders, and a woman—not a

Christian, mind you: a citizen of the metropolis—was killed as a result. Punishment must be exacted, unless we're ready to accept chaos in the streets."

Tralles, who had willy-nilly summoned the squad leader at Aelius's request, attempted to brazen his way out. "Rabirius Saxa has asked for no such punishment, and what he says, goes."

"I will speak to Rabirius Saxa if I must. You understand this has nothing to do with antisuperstition laws; the squad was ordered to protect the defendant's family, and failed to do so. Worse, it deserted under attack. If the first charge doesn't stick with Saxa, you may be sure the second will."

"You are being difficult, Aelius. The crowd cheered the men as they marched back to the barracks. You don't see civilians applauding soldiers too often these days."

"In the old times they'd have been beaten to death, the lot of them."

"The old times are gone." But already Tralles was relenting. Not out of any deeply felt loyalty to the squad, as far as Aelius could tell; simply to avoid trouble for himself. "If you ask for the squad leader's transfer, I won't stand in the way."

"I'll ask for what I see fit, Gavius."

Tralles groaned, throwing up his hands. "As long as you don't embarrass the troops."

"They have embarrassed themselves."

"Oh, what the hell? You never were this way in the old times."

"Yes, and the old times don't exist anymore."

Consulted by both officers, Rabirius Saxa was pragmatic. "We can't execute the man, and we can't ignore that he stood back."

"Fled," Aelius corrected.

"Well, maybe. But it wasn't in battle, Spartianus. I will agree to have the squad leader transferred downriver to Doron Theou, but not to demotion nor permanent reprimand on his record."

"Doron Theou is a better assignment than this, *epistrategos*."

"It was during the Rebellion. Now it's rife with water thieves and other marauders. Our man will have his hands full over there."

Neither Tralles nor Aelius was happy with the decision, as Tralles had hoped to keep the squad leader within the territory of the metropolis (he'd thought about transferring him to the Philadelphia suburb), and Aelius had wanted demotion at least. Meanwhile, though, this was what they had to settle for, and two days later, when Pudens's trial resumed, the result was a foregone conclusion. The *locus solitus* for execution at Antinoopolis lay on a side road by the horse track, and Aelius went to witness it. Owing to confiscation of the defendant's goods, and the death of their mother, the engineer's children were left destitute. Through Culcianus's referee, Aelius was able to secure their removal to Karanis, and a promise that some assistance would be provided for them.

Harpocratio meanwhile, as he found out, had managed to grab a few of the dead man's books still stored in the metropolis' jail in anticipation of a second public burning. On the fifteenth day of June, he and Aelius met to go through them in a small flat Serenus's lover used occasionally downtown. Most were religious books— Tertullian's works, Irenaeus's *Against the Heretics*, a tract by a man called Lactantius—but there were occasional essays, anthologies, and a few history books. Aelius was thrilled to find Books 68–70 of Cassius Dio's *Roman History*, covering the rule of Trajan through Antoninus Pius, including the biography of the deified Hadrian.

"You can have them," Harpocratio said. "There are scribbled comments all over the margins, and I couldn't sell them if I wanted to. I'm sure I don't know why folks have to deface books with their bigoted drivel."

Eagerly Aelius skipped to the chapter on Antinous's death, and found the comment, presumably in Pudens's hand, *And no man putteth new wine into old wineskins; else the new wine will burst the wineskins, and be spilled, and the wineskins shall perish. But new wine must be put into new wineskins; and both are preserved. No man also having drunk old wine straightway desireth new; for he saith, The old is better.*

"What is this?" He showed the passage to Harpocratio.

"I don't know, it's Christian talk. I say, it depends on the wine."

"But why would he write this as a reference to the Boy's death?"

Harpocratio lifted his nose from the copy of Seneca's dramas he was perusing. "I have no idea, but I know someone in the metropolis who knows everything about the blessed Antinous. I daresay he might like to meet *you*."

21 PAYNI (16 JUNE, FRIDAY)

Whether it was to be forgiven for his hesitation about punishing the squad, or merely to prove a point, Tralles came to visit Aelius that morning. He found him writing, with history books spread on the floor around his chair, and a "to do" list by his inkwell, on which he'd jotted down Pammychios's address.

"Well, I found your murderer," Tralles told him, picking up the list from his colleague's desk. "You see that results are achieved even without the need of special envoys."

Aelius put down his pen. "Well, who is it?"

"A local cobbler by the name of Crispinus Crispinianus. Confessed everything, and the freedman's case is closed."

"Has he given a motive?"

"Said he will only give it to the judge when he's brought to court, and not until then."

"We'll just have to bring him to court, then." Quickly Aelius gathered and put his things away.

"Where is the man held?"

"At the command post. My men brought him in."

It would turn out that the cobbler had actually come knocking on the command's door, accusing himself. Aelius summoned his minutes-taker from the room outside his studio, where the young man was copying his shorthand from Pudens's trial. "Go to the courthouse, check if the accused has a record, and bring it to me at the command post." Turning to Tralles, "Could I ask your cobbler a few questions?"

"I don't see why not. I'm about to interrogate him. Come along."

If ever a name was rightly applied, this was the case. The cobbler had wild, curly black hair forming a crisp, wiry ball around his head. Rubbing his hands, he stood under that gorgonlike namesake tangle with what seemed to Aelius mindless glee at having been found out. Hearing that a man from the court would question him, he seemed positively thrilled, and said that in that case he was ready to explain himself at once.

They met in Tralles's office, where Aelius was handed what written information had been gathered thus far. "He goes to the judge as soon as we say so," Tralles told him in Latin, to keep the prisoner out of the conversation. "You were the first authority on the scene of the crime, so feel free to cut in any time." With his eyes on the document before him, he then asked, "Are you Crispinus Crispinianus of Antinoopolis, cobbler and resident in the *grammaton* or district of Philadelphia, on the *plintheion* of Hercules the Victorious's Street?"

"I was."

"What does that mean, you *were*?"

"My name is now Kopros."

"True?" Tralles looked over to the soldier who had taken the man into custody.

"True, sir. He goes by that name though he never legally changed it. The rest of the information is still the same."

"Very well. Whatever your name is, did you kill Pammychios, also known as Loretus, of Hermopolis Magna, freedman of the late army supplier Serenus Dio—"

"Sure, I did."

"—who on 8 Payni was found dead by the esteemed Commander Aelius Spartianus, here present, in the victim's own house on Dovecotes Alley, off the road to Cusae—"

"I did, I did. I tell you, I killed him."

"—and whose property was ransacked during the assault?"

"Yes."

"I told you," Tralles whispered to his colleague. "Take it from here if you want to."

Aelius had been sitting back from the desk, overtly minding the circles of flies in the middle of the room. Now he looked over to the cobbler, who responded to the attention with an expectant grin.

"And how did you kill him?"

"I stabbed him, sir."

"The victim was not stabbed."

The cobbler held his stare. "Well, I was going to stab him, but he managed to take the knife from me, so I strangled him."

"His head was bashed in from behind."

"Precisely. I had to make sure he was dead, after strangling him."

One of the flies had alighted on Tralles's desk, and appeared busy sucking in some remnant of food or drink from the surface. It took off again when Aelius stretched to retrieve the docket and read from it. "You say you were at the victim's house, but no one saw you on the road or at Dovecotes Alley on that day. On the other hand witnesses—including your own neighbors—maintain you were in your shop across the river at the time the murder was committed. Which one is it?"

"I was on Dovecotes Alley, Commander."

"Which means the witnesses lied, and perjury is a grave offense. Surely the judge will have the constable draw a list of the witnesses, and bring them in for questioning."

"I never said they lied—they mistook me for someone else, that's all. I am a common-looking man: you see one, you've seen us all."

"Well, why did it take you two weeks to turn yourself in?"

"Because my conscience didn't trouble me until today, sir."

"And now it does. It seems to me that you're smiling."

"Why, does it make a difference what face I confess with? I killed the man, and that's that." Because Aelius did not encourage him, and neither did Tralles, "I am a murderer," the cobbler added, somewhat perturbed. "I confessed to the crime. The penalty is execution, so let us have the trial and be quick about it."

Aelius had been watching the progress of the fly along the edge of the desk, and concentrating on the insect placed the rest of the room out of focus, so that Kopros's voice came from that haze, as the background to the progress of a fly. He said, frankly annoyed, "Let *us* be quick about it? What have *you* to say about judgment? You haven't even given the reason for your actions."

"Theft."

The fly began rubbing its forelegs. "Of what?"

"Gold."

"Not silver?"

"Also. Gold and silver."

Tralles leaned back, to be able to exchange a few words in Latin with his colleague. "So, what do you say?"

Aelius shook his head. "I think he's as crazy as a loon. There are six or seven people who swear he was nowhere near Dovecotes Alley. He'll say anything that might help convict him. What is a court of law to do with him?"

"I say, let the judge give him what he wants. Cobblers are a dime a dozen, and fools even cheaper. He confessed: As far as I'm concerned, that settles it. Besides, what else is there to do with one who's cracked enough to change his name to *Dung*?"

Aelius looked past his colleagues, at the cobbler. "Since you've been there," he took up in Greek, "give us a general description of the victim's house."

The man shrugged his shoulders. "I don't remember it. I was scared and angry, it was all a fog."

"Is his property on the right or the left side of the road?"

"The left."

"The right side." Aelius had heard all he was going to hear. He stood and headed for the door, where his minutes-taker stood with a ledger under his arm. "I say this man never was even near the place of the murder—whatever his reasons for accusing himself, he did not kill Pammychios. Either he's covering up for someone else or he hasn't the sense of a gnat. I'm no lawyer, but in either case the evidence of his misguided attempts is such that I doubt he'll ever get to trial at all."

As he stepped out, the cobbler tried to reach for him and was held back by the soldier guarding him. "I am a wretched man," he cried out, "why can't you help me? You come from court, it costs you nothing to give the order that I be tried!"

Just outside the door, with Tralles curiously looking over from his desk, Aelius read where his clerk pointed on the ledger. He said nothing just then, but shortly was back in the room, and in his chair at an angle from Tralles's desk. "Cobbler, the court records say that under your old name you used to be a deacon in the Christian congregation of the Matidianum district of the metropolis. Is this true?"

There was no answer, but Aelius was not done talking. "The records further indicate that a year ago you collaborated fully with the government by surrendering cult-related books. You were a witness for the prosecution, and also turned in Church revenues." The accused squirmed, mumbled something under his breath, but that was all. "You volunteered," Aelius specified, "no one prompted you. And now, with a self-abasing name, living in a different district, you expect the government to help you silence your guilty conscience. Well, the government is not in that business. Do not presume to waste the government's time. You may be sure the judge will dismiss the case, and you with it."

"I wouldn't go as far as that," Tralles whispered in Aelius's ear. "What difference does it make? We can ask the judge to go ahead and make it speedy."

"No."

The cobbler began to weep. When Aelius left the office for good, with a wave of farewell to Tralles and no acknowledgment of the cobbler, again he tried to break out of the soldier's hold. "But you can't keep me from going to trial! You can't! You can't!"

W hen in doubt," Diocletian had once remarked during a speech, "go to the baths." Which is what Aelius, having sent ahead a servant with his writing kit, did after leaving Tralles's office. Not to his own, or the dingy army baths where he'd have to relate to

Tralles's colleagues, who suspected special envoys and would not share with him any worthwhile information. The small but elegant city baths on Philopator Street, toward the Eastern Gate that led to the horse track, had been the travelers' baths eight years ago, but now were, as Aelius found out within minutes, the homosexual meeting place in the metropolis. Still, he had come, and he might as well remain, all the more since they'd been built by the deified Hadrian—which of course gave him a plausible reason to be here to do research.

The marbles and tall columns, the eccentric spaces lit by invisible windows recessed in vaults that split into sails, edged by jutting cornices, gave an impression of intermittent semiobscurity and broken light that disturbed and fascinated the eyes. Water darted around reflections like fireflies on the walls, and wet marble tiles, mirrorlike, catapulted the ceiling onto the floor, so that one felt altogether lost in the illusory space, and only sinking into the pool with one's eyes closed restored one's balance somewhat.

By the public mail, the night before he'd sent a second letter to Diocletian, reporting on the state of affairs such as he'd found it and could judge for now, and attaching specific examples as needed. This time, in hopes to expedite delivery, he'd secured the services of a land courier once the letter should reach southern Greece by sea. It was in Hadrian's baths, having declined multiple offers of massage and more private encounters, scrupulously keeping his undershorts on the whole time, that Aelius began a third letter, and reread some of the notes he'd put in longhand after his conversation with the priests days before.

N otes taken by Aelius Spartianus while inspecting the deified Hadrian's imperial barge in the collection room of the temple of Antinous:

> On the main deck, a fine mosaic (of the type architects call "grub-shaped," opus vermiculatum), representing the upper

course of the Nile, that is, from Philae southward. A well-appointed barge is seen plying the waters, with Ivory Island at the lower edge (forefront), shown as a platform with two elephants facing in opposite directions. There's an obelisk between them, which I don't recall seeing there, so it makes me wonder whether one existed at that time, or perhaps the artist never saw the real place and derived it from descriptions alone. On the barge are figures in Roman garb, which I assume to be representative of the imperial party. The deified Hadrian is seen with a group of men with the appearance of rhetoricians or philosophers. Ladies are sitting under an awning, one of whom being more richly dressed and slightly larger in size, I surmise to be Empress Sabina. Two young men are at the sides of the emperor, one of them—I venture to say—being Antinous, with incipient sideburns like Alexander is represented in some of his portraits; the other young man might be Alcibiades Junior, who I know was on board, or another age-appropriate companion selected for the Boy.

In the barge's dining quarters, the floor decoration is divided into eight squares, each representing a couple of companion or father-son figures. From left to right, top to bottom, I identified: Achilles and Patroclus, Euryalus and Nisus, Castor and Pollux, Priamus and Hector, Romulus and Remus, Odysseus and Philoctetes, Hermes and Dyonisus, Horus and Osiris.

In the ladies' quarters are three medallions at the center of a perfectly white mosaic, at the corners of which are medallions with the four seasons. The three central medallions represent: Orpheus and Eurydice, Hades and Persephone, and Admetus and Alcestis.

In Antinous's quarters, the majority of the mosaic is a complex pattern of vines, birds, and insects, like an intricate arbor, at the center of which is a square framed by lotus blossoms. Within the square, is a Romanized rendition of Horus

*striding on two crocodiles, with Egyptian characters on the
right side, which I do not profess to understand at all. The
priests in the temple say it reads, "Sobek gives no sound, of him
above the rest fear is uncontrollable: and yet Thou hast power
over him," and that they have this interpretation in writing
from the days of the deified Hadrian's visit. They insist the
words refer to the Boy, identified as Horus, having been spared
by crocodiles.*

*The least identifiable—not in terms of clarity, but as re-
gards its direct or implied meaning—is the small mosaic near
the prow of the imperial barge. It reads like a heavenly chart,
showing Orion, recognizable by those stars Ptolemy indicates
as* "splendida quae est in humero dextro et est subrufa'—*the
reddish one on Orion's shoulder—and the shining one at the
tip of his left foot:* "splendida quae est in extremitate pedis
sinistri communis cum aqua." *There are also the constellations
Lepus, Argo Navis, and Canis Major (with the brilliant star
marking the Dog's mouth, which Ptolemy calls* "quae in ore
fulgentissima est, et vocatur Sirius"). *What significance these
particular groups of stars might have held for Hadrian or Antinous, must remain for now a matter of conjecture. Do they
indicate a prophecy, or a horoscope? They matter, somehow,
but there are no other indicators on the flooring itself—and
even the priests are mum or know nothing about it.*

Scenes of farewell, he thought, of departure and return, of salvation,
or sacrifice. He wondered whether it was a coincidence. They were
stock scenes one saw a bit everywhere, but had they been placed on
the barge's deck by the emperor, and, if so, before or after the fateful
trip? Were they a commentary by later rulers, who were known to
have maintained and added to the collection? The sky chart mosaic
especially intrigued him, all the more since the astronomer Ptolemy
was active in Egypt in Hadrian's day. He'd have to inquire as to which

month of the year that combination of constellation shone in the heavens.

Like triplets, three identical statues of Antinous occupied the trilobed end of the well-lit room where Aelius sat, their nakedness enhanced by gilding. It might be worthwhile pursuing the lead of Serenus's friends, he thought, watching how the sunlight streamed directly into a round pool until everything—oculus in the vault, shaft, water—blazed like gold, and the space around seemed dark in comparison.

25 PAYNI (20 JUNE, XII KALENDS OF JULY, TUESDAY)

It was Harpocratio who presented him to the homosexual community of Antinoopolis. It congregated every third Tuesday of the month in the Hadrianeum district, on Berenice Street, a place bordered by elegant barber shops and wig-makers, perfume stalls and shoe stores, with daintily kept flats in rows of well-maintained houses. The community was surprisingly mixed, music teachers, tattooed sailors, physicians, traders, burly fishmongers, and playwrights, and having its monthly luncheon in the private, vast hall in the back of a corner bookstore. The shop seemed small, as if squeezed into the corner of the city block, but the banquet hall opening immediately past its rear door occupied the better half of the block itself. Harpocratio accompanied Aelius to introduce him and explain things, as he said, *to avoid misunderstandings.* About fifty men of various ages were standing around, chatting, for all the world like any other business meeting of merchants, but for the finicky attention to clothing, the scent of perfumed oil, and the sidelong glances coming the newcomers' way.

"And who is *he*?" Someone asked, pointing to Aelius behind the cupped hand, not so under his breath as not to be overheard. "Will you look at him?"

"Nice, nice."

"I've never seen *him* before."

"Wasn't he at the baths the other day?"

"I told you uniforms look good on tall men."

"Looks straight to me, I bet he's straight."

"I hope not." And so on.

The wearing of the uniform had been Harpocratio's idea, to impress just how much Aelius was here on official business. Heading for a table where drinks were being served, "Anything that has to do with antiquity as it relates to *us*," he said, "you may ask Theo, the spice merchant. He's widely read in the classics and in religion, and though not known to the army as such, his sister Thermuthis is, as she kept the best brothel in town during the Rebellion."

Thermuthis's name was legend in the ranks. In terms of personal comforts, she was to the army what Serenus Dio had been as regards other provisions. Aelius remembered her well. A red-haired, handsome woman of Berber ancestry, she'd bedded them all in her fancy quarters behind Heqet's temple, and rented girls out to them when she'd gotten weary of these northern officers who flocked to her because of the color of her hair. Anubina was one of her younger girls, and Aelius had been easy to convince to switch.

Theo had none of her good looks, but he was a big, engaging fellow. Bald as a priest, he dutifully drank to the emperor's health, and that of his coregents, knowing that Aelius would appreciate that. He then invited him to a separate small table set in a recess of the wall, where the chatter of guests was less distracting. Aelius summarized his intent, added a few details, and began by showing a sheet of paper, on which he'd copied the comments on the margins found in Pudens's book. "In a used text, I saw this passage scribbled alongside Cassius Dio's account of Antinous's death. What can you tell me about it?"

In the dim light, Theo squinted to read the words. "It's from one of the accounts of the Christ's life," he pronounced after a moment. "It refers to new religion versus old religion, but in this context, well, let me think. An old man and a young one—the risks of such a relationship, I want to say. The possible supremacy of the elder." He placed the paper on the table and smoothed it with his fingers. "Naturally

Cassius Dio had his biases, and in my opinion he'd have been better off trusting what the deified Hadrian had to say about the incident, seeing that he was there and the historian wasn't even born yet."

Aelius knew he was on to something. Encouraged, he said, "The priests told me that Antinous is buried here in the metropolis, but I would like confirmation. Harpocratio thinks you, or someone among you, might be able to tell me what really happened to the body."

Theo rolled his eyes. "So, that's how it is. Any reason not to trust what they told you at the temple?"

"Not really. But one should always double-check one's sources."

" 'Not really' is not the same as 'not at all.' "

"That's true." It was clear that Aelius wouldn't say more than that. Theo surveyed him from across the table, fingering a hefty gold ring he wore on his left hand. The ring seemed too wide, and he turned it to make the bezel face up. Noticing how Aelius's attention migrated to the stone intaglio, he placed his hand in full view. "One thousand years old, Commander. If you're ever in the market for old jewelry, I can point you in the right direction."

Aelius smiled. "The only *jewelry* I ever wore was the lead signet when I enlisted. I think soldiers are better off bare-handed. What about Antinous's body?"

"Well," Theo said, putting the ring back on, "surely the deified Hadrian wouldn't be leaving his beloved behind in Egypt, or anywhere else where he was not."

"I thought of that. Except that the deified Hadrian continued his travels right after the Boy died, and for years to come before returning to Rome."

"Dead lovers are easier to convince to come along than live ones."

"But the cult was started here, the priesthood originated here."

Impatiently Theo waved off the girl-faced servant bringing finger foods. "I thought you wanted information, Aelius Spartianus. Do you *know* about this, or do you want to find out? Because if you want to find out you have to listen."

"I want to find out from the start. From when the accident happened."

"That's more like it. But we can't talk here, there's going to be far too much noise when lunch starts. How about a walk?"

From the Hadrianeum district one could, following Berenice Street clear across downtown, reach a paved promenade that overlooked the Nile and the lower tip of the southernmost island. A small wharf for leisure boats was busy in this early afternoon, but would soon close for the season as the flood approached. Seen even from here, past the tangle of snapping awnings of stalls and sails, the water ran north visibly murkier than even the day before, carrying willow branches on its froth. "I hope all this green water doesn't mean there's drought past the cataracts," observed Theo. "Wholesale prices of pepper and cumin go up even when there's just talk of a drought. I say, willows upriver break easily even when there's no dearth of rain." From a boy vendor, he bought two *kuroi* cakes, handing one to Aelius. "Start at the head," he said, "there's more wine in the paste."

Aelius put his cake away for the time being, conscious of the *gravitas* expected of his rank. Theo rightly took it as an indirect goad for him to resume the narrative started in the hall. "So," he spoke after taking a bite, "right after the Boy died—there's no written record, so don't look for it, but we have ways of committing to memory what matters to us one way or another—there was a frantic search for the body. All along, the Roman navy had been beating the river in advance of the imperial party in order to minimize the presence of crocodiles, but they are devious creatures, and fear was high that he'd been devoured all or in part." Another bite took the feet off the mummy-shaped cake. "Have you ever seen a body half-eaten by a crocodile?"

"I have."

"Then you know what it means, how horrific it is. We're once more confronting that sad reality now that our dear colleague Serenus was taken from our midst. Anyway, it was close to ten hours

before Antinous's remains were discovered. It was about halfway between the place where the travelers had briefly anchored for dinner
on the evening before the death, and the place where morning found
them, when the Boy's disappearance was discovered. It's a lovely spot,
you ought to go there. There's a sandbar now that slows the current
down considerably, though surely there was none then, and the current was swift along that bank. But the papyrus grove must have been
there even then, with its herons and other wild birds, because the
name of the spot—again, don't look for it on maps, it's not marked,
was and is called by the locals Benu Grove. The body lay half in the
water and half on the sandy bank, as though the Boy had nearly come
to safety, or were affirming his own status of half-man, half-god. He
was intact, thank God, not even the fish had nibbled at him." Having
disposed of the cake, Theo said something about reaching the duck
pond ahead, and feeding the ducks. "I can see the scene. His beautiful
braid had come undone and looked like water plants, and his whole
body was just like marble. The deified Hadrian pulled him out to dry
land himself, though the Boy was tall and muscular, and—dead—
must have weighed much. There are things that cannot be said, so I
will say nothing about the grief that accompanied the discovery. The
empress was there, too, by the way, just a bit up from the bank in her
litter, and she was weeping. Pancrates wrote a distich about her tears
being shed and resembling pearls or something, a very tasteless little
exercise, but it's telling that she would be crying over him."

"—Or her husband's grief."

Theo gave him a dry look. "I doubt that. Anyway, there was the
matter of the heat and the waterlogged body, and what would shortly
happen to it. The choice was either to mummify it, as tradition requires around here, and that would take seventy days at least, or cre-
mate it. Inhumation was not considered, as it would abandon the
Boy to the most disgusting of decays."

"What did the emperor decide then?"

"Well, first of all, a marker was placed on the spot where the body
was discovered. It's out of the north gate, I'll give you directions. You

might have to hunt for it because of the rank growth of plants, but it's still there. I saw it as a youngster, because it was a place where we often went to bathe."

"It is not a grave site, though."

"Some say his braid was cut and buried there. You might want to consider it a partial burial, a glorified cenotaph. Not a grave site."

Aelius made a mental note about traveling there and checking the place out. "What about the body itself?"

Now that they had walked past the line of stalls, the scenario opened on the riverside. Across the Nile, Hermopolis shone with its temples and public buildings, like a flowerbed across the bridge; on this side, carved from local limestone about a hundred years earlier, an hexagonal basin created an artificial pond out of river water. Lotus rimmed it, and a colony of ducks squabbled and kept other water fowl away from it. They were a new colony, since the previous one had been killed for food during the Rebellion. Theo said, sitting on a bench that overlooked the pond, "What the priests told you is true so far. The deified Hadrian did order that he should be mummified. After all, he was to remain in Egypt, the emperor, for months to come, and there was ample time to ensure the operation was carried out according to the best funerary traditions. The organs were removed shortly after discovery, of course, and it was with Antinous's heart—against all tradition, to be sure, for Isis's invocation goes, 'Your heart is however your own. It will stay in its place for all times,'—that the deified Hadrian traveled south to Ptolemais and Thebes. It was kept in the liver jar, bearing as a cover the human head of Imseti, which is under the protection of Isis. The other three jars containing the organs were left in care of the priests, and by the sixth day after the Boy's death, when Antinoopolis was officially founded, these were the holy relics and prime reason for the construction of the temple. I am sure you were shown the jars."

An old woman came by selling stale bread to feed the ducks, and Aelius bought a round loaf from her. "Yes, but I was shown four of them, including the human-top."

"Well, that is empty and a copy, because the original was taken along by the emperor. The same goes for the body, missing as far back as Marcus's reign. It was then that his idiot son Commodus Antoninus had the bright idea of wanting to see what a dead favorite looks like, and was disappointed. As the doggerel went in those days 'No mummy, no body, no bones / not a dust particle did Commodus find. . . .' Why the pious fiction, then? It's obvious. There's much revenue resulting from the cult of Antinous, so the priests have all the interest in maintaining that the Boy is here, and that oracles and miraculous cures emanate from his remains. Of his, hereabouts there's the hair by the riverbank, and the intestines, stomach, and lungs in the other three jars."

Aelius decided to pass under silence Theo's judgment of Commodus Caesar. Instead, he gave half of the loaf to Theo, adding, "The first cutting of his beard is kept at Eleusis, I have read it in Pausanias. So, what about the body?"

Theo wagged his head. "Were you given one of the mummy cakes they make at the temple? A bit too much anise compared to those you buy on the street, but they aren't bad. It's the wine in them that makes them reddish and makes them last a whole day, if you nibble on them."

"What about the body, Theo?"

Studiously the spice merchant broke the bread in small chunks, piling them on his side of the bench. "Well, it gets complicated after the imperial party leaves Egypt. You know how it is with us Egyptians. No one really knows where Alexander is buried, though they claim it is he under the crystal canopy in Alexandria, but Pella and Ammoneum and a couple of other places claim him, too. The same with Cleopatra and Marc Antony, and were it not for the deified Hadrian who restored the grave site of Caesar's old enemy, Pompey, we wouldn't be sure where that general is interred either." With a moderate gesture, he tossed a handful of crumbs over the banister. "There are several traditions. One maintains that the Boy was buried in or around Rome, in one of the imperial properties there. It is a believable tradition, since several of the dead favorites had been similarly placed by their masters, somewhere nearby, like pets who are stuck in the flower bed with a lily planted over them. Another tradition holds that the remains were carried along to Baiae, where the deified Hadrian passed on, and left there even when the emperor's body was translated to Rome and into his mausoleum by the Tiber."

"Credible?"

"Credible, but I doubt it, as by the time of his death Hadrian, though desperately ill, was still hoping to live to see his Tiburtine villa again."

Spoiled and well-fed, the ducks thought it over before approaching the floating bread, then by habit started eating and soon fighting over it. "Yes." Aelius stood by the banister to feed the birds below. "What about the Tiburtine villa?"

"That is another possibility. Many are sure it is exactly there that Antinous lies to this day. You know that great villa is like a city, like a world, and in it the emperor put up copies of the sites and buildings he liked most, or meant most to him, including the sacred temple at Canopus. I have not visited there myself, but was told by a good friend that the Tiburtine Canopus is like an enormous shell placed at the mouth of a river. In this shell, which is gushing with water on all sides, there are statues of Antinous in the Egyptian style, copied from the cult image here in the metropolis, large and showing him like Osiris. Hadrian set up an obelisk there, too, marking in Egyptian characters the spot where the Boy was buried. So, my vote goes to the Tiburtine villa as a grave site."

"Anything else?"

"Hm, let's see. I heard tales about the great temple of Firstborn Fortune at Praeneste as a possible resting place for the Boy, but don't know much more than that. Except that there is a mosaic in the temple—some say it belongs to the age of Alexander, some that it was placed there by the deified Hadrian after his return from Egypt— showing the whole course of the Nile. So it's an Egypt in effigy, so to speak."

"Similar to the one on the deck of the imperial barge?"

"Something like it, no doubt. I wonder how likely it is for Antinous to be buried at Praeneste, but it is a commanding monument from what I hear, and the cult of Antinous is celebrated there, too. But, of course, so it is in Bithynia, throughout Greece, at Lanuvium, Alexandria, the Delta, and so on. All I can tell you for sure is that the body isn't here at Antinoopolis, mummy cakes or not."

Systematically, Aelius had divided and cast some of his bread, favoring a crooked duck that swam with a list. "One last question."

"Related to this?"

"No. It is about Serenus Dio: Do you think it was an accident?"

"I do not. However, I have no suspects in mind. I think it was a vendetta of some kind. By whom? Take your pick—Serenus had a finger in every conceivable moneymaking scheme, and often feared repercussions. Harpocratio pleads poverty these days, but I bet the thieves didn't find one tenth of what those two had stashed away."

Aelius glanced over. "Would he entrust some of his riches to others?"

"Friends, you mean? No, he was smarter and not so deluded about human nature as that. He occasionally gave us who knew him best this or that antique he didn't want to put into storage or clutter his house with, but nothing ever of real value." Theo tossed the rest of the bread to the ducks, freeing his palms of the crumbs with a clapping gesture. "Take me, for example. Toward the end of Pachon—yes, about the third week in May—Serenus gave me a wooden crate to keep. After he died, I figured it wouldn't hurt just taking a look inside. Well, what do you think? There were a couple of cheap carpets rolled up inside, and a leather saddlebag so worn and brittle, it must have come to Egypt with Julius Caesar. No, I didn't open *that*—what was the point? I still have the crate in my junk storeroom, and unless Harpocratio asks for it, I'm going to have it hauled out to the dump."

It took all of Aelius's self-control (he'd been complimented on it by His Divinity on one occasion, and had worked at perfecting it ever since) not to betray his interest. He busily tore bits of bread from the

loaf and tossed them to the ducks, giving himself time to sound natural before speaking again.

"I see your point," he said carelessly, though he was actually raking his brains to find a way to secure a look at the crate, or the saddlebag itself, without giving any of his information away. "One more
thing, on a completely different matter. Does your sister still stay at
the same place?"

"Which sister? I have two."

"Thermuthis."

Theo laughed. "Of course, I knew that. I like to make men own up
to it, though. Yes, she's there. And while everyone else in the business
scaled down after the Rebellion, she's added one floor to her *house*."
Pulling back from the parapet, he went to sit on the bench. "So, you
really went to *our* baths on Philopator Street just by accident, as Harpocratio says. Some of my friends were asking whether you—"

"No, I meant to go to those baths, not knowing. If I went again,
it'd have to be by accident."

"Pity."

In his studio, after leaving Theo with an acquaintance who'd met
them as they walked back, Aelius had to force himself to sit down
and think things over. Antinous might not be buried in Egypt after
all, which begged the question of where his historical search would
lead him next. Meanwhile, coincidence or not, two men in whose
possession Hadrian's letter had been, were dead. There was no assur-
ance that the saddlebag Serenus had left with Theo was one and the
same, but in good conscience he could not expose the spice merchant
to risk danger for it. Visiting the merchant's storeroom would alert
potential killers, so he had to send somebody unsuspected to fetch
the saddlebag. He hoped against hope that somehow, after writing to
him, Serenus had changed his mind and either not entrusted the imperial letter to his unlucky freedman Pammychios, or taken it back
from him to deposit it with Theo.

Once more surrounded by his books and journals, Aelius went over the options he'd been considering ever since his conversation by the duck pond. None of them, he feared, would ensure the secrecy of his errand. Whether he sent word to Harpocratio or went directly to tell him he wished to acquire the crate at Theo's, he'd alert him to the possible value of its contents; the same would be true if he directly showed an interest with Theo. In either case, were Hadrian's letter miraculously still inside the saddlebag, its very existence would be revealed. If the saddlebag was empty, he'd have to admit that—for whatever reason—someone else was interested in it enough to kill.

He leafed through his papers without seeing them, consumed by the need to solve his immediate problem. Asking about Thermuthis had deflected any appearance of keenness about the saddlebag on his part, and now he saw that it had not been mere diversion. He had meant to ask about her, for reasons of his own. Perhaps—once he was done reading a miscellanea of purported sayings, jokes, and anecdotes by the deified Hadrian—it might come in handy to go see her in the morning.

Joke ascribed to the deified Hadrian:
A lusty matron was so fond of her horses that she wished they were young men to sport with. Especially, she loved her favorite roan Incitatus, and ardently prayed to Diana that she would metamorphose it into a man. During the festival in her honor, the goddess herself appeared to the matron in a dream, and bade her go to the stable to see her wish come true. The woman did so, and to her delight discovered that the roan had become a handsome fellow, and well-built and tender as he'd been as a horse, so he was as a man. At once they threw themselves into each other's arms, kissing and caressing and calling each other pet names. Before long, the thrilled matron urged him to join her in her alcove, but at this the handsome Incitatus fell to her feet weeping and pulling his hair. "Mistress,

mistress," he cried out, "do you not recall you made me into a gelding?"

26 Payni (21 June, Wednesday)

He knew the way there, what with its nearness to the frog goddess temple, what with the unmistakably expensive street on which the four-story bordello looked. He'd spent a small fortune making love to Thermuthis first—as had Tralles and the rest of the well-paid young field officers—and then nearly as much hiring Anubina night after night, twice arriving there with the blood of battle still on him, until Thermuthis had suggested that he take the girl for the season. The first thing Anubina had asked for was a doll. Now the same Anubina could say, looking out of the door of her blue house, "We're building. I'm happy," and likely mean it as much as he still meant it when he'd told himself that he still loved her a little.

Thermuthis's hair was less lustrous, but still red and wavy and tastefully arranged, as indeed everything was elegant and businesslike in her establishment. She received him in a small parlor that could have been the front office for a charitable institution as much as for a music school, so unrevealing it was of the riotous possibilities just one floor up.

When Aelius said he needed an answer from her, and a piece of advice, she raised her eyebrows. "Is that all?" she said. "I had heard you were in town. It's taken you some time to come see me. For a moment, there, I thought you'd decided to patronize the Alexandrian."

"Isidora? Not likely." Mention of her great rival during the Rebellion made Aelius think better than to try to hug her, since Thermuthis was not one to be coaxed. After all, he needed her help to secure the saddlebag, madams being better informed and connected than anyone else in this, or any, town of the Empire.

"Well, no matter," Thermutis was adding. "You look well. I knew you'd grow gray early, thick-haired blonds always do. So, do I set you up for the night, or are you looking for a longer arrangement?"

"I actually came to talk about Anubina."

"Ah, so that's the question. You'll have to take it up with her husband then. She's married, don't you know?"

"I know."

Thermuthis had green eyes, and even when she spoke sympathetically, they seemed cool because of that catlike color. "You can do much better than that. I have young things two-thirds her age."

"No, I mean to know about her daughter, whether she's mine."

"Just what do you have in mind, Aelius Spartianus?"

"Nothing of that sort. It matters to me to know if I made her."

"*Made* her. How typical. You men don't make anything, except love. It was Anubina who made her two children."

"Whatever, Thermuthis. She won't tell me who the father is."

She pointed to a settee. "And I will? Come, Spartianus, you can't be in a hurry. Sit down and let us catch up with one another before getting down to *any* business—including the help you want from me."

30 Payni (25 June, Sunday)

The place was as Theo had described it, only wilder. The north-south ledge road that ran above it, shadeless, devoid of houses, fences, or shrubs, ran perfectly straight, and from where Aelius stood, it seemed as though following it might lead to the end of the earth. To the north lay what had once been the irrigated estates belonging to the long-vanished community of Her-wer, in the old XV nome of Un. Bought and kept up until a few years ago by Roman veterans, they'd been left fallow on account of a dispute since the Rebellion, and would unlikely be brought back to fertility during his lifetime. The wind had desiccated them and combed them over with dust.

At the foot of the ledge, straight below, in sharp contrast, the river bank appeared unruly, lush. The Nile, swift and already muddy at the center, ran sluggish on this side of the sandbar, by which alone the site of the body's finding could be identified. A couple of pale willow trees struggled to rise up from a rank growth of papyrus plants, and these, crowding the water's edge, shaded it with their reddish, feathery flowering heads. Too impractical to reach, this grove had been left untouched by the recent harvest, and now some of the plants measured eight feet at least of brilliant emerald green. Within two weeks it would all be under water.

Judging it too intricate and undisturbed a vegetation for crocodiles to be hiding in it, Aelius left his horse on the ledge and came down, sliding on the sandy loam first, then on the grasses, until he reached the water. His boots sank into the mud, then found rocks to stand on. Up to his knees in the river, he oriented himself according to Theo's details. The empty surface of the river, high already, and likely to cover sandbar and inlet even before the precipitous July tide broke through, flickered like brilliant embers as the wind raked it, and the coast beyond it drew itself minimum-red. No doubt, even since Theo's youth, the sandbar had shifted and been reshaped by the yearly floods; so Aelius determined the possible position of the marker from the profile of the bank on this side of the Nile. According to Theo's directions, the river created an inlet, at whose center the marker lay. Reeds and papyrus plants made the edges of the inlet hardly visible, but the ledge was recessed, and by stepping to the right he ought to approach the central point of it.

The odor rising from the place was of decaying plants, of earth dissolving in water, of different leaves giving out a wet, green scent. On the sandbar, herons and awkward red-legged blue birds stood among the rushes and did not mind him. All around, as Aelius regained the marshy bank, darting movements in the grass were too inconsequential to indicate danger, unless by snakes, and the army boots could withstand snake bites and more.

So, this was the site of a long-past episode of grief. There was nothing in the calm of the day to indicate any of that, human emotions dissolved as if they had never existed. Aelius began looking for the marker, supposed to be a truncated pyramid or other such solid, according to Theo's words, about three feet high. And the uncontrolled papyrus stalks here and there had the diameter of a man's wrist.

It came to his mind as he searched—out of the odd void where-from memory flows—that the night before he'd dreamed of his own childhood on the frontier, a winter day of shoveling snow. The day his father had sent him out and drowned his dog Sirius, because in the new assignment no animals were allowed. Digging in the snow bank, he'd unexpectedly found Sirius's collar, and had picked it up with a sick feeling, stumbling back into the family quarters in time to see his father toss the drenched carcass of the dog out of the back door. Tears—a reaction amazing to him—came to his eyes even as he leaned over to part the muddy grass, because he had never wanted to remember the day, never wanted to own a dog again, and never for-given his father for it. It seemed somehow a safe and lonely place to let go a little, and be himself even as he carried out Caesar's bidding. Other melancholies, other regrets were surely at play, but those—those had best be left alone for now.

Bubbles came up from the lukewarm mire as he stepped into it, insects flew and flitted in clouds, stumps of dead trees and mucky alluvium collapsed and caved in under his boots. A water snake slith-ered before him, seeking the river. The green of the leaves reminded him of Thermuthis's unwavering glance, when, at the end of their conversation four days earlier, she had suggested a solution to the dilemma he had brought to her, and told him that she would take care of things. Today, if all went well, he would discover Antinous's marker, and hear back from Thermuthis. In a cloud of gnats he bent the grass with a stick, parting the papyrus stalks as he went, eyes low. The feathery heads of the paper plants tickled him and fluttered above him, gracefully bending this way and that.

It was stumbling upon its base that allowed him to find the marker. The growth was thickest here, well above his height and mixed with marsh grass with cutting serrated edges, but meeting the hard corner and edge with his foot gave him the clue. He parted the grass and saw the inscription, three Greek words—*Ántínou tó sama*—to indicate that the Boy, or part of him at least, had been buried here. Not hardly the *memoria Antinoi* quoted by Serenus, nor the place to conceal state secrets: but a start, and one more addition to his careful research notes. A green blue residue from the many intervening floods stained the pyramidal stone, and feeling with a stick around its base, it was obvious to Aelius the small monument had sunk as well, and would eventually disappear into the river.

He studied the marker long enough to be able to describe it. With his foot, meanwhile, he pushed and patted down the grass around it, facing the river, halting only time enough to wave off the swarms of mosquitos that crowded him and sought his sweaty skin.

It was only because of the herons' taking flight from the sandbar that he realized something was behind him, and his first instinct was to turn, but he was already being pushed with great force forward as a man fell on him from the ledge. Aelius lost his balance in the marshy soil and sank farther, bracing to avoid falling face first, and already a second attacker joined in. The combined weight caused him to collapse in the reeds. Trying to get out from under it, he slipped in the slime down the submerged sandy slope of the river bank proper, a disintegration of loam under his boots, soft and malodorous and cool, a feeling of being sucked downward, and he was into the water to his waist, his chest and neck, and over his head. Hands and elbows bore down on him; to avoid being held below the surface he let himself go down farther into it, without fighting the pressure, escaping the scramble to sink him long enough to drop deep into the water, conscious all the while that crocodiles waited for commotion at the water's edge to rush in to feed, lashing their tails. Keeping his eyes open was difficult, and nothing but a murky detritus-bearing greenness surrounded him anyway, with dark sand being kicked up from below, the taste of rotten leaves and roots stripped from their matrix filling his nose and mouth.

Aelius fought to double over in order to reach for the army knife he carried in his right boot, holding his breath, but he feared blacking out and tried to come up for air instead. They would not let him and he grew furious, grabbing at arms and waists, cloth floating about, until he got out of the water in an instant that gave him the sky like a burst of whiteness, time to exhale, struggle to stay up to take another breath, refusing to be drowned without a strife. All had escaped his mind, meanwhile, except the exigency of living through the next few moments, and only when he was finally able to feel un- der his fingers, after a backbreaking effort to gain hold for it, the handle of the army knife. It all came real and in perspective again, the attack, the danger of crocodiles, the forlorn length of the Nile, the er- rand, Antinous having drowned in the same water, washed ashore in the same spot, Sirius drowning by his master's hand, and what it must have taken to drown him, too. His knife met nothing at first, waving slow arcs in the green water, but he found meat or bone later, just a glancing stab but sufficient to create a red spill in the water, a swirling haze, more cloth flapping about, the white sky and splashing and sinking again, another hitting of the mark and some freedom, more blood oozing up.

He was suddenly out from under the pressure and the weight. The buoyancy of his unencumbered body brought him up, head out of the water, with his back to the bank so that only the seemingly endless width of the Nile was before him, and a sky with no bounds. Aelius turned to see his assailants flee, scrambling back up the ledge, whichever of the two was wounded, or both, their faces invisible as they covered them again in black cloth, and regained the road and, judging by the clatter, their expecting mounts.

Motion and blood in the water could not fail to attract preda- tors. As quickly as he could, Aelius waded ashore dazed and weighed down by moisture, cut his hands against the broken stalks of the reeds and into the papyrus grove, downriver a piece from where he'd fallen in. The crocodiles were, in fact, coming, their knobby spines breaking the surface of the water with undulating smoothness, but by this time Aelius had splashed through the marsh and back to firmer ground, from which he climbed the ledge and hauled himself over it. The road, the cliffs beyond it, everything seemed red and unbearably brilliant. At his whistle, with the evenmindedness of the battle mount, his horse came back from where it'd trotted away, and Aelius gave himself time to take his breath and straighten his uniform—his cap was lost and likely to be borne by the flood all the way to the Delta—before getting in the saddle to return to the city.

FOURTH CHAPTER

Antinoopolis, 1 Epiphi (26 June, Monday)

He wasn't even angry when he returned to his quarters. A failed ambush has so many aspects that are altogether ridiculous, in terms of surprise gone awry, that he found himself rather in a good humor. When he told Gavius Tralles on the following day, meeting him after the sacrifice of a bull to the genius of Severus Alexander, he got a blank look back.

"Whatever makes you think it was Christians, Aelius?"

"Well, who else could it be?"

"They've been under control for the past three months in this district, I assure you. It falls within my bailiwick, and—think what you will—I'm not one to do less than a thorough job. No, you got yourself into something else."

"Highwaymen?"

"As above. This isn't Hermopolis, you know. Around this city, I hanged and crucified them until they cleared the roads. Now, if you'd gone out of the territory of the metropolis, I couldn't vouch for that. The scene would be easier to reconstruct then: Ruffians would notice your horse standing above the river bank—you should always hobble your horse, you know that?—and owing to your gray hair, they'd take you for an old geezer, and try to jump you. But seeing where you were, not that far from the city limits, I'm stumped." Although Tralles made light of things, Aelius smelled anxiety in him. It wasn't the same passing the buck as to any responsibility in the riots after Pudens's trial. It felt like a personal concern, related to his arrival in Egypt, and the irritant of an incident that might mean more than it seemed.

Aelius said, "They had their faces covered like desert dwellers and no weapons. Had anyone wanted to kill me, he'd have smashed my head with a rock or strangled me—not tried to drown me."

"They had horses, though."

"They didn't steal my saddle, much less my horse."

Half-heartedly, Tralles laughed. "Well, anyway, I told you the army was disliked."

"Ah, yes." Aelius could not resist the dig. "I forgot about the army. There's always the squad that let the mob kill Pudens's wife, and whose leader I got sacked."

"Now you offend me, Aelius."

After this, there were no more pearls of wisdom emanating from Tralles. Aelius was left to ask himself whether the attack had anything to do with his duties here—though only Serenus Dio's fears and his freedman's coincidental death made him even think that anyone cared at all about historical research, much less about decrepit imperial letters. Maybe he saw conspiracy where none existed. Yet, two men were dead, and the saddlebag sitting in Theo's storeroom might answer some of his questions: What exactly did Hadrian's letter imply, and was there a connection between it and those deaths? Who in the world would have an interest in the threats Rome had faced decades ago? Would they attack an imperial envoy for it? Watching himself was something he did as a second nature, and he did not worry about his safety, really. Just this morning, Diocletian's reply to his letter had arrived, with the thrilling words of encouragement—secretly hoped for—to follow his curiosity in all directions. On the other hand, the fact that His Divinity had been asked in writing that he be recalled from Egypt, was a piece of information Aelius would keep for himself until he could discern more clearly how things stood in Antinoopolis for Caesar's envoy. In that light, he wondered why Tralles now insisted about social unrest in the province, while swearing that here everything was under control. Even more, he was baffled at the thought that someone should try to intimidate him, but altogether not concerned enough to summon his escort from Cynopolis.

This being the day Thermuthis had given him an appointment at her house, Aelius went there directly from the command post. In his prudence, he wasn't hoping for much, and was thoroughly amazed when the madam handed him Serenus's saddlebag. Risking his life on the river bank for a granite marker seemed idiotic and absurd, in the face of what this well-groomed woman had accomplished without apparent difficulty.

"How did I manage?" She smiled, condescendingly. "Why do men always have to find out how women manage things? It should be enough for you that we do, and very well, thank you. It was easy. You posed the problem, and straightaway I told you it'd be a good idea for a woman to go to Theo's. Then I thought to myself, give her a basket to put it in, and the older the better—women are invisible past a certain age. So I sent the porter—did you notice her, below?"

"No, I didn't."

"See what I mean? She was sitting there, let you in, you probably even took the trouble of muttering a thank you or tossing her a coin, and you didn't even *notice* her. And to think that she was one of the Younger Gordian's twenty-two concubines in her day!"

"Was she?" Aelius was feverishly anxious to open the saddlebag, but restrained himself a bit longer.

"I might ask her for details on that prince's reign."

"Yes, the whole one month of it." Thermuthis poured *serent* in a glass. "The old woman will tell you that it isn't true that he died in battle with the governor of Numidia."

"Well, his body was never found, but—"

"He escaped. She hid him in her room for three months, until his silly nephew ended up on the throne, and even then Gordianus never went back to Italy. Lived anonymously the rest of his life here keeping a pub, which given how much he drank, was a natural choice for him. Ask her, when you go back down, she'll tell you." With her glass of apricot juice in hand, Thermuthis walked to the door. "You're dying to open that stupid bag of yours—go ahead. I'll be outside."

It was not very different from document pouches used by army dispatchers these days; Aelius saw why Serenus Dio had rightly identified it as a Roman piece of equipment. No legion or unit mark appeared on the outside. Dryness and age, exposure to the sand-bearing wind had made the thick leather fragile, and he had to steady the eagerness of his hands in order to unfasten the corroded buckle without tearing the strap. Inside was a note, tied with an incongruously new hemp string around a much older, cylindrical wooden letter case. This, he couldn't bear the possible disappointment of finding empty, so he unfolded the note first, and read it.

It is my hope, esteemed Commander Spartianus, that it is you—with God's help, and following the directions that my freedman Pammychios undoubtedly gave you—who tracked down this saddlebag and its contents to its present location. If you did, it likely means that I have met an untimely end, as I fear might happen. Should anything have befallen my freedman also, know that, two days after I wrote my previous letter to you, he endeavored to meet me as if by chance at the store of Theo the spice merchant's, where I always go at that time of the week. He told me that for the last several hours he had noticed suspicious people prowling up and down the road near his place on Dovecotes Alley. He wasn't afraid for himself, but feared that, should thieves or other marauders succeed in robbing him, the document I had entrusted to him (he has no idea of its nature) might be lost. Pammychios brought the

letter of the deified Hadrian in a shopping bag—ask him for
details of our meeting in case I should not be alive. I was just
then in the process of asking Theo whether I could leave with
him a crate of old rugs, in which I had already placed the
empty saddlebag. To summarize things, I replaced the letter in
the saddlebag, it inside the crate, and the crate is being stored
today at Theo's place.

It is up to you, if all that I dread should come to pass, to
find out why such a long-lost, ancient document seems to cause
such turmoil. I am on my way to Upper Egypt to visit lands of
mine and to do business. God willing none of this subterfuge
will have been necessary, and it will be the undersigned Serenus
Dio who shall receive your offer to acquire the letter for your
own purposes. Written on 19 Payni (14 May), the ninth and
eighth year of D. and M. consulships.

The rambling note pointed to Serenus's last-minute afterthought.
Thermuthis's decision not to let her brother Theo know that the saddlebag was being removed from the crate seemed wise in the context.
Thermuthis had asked Aelius no questions, showed no interest in the
saddlebag ("Men's games, play them all you want"), and offered to
keep it in her safe if needed, or else return it to its place in the spice
merchant's storeroom. Now it all depended on what, if anything, was
in the letter case.

Aelius could not bring himself to open it, much less read its
contents in a brothel. The girls' laughter came from the upper floor,
whose small, charmingly furnished rooms he remembered well. Thermuthis, businesswoman that she was, would likely put one or the other
of her better prospects in his way if he stayed. He'd made up his mind
he'd let her do it, but this wasn't the time. Accordingly, he left her a
note with instructions to keep the saddlebag in custody for the moment, and left.

The brothel's back door opened on the interspace between the
podium of the frog goddess's temple and the neighboring building,

an alley so narrow that a man could not fully spread his arms in it. Aelius followed it, expecting to rejoin the main street if he took a right at the end of the alley, but new constructions had gone up in the years of his absence, and he found himself at a dead end. Doorless walls around him, he didn't like on principle, so he retraced his steps in order to take another narrow street, and through a maze of lesser lanes crowded with children, clicking with the sound of looms, he emerged eventually onto known surroundings. Down a porticoed boulevard, past the command post, he aimed for the city mall, and the busy thoroughfare where his flat stood. It was an effect of carrying on his person Serenus's note and the yet unopened letter case, no doubt, but it seemed to him he had eyes behind his head. He noticed movements, faces, gestures with the keen accuracy of his war days, which in retrospect seemed to have much more in common with the behavior of the prey than that of the hunter. Passersby didn't notice him any more than they would any other man in an officer's uniform, whatever the times were, hardly a novelty in this fourth century of Roman rule.

Yet, out from under the awning of one of the book stalls where he'd often stopped, he did notice the sudden stealthy motion of a man at his passage. Aelius was by now a hundred paces from his doorway, and it was a temptation to hasten toward it and lock himself in; but he had been trained not to face danger without a fight. So he changed his plan, going down the street that led to his flat but then walking past the entrance, crossing the street again to enter the mall from one of its side gates. The man, who'd followed him around the corner and down the street, once or twice becoming lost in the crowd of shoppers and pack animals, was still behind him. Aelius let him draw closer, pass him, slink ahead among the white donkeys, porters and market-going women, and when he recognized him desperate for an assault, with a letdown of tension he saw it was the cobbler Kopros, who'd never had his day in court. Bare-handed, a delirious look of fear and anger on his face, he was recklessly charging without covering himself. Aelius stood his ground unconcerned, with the outstretched right fist smacking him on the side of the head hard enough to fell him, and left him there. Then he cut through the press of idlers immediately assembled, regained the street, crossed it, and went home.

His studio, once the servants had made themselves scarce, afforded him the luxury of silence, facing as it did the inner court. Aelius locked the door, went to his desk, and unscrewed the light wooden cylinder from Hadrian's day. Inside, rolled up to fit it perfectly, paper darkened by age met his fingers. The texture reminded him of a dry leaf, but the weave was resilient, and came out easily.

As expected, the text was in Greek. The handwriting, quick and ornate, with idiosyncratic strokes, showed how the brush had been used to apply ink with a painter's taste for shape and calligraphy. The words swam before Aelius's eyes, as he'd read many copies of Hadrian's letters in anthologies of imperial correspondence, and his critical mind was searching for stylistic clues even as he devoured the subject matter laid before him.

Hadrian to his most honorable Caesernius. What you heard about me is true, dear friend: this old man's soul is a willing Proserpina, but Hades will not bother to rise up with his chariot to snatch her. Likewise it is true what they say of man: that he spends the first half of his life pining after this and that, and tragically expostulating, "I can't live!", while the second part of his life he passes crying out, "I can't die!" Our Antinous's memorial resting place, about which so solicitously you asked, is all but finished. Inside it, alongside those objects such as love requires that be placed with one who modestly and graciously conquered the palm at the Great Human Friendship Contest for all the years I knew him, I plan to lay a document which I commend to your attention and memory. As consul, you guide the fatherland. As Hadrian's friend, you are bound by your affection for me to love the fatherland even as I did. Know then that in the memorial resting place of our Antinous is kept the

record of the great and ever-present peril to the welfare of the
Roman state; that you are not to reveal this detail to anyone,
but judge from the receipt of this letter that I entreat you, in
my infirmity, to carry out the orders I gave you when we last
met to rid Rome of such danger, orders from which you were to
refrain as long as I was silent. Were we not to act swiftly now,
the threat should fester for years and centuries to come, and
the very well-being of the empire enfeebled by it. Farewell.

As Serenus said, the letter was not dated, but Aelius understood nearly at once that the merchant had mistaken the reference to the emperor's last illness for distress related to the loss of Antinous eight years earlier. The recipient of the letter was no doubt—he kept a list of the consuls at hand at all times—the former *comes per orientem* Caesernius Quinctianus, but in his role as consul in the year of Hadrian's death. Without a place of provenance it was difficult to tell, though it was reasonable to infer that the letter had either been written in the imperial villa of Tibur or even at Baiae, where the emperor died on 10 July of the 891st year of Rome. Since most likely the consul was in or around the City at that time, there was no accounting for the letter's being found in Egypt, and in the Western Wilderness of all places. The seal having been only broken by Serenus upon discovery, one could further suppose that the message had never reached its destination, and no action had been taken regarding the unnamed threat to the state adumbrated therein.

He spent the rest of the day checking the letter before him against those collected by historians. Was this Hadrian's style? Would he use these phrases? Fingering the paper, too, he thought that it had been touched by the same hands that had pulled out of the water the body of a dead favorite. Why did the deified Hadrian, who spoke of himself as "I," refer to the Boy as "our" Antinous? Most of all, where was the grave site he referred to? Until late at night Aelius worked at his papers. He had far more information than he was expected to put in the imperial biography, and even as he compared the perspectives of

Hadrian's reign as put forth by various authors, he sought references to significant threats, dangers, conspiracies in those days. Back and forth, try as he might, all he could find were references to the great Jewish revolt, and to the apparently mad suspicion of Hadrian's last years, when even those close to him, even the old and infirm, had been put to death on apparently frivolous charges. He read and wrote into the early morning hours, and went to bed exhausted, with the boxed imperial letter under his pillow.

2 EPIPHI (27 JUNE, TUESDAY)

In the morning, he was up relatively late, and took a leisurely break-fast. Rereading about the Jewish revolt had made him think overnight (he'd slept fitfully, dreaming of getting lost in dark alleys and being pursued by enemies old and new) of the man he might have to see to get a perceptive reading of the present circumstances. As he readied to leave the house, he ran into the housekeeper, returning—as she put it—"from birthing twins uptown." With the directness typical of her profession, she addressed him first, "Have you heard the commo-tion this morning?" Because Aelius said no, she continued with the undisguised pleasure people always have when they find out their news is not yet known. "There was a fire in one of the fancy shops' storerooms, down the theater way. No, they didn't break in, they just threw burning rags soaked in pitch and oil into one of the windows, through the iron grill. By the time the slaves organized themselves and the fire patrol was sent for, the place was a total loss. Smoke everywhere, I had to take the long way around the block."

Aelius had more than an inkling of what might have happened. Without asking further information, he set off in haste for the gen-eral direction of Theo's store, which the spice merchant had shown him in passing during their walk a week before. The street had been cleared by the authorities, but Theo's slaves were still picking through the rubble of the gutted building, a block down from the store itself, which was open for business.

Theo himself was inside the store, chatting with friends who had rushed in for the news. Aelius bought ginger and *carum* for his mother, and waited until the floor emptied of gossipers and the curious. Theo cordially joined him and attended to his acquisition himself.

"You find me at a rather odd moment, Commander," he said with a crooked smile. "I'm like that farmer who lost one of his sons, but consoled himself saying, 'At least he wasn't my strong-backed son.' "

Aelius found it politic to feign ignorance. "What happened?"

"Arsonists. They took out one of my buildings, bold as brass. Why? I don't know. I'd like to say it was competitors—there's one in Hermopolis who's nearly bankrupted himself trying to undersell me—but if so, they failed."

"But it's a loss, isn't it?"

Theo shrugged the incident off. "It wasn't where I keep my spices, just my junk storeroom. Nothing but a storage of old furniture, harness for my animal packs, fodder, easily replaceable. I wouldn't be so blithe if they'd set my other storeroom on fire. As it is, I think I can stand the loss."

The *junk storeroom.* Aelius remembered Theo mentioning it as the place where Serenus's crate had been kept, and from which Thermuthis's old porter had removed the saddlebag. Theo prevented his asking anything about it, by volunteering with a raising of eyebrows, "No point in even bringing up to Harpocratio the old rugs Serenus gave me to keep. They went up in smoke with the rest, but then they weren't worth fifty drachmas." He smiled at Aelius. "If you don't tell him I even had them, *I* won't."

Aelius left the encounter itching to put his thoughts down on paper, and to find the man who'd come to his mind as someone from whom he might get a clearer vision of what was actually happening at Antinoopolis and in the Heptanomia.

Baruch ben Matthias was as secular a Jew as anyone could expect to find in the metropolis. He'd been much less secular a few years back, when he'd come close to killing Aelius during a well-planned ambush near Coptos. It'd taken two weeks for Aelius to get over spitting blood from a pierced lung, and then he'd prosecuted with enough vigor to make ben Matthias despair of saving any of his own. They'd come to an agreement of sorts at last, and had left one another with a wink, convinced they could trust one another now that they'd cleared the air of ideological and personal matters, but for the world it could not really appear as though they'd come to that.

Secular Jew that he was, ben Matthias had started a flourishing business as a painter of mummy portraits, and now employed over ten workers. His shop stood a bit back from the road, in an alley shaded by immaculate awnings, and outside the door, on both sides, big-eyed, bearded, woolly headed and heavily made-up, a variety of dead Egyptians looked down onto the visitor, so lifelike as to resemble people at small windows peering out.

The workers mixing colors in the alley facing the entrance, three tough and dark young men with the build of fighters, eyed him suspiciously when Aelius approached, and followed him in as he crossed the threshold. As for ben Matthias himself, there was no doubt that he'd recognized him. He turned at leisure, though, and—remaining seated at his easel as he put the finishing touches on the portrait of a lamentably young child with puffy cheeks—said, "You have some gall showing up here." He told him in all coolness, "You've given us trouble before, cost us plenty, and it's only because the balance of power is on your side that I don't have you thrown out on your ear on the public street. With all respect."

Aelius found himself having to choose so precipitously between anger and amusement, by natural inclination he chose the second. "I can't blame you, Baruch. But the trouble was mutual, and you seem to have recovered well enough from my throwing *you* out on your ear."

The young toughs seemed within an inch of acting on their own, but a motion of ben Matthias's hand stayed them like an invisible leash. "Well, we're both older, though you could be my son—I started early, had my first at sixteen—so I suppose we can be civilized about this. Am I to think Nicomedia has grown stale and unexciting?"

Which was as clever a way as Aelius could think of, to let him know that ben Matthias not only remembered him, but had also kept up with his career, and even his latest assignment.

"As you've gone that far in fact-finding," he replied, "you ought to know why I'm here."

"If you don't watch it, to get one of these painted of you, from what I hear."

Aelius carefully showed no reaction, but ben Matthias, dragging the brush against the paint pot to remove the excess of color, winked. "Near the Benu Grove, and the sandbar with herons. Does that ring a bell?"

"I'll never know how I managed to get the best of you, I swear."

"Ha." Ben Matthias made a wide gesture, brush and all. "I think I let you. But the brunt of the whole Roman army might have had something to do with it, too."

"I'm glad to see you well and profitably employed."

"Same here, same here." Wiping his hands, the old rebel waved his young toughs back to work, and grinned an invitation for Aelius to follow. "Come out back."

Out back was a small room at the end of a passage so narrow, Aelius suspected it might have more than something to do with the old habit of ensuring safety. The room itself opened on an inner court, paved in ashlar, with a well at the center, sided by blind walls at least three stories high. Still, the sun fell into it so precipitously, the brightness it threw into the interior sufficed to illuminate it fully.

"Sit down, will you?"

The chairs, the table, wine in a cooler, glasses, all the utensils were Roman, imported, good quality. The wine, better than good. "Have an almond cake," ben Matthias was telling him. "My daughter makes them." Then said, "What in the world leads you to study the life of the Butcher of Jerusalem?"

Aelius had once more grown accustomed to the Egyptian way of feeding one's questioner or guest, and reached for an almond cake. "You people haven't gotten over the deified Hadrian's victory yet."

"Never will. We're still talking about Pharaoh who went after us from this patch of desert land some thousands of years ago. It pays to remember."

"Which is exactly why I am studying the life of the deified Hadrian."

"What can you add that he hasn't already abundantly bragged about in his *Anamnesis*? That's what he called his memoirs, if I recall correctly."

"Well, I'm rather interested in what he might not have said."

"About the Boy?"

"Also."

Ben Matthias poured wine for Aelius in a clear glass goblet, on which a bear was painted in bright colors. "You know, that was just about the only charming thing about the man—that he had a soft spot for someone, at some point. Come and think of it, it was ill-advised of bar Khokba to start the Jewish uprising shortly after Antinous up and died. Never start uprisings when monarchs are in a bad mood, I say."

Aelius was careful not to acknowledge the statement in any way.

"If you drag me by the hair, Commander—which would be a feat in and of itself in this balding season of my life—I may be able to supply you with some interesting tidbits about the Butcher."

"I'd be much obliged, if we agree on a nomenclature midway between his deified state and your insult."

On ben Matthias's glass, a man fighting a bear was painted in reds and greens. "But if gossip is even half close to the truth, there's more to your visit to Egypt than retracing ancient steps. At first I said to myself, 'He, he—he comes to pick on the Christians. It took him long enough to get around to it.' Then I said, 'No, he's here to report about all of us to the old man.'"

"Do you intend His Divinity?"

"God is one, Commander, and His ineffable name is certainly *not* Diocletian."

"Well, so—informed as you are: how *is* Egypt?"

"Ah, it's a mess, Aelius Spartianus. It may look like the granary of the empire yet, but it's crawling with rats. It's a rotten beauty, a poisonous well."

"Good metaphors, but they tell me nothing."

Ben Matthias glanced at the scattered shadow of pigeons taking flight from the roof across the courtyard. "Let me put it simply to you: If you have come here unscathed, and are asking these questions, it's because someone let you."

Aelius burst out laughing. "Truly? And who is that, who allows me to go about my official business?"

"I wouldn't tell you if I knew." Ben Matthias's long, bearded face had the expression of a merry goat, so that Aelius didn't know how seriously he meant the words. "Judges are bought and sold by them, or leave their posts in disgust. Merchants pay dues to them, the corner cobbler who doesn't go along gets his boiled urine tossed in the family well, or else they break his legs in a dark alley. You want to build a house? You buy the land, pay the permits, hire the masons, but nothing gets done unless you drop the coins into the right slot. Your daughter won't get married with wine and music unless you pay up." Looking sharply at Aelius, he added, "Army suppliers fall off their boats, and nobody knows how."

"Am I to understand that Serenus Dio might have been killed for lack of paying protection money?"

"Heaven knows. In his business, for every penny he made, he undoubtedly had to pay two to someone. Goes to prove how much he was actually making, rich as he managed to stay. Now, to you, they will tell nothing useful, Or, rather, they will point you into a couple of fine leads, and only when you're three quarters of the way there you'll discover they're going into diametrically opposite directions. Either that, or they bring you back where you started from."

"*Them, they*—this is all haze and smoke, Baruch. Make it short. Whom can I trust?"

"No one, not even myself, since you have no way to know whether or not what I'm telling you isn't part of the scenario."

It was like being in the broken light, the illusory spaces of Hadrian's bathhouse, sinking up to the nostrils in lukewarm water. "If you could tackle the power of Rome, you surely aren't about to knuckle under any of this," Aelius observed.

"Who has spoken about knuckling under anything? I may have my reasons and reap my benefits from the deal." Wagging a paint-smeared finger at him, ben Matthias had that amused expression again, but it might only have been out of contempt for the way things were. "Take a good look at something you would never get into unless you were told: the accounts of farmers and small artisans. Care to see mine? I call it as it is, Commander: For every drachma I spend on supplies or wages for my workers, I spend ten times as much in bribes. That is, whenever the bully is too powerful for me or the boys to go over and break his head. I think it's the rottenness of every empire, which starts to show at the extremities like gangrene, but begins with some inner disease of the core."

"I have heard just about all I'm going to hear about this."

"Which goes to prove that you, too, historian as you style yourself, are deadened to the reality of things."

"It's human nature: It will tend toward corruption regardless of the political form, which is why His Divinity's reforms must be enforced. Do you mean to tell me the Rebellion was motivated by honorable sentiments?"

"Probably not. Me, I had nothing to gain but harassing Romans, which sufficed at the time. What can I say, Commander? It's in the blood. I fought the Romans with Achilleus much as my father fought them along with bat Zabbai."

"And who was *he*?"

"*He*? She, you mean. You call her Zenobia, and she gave you a run for your money. But you were barely born when she was queen of Palmyra, so you were spared that embarrassment. As for me, now I harass Romans in different ways, fleecing them through high rents of vacation houses and expensive tours of the interior."

"You are cynical."

"I hope so. It's as good a philosophy as I can think of. I'm not a religious man, you know. I'm not even Egyptian. I just don't like Romans. You, on the other hand, are actually convinced you might lift the veil of the past, and find a pretty bride; all you might find is a grinning skull, moldy and worm-eaten."

"That is, assuming that I am seeking a bride at all."

"Doesn't everyone, except for those who'd rather have a lad? The Butcher brought his boy here like a puppy, drowned him like a puppy, then made him into a god. I knew two sisters in Arsinoe who did the same with their sickly lap dogs, and had me paint portraits of them."

Aelius bit his tongue. "How would you know he drowned him?" he asked then.

"That's not the right question to ask. The right question is: Was this man, this blasphemer who could kill thousands, likely to have let his favorite be done in under his very eyes?"

"Domitian was a morbid and suspicious prince, but someone assassinated him anyway; and so Commodus."

"Ha! Do not compare those two half-wits to Hadrian's malice. On an imperial barge, with military escort, none but he could have thrown the Boy overboard, or ordered him to do so. Follow the wisdom your gray hair suggests you have: The trail of this murder is so old, there's precious nothing for you to go by."

"And if it's not a murder?"

"Accidents are even harder to prove—and at such distance of time. Why, Commander, those were the ancient days when Rome first dragged your unwilling ancestors by their blond beards out of their barbaric dens!"

"You purposely insult me."

"Well, I can't very well help it if your ancestors were walking on all fours or close to it, and my people were already leading a national resistance against the invader of the week."

"At least Pannonians thrive at Court, while Jews are scattered to the winds."

"Sadly, I can't argue with that." Raking his grizzled beard, ben Matthias found bits of paint, and pulled them out gently. "If I were you, and if you're as interested in finding out what happened to Serenus as I think you are, I'd take a look at the Christians anyway. You know, it's their holy men or *anchorites*—that's what they call themselves, just like those who run off to escape creditors—who take over abandoned tombs to do their solitary living. And what is there— or can be—in abandoned tombs?"

"Christians are not motivated by gold, as far as I can tell."

"Maybe not, but they wouldn't relish someone barging in to disrupt their prayers in order to *get* the gold. And don't tell me they wouldn't kill because they would, and you know it."

"They wouldn't go to kill him in his boat."

"And why not?" Cocking his balding head to one side, the old rebel seemed to evaluate him, and Aelius assumed it was out of their old enmity, or perhaps to gauge his resolve. "But then, everybody gains from Serenus's death. His blubbering lover, his debtors, his competitors, the Roman fisc, real estate agents from Oxyrhinchus to Philae, a couple of art dealers I know. Even the priests of Antinous, who stand to get a good chunk of his inheritance as soon as the legal tangles are undone, as they will."

"None of these people was on the boat with him."

"Anyone could have gotten on the boat and off again, unless hired sailors have changed from my days."

From the floor by his chair, ben Matthias had picked up a piece of slate, and took to sketching with it, in an off-hand way, looking up now and then. "The river is long, much can happen alongside it. There are definitely two or three places along the way where even folks with less wealth than our Serenus would risk their lives, sailing by in their pretty boats."

"River thieves?"

"Water thieves, we call them—yes. The previous administration had managed to stamp them out, but they cropped up again in the past five years or so. Sending them into internal exile was no solution, I knew all along, but they must have greased the right palms in the right quarters. The army and the river patrol swear up and down that they've rid us of them, but it isn't so. They're stronger than ever, and mean business."

"But they are not the same *they* who *allow* me to go about my official business."

"Not that I would tell you."

Aelius munched thoughtfully on a second almond cake. "My mother makes them somewhat like this."

"Good?"

"Very good. So, are you sketching the course of the Nile, to give me a hint?"

"No. I'm sketching *you*, just in case I need to fit you with a mummy tablet."

N otes taken by Aelius Spartianus on the first week (V Kalends) of July, to be then transcribed in letter form for the benefit of His Divinity:

Things in the Heptanomia don't seem well. Local authorities are in turn lax or abuse their powers (cite interview with Baruch ben Matthias, erstwhile supporter of Achilleus during the Rebellion), the roads are not safe, crime does not elicit the attention of investigators or prosecution. The prices of basic foodstuff (attach list separately) are at great variance with the maximum allowed by the edict. Court proceedings against the Christian sect continue, and in the three weeks since my arrival

*in the metropolis alone fifteen men (four of them military)
and two women (plus one killed by the street mob) have received capital punishment. Sentiment against them is strong
among the populace, as a rift among the Christians is perceiv-
able between those who recanted as a result of past prosecution
and those who persevered in their folly. Recusants and informants are personae non gratae amidst their own, have to move
from their neighborhoods and often change their names.*

*In other matters, I am now convinced that the army sup-
plier Serenus Dio and his freedman Pammychios were assassinated in order to obtain, and probably dispose of, a letter from
the deified Hadrian pointing to a threat against the empire;
with the same goal in mind, persons unkown have also set fire
to the spice merchant Theo's storeroom. While there is not
enough evidence at present to assume that attempts to intimidate me and to have me removed from Egypt are also ascrib-
able to the same person or persons, it is evident that the mention
in the letter of documentation about a conspiracy or plan has
aroused in some quarters fears of Roman retribution, should
the documentation be discovered. If Serenus Dio, as he alleged,
mentioned his discovery to no one, how did anyone know he
had the letter? I believe he spoke to someone, perhaps in confidence, and the indiscretion cost him his life.*

*Well aware of the political risk, I intend to request per-
mission from the local priests to open the Boy's grave in his
temple, ostensibly to carry out His Divinity's command to
pursue my historical research. In reality, to avoid being beaten
to it by parties unknown. Were I refused, I must be ready to
act upon the authority vested in me, and order the opening
of the coffin. In this second instance, either I endeavor to act
expeditiously—indeed tomorrow, owing to the fact that 3 and
4 Epiphi are listed on the Egyptian calendar as days most
adverse to all enterprises—or I must wait a full week before
the next propitious day. At all costs I will avoid even the*

perception of sacrilege, though in case of forced entry, military
escort will be necessary.

Gavius Tralles had the face of fear. The bureaucrat's face of fear, half-grinning, with an apologetic cast that was ready to harden as soon as one doubted the intensity of his refusal to help. Aelius had learned to recognize it long ago, before battle mostly, but even on the battlefield, when least one could afford a colleague to fail.

"It's impossibly complicated," Tralles was saying, because, of course, it was never a matter of not being able or willing, but always a question of sheer, fatal impossibility. "You don't remember Egypt well, things have changed in these last years, it's not like it used to be."

"I saw Egypt at its worst. I doubt it's worse now." In order not to lose his patience, Aelius had to look elsewhere in the room, past the disorderly desk and into the semidarkness of the office he was beginning to know, with a window small and narrow and so bright that it seemed to burn with the white fire of midday. "All I need for you to do, should the need arise, is to head the local militia to guard the temple while I go about my duties inside. The matter has to be dealt with, I don't care how complicated it is."

Tralles was his friend, and for all his vacillation, had been a fine officer. Here he stood at his desk, much as the first day they had renewed their acquaintance in the metropolis, big and burly and every bit as much a Romanized product of the army as himself, so similar to him in so many ways that Aelius felt his refusal acutely, like a personal failure. As if he were the one not wanting to tangle with the priests or the temple of the blessed Antinous. The meeting was like the sharp point of a pin, deflating their friendship, creating a void around them. In the void, Aelius became keenly aware of the nestled nature of this exchange and its larger implications. Here they stood in this small room, and outside of it in ever-larger dizzying circles the walls of the command post, the army compound with its Roman and Romanized garrison, the streets of Antinoopolis, the ledge behind the city, Hadrian's Way departing for the mountains and the Arabian coast like a great snake swallowed by the desert, the vastness of Heptanomia stretching from the Delta to the Thebais, cleft by the Nile like a green running wound and hemmed in on all sides by sand and sky, endless but for the deep oasis of Ammoneum, emerald of God.

"Well, Gavius, if you don't do this, who will?"

"You will. You are Caesar's envoy. No relations here, no attachments. You can."

So, that's how things stood with Tralles and the rest. Whatever had happened here in the last eight years, as ben Matthias said, there was no fighting it directly just now. Rabirius Saxa, who'd nominally said yes, had already declined to become personally involved, and there was no time to enlist the support of Prefect Culcianus from Alexandria. Aelius's escort, twenty cavalrymen from his Armenian campaign unit, had hastily been sent for by courier, but would not get here from Cynopolis, fifty miles away, before noon the following day. He had a rude desire to berate Tralles but it'd do no good, so he remained where he was instead, and decided to salvage out of the relationship with him what was possible out of their mutual disappointment. He said, sitting across from his colleague on the other side of the desk, "At least tell me why you have lost your nerve, Gavius."

Having crossed over into the no man's land of justification, Tralles was defensive by now.

"It has nothing to do with nerve," he said grumpily. "One needs to do what one needs to do in order to function here. What's the problem? You need to *adapt*. It's by degrees anyway, like ratcheting down a couple of cogs now and then. It's not like they ask you to turn yourself upside down. I had to make some adjustments from the old days."

Aelius had been staring at him, chin on his knuckles, and now lowered his eyes; but not to release his colleague from observation. To protect himself somehow from what the other was saying. The argument was the same everywhere one served, everywhere one had dealings. Tralles had discovered nothing other than his own inability to differ.

"And so?" he mildly prodded him. "Let's leave the matter at hand aside. You did—what?"

"Nothing illegal, if that's what you mean."

"It's not what I meant."

"Went native a bit. I mentioned it to you."

"Native as in—Greek? Egyptian?"

Tralles had hinted at these enterprises before, but now made them look new and more relevant, as if because of them he could not lead a body of soldiers in the morning. "Native, however you define that—like the folks who live here. Got myself a couple of slaves left as newborn on the dung-hill, raised them to their teens, sold them at a great profit. That's just good business, and not especially local, you'll say. But I did raise them to be castanets dancers, which fetches good money around here, for wedding feasts and such. Bought three farms at a discount after low flood and a bad crop, put peasants on them, turned them around by planting tree-wool. I took a sister-wife—"

This, Aelius had not heard before. "A *sister-wife*?" he burst out. "What are you saying? You never had a sister."

"Well, not exactly, but I have a first cousin, and passed her off as my sister. To fit in, you know. That is, before it was made illegal for Roman citizens six years back. We have children together, and as she was married before, she has children of her own; now her eldest girl is expecting, and the boy she married has moved in with his parents and uncle. I got a bigger place, and everybody's happy." Tralles took a deep breath and let it out again. "Which is why I don't want anything happening to me or mine." Outside, the wind was up again, and some fine sand came twirling in through the window, sparkling in the light. "It's not like I don't do my job, Aelius—I do. Ask anyone, my record as a keeper of order is the best they've had in years, around here."

"As long as you can expect no retribution."

"You know what? Curiosity killed the cat. That's my motto. You always made it a habit of being curious, being a dabbler in history or whatever it is you dabble in during your spare time; you also never settled in a place long enough to be a part of it, never participate fully, never became one of the group. It's easy for you to talk. Now you're Caesar's friend, so take advantage of your rank." Tralles put his open hand flat on his chest, to show his sincerity in the matter. "I can be of help to you, I really can. Just do not ask me to do what I can't do."

"Or won't do."

"Whatever. Short of that, I'll help."

Because Aelius had stood from the chair and was leaving the office, Tralles spoke up without rising from his desk. "Why do you travel on your own, Aelius? Where's your retinue right now?"

Aelius did not look back. "I travel on my own, by choice. Serfs and books and escort precede or follow, depending; I use the escort only when I *have to,* and for the rest I rely on bank drafts, letters of presentation, signet ring, and basic conversation dictionaries. I never traveled so comfortably before in my life."

"But you're alone, with all that's going on."

Now Aelius did turn back. "I'm not aware that anything is going on. According to you, even when you have no answer for violence or theft, it's not our business or there's nothing we can do about it. I'll watch myself, don't you worry."

3 Epiphi (28 June, Wednesday)

By a miracle of logistics, having rushed overnight, Aelius's armed escort was in the metropolis at sunup. By this time, he'd already sent a message to Antinous's temple, and was invited to an interview with the two priests who had shown him around. They met in the priests' house, and to his amazement they posed no significant obstacle to his request. They spoke of extreme concern for the irregularity of it, of the absolute need for secrecy "in order to avoid a scandal among the faithful" and demanded a number of privileges for the religious collegium (mainly exemption from dike taxes and corvees for their relatives). Other than that, they seemed amenable.

"Of course we do not have the manpower to do the work today,"

the short, fat priest added, "and we'll have to send for trustworthy engineers and masons at Panopolis. So it will be the eighth of Epiphi
before we can oblige you."

"I prefer not to wait that long."

"That is unfortunate, *legatos*. But you understand that exposing
the remains of a god, regardless of your scientific interest, must be
done on a propitious day."

*They are fully aware there's been nothing in the grave since Com-
modus's days,* Aelius thought, *but I must make sure for myself. They're
trying to buy time.* "I have an engineer on my staff," he said, "and men
enough to handle the rigging."

"Well, it may be, but it cannot be done today. We have ceremonies already planned. It's out of the question."

Aelius wanted to put his foot down, but thought better of it. "My
men are outside. Research calls me elsewhere, and a week is too long
an interval. I promise to obtain from His Divinity, and in his name, a
hereditary life annuity for the personnel of this temple as a token of
gratitude, if I am allowed to open the grave *now*."

The tall, lean priest shook his head. "There will be riots in the
metropolis if there's a perception of army violence in the temple."

It came down to more promises, but within half an hour the temple servants were dispatched to the city with excuses, the gates of the
sacred precinct closed to the public, and the baboons fed fruit in the
grove. Aelius's squad, handpicked veterans from his own country,
stood ready to carry out orders. Followers of Mithras, all of them, they
had neither awe for, nor concern about, exhuming a Greek god.

Inside the temple, the priests removed an armful of flowers from
the sarcophagus of the Boy, awakening a billow of scent and small insects. Incense was used to purify the men, their tools, and indeed the
entire cell, until one's lungs felt as embalmed as any Egyptian dead.

The seals of the sarcophagus, the engineer commented, had been
tampered with and soldered back together, an old repair job.

"More than a hundred years old?" Aelius asked, thinking of
Commodus's visit.

"Not that old."

The answer altogether made him wonder, but it made little difference to an empty coffin.

Given the weight of the lid and the difficulty to set up machinery to hoist it, the engineer concluded it should be merely shifted at a forty-five degree angle, in hopes that the thickness of the sarcophagus itself were not so massive as to impede looking within. Under the impending shade of Antinous's massive statue, in an ever-renewed cloud of incense, the soldiers labored to introduce wedges and raise the lid from its groove enough to make it rest on the outer rim of the coffin. It took them ten hours to succeed in doing this, by which time Aelius wondered how could the priests remain as collected as they did, and whether they would sham surprise at the sight of an empty grave.

But the grave was not empty. When finally the upper stone was hinged off-center and he could look in, with the help of a lamp, he met the haunting painted face of a young man with large brown eyes, dark curly hair, a pinched, cleft chin, staring upward as if the light had awakened him. Around the portrait tablet, gilded cartonnage wrappings were tightly bound in a crisscross pattern, so adherent to the body as to make it quite impossible to conceal a large document. Unless, of course, the "proof" Hadrian had spoke of had been used, with the rest of the glued papyrus material, to shape the mummy cover. Aelius's mind was swimming in ideas so opposite and quick as to stun him into silence. Theo was wrong, Commodus *had* found the body of Antinous, there were no other burial places but this one. How thinner and less impressive than his official portraits, how shorter than he imagined him—a common youth, cut down before becoming plain. Such love, such remembrance, for a common youth. The haste of the burial explained the fairly inexpensive material used to send him off into eternity. No grave goods were visible, and even peering closely, Aelius could make out nothing whatsoever around the mummy. Had anyone the gotten here before him, and removed the document? He leaned over to look into the corners of the coffin, ran his hands under the stiff mummy wraps, for a few moments he forgot who he was and where he was, such was his need to *know*. Nothing, there lay nothing else but the corpse of an average youngster. Temples, statues, poems, an entire imperial villa to keep him in, like a precious and exotic bird: Hadrian had created a legend around this thin-faced, insignificant-looking boy. Aelius thought disappointment would choke him, but evidence stared back at him from the cheap death mask.

His soldiers, curious or not, stood back, including the engineer. As for the priests, they had never moved from the folding chairs in which they sat, like judges at a sports event or politicians at a lengthy meeting. Aelius turned to look at them, and the fat priest did finally draw close, though not enough to look inside the sarcophagus. "My colleague and I were shown the blessed Antinous on occasion of repairs and embellishments to the temple, during the *pro-Egyptian* reign of Probus Caesar."

Aelius was still too surprised (*I'll never be able to get the document now,* he was thinking, *and even if it's still here, stuck somewhere inside the belly of this mummy, it's out of reach*) to comment on the slight political dig. He spent the following hour in gloomy silence, taking minute notes about the corpse and its coffin, and after prescribed ceremonies of purification and offering, cleansing and sprinkling of incense around the altars, eventually left the temple. His men went to billet at the command post, and he back to his flat, where he wrote and pondered into the night.

FIFTH CHAPTER

4 Epiphi (29 June, Thursday)

Despite the brush in his hand, Baruch ben Matthias held a finger to the side of his long nose, as if to signify he was on the right scent.

"I'm not going to ask you why you want to know, although—left to my own devices—I'm pretty sure I'll figure it out." He'd just begun the full-length portrait on linen of a sour-faced woman, whom Aelius had met on the threshold as she left her sitting with the painter.

Mixing colors from various pots, the Jew returned his attention to the easel, on which a starchy shroud was pinned. The cloth still showed little more than a gray background with a sketched face and basic lines, and the air in the shop hung thick with the smell of resin and the sappy odor of melted beeswax. Baruch had smeared his nose with red, and now wiped it clean. "If your description of the mummy is accurate—"

"It is."

"If it is accurate, you were not looking at a mummy of the Butcher's days."

"No?"

"No."

"Later, then?"

"No. *Earlier* than Hadrian, by about fifty years. Style of painting, hair treatment, the way you described tablet and casing, its shape—I want to say, give and take five years, that the mummy you saw was made during the reign of that other butcher emperor."

Aelius understood the reference to the first destruction of Jerusalem. "Titus?"

"That's right." Ben Matthias quickly stirred the pigments in his pots, applying bold strokes to the cloth. "And I suggest that the mummy was not a local product, either. Maybe Arsinoe, where they leave their tablets square. You ought to know, if you don't, that moving dead bodies isn't anything new in this country." He glanced over his shoulder, like a ram checking if the herd was behind him. "The long cliff not far from the city—yes, the Antinoite ledge, as they call it—used to be filled with burials when I first came, rifled all of them centuries ago, but some still containing their mummies, stripped of all valuables. The tombs were actually old quarry holes, so when the metropolis decided to exploit them again, they hauled the bodies out and buried them in modern coffins, outside the east gate. Why do you look so elated, Commander?"

Aelius would not say. Theo might have been right after all. Commodus had found nothing in the Boy's coffin, perhaps because the deified Hadrian had already emptied it upon returning to Rome. However the news had been kept from spreading, the temple priests had quickly taken the opportunity to place an extraneous mummy in the coffin, just in case other powerful visitors tried to view the body. Cult ceremonies and revenues went on as if the body were Antinous's. But now traveling to Italy became a distinct and urgent possibility, which renewed Aelius's hopes of discovering the truth.

"I thank you for the information, Baruch."

"Costs me nothing."

He left ben Matthias's shop with a mind to take a ride in the country before the wind picked up enough to generate a sandstorm. Fine silt, like ground glass, was already blowing down from the ledge outside the east gate. Here Aelius stopped to lift the neck kerchief to his face under the triumphal arch of Carus and his two sons. Emperors before Diocletian, those warring upstarts had all been killed years ago. Their commemorative inscription still carried the chisel marks of Aelius's troopers, commanded during the Rebellion to erase the three hateful names: never mind that from that intrigue of ambition and fratricide, His Divinity had paradoxically risen as avenger of Carus's youngest son and as new ruler.

The horse track down the road, set at an angle from the city wall, ran in a precise east-west direction, and funerary monuments lined the verge between here and there. Some of them predated the colony and bore no name, or the name was written in incomprehensible pictographs. He'd twice ridden this way lately, when Christians had been executed, army men who'd without complaint gotten their heads lopped off *in the usual place.* A fortified cistern of the type they called *hydreuma,* hastily put up during the Rebellion by Achilleus's troops (by ben Matthias, for all he knew), had been since left to silt up. It was behind that very wall that the army executed its Christians.

Beyond the horse track, an elongated, natural butte seemed the convex version of the concave stadium. At less than half a mile of distance, like the ledge above it, it had at this hour the brightness of a copper mirror. It was hard to believe that this was the same rock and the same Antinoite ledge that in the morning was bluer than the sky past it and simmered red in the afternoon.

He headed for the old hillside graves and quarry holes, so between the rounded end of the horse track and the butte, he left the road and took a sharp right in the bare and shadeless expanse, to seek a climb manageable on horseback. At the foot of the butte he encountered a small, timeworn shrine to Hathor, and through the cloth of his kerchief, by habit, he touched his lips out of respect. Inside her niche, the statue of the goddess stood as if to greet him back. Her curving brow, narrow chin, wide temples, mild, sweet expression, and heifer ears made her into a divine hybrid of farm animal and goddess that reminded him of Anubina's face. He planned to go to see her at the store before leaving Egypt, and to that end he'd bought a doll for her daughter and would bring sweets to the boy. Should her husband be around, well, he'd meet him too, fortunate chump that he was.

There had never been a direct, paved way from Antinoopolis to the quarries, and Aelius's best bet was to follow the bone-dry, pebble-strewn bed of a seasonal torrent, rising moderately at first and then curving at a sharper northbound angle to the rim of the ledge. Minor branches of the torrent spread like fingers of a hand stretching to reach the eastern wall of the metropolis. Scorpions darted from under rocks as the horse clattered up the incline, and the ledge that appeared low and scalloped from the city seemed to grow in height and steepness as he drew close to it.

The entrance to the principal quarry was not at all like the regular, squared ones he'd seen north of Aspalatum, from which His Divinity's palace was being fashioned. It really resembled the jagged mouth of a large grotto, and the moment he stepped into it the wind died down in his ears, with a hollow effect of utter silence. Powdery silt followed him in, and settled as well. A few steps ahead, errant rocks and abandoned rubble on the floor revealed that the quarries were once more vacant. In older days, if one could trust the sources, travelers had to be careful about lions and such taking refuge in caves. Now there was scarcely need to smell the air before going in to make sure it was not a den. Lions were so rare, he'd seen signs posted in the city advertising premium pay for a single pride to sell to the circus.

As Aelius stepped farther in, he met darkness broken by an occasional light shaft cut into the quarry ceiling, to which on the floor corresponded a cone of pebbles and sand fallen from above during sandstorms. Marks made by mattock and pickax pocked the walls like fish scales. There was also dressed stonework where ancient graves had been carved out of these spaces midway through the life of the quarry, and then gutted to extract stone again, perhaps in the days of the deified Hadrian and the building of Antinous's memorial city. The murkiness that at first had veiled his eyesight after abandoning the outside cleared enough for him to distinguish shapes and objects all around.

On the ground, at the end of the corridor of dressed stone, he saw what seemed to be timber piled out of the way. Close up, the heap revealed itself to be cut, planed, and painted boards and planks, most of them shattered and broken through. Aelius lifted one carefully and used it to prod through the others, causing a race of spiders and jellylike scorpions to surge in all directions. Astonished painted faces, the gilding of wreaths and lips removed long ago, looked back at him from the dust and decay of the pile as he exposed mummy tablets not unlike the one found in the Boy's coffin. Going deeper into the rubble-strewn corridor might reveal more such remains, but he had no interest in visiting rifled tombs. Still, he spent some time exploring other openings. In some he found human excrements, broken pots, the signs of at least temporary habitation. Afterward, standing at the mouth of one of the quarries, he was afforded a sweeping view of the country below him. Hawks caught the ascending currents of warm, dusty air and balanced themselves on the wing against the green fringe along the bank, the Nile, its islands, and Hermopolis across the water.

From up here, one could see how the level of the river had risen, and already the lower-lying areas to the south had been flooded, so that seasonal huts of unfired bricks crumbled into mud again and washed like every other detritus to the Delta. Farmhouses farthest to the south were reduced to a small space around the knolls on which they were built, fields were completely underwater, palm groves looked shortened as the lower parts of the trunks were submerged; water fowl—resembling swarms of gnats from the hazy distance—flocked to swim in newly formed ponds. Soon farmers would get around in boats and dinghies, and one would travel by water; mosquitoes, other insects, frogs would follow, and for the long time of the retreating flood everything would smell like mud and rotten stalks, but grass would sprout up with flowers everywhere. It seemed to him that this yearly expectation shaped the people here, making them both secure and fatalistic, believers in the quirky eternity of seasons, cycles, and stars. He had none of that fatalism and security, relying on himself and what he knew. Trusting less in traditional and remote gods than in philosophical virtues taught to him by good teachers, chosen by his father's ambition for him.

But there existed an eternity of sorts, and out of that timelessness into which all who died tumbled forever, he was trying to learn what had happened to Antinous at the now half-sunk Benu grove, or to Serenus Dio and his freedman.

Overnight, accompanied by a sandstorm, the flood broke through the narrows of the First Cataract, three weeks ahead of schedule. Though it would take another week for the full rage of the water to travel four hundred miles and wash over the banks here, its color was suddenly reddish brown and the level menacingly high. Rats swarmed up from the lower-lying areas and basements, fleeing the seepage that would eventually drown them by the thousands. Across the Nile, the river harbor of Hermopolis and the whole left bank, lower and less hilly, must already be under a foot of water.

Despite the blowing sand, in Antinoopolis the temples opened early, and there was concourse of the faithful everywhere. By noon, however, the storm was fierce, and the streets depopulated, the shops closed.

Aelius came back from the city library just in time to avoid the worst of it. He'd found out at the mall when the first ship leaving for Italy would take sail from Alexandria, and made his plans accordingly. For the rest of the day, there was nothing to do but stay out of the weather. Sand managed to enter the smallest chink of doors and windows, and reading in a small inner room afforded the only respite from the confusion. Night took forever to come, and in the dark the wind kept on, to abate only shortly before dawn, as if gates had closed against it in the south, and only the flood were allowed to continue.

> *Joke ascribed to the deified Hadrian, also known by the title*
> *"Even the Powerful Are at Times Mistaken"*
> *As everyone knows, my father, the deified Trajan, was in the habit of visiting the poor in the City, distributing largesses and consoling them in their plight. One morning, as he walked the streets of the crowded Transtiberim district, accompanied by officers of his revenue who often turned up their noses at the misery encountered, he happened onto a particularly neglected family.*
> *Huddled in their smoky quarters, mother, father, and a brace of children looked the picture of poverty. Under their breath, the deified Trajan's officers laughed at their rags, and remarked on the utter ugliness of the youngest child, whom they called "misshapen abortion" and "gruesome tyke." Meanwhile, the excellent prince handed bread to the mother, placed a handful of coins into the father's trembling hand, and patted the older children's heads. Busy in his generosity, he had heard none of the cruel remarks by his retinue. Finally, having come to the corner where the youngest sat, he snapped his fingers to the slave bearing food, and loudly said, "Quick, boy, let us leave no one without: Hand me walnuts for the monkey!"*

6 Epiphi (1 July, Kalends, Saturday)

When, half packed already, on the third hour of Saturday Aelius went to deposit letters for friends and family at the command post, Tralles saw him through the door of his office. He came to meet him in the hallway, where orderlies swept sand and dust from the floor. "Wasn't it one of *those storms?*" he said by way of a greeting. "I managed to get sand even inside my pants!" Because Aelius kept aloof he said, "You'll be curious to know what happened to our old friend with the shitty name," he added. "Kopros the cobbler, you know. He finally managed to get himself arrested for setting the house of a tax agent on fire and raved like a lunatic about religion enough to be hauled before the judge as a Christian."

"I should have hit him harder in the marketplace. Well, what did the judge decide?"

"Found him guilty on the counts of arson and superstition, and condemned him to death."

Aelius resumed walking, bound for the rooms where his bodyguard quartered. "I wouldn't have given him the satisfaction. Now they'll make a martyr out of him though he was the one who turned others in."

"That's where the judge thinks the way you do, Aelius. He commuted capital punishment to hard labor in His Divinity's new baths in Rome."

They hadn't spoken to each other since the day Tralles had refused to support him, and Aelius had to make an effort to be polite. Cutting the conversation short, he left his colleague for the sand-strewn inner court, where the noncommissioned officer heading his escort awaited. He gave the man orders to precede him with the bulk of the troop to the Delta, carrying luggage, the books, and leaving behind a nominal force of three cavalrymen to accompany him.

For the balance of the morning, having decided to retain lease of his flat through the summer, he raided the bookstalls once more, and solicited copies of documents he could not acquire or borrow from the shrine library at Hermopolis. To Thermuthis, according to an agreed-upon code, he sent word to "keep the advance," by which he meant the saddlebag, "until I come back and can settle the account." A quick lunch was grabbed at the mall. Afterward, a constitutional alongside the river, where he and Theo had fed the ducks, showed him how moorings, piers, even the hexagonal basin for the duck pond, lay under a turbid veil of water. Birds pecked at a dead rat, and in the air hovered an indefinable smell of wetness, decay, and green leaves torn and mashed. Across the racing current, slapping and frothing around the piers of the bridge over the partly submerged islands, Hermopolis took in the sun and—as expected—was already flooded to the foot of the harbor wall.

At his quarters, Aelius found a long-winded invitation from *epistrategos* Rabirius Saxa to attend a series of boxing matches in honor of the deified Julius Caesar, whose month it was. He accepted, though it would not keep him from reporting to His Divinity that Saxa, too, had in a pinch declined to help.

8 EPIPHI (3 JULY, MONDAY)

The pretentious central gymnasium, looking wholly Greek except for the potted palm trees, was filled to capacity with crowds arrived in town to witness the trial of Christian clerics, and disappointed by their abjuration. "We've been robbed," Aelius overheard an uncouth visitor tell another. "My friends and me, we came all the way from Ombos to see them suffer, and them Christians turn coat just like that. *Robbed,* I tell you! This here boxing had better be worth a Christian trial."

In that, he was likely more satisfied than Aelius, who cared little for the waste of energy in the ring. Throughout the afternoon, beefy young men with hands bound in leather and lead bloodied one another in earnest, and even in the less violent *pancration* a couple of well-aimed blows of the bare knuckles did commensurate damage.

Theo the spice merchant and Harpocratio were in attendance. Sitting in different rows, both waved kerchiefs during the intermission to let Aelius know they'd recognized him. Afterward, in the sweaty crowd that streamed out of the gymnasium, they waited only long enough for Aelius to part ways with Rabirius Saxa and other officers to approach him. Aelius told them he planned to leave the metropolis on Friday, though in fact he meant to be gone by Thursday morning at the latest.

"I am going to Rome to pursue my historical work," he said, and as he spoke he formulated ideas about how much, or little else, he would reveal. "Since I have never been there, I should be grateful for names of contacts who might help me in my research. Of course, I'll be delighted to carry any messages or objects you might want to send along to the capital."

Harpocratio looked interested. "What ship will you sail in?"

"I don't know yet." It was not true, but Aelius thought he'd keep the information for himself. "Likely a military transport, unless I can do better. In the past, like everyone else, I had good luck with cereal cargo ships heading to and from Ostia."

It turned out that Theo had letters to send and Harpocratio a box of books. Both of them showed themselves eager to expedite shipping through Aelius. Theo volunteered, "You must positively get in touch with my good friend Lucinus Soter, in the III district. He lives on Copper Alley, kitty-corner from the Baths of Titus, anyone will be able to point you to it. He's a textile wholesaler, and knows everybody among the Egyptian expatriates of Rome. I'll send his address to your place along with the letters. If you're going to the *Iseum Campense* or to the other worship places, they'll give you a line of official tales there as well, so you'll need someone like Soter to sieve through the nonsense."

With this, and warm wishes for a safe journey, Theo was on his way. Harpocratio mentioned he had some names in mind as well, especially among the booksellers and book collectors of the City. He had come to the match accompanied by an athletic young man with a remarkably sleepy face, whom he now sent ahead in order to speak privately to Aelius. "If you have time before you leave, Commander, let us get together at my place," he said, and when Aelius inquired further, he added, "It's about Serenus."

Having made an appointment to meet Serenus's pal in the morning, Aelius walked the streets where shadows lengthened, still noisy and warm, clogged here and there by youngsters who worked out the excitement of the boxing match by repeating the athletes' moves and shoving one another. A full moon had risen and hung in the polished sky opposite the sun, trembling in the heat that streets and roofs gave out with the coming of evening.

Anubina's shop was a heartbeat away from the amphitheater that had been built near the south gate, but now was stranded between the houses built in the days of the deified Hadrian and a newer district outside the old walls, less orderly than the Hellenic grid plan and rather organic. Presently, a pleasant odor of frying meat came from the food stands under the arches of the amphitheater; idle young men with unruly heads of black hair loitered nearby, chewing on skewered bits of fried lamb. Aelius wondered whether Antinous had looked like them, the sort of soft youth one feels like shaking into discipline, starting with a haircut.

The next street, curving sharply and completely in the shade, was where Isidora's brothel had its main entrance. It featured mostly older women from Alexandria, who'd passed their professional prime and sought a second career in provincial towns. Boys and older men tended to patronize it. Aelius had been there once, to pick up Tralles who'd gotten drunk and knocked a woman down a flight of stairs. They'd given him a free pass, but Aelius had always preferred Thermuthis's place.

On the wall alongside the entrance of Anubina's shop, a blue sign was painted directly on the plaster. In a public scribe's facile hand, it read Πλουμαρία, embroiderer, and—in Latin—PLVMARIA. She employed four girls who decorated flax, linen, and linsey-woolsey tunics and dresses, a flourishing industry in the area. She herself drew the patterns and did much of the sewing. This evening, the girls started giggling and craning their necks at the sight of the fine uniform and the fair-skinned man in it, so Anubina pulled the drape that divided the workshop from the sales room, and met him there.

Skilled at sewing as she'd always been, Anubina had always dressed well, and even at the brothel her sheets and towels had been beautifully stitched with openwork and appliques. She wore city clothes today, indigo-colored, and if it weren't for the exuberance of her black hair, her coiffure would have been as slick and contained as

Aelius had seen ladies wear at Nicomedia: wavy at the sides, gathered at the nape of the neck in a flat bundle turned back to be pinned at the top of the head. With Anubina, it was as if rays of night always escaped clips and hairpins.

"You went to ask Thermuthis," she told him, a little provoked. "Aelius, why can't you take no answer as an answer?"

"If it's any consolation, she wouldn't tell me either."

On the counter, where samples of embroidered hems were displayed, she saw what he had brought.

Still, "What is this?" she asked.

"It's a doll."

"I see *that*."

"For Thaësis." It was an expensive ivory toy, jointed and delicately sculpted, with a miniature glass mirror at her belt.

"And the sweets?"

"For the other one."

Under the bag of sweets was something else, which Anubina uncovered but would not touch.

"That's for Thaësis, too," Aelius hastened to say.

"A gold necklace with carved stones and a locket?"

"For when she grows up. You can wear it until then. If you want."

She set doll and sweets aside, without looking at him. "These, I will accept. The necklace is no gift you should be giving to either one of us."

"I am only giving it because she could have been mine. I'm no longer insisting that she is, and am not asking you anymore."

"And what should I tell her when she's old enough to wear it?"

Aelius pushed the necklace alongside the other gifts. "You can tell her it was a present from her uncle, Anubina."

She looked grieved, for the first time since they'd met again. A line drew itself between her eyebrows, and testily she lowered her head to keep him from seeing her frown. Still, he could make out the richness of her throat, the rounding of her shoulders. Her belly hadn't grown from the day at her house, so she mustn't be pregnant.

Aelius was glad of it, though he hardly had a reason for it. "I'm leaving soon," he said. "Take care of yourself."

Anubina stayed half-turned. It took him a moment then to realize that she was laughing to herself, as women sometimes do when they don't want to give men credit for making them weep. "Do you remember when I boiled rice and you put butter in it?" she said out of the blue, holding the doll in her hands and still avoiding his scrutiny. "Crazy northerner, putting butter where it doesn't belong." Such a little episode from their past, and yet it was like the unexpected completion of a circle. Meaning no more than it said, but still a sort of healing—of today's melancholy at least.

9 EPIPHI (4 JULY, TUESDAY)

Fresh from a swim in his pool, and from having his hair dyed and dressed, Harpocratio received Aelius in his living room, where silver and fine plates were displayed behind grids inside stout furniture. The marble floor—worth a fortune no doubt—was so shiny as to seem wet, and tinted by the rose-colored ceiling-to-floor drapes, bearing woven medallions of youthful centaurs and piping shepherds. The wind made the light cloth billow in from the garden with the impression of sails, as though the whole room floated comfortably across an invisible ocean. Lined with appetizingly crowded shelves, the rich library showed through the door of the next room.

Harpocratio had a gift for him, a codex with a new epitome, a shorter version of Herodotus's travels through Egypt. Aelius, who harbored a little discomfort for having secured Hadrian's letter at no cost, hesitated before accepting, but was not willing to offend by refusing. After all, Serenus's friend was safer ignoring the existence of the saddlebag altogether. If he'd learned the way these people operated, a gift was often preemptive, either of a request for favors or an apology. Accompanying the gift with a bow of his head, Harpocratio was in fact saying, "I am afraid I haven't been completely candid with you during our previous encounters, Commander."

Aelius laid the codex aside. "Really? On how many counts? I

figured you didn't tell me one third of what you knew about Serenus's death, his last trip, or his expeditions to the gold-filled graves."

"That is true, but I had good reasons for it."

"Fear I'd turn you in to the fisc for not declaring your wealth? Roman tax collectors are dogged, but I'm sure you'd find your way out of it with the help of smart Alexandria lawyers."

"You do me an injustice, Commander."

"I doubt it. But enlighten me on the rest. You know I'm off soon."

"I'll make it short, I'll make it short. After Serenus came back from the Western Wilderness, we gave a small reception at our house. What's *small*, you ask? No more than fifty people, I'd say. Serenus hardly ever indulged in drink, but he'd been so on edge lately, he put away a few. We were sitting in the arbor where you and I first met, when he told me that he'd been to Ammoneum and received an oracle that thoroughly unnerved him. He'd gone to the desert shrine for an offering—he was particularly devoted to Zeus Ammon—and decided to sleep in the incubation room, as they do here in the temple of the blessed Antinous, but on a grander scale. I was at once concerned, knowing how sensitive he was, and asked him whether the god had come to him in his sleep. He said no, but that the blessed Antinous had, and seemed to be dipping a ladle into the Nile to take water from it." Aelius took notice, but did not comment on the detail. He said, "Thus far it seems to me that Serenus had a bad conscience about stealing water from a neighbor in the spring."

"How would you know about that?"

"I read it in the dockets."

"But the dream didn't end there. The deified Hadrian was in it, too, and seemed cross, either because of the Boy's action or at Serenus himself."

The matter became more interesting now. "I see." Aelius spoke looking at the feminine swell of the rosy drapes. "Did your reception take place before or after Serenus left the letter for me at the Hermopolis post exchange?"

"It was on the evening of that very day. I remember because

Serenus came back late and had to change in a hurry from his street clothes."

"Do you have a list of the guests?"

Harpocratio made a fussy gesture of denial with his hands. "It'd do no good. We always, always used to invite five or six old friends, and told them to bring along anyone they wished. There have been times at our parties when some unknown boor even bad-talked Serenus to me, not knowing who I was!"

"Still, I'd like the list."

"It's in the library. I'll get it for you."

Following Harpocratio next door, Aelius scanned the shelves, filling his nostrils with the good odor of books and boxed volumes. "Just out of curiosity," he asked, "did Serenus have an inkling on the meaning of the dream?"

"He wouldn't go into detail, Commander. He did say the oracle at Ammoneum was not favorable. Ah, here's the list—take it. He debated whether he should travel on business to his property at Ptolemais or not. I offered to go for him, but he refused."

"Dreams are interesting, but I don't see how all this helps me."

Leading the way back across the living room, Harpocratio cleared his throat. "Serenus also confided to me that he'd been talking a bit too freely during the party, and that getting out of town for a while might be a good solution after all. Now don't get excited, you must believe me if I tell you that I have no clue, no clue at all, as to what he might have said, about what or to whom. I could make neither head nor tail of his concern about the dream: We pay our respects to the blessed Antinous, send money, pay for a wreath on the festival of the deified Hadrian, but other than that we have little to do with them. The following day, he pretended not to remember our conversation and minimized any indiscretion during the party. But something was definitely amiss."

"But you won't say officially that you suspect foul play because of the stipulation in his will."

"Is it wrong? Serenus wouldn't want me not to benefit from what

I helped him accumulate." Harpocratio looked contrite, but who knows what layers of less worthy emotions resembled contrition on his florid face? "I know you have been making inquiries into Pammychios's death, and that you seem to think his end is somehow linked to my Serenus's. Should you find out what happened, wherever your research leads you, I beg you to let me know. It will help me put my heart at ease."

"You had better get those Alexandria lawyers cracking, then, because I can guarantee you it is murder. And as long as you are in a mood of sincerity, it'd help if you told me whether you think the ransacking of this house has something to do with Serenus's loose talk during the party."

The mask was going back up for good, because it was about money again. Harpocratio's contrition became levity, as he looked around the well-appointed room as if to make sure all the beautiful things in it were still here. "Yes, I am sure. He probably said more than he intended about his fortunate discoveries of grave goods, and the word spread enough for thieves to think we'd keep the gold under our beds."

The second letter from Aelius Spartianus to Diocletian Caesar:

> *To Emperor Caesar Gaius Aurelius Valerius Diocletian Pius Felix Invictus Augustus, in obedience to His commands to be addressed heretofore as Lord, his Aelius Spartianus, with gratitude and greetings.*
>
> *Upon arriving in Egypt a month ago, Lord, it was my intention to remain until the flood should recede and continue my local travels in search of details pertaining to the deified Hadrian's permanence in this province. As it is, I feel I must depart even before the flood reaches peak stage, in order to pursue more immediate leads in Italy. All I have seen and heard to date makes me believe that the document the deified*

Hadrian alluded to might have been once—if ever—inside the sarcophagus in the Boy's temple at Antinoopolis, but that the memoria Antinoi *of which that prince spoke is not, nor was ever, in said temple. Another funerary shrine or monument is intended, which—for want of details—I am at this point only assuming exists or existed on the grounds of the Tiburtine villa, in Rome, or at Baiae.*

Mindful of your encouragement to pursue this investigation where it will lead, I am preparing to leave the Heptanomia and sail for Italy. Thanks to your letters of presentation, Lord, I am spared the delays and contretemps that are the bane of most travelers and count on boarding the good ship Felicitas Annonae *when she sails from Alexandria-near-Egypt on the sixteenth day of July. If the document still exists, my hope is to secure it in advance of others, and to deliver it into your hands. In the process, being now convinced that Serenus Dio's as well as his freedman's death are connected to it somehow, I hope to solve the crimes as well.*

As by your request, Lord, below is a summary of selected prices, as found in the metropolis and surroundings (on average, in denarii and Roman measures, as equated by myself from drachmas and Egyptian artabae *and other measures, unless noted otherwise):*

wheat *(1 army camp* modius*)*	147	denarii
rice *(cleaned, 1 a.c.* modius*)*	230	" "
rice *(uncleaned, 1 a.c.* modius*)*	200	" "
pork *(first quality, 1 Italian pound)*	20	" "
pork *(second quality, 1 It. pound)*	10	" "
pork mincemeat *(1 ounce)*	3	" "
army boots *(w/out hobnails)*	125	" "
notary public *(per 100 lines of text)*	12	" "

The smallest variance in excess of the prices set by the edict amounts to 20 percent (notary public fee), and the highest to 47 percent (wheat). Of all the items I priced, only Egyptian

beer and second quality river fish were at or below edict prices.
Soldiers and civilians alike suffer from the high cost of living;
money is plentiful, but its value much abased.

Separately I am sending a detailed report on the proceed-
ings against Christians, and of the response by local authori-
ties to requests of support in my duties.

Written in Antinoopolis, on the fourth day of July (III
Nones), in the twenty-first year of Our Lord Caesar Diocletian's
imperial acclamation, the seventh year of the consulship of
Maximianus Augustus, and the eighth year of the consulship of
M. Aurelius Valerius Maximianus Augustus, also the year 1057
since the foundation of the City.

10 Epiphi (5 July, Wednesday)

Having heard that Aelius was leaving, Tralles seemed all of a sudden anxious to be of help. He came to see him early in the morning, joined him in the private baths where he was soaking in lukewarm water, and spoke his well-rehearsed little piece.

"Just to show you that I care, Aelius, for old times' sake, and for the money you lent me once—I know you don't recall, but you did, and I'm afraid you're not going to see it again any time soon, now that I have a large family to take care of—I wrote to someone who might be useful to you in Rome. Useful? What am I saying? He *will* be useful. Why, he's brilliant."

Aelius sank completely under water before emerging with his head again. "Is he army?"

"Ex-army."

"Qualifications?"

"You name it."

"Available?"

"Even now."

"Cost?"

"Pensioner. No cost."

"What's the catch?"

"He's blind."

Hauling himself out of the water, Aelius laughed out loud. "You cannot be serious."

"Oh, but I am. And not to worry, he has a boy who takes him around where he needs to. Won't give you a bit of trouble. You need this man, Aelius. He can help you reconstruct what happened on the imperial barge with Antinous and the deified Hadrian and the rest—has professionally solved murders before and after losing his eyesight."

"And what makes you think he'll be disposed to up and support me in my research, and for no compensation?"

Promptly Tralles handed a towel to his friend. "The man is a wanderer, inside and out. The idea of traveling and doing things is all he lives for. You have to give him a try, Aelius. You'll be glad you did. Besides, I wrote him already, and he'll be waiting for you when you get to Italy. Here is his address. Just send word ahead of where and when you'll be landing, and he'll do the rest."

The last person Aelius went to meet before leaving Antinoopolis was ben Matthias, who gave him an earful about the nastiness of the capital.

"You won't like Rome, you know. Noise everywhere, idlers by the cartload, they'll steal the soles of your boots from under your feet if you don't watch out."

"Well, I've been to Alexandria and Nicomedia, I'm not entirely rustic."

"Ha! Listen to him. Alexandria and Nicomedia—provincial cynosures for the army traveler! I've been there enough times myself to know that I don't—and you won't—like it."

"Thanks for spoiling my expectations, Baruch. Now I want to ask you something I'd only ask a former enemy: advice about the wisdom of a possible alliance."

Ben Matthias clapped his hands in amusement. "I'll have to make an effort not to look smug, but go ahead."

"A man by the name of Gaius Aviola Paratus has been recommended to me in connection with my historical research. I am to meet him in Italy later this month or early in August. What do you know about him? He used to serve on Domitius Domitianus's staff, but left him when the general started the Rebellion, and fought in the Delta on our side until the victory in March."

"Paratus? I recall him well enough, though 'fought' is hardly the term I'd apply to a blind veteran who was head of intelligence. I expect he'll serve you as well as he served your common master during the Rebellion. His birth name is Breucus, if I'm not mistaken. Pork- and Danube-fed like so many of you. If I find out anything else about him before you leave, I'll send you word."

"Any words of wisdom before I go?"

"Well, it's just a hunch. But two killings, two thefts, and two attacks against you—if the crazy man who tried to jump you in the street counts as much as what happened to you on the river bank— point to something more than coincidence. Mind you, I'm not asking what about any of these crimes fascinates you, but it's been noticed you're *interested.*"

"Come out with it, then. Do I have enemies?"

"I'm not an oracle, Aelius Spartianus. Ask the priests at Antinous's temple: They are in that business." Ben Matthias turned to the easel and busied himself with a small paint pot, out of which, with a fine brush, he gathered just enough white to highlight the scowling eyes of his sitter. "Enemies, we all have. I'd watch my back all the way to the harbor, and unless you know the crew, aboard the ship as well."

Aelius was less amused than he sounded. "You wouldn't have anything to do with any of this, Baruch, would you?"

"Me!" Once more the painter faced him. "If I'd wanted to kill you, I'd have come myself and made sure the arrow went deeper than last time." But the way ben Matthias said it, cocking his head through half-closed lids, made Aelius wonder how much of what the Jew told him could be taken as true.

The housekeeper was supervising the covering of furniture with linen throws when Aelius returned home. She was quite happy to keep the flat rented during the hot season, when tourists dwindled to a few consumptives hoping to roast away their disease.

"Commander," she said gingerly at his entrance, "a few minutes ago there came a young girl with a package for you. I had it brought to your bedroom."

Aelius had bought nothing today. "What sort of package?" he asked, and, "Was there a message?"

"No, no message. The girl was dressed like an apprentice, so I figure it's from some shop you went to."

Aelius went to see. On his bed, there lay a bundle of cloth tidily wrapped and tied with wool yarn, which he undid at once. Folded with care inside, a finely stitched tunic with dark blue applied strips—those called *clavi*—down the front. A sober decoration, which only at a close exam showed the minute embroidery of blue jackal heads, for the whole length of the strips.

From the doorstep, the housekeeper's voice caused him to turn.

"Why, that's from Anubina's shop. What a great piece of work! That girl has done well for herself."

11 EPIPHI (6 JULY, VIGIL OF THE NONES OF JULY, THURSDAY)

On the morning of his departure, ben Matthias's coming to his flat surprised him, but the Jew was there, keenly eyeing the luggage to be packed on mules for the land travel to Alexandria. He said something to the effect of being headed for Oxyrhinchus himself. "So, since we're to follow the same route, I thought we might join up."

Aelius had just folded Anubina's gift tunic into his trunk, and felt a little vulnerable at the moment.

"Is that why you're here uninvited?" he said, briefly.

"Actually, no. I came because you did ask me to find out about the contact your colleague suggested."

Ben Matthias, too, was in traveling clothes, and armed. Aelius had to wonder how many of his young toughs would go with him, and how believable this sudden travel of his was. Clearly he knew his party planned to travel along the right bank from Hermopolis through the Arsinoites basin to the sea.

The Jew seemed unfazed by the officer's scrutiny. "As far as I can tell," he continued, "Aviola Paratus is all right. Had been volunteering as a language instructor at the metropolis command post, and left to rejoin his family in Italy about a month ago. Quiet man, pays his bills, manages to stay active despite his blindness. Began as a policeman in Rome, made the grade, and then joined the army. Has an uncanny ear for languages and dialects, and his specialty until he lost his eyesight was cryptography." Ben Matthias took one step to the side when the house servants lifted the trunk and took it out. "It was a loss to the Rebellion and to our Jewish unit that he went over to Diocletian."

"I thank you for the information. And if it's all the same with you, Baruch, we'll travel separately."

"Suit yourself, Spartianus. I've never been one to insist when I'm not wanted. However, I plan to be in Rome sometime during the fall, to check on real estate I have north of Nero's Meadows. I might see you then if there's occasion. And if you travel to Tibur on the Butcher's tracks, make sure you bring my greetings to Queen Zenobia's grave. I bet no one remembers the old girl these days."

Travel Notes by Aelius Spartianus:
We departed Antinoopolis today, 6 July, crossing over to Hermopolis, and from here heading north. I had originally intended to follow the route on the left side of the river, and to cross over at Babylon in the Delta on my way to Alexandria. Given the state of the river, this is now quite impossible, be-

sides, the river police discourages all travel on that side, on account of recent raids on caravans. When I objected that I did not see this as a peril for myself and my men, I was told by Rabirius Saxa himself that the local authorities did not wish to take upon themselves the responsibility for any accident, and I had to acquiesce.

There are evident advantages to traveling along the right bank, as one needn't ferry across the Nile at any point to reach Alexandria, but the river branch that parallels on this side the course of the river from Abydos to the sea, nearly five hundred miles in all, presents its own obstacle now that we are in the flood season. As this bank is lower than the other, much of the riverside is already impracticable on foot and in most places on horseback as well. Hence we will have to keep on the ledge road. My intention is to maintain as much as possible an average speed of forty miles daily, stopping only to rest, and to visit a couple of sites associated with the deified Hadrian, but my aim is Alexandria, its harbor, and the Felicitas Annonae.

As we left the city by the north gate, no hide nor hair of ben Matthias and his crew were to be seen on the road. It strengthens my suspicion that he never meant to travel on his own but to follow me, if possible. I do not trust him or his, and will keep on the lookout should they appear to be in the neighborhood. I have the advantage of immediate access to the army posts along the way. Not having traveled this way since the Rebellion, I assume some of them will be much depleted or in disuse, still this is a more populated trek than on the Antinoopolis side. At Oxyrhinchus I plan to do some asking of the Libyan Wilderness merchants, who tarry there at the terminus of the caravan roads.

Day One. We have come without impediment the distance agreed upon. Four militarily trained men can compel local mule drovers to do miracles. We avoid the midday sun, unbearably hot, and stay away from the water's edge at night, when insects blacken the moonlit air. A couple of fortified cisterns, wholly useless due to lack of maintenance, had the sand around them so well smoothed out that I suspect someone might have actually concealed traces of having stopped there shortly before our passage. I may be wrong, or it may be any one traveler heading north even as we are, but I gave orders to keep weapons at the ready anyway. The natural branch of the Nile splits in two and braids back again in this area, but if one didn't know from the map, one would not notice: The land is flooded over all. We crossed a couple of dilapidated villages, built on the titanic ruins of ancient temples or fortifications. These, too, being built of sun-dried bricks, have crumbled through the centuries, leaving behind mountains of detritus rich in salt. Goats lick the collapsed walls. Precious nothing visible on the other bank. A hot norther blows continuously. Mosquitoes most annoying.

Day Two. Cynopolis. The foundation day of the Ala Ursiciana, my Armenian unit. The men and I offered sacrifice in the temple of Hermanubis, which is in very bad shape. Its outer perimeter has given way, and although we read in books that this was once a famous center for the cult of the jackal-headed god, Dog City is now little more than a village—where incidentally everyone complains about taxes, and started running at our arrival taking us for tax men. Once it was clear we were not, I managed to converse with one of the local elders, whose Greek is so abominable that, were it not for the little practice years ago with Anubina, I should have been left scratching my head. Still, he told me that a group of ten or twelve men is riding ahead of us by half a day. They didn't come through town, and he only knows because his sons, who were on a dinghy transporting some thing or other, saw the group filing on the ledge road. Again, it may be a coincidence, or not. It is likely that sooner or later, either because they slow down or we gain speed, we will meet along the way.

Day Three. *At Oxyrhinchus. Our mysterious predecessors have entirely vanished. No one has seen them, and I'm thinking that—it being Saturday—it could very well be that it is ben Matthias and his band shadowing us, but being careful not to break the Sabbath. They're hiding somewhere in the whereabouts, I wager. The town, antique and venerable, suffers from faulty maintenance like so many other Egyptian sites. I had great hopes that the Temple of the deified Hadrian would comprise a library, and was terribly disappointed to find that it is not even being used as a place of worship. An itinerant judge travels to it once a month from the Arsinoite to hold trials, and the annex of the temple is being used as a prison. Three Christian priests or deacons (I am unsure which) are kept there awaiting trial. The town's other temples (to Kore, Serapis, etc.) are minimally kept up; even the capitol is used as a jail. A depressing sight. Antinoopolis in comparison seems like a thriving beehive.*

The only good thing happened when I surprised some workers behind the marketplace, busy removing limestone slabs from the gymnasium courtyard. "For reuse," they said, but they're likely selling it or making it into lime, judging by the combustible material they were also getting ready to cart off. Most of it came from Christian households (codices, books, other written material), but some had been hauled in as kindling and scrap by caravans returning from the Libyan Wilderness. A treasure trove! An entire city archive from the days of the deified Hadrian, coming from a small desert edge community called Ptolemaion, plus an odd tract in Latin, bearing the title The Death and Resurrection of Antinous. *There is a small shrine to the Boy, incidentally, nicely kept. The sexton, who looks old enough to recall Hadrian's travels, or even Caesar's coming, told me that a local tradition maintains that the emperor had a dream at Oxyrhinchus, commanding him to kill Antinous in order to break the long drought. We'll see if the tract tells the same tale.*

Day Four. *A long solitary stretch with no towns, and even now we are still south of Herakleopolis. The men are edgy, and so am I.*

Day Five. *A soldier's instinct never lies. When we stopped yesterday, the solitude of the road, the ruinous state of the watch towers, and an indefinable quality of tension in the air caused us to take extra precautions when camping out. I had barely begun penning my diary entry when we were attacked by a handful of mounted bandits, coming from the north. We resisted, although outnumbered two to one (servants are wholly useless in situations like this, and one of them managed to get himself killed by not taking cover). It looked ugly for about half an hour, as our group was behind the ramshackle wall of an abandoned building with nowhere to go, having the desert behind us. Once we pushed them back, since they only had swords they couldn't pluck us off from a distance, but sooner or later they were likely to storm our redoubt and do us in.*

My only consolation lay in having taken precautions as regards any valuables, having shipped them off with my escort well ahead of time. This way, we only had to lose our lives. Then, just as I calculated the bandits to be planning an irresistible assault, here comes a handful of men on horseback, with bows and arrows enough to kill three of our attackers on the spot, and convince the rest to flee, but not before scooping up their dead and taking them along. Both groups had their faces covered, in the manner of desert dwellers. I'd say they looked like those who attacked me at the Benu Grove, but they all look alike. Our rescuers didn't stop around enough for me to jump over the wall and come to thank them. As quickly as they had ridden onto the scene, they wheeled back, and they, too, headed north again.

For a moment I was tempted to recognize ben Matthias's men in the second group, but it is more likely that the old rebel was the one who ordered the assault in the first place, and—seeing that we resisted, or else fearful that there would be serious consequences for killing Caesar's friend—he thought better of it and fell upon his own to ensure they wouldn't betray him. I am beginning to suspect he sketched my portrait on the sly so as to make me recognizable to his followers. Who is to tell? In any case, if he or someone else were looking for the deified Hadrian's letter, it is already safely in Alexandria with the head of my escort. As for us, we buried the servant, and forgoing our rest, rode on to the Arsinoite.

We are actually encamped at Aueris, where the necropolis of the city of Arsinoe has been for centuries. Most of the folks here make a living by being associated with mortuary activities. There's an embalming school, a shroud-making factory, and mummy tablet painters thrive (one more reason to think it was ben Matthias's men we met yesterday). The army garrison—if close to ineffectual—is open for business, and here I was told that brigandage is a way of living in the oasis. No tourists come alone, and the crocodile population has increased enough to scare off even the cartloads of sightseers who used to trek down from Alexandria during flood season. Water everywhere. Lake Moeris, the creeks, false rivers, and canals form one uninterrupted table of water spreading over the oasis.

We are guests of a Roman landowner, "the last of his kind," as he puts it, whose estate along the ledge road near Philadelphia Arsinoites is amazingly and delightfully cooled by the wind. Up here most of the other estates have been eaten up by sand, due to the disastrous state of irrigation.

Sixth day. *At Letopolis. The Egypt most travelers know: cities and villages close to one another, temples and pyramids, markets and orchards. Essence of roses being sold at reasonable prices (comparably speaking). We left behind the rice and flax fields of the Arsinoites, and now we are beginning to encounter traffic, fancy caravans, decently uniformed army*

units. *It being the birthday of the deified Julius, and having
purposely timed our march so as to arrive here for the occasion, my men and I sacrificed an ox as is required. I then re-
leased them to attend a ceremony at the Mithraeum of the
army camp, and went to the exquisite small temple of Antinous, known here as Antinoeion but also Hadrianeion, inter-
changeably. It is associated with an oracle, and its priest is a
cultivated man who lived at Nicomedia a few years ago. He
made no pretense to believe that the gilded eggshells kept in the
temple museum are actually what remains of Antinous's last
meal before drowning. Personally, he told me he believes the
Boy took his own life. He thinks he is buried in Hadrian's
Tiburtine villa, on the strength of epistolary evidence he read
as a young man. When I declined as gracefully as I could to ask
for an oracular response for myself, he asked me whether I did
have something to ask, unrelated to my person. Serenus Dio's
death came to mind, so I let myself be convinced, and wrote on
a scrap of papyrus the question "Who killed the merchant
Serenus Dio?" This, I folded into a minuscule packet, which
I tied with a string and tossed into the fire built on the altar.
Usually, as I heard, one merely deposits an oracular question,
and gets also to write "yes," "no," or other possible answers,
which then the priest picks at random. Here, however, the
question was consumed by the flames. The answer, I was told,
would be found in the oracular book, which without looking I
was to open in the priest's presence. I was nearly—nearly!—
starting to be excited about the possibility, when my eyes fell
on the first line of a page reading "He died like the blessed Antinous." Well, I hardly needed an oracle to tell me what I knew
already. Since every page, as far as I can judge, has a list of pat
sentences beginning with "She will marry . . ." "He died . . ."
"He will lose/gain money . . ." there seemed to be hardly any
supernatural intervention at play. Still, I offered a sacrifice,*

*left an offering, and politely took leave of the priest, about
whom now I think a little less.*

Seventh day. *Caught a fever or something. I feel miserable. We are somewhere past Terenuthis, and the great pyramids are not far. The Delta is flooded.*

Eighth day. *Sick as a dog. We are staying at a house in
Hermopolis Minor. The men want me to stop over, but I
won't. The* Felicitas Annonae *sails day after tomorrow, and
I'll be on it if it kills me. Water everywhere.*

Ninth day. *Still sick, but the fever is breaking. We are not
far from Alexandria. Everything looks too bright, too noisy,
and I wish I were back in Antinoopolis. I miss Anubina.*

Tenth Day. *What foolishness one writes when one doesn't
feel well! After an absolutely dreadful night of sweating and
tossing. I am back to my old self. The city, fully reconstructed
after the Rebellion, is as beautiful as ever, and if I had time,
I should bury myself in every library it contains—but another
duty calls. The army doctor gave me a clean bill of health, so—
having been rejoined by the bulk of my escort—I am about to
head for the Eunostus Harbor, exit pass in hand, with perfect
weather, and no more threats from shadowy highwaymen.
The ship is a massive craft, more than 170 feet in length,
which happens to be transporting a cavalry unit to Sicily. That
means I'll have a couple of officers to chat with. By great luck,
there was also one available cabin aft, which will afford me
privacy to think and review my material. The skipper is an en-
ergetic man from Salonae, married to an Egyptian, and whose
son is one of the engineers working at His Divinity's palace. As
for the master of the ship, he's a taciturn Neapolitan, Expositus by name, all business. The crew is entirely Egyptian, loud
but—at least at first sight—competent and hardworking. According to them, the* Felicitas Annonae *is the pride of the
Rome-Alexandria trade route (a claim I heard about other*

ships before), but it does carry some 15,000 artabas of wheat, enough to feed an army, plus I don't know how many wild animals for the circus, and several pounds of silk worth at least half a million. All propitiatory sacrifices are favorable, and no delays are expected.

Grain and silk, cavalrymen, crew, animals for the circus, my escort, and myself; then—on or about my person at all times—there is the precious letter I carry with me to Rome.

PART II

The Soldier and the Assassin

SIXTH CHAPTER

The skipper of the *Felicitas Annonae* had been traveling the Rome-Alexandria round-trip route for fifteen years. From the time they left the harbor and freed themselves of the reddish currents pouring out of the Delta, he could tell that travel would be fine in the first leg of the journey, notwithstanding the contrary north-south winds.

"We'll likely meet with stormy weather later on, but if push comes to shove, we'll stop along the way or adjust our route." He said the words under the great red-trimmed mainsail—sporting a painted horn of plenty overflowing—as if he had personal information on all the possibilities that lay ahead. Then again this was a man who'd made record runs from Rhegium to Alexandria in a week's time, and even with the contrary Etesian winds had managed to complete the distance in the opposite direction in under two weeks. Aelius listened, fully intentioned to disembark in Sicily—where the scheduled stop was at Catania—and raid the bookshops there, ready to hitch a separate passage to Bruttium if it seemed that sea travel would be very much delayed.

Meanwhile the cavalry officers—two brothers from Aquileia—

had turned green at the first swells of the open sea, and disappeared below deck. As for the two hundred or so troopers, counting both Aelius's and the others, they were visible in proportion to their level of comfort with sea travel, while the rest of the people on board— crew, animal handlers, merchants, and Aelius himself—were doing fine and going about their business.

In Aelius's case, it was a matter of putting the forced idleness of travel to good scholarly use. Checking Harpocratio's list of guests may have to wait until his return to Egypt, but there was more to do now. He began by perusing *The Death and Resurrection of Antinous,* the tract he had saved from the scrap heap at Oxyrhinchus across the street from the shrine to the Boy. The copy was old, perhaps dating back fifty years, and judging from the quaint syntax, a translation from provincial (likely Egyptian) Greek verses. Having found a shady spot on deck, out of the sailors' way, he sat down to read and take notes in a scribbled shorthand, as the waves, chalk, and the slate tablet allowed.

It was a traditional narrative of metamorphosis, complete with heroic details, mythological parallels to other youthful victims of fate, and final apotheosis. What intrigued him was the rhetorical style, a bit precious, which he dated around the time of the deified Hadrian. Further proof that the tract was nearly contemporary to Antinous were the flattering and hopeful references to Hadrian's successor-elect Aelius Verus, who had died a few months before the emperor himself. A paraphrase from Homer—"his eyes shrouded in haze, he did not see / the godly hand pushing him from behind"— was too provocative to ignore, but too ambiguous to draw conclusions from it. On his ever-ready tablet he jotted down, *Does it mean Antinous was killed by Fate, or by someone acting out Fate's will?* The quotation referred to Patroclus, of course, an appropriate mythological counterpart for the Boy, if one considered the deified Hadrian as Achilles. A young man borrows his friend's armor and dies in battle, his powerful friend avenges him. The hero goes on to live forever among the stars. Had Hadrian avenged his friend while still in Egypt?

Aelius had found no mention of that in the archives of Hermopolis, none in Antinoopolis. Unless the murderous "godly hand" was Hadrian's, as some historians maintained. He made a note to himself to pick up a copy of *The Iliad* as soon as he landed, and go through books XVI and XVII with a fine-tooth comb.

The *Felicitas*'s route was a much-traveled one, and every day there would likely be at least one encounter with a military or mercantile ship, though often it was only a sighting of one another from a distance. On the second day out they were overtaken by the *Penthesilea*, an upper-end, heavier-than-most vessel of the *lousorion* class, speeding northward from Caesarea to Cyrenae with a wake of dolphins. The sailors exchanged greetings and wishes, and—used to the swearing of the battlefield—Aelius never ceased to be amazed by the superstitious control over blasphemy that sea people observed from the moment they made sail to that of mooring securely in harbor.

At night, the immensity and brightness of the starry sky in the open sea rivaled the watches kept at the desert's edge, or in the mountains of Armenia, so different from the overcast, fog-shrouded nights of his childhood that at first he couldn't look up without feeling dizzy. He'd grown accustomed to them in time, but now the lack of reference points around, and the apparent continuity between sky and water brought back that feeling of astonishment and suspension, crossed by the occasional brittleness of a falling star. The constellations stood out from the utter darkness in their summery pattern, with Cancer following the Twins, and Serpentarius (that which was said by the almanacs to bring stormy weather) setting in the morning. Among all, the great star Sirius pulsated as if the dog at Orion's heel were blinking or panting; but in Egypt, carrying Isis's name, it made the flood overcome the cataracts and race unchecked through the land.

Sitting outside his cabin, Aelius closed his eyes to shut the reel of stars out. Traveling between Egypt and Italy, he belonged to neither, and his own sense of homelessness was more acute, as he considered how far he'd come in every sense from his early days. He began to understand why his father was so proud of the house he'd built near Mursa, two-storied, with its pinkish stucco finish, stables, pens, the markers of a settled life; and yet he saw the finite nature of that ambition. Anubina had asked him about his parents, and he'd said that as far as he knew they were well. *But I'm not going back there,* he was thinking while talking to her. *Every book I read and every promotion I received, every trip I took, removed me from that brick-and-mortar sense of place, and if I long for a home, it isn't my father's.*

A dog's distant bark startled him, and Aelius had to gather his thoughts for a moment to remember where he was, and from what direction came the call, so muffled and seemingly far. Ah, yes. The master of the ship said that a pack of dogs destined for the arena was being transported to Italy. It was not distance, but the depth at which the dogs, along with more exotic creatures, were kept in the hold. The sound and the thought of precious and not so precious animals traveling to their death made him pensive, and Aelius waked in a melancholy frame of mind, while here and there on deck, sailors and troopers slept in the open air and the watchman called the hour from his invisible perch.

24 Epiphi (19 July, Wednesday)
On the fourth day out, they encountered the *Lamprotate,* sister ship to the *Penthesilea,* returning from Rome with a large load of wine to sell at Canopus. Like the *Felicitas,* it was crowned by a bright red topsail that first emerged from the horizon like a rooster's comb, and then by and by its starburst sail design made it recognizable to the crew.

It usually broke the voyage by anchoring at its home port in Crete for two days to pick up spices, but—as the skipper (a Soknopaios, originally from Canopus) explained coming on board—it had been blown off course by a storm south of Syracuse, and now was trying to regain the time lost by making straight for Egypt. This was the only reason, he added, why he had to excuse himself and not accept an offer to dine with the officers of the *Felicitas*. "But I do have news and mail from Rome," he volunteered, "and ask the esteemed master of the ship, Expositus, to carry along our mail to the City when he arrives there."

A man of few words, Expositus said that of course he would. "What news from the City, then?"

An update on business, people known to the merchant marine, warehousing, and harbor details followed, hardly what Aelius would call news in the general sense. "Also," the skipper of the *Lamprotate* continued, "all of us Egyptians of Rome unite our prayers to those of our brothers in the province, hoping for a fortunate level of flood and prosperity in months to come. The community sends greetings and wishes of happy new year." He meant the Egyptian New Year's, four weeks away, but superstitiously mentioned as already at hand.

Aelius, as the highest-ranking passenger, was allowed to participate in the meeting. He let the exchange among mariners go on before asking about Lucinus Soter, whose prominent position in the expatriate community of merchants must be well known to the speaker.

Soknopaios looked mildly surprised. "I was about to speak of Soter. Did you have business with him, Commander?"

"What do you mean, 'did I'? I *do* have business with him."

"I'm afraid you won't. Soter is dead."

"Dead? Since when?"

"He died two days before we sailed out, a most unfortunate accident. Burned to death in his house near the Baths of Titus. I heard that a lamp overturned in his studio, and given the hot season and the many textiles he had in storage, the whole thing went up in flames before the fire patrol could intervene. They barely managed to save the houses nearby. His secretary got badly scalded attempting to save some of the correspondence, and they're not sure he'll live." Appropriate expressions of shock and condolence were exchanged among the mariners, then Soknopaios switched to other news, and

Aelius was left with the odd feeling that coincidence—if nothing else—had just taken from him a potentially important source of information in Rome. He followed Soknopaios while he headed for the rowboat that would return him to his ship. "Captain, what does the Egyptian community say about Soter's death?"

"There's no arguing with fire at the height of summer, Commander. It is a loss to all of us, as he was a well-educated man and used his wealth to further our interests. In these hard economic times, several of the Isiac shrines in Rome depended on his patronage, and who knows how they'll fare now. Whatever your business with him was, your only hope is to find the secretary still living. His name is Philo, and I believe he was brought to his brother's house outside the Ostia Gate."

Nimbly for a middle-aged man, Soknopaios was letting himself down by a rope into the rowboat when Aelius leaned over the gunwale, asking, "Did he have family? Will I be able to meet with them?"

"He lost his family during the Rebellion, Commander. The secretary is your best bet."

As the skipper had predicted, the weather turned unpleasant on the fifth day out of Alexandria, beginning with a haze at the far northern horizon. There, already early in the morning, the sharp line between water and sky grew blurred and disappeared, creating the illusion of a foggy wall set to hide the end of the world. The rising sun could not penetrate it, and rather was refracted by it with a muted tinge of pale yellow, not unlike a sandstorm coming. Skipper and sailors went about their daily routine, with an eye on that pale barrier. Outside his cabin, Aelius read through the old archival documents from Ptolemaion, and took notes.

The sea stayed calm until midday, by which time warm buffs of wind began scudding from the north, smacking the mainsail; gradually the water turned turbid, spitting faster and faster white crests that crisscrossed like netting over the tumult. Reading was still possible, but Aelius had to forego note-taking as the motion of the ship grew erratic. Overhead, the rigging creaked at every gust, and soon from the sides and below arose the other assorted sounds that wooden hulls make under pressure. Pitching began in earnest in an hour's time, so that trying to read made Aelius nauseous, and he had to give it up.

At least he had had the forethought of securing the few loose objects in his cabin, and was spared the scampering across deck in which his cavalry colleagues engaged, to catch cups and personal belongings tossed this way and that. Worrying about horses and the other animals, troopers and handlers kept below deck, but if the wind kept on, and a squall was headed this way, soon enough they might all be called back up to help with the canvas. The sun was still shining but more and more lost contours as the haze drew closer, or perhaps the ship ran into it, until the sky's brilliance dimmed. Aelius had hammered nails on the deck to secure his writing box at the corners, and now did the same with his trunk. When he stumbled out of his cabin, high water sprays were running up the prow and the color of the sea, changed with the disappearance of the blue above, was an ugly gray. Neither the skipper nor the master of the ship seemed worried, but as one of the tottering cavalry officers glumly reminded Aelius, sailors are known to go to their watery graves without flinching.

"I don't think it's as bad as that," Aelius said, though truly he had no idea how good or bad things were. "I'm going below deck in a moment to check on my horse. You're welcome to come along."

"No, no. If it comes to sinking, I'd rather see it coming than being trapped below."

In fact, the storm was rough, and even though with able maneuvering the crew succeeded in skirting the worst of it, still the haze became rain. Soon it poured from above and the sea churned below, a fact all the more exasperating as the southern horizon, beyond the agitated veil of rain, looked yellow-skied and cloudless. Deep in the hold, the animals were terrified, and it'd be a miracle if the ostriches didn't break a leg or die of fright; the stench of excrements and growling came from the lions' cages, and the grazing animals, sedated as they were, were heaped in a shivering tangle. That creature terror, chained and imprisoned, revolted Aelius, whose horse—on its fourth sea voyage—looked no less frightened than the other cavalry mounts. Tied to their chains, the dogs had been howling but now cowered, and when Aelius tried to pet one of them, he was bitten in return.

All the while, despite his optimism, he kept an ear perked for a crash of water that might indicate the breaking of the hull, but the grain-laden, groaning *Felicitas Annonae* seemed to maintain both seaworthiness and a reasonably dry bottom. It pitched badly, but did not list, and if one forgot all about the danger and the eventual coming of night, one could nearly enjoy the wildness of motion. It was more than Aelius could say for himself or anyone else as the dark overtook them, and God knows how mast, canvas, sailors, and raging water interacted on the deck, where no one else was allowed. As he tersely jotted down later in his notebook, the powerless passing of those hours was "best forgotten."

26 Epiphi (21 July, Friday)

Exiting the squall was as much a willful act on the part of the skipper as it was a matter of weather simply going past them. On the morning of the sixth day, the quality of rearing and sounding up and down the swelling waves changed perceptibly; the angle became less acute, rain ceased. Froth still jetted above the prow, but not as violently. When they came far enough from the edge of the storm for the waves to roll less frantically, Aelius—drenched and alone with the sailors on deck—could see that a few ship's lengths back the churning continued, with rain going in circles and haze blotting the incipient light of day.

By now Crete lay to the northeast, Expositus said, farther off than if they had stayed the course. "We're heading for Africa the way we're going, but we won't for long."

This stretch was where they usually crossed vessels plying the Gortyna-Cyrenae route. None were visible, as the storm must have scattered them as well. At sunup, the sailors pointed out floating timber on the port side. A broken keg went by, half-sinking, and an ominous iridescence in the water ahead indicated the wreck of an oil cargo ship. For two hours the *Felicitas* circled the area in hopes of finding survivors, to no avail. When a piece of sail bearing the name *Thetis* was seen go by under a veil of water, Expositus ordered a man to tie himself with a rope and dive to retrieve it. "I knew the skipper," he said shortly, and that was all the mourning allowed on the ship.

Until the afternoon they dragged themselves out of danger, and it was toward a relentlessly slow westering sun that the *Felicitas* at last escaped the outer rims of the squall, wind-tossed but intact, its great sail gathered and soaked, and nothing but the tightly packed grain still in its original place. On the wide deck, water ran ankle-deep to the side of the ship that happened to be lower at any one time, but vigorous mopping and the dry weather they were going into would solve the problem before long. When the sun struck the pool of sloshing water, handfuls of gold seemed to be back and forth heaped and raked along the planks.

"As God is my witness," one of the cavalry officers walked by, talking to his brother, "I am taking a desk job when we get to port, and this is the last sailing I do."

It was in that brisk salt water that Aelius washed his livid and stiff right hand, which the dog bite had punctured open on the palm and back, around the thumb. If he closed his eyes (and he hadn't closed them much the night before, like everyone else), he could imagine himself on the river in Egypt, like the first time he'd come up the river, bound to fight the rebels. Or even this last time, when his only charge was to study the deified Hadrian, and he didn't yet know that Anubina had married, and twice given birth.

At this hour, he thought, back in Egypt the flood must be rising unchecked over the brim of ditches and canals, washing over levies and into the black land, crumbling boundary mud walls. Ducks and gulls surely fought over garbage, basements filled up, rats drowned. The sleepy crocodiles must slide down into the pervasive brown water, invisible to their prey until it is too late. How bearable the sting of his broken flesh was, compared to what had happened in the Nile to Serenus, and to what, for all Aelius knew, might have happened to the blessed Antinous himself.

"It's smooth sailing from here to Sicily," he overheard the skipper prophesying, and the reserved Expositus grunting back.

Pressing on his palm, Aelius forced the wounds to spurt fresh blood and serum. As he finished rinsing his hand, he noticed one of the animal handlers coming up from the hold, and quickly stood from his crouch and walked toward him. The man, a bowlegged little Sardinian with a squint, acknowledged him and said immediately, "The dog was beaten for it," expecting an angry scene about the bite during the storm.

Aelius cut him off. "How many animals are you taking along?"

"Oh, that." The handler swayed a bit, reaching for the closest rope to steady himself before the next wave. "Why, Commander, about seventy-five. Six pairs of lions, a dozen ostriches, leopards, and a herd's worth of gazelles, plus porcupines and wild dogs to sic at the pygmies."

"How much do you want for the dogs?"

"They're sold already."

"How much? I'm sure it isn't the first time you've sold animals twice."

The handler looked virtuous, whether because he refused the accusation, or smelled an affair. "Well, they're not just dogs, Commander—they're *wild* dogs."

"They're mutts. You may have found them in the wild, but they're plain mutts. One of them even bears the marks of having worn a collar."

"That may be, but it cost me as much trouble to catch them as to catch wolves or hyenas."

"How much are they paying you for them at your destination? Don't lie to me, as I have means of finding out the truth."

The handler coughed up the price. "And that's without the freight I'm paying for them."

"I'll buy the lot."

The Sardinian held out his hand, seeing that—like all on board in rough weather—Aelius carried his coin pouch about the neck. "And do what with them, if I may ask?"

"That doesn't concern you."

The pitching and rolling of the ship continued well into the coming of night, by which time the swell subsided at last, and once more the *Felicitas* made good time, though it was still toward the southern coast of Sicily that according to the skipper they were heading. Morning of the eighth day came before they sighted Malta, and even then a continuing strong nor'easter pushed them westward, so that they were unable to make immediately for Catania and the strait.

1 MESORE (25 JULY, TUESDAY)

The place on the coast, sunbathed and solitary, was termed Chalis on Aelius's map. From history, he knew this had been once the site of the great ancient Greek city of Gela, of which Herodotus and Diodorus had written. Utterly destroyed and abandoned for nearly five hundred years, from the ship, only the estuary of its namesake river and pitifully overgrown ruins marked it to the visitor now. Aelius would like to be able to say he recognized Timoleon's glorious walls, and the places where Carthaginians and Greeks had camped to fight, but nothing remained. Indeed, there was no harbor either, just a beach with half-sunk breakwaters. A little recessed from the strand, fishermen's huts had cropped up, with their boats, oars, and nets high and dry.

Still, a small military ship lay at anchor nearby, and there was some activity ashore. Boxes, kegs, and building material piled up, while pack animals already laden waited for their drovers to lead them off. With the *Felicitas* anchored within calling distance from the navy boat, Aelius introduced himself and inquired of the captain. From him, he learned they were escorting the shipment of fine art and precious materials for the new villa of Maximian Augustus.

"I don't see any sign of construction," Aelius observed.

The navy officer made a vague gesture indicating the land rising beyond the beach. "It's not around here. It's two days' march inland, by Philosophiana."

Aelius checked his map for a few pensive moments. "Is there a road to it?" he asked then.

"Not from here, not yet, but once you get there, you're right on the Agrigentum-Catania military highway."

Meanwhile, the skipper had decided to do the best of the situation, and get fresh provisions as well as fresh water; minor repairs to the sail were needed, and it was as good a place as any to take a breather after the storm.

"How long do you plan to stop here?" Aelius asked him.

"Until tomorrow. Then we sail back and round Pachynum for the Catania port of call."

"When will you get there?"

"Gods willing, by Sunday noon."

Aelius nodded. "I'll meet you there, then. I'll get off here with some supplies and men, and will travel by land to Catania."

"As you wish, Commander, but we stop there one day, and I'm waiting for no man once the anchor's aweigh."

"Fair enough."

The dogs, freed from their chains, raced up to the deck and festively followed their handler down the gangplank, where they stood in a semicircle sniffing the sand and the tangles of seaweeds washed ashore by the storm. "Now what?" the Sardinian asked. "If you have a mind to kill them yourself, Commander, let me at least have the carcasses for the lions."

Aelius waved in annoyance. "They come with me to the interior."

"Well, why take them so far to kill them? I never heard of such nonsense!"

Travel notes by Aelius Spartianus:
Three men and I left the shore as soon as our dutiful attendance

to the thanksgiving sacrifice was done with. After negotiating a bit, I was able to secure excellent horses from the locals, as ours would be wobbly after the sea voyage. Fortunately, although there is no paved road, as the navy captain mentioned, the traffic of mules, donkeys, and laborers back and forth along the trek toward the site of the imperial villa has cleared a path easy to follow. Indeed, there are small stations along the way where water and food are to be had, and we made good time, notwithstanding the motley company of the dogs. Twice we thought we lost one of them, but he returned both times, and proceeding without delay in the best cavalry fashion, we arrived at our destination, a road station on the military highway called Gelensium Philosophiana, early on Friday. The construction site nearby is spectacular, and had I not seen His Divinity's construction at Aspalatum, I'd have been floored by what is going up here. The foreman took a look at my ever-useful letters of presentation and immediately offered me his room, ordered dinner, and—convinced as he is that I travel here on official business—began at once to show me around, all the while dictating a list of the details he will explain tomorrow. See below regarding my intention to comply.

Brick kilns and stonemason huts surround a huge area already partly built, and the tesserae to be used for mosaics are so numerous as to be heaped like hillocks of various colors. African workers have been brought in to work on the patterns, and despite our long ride, I was shown one after the other of the cartons of what promises to be acres of mosaics showing landscapes, hunting scenes, and all kinds of seasonal activities and entertainment.

Having declined with a polite excuse to impose on the foreman's table and bed, I ate in the open with my men, and just before sunset hiked to a nearby mountain shrine to the deified Hadrian (who visited these parts after his famous climb to see the rainbow atop Aetna). The shrine, elegant and small, stands abandoned, and the laurel grove around it that once must have been carefully tended is a shapeless jumble I had to cut through with my knife. I had with me enough incense to offer on the altar, which was so overgrown as to stand tilted where the laurel roots have undermined it.

I learned that the locals have their own explanation of what happened to the blessed Antinous after his death in the Nile, believing that his body was never retrieved after drowning, but emerged north of here from the waters of Lake Pergus, after traveling in the underworld for several days. As a proof of this, the foreman pointed out to me a fine bronze statue of Apollo—likely dating back to the times of Sicily's Greeks—which they mistakenly call "Antinous the Reborn." The statue was discovered on the lakeshore years ago and brought here by the road station, where it stands covered by a little roof, an object of some veneration by peasant boys and their mothers.

Pergus is certainly the lake by that name mentioned in the fifth book of Ovid's Metamorphoses, in the neighborhood of which Proserpina was abducted by Hades. The foreman described vividly its brackish water, turning to blood in this season "ever since the death of the blessed Antinous," his very words. It might have been the late hour, but the way he spoke of the place well-nigh spooked me. On a happier note, half of the birds in Sicily (apparently not only the swans mentioned by the poet) make their home on Pergus's shores.

Just out of curiosity, as we were on the topic, I asked the foreman whether there are any local theories about the circumstances of Antinous's death, and he said that "he died like Patroclus." I confess I was rather surprised, as this is what the tract I bought at Oxyrhinchus also says. "But Patroclus died in battle," I objected, to which the foreman replied tossing back his head and clicking his tongue, a ubiquitous Sicilian response that left me as ignorant as before.

Anyhow, I acquainted the man with the fact that it is my

wish to leave the dogs here, under imperial protection, and
that their care will fall upon him. He showed himself much
more pleased than I expected (civilians grumble first, whatever
you ask them, to let you know they're doing you a favor), as
apparently foxes and wolves have been prowling around the
construction site, and a pack of dogs is welcome.

I write this late at night, as it is my intention not to sleep,
but to depart with my men well before sunrise, and travel the
well-designed military highway to Catania. We will rest to-
morrow night, probably at Capitoniana, and reach the harbor
well in advance of the Felicitas Annonae's *date of departure*
for Rome.

CATANIA, SICILY, 4 MESORE (28 JULY, FRIDAY)

At Catania, Aelius discovered that the cavalry troop and its captains
had disembarked and were on their way to their assignment, and that
all the ostriches, two of the lions, and several porcupines had been
delivered to the local entertainment officials. Trials against the Christians were being held this week, and though the squinting Sardinian
maintained they were to be tortured by having porcupines tied to
their backs, Aelius had his doubts. With his men already on board,
there was enough time for him to stop by a bookstore behind the
odeum, where he found an account of Hadrian's trip to Sicily in the
eighth year of his rule.

The skipper was as good as his word, and they were off by midday. Soon, leaving behind Aetna's brooding massif, they sailed up the
eastern coast of the island, keeping in sight the shoreline highway
heading for Messana. Past the narrows of the Sicilian Strait, which
the *Felicitas* negotiated without trouble, for the first time in his life
Aelius entered the Tyrrhenian Sea. He scribbled without pause, making notes to himself for later elaboration:

Swordfish being fished at this time, large blue schools of it
streaming, a sea incredibly rich. Dolphins capering, begging

*for food and grinning all over. Each place on the shoreline
an important historical spot. Rhegium, Cape Palinurus, Velia,
Vesuvius, Goat Island, Cumae, Formiae—we sailed or are
about to sail along all these, and more. Too excited to sleep.
Wonderful weather, though the skipper smells winds that will
likely push us north of Ostia. Expositus grumbles, but it's fine
with me. I will gladly enter the City from the north, as the
tomb of the deified Hadrian is near Vatican Hill.*

In the waters facing Tarracina—where the sailors hailed out loud the
terraced mountain temple of Jupiter—the *Felicitas* met the small,
slick and brand-new *Providentia Deorum II,* speeding south with favorable winds on the Antium-Lepcis Magna-Cyrenae-Alexandria
route.

There followed the usual exchange of pleasantries while idling in
the water side by side, wishes of good luck, and mail. "Is there mail
for me?" Aelius inquired. "It would be inconvenient for messages to
arrive to my quarters in Egypt while I'm about to reach Rome."
Quickly the letters were checked, and three messages addressed to
Aelius Spartianus were handed to him. Two were replies to inquiries
he had sent weeks earlier—confirmation that an official inventory of
the buildings erected under Hadrian's rule existed in the State
Archives, and a bookseller's price list. The third letter, in a strange,
cramped hand, was from the prospective collaborator Gavius Tralles
had contacted for him. Dated on the previous Thursday, it'd been
taken aboard the *Providentia* the following day, and indeed provi-
dentially met him here on its way to Egypt.

L etter from Aviola Paratus to Aelius Spartianus:

*Gaius Aviola Paratus to the esteemed cavalry wing com-
mander Aelius Spartianus, good health and greetings.
    It is with a deep sense of joy, sir, that I heard from your*

*erstwhile colleague Gavius Tralles that you might see fit to em-
ploy my professional skills in what I understand to be an important historical survey relating to the reign of the deified
Hadrian. While I do not presume that you will indeed decide
to do so, the very opportunity of being once more of use to my
emperor through you, fills me with hope and affords me great
consolation. From your own military experience, undoubtedly
you understand the plight of a veteran who still has energy
enough to serve, despite the limitations of his infirmity. It is
my fond wish that my knowledge of Egyptian matters, history,
languages, and several sciences (including, but not limited to,
paleography, astronomy, and geography) may be worth your
consideration.*

*Presently, as your colleague may have told you, I make my
home with family at Minturnae, but stand ready to meet you
and offer my services in person whenever you desire. Should
you elect to grant me an interview, it will suffice to send word
to me care of Innkeeper, The Bear in a Skullcap Tavern, outside the Roman gate of Minturnae. As of August 1, I will be instead at my own establishment at the XII mile of the Via
Labicana, At The Glory of Our Lord Aurelian's. I will promptly
travel to your location in Egypt or elsewhere. Should your travels take you to Italy, of course, I will be on hand if needed as
soon as you come ashore.*

*In recollection of our common fight during the Rebellion,
and with all good greetings, I am respectfully yours, G. Aviola
Paratus (having written the present brief in his own hand, the
calligraphic uncertainties of which I hope the Commander will
forbear, on the twenty-sixth day of July at Antium, which
I am visiting on family business).*

It was a promising break in his search, this offer of competent help.
Delighted with the letter, Aelius looked forward to landing according
to schedule, but the skipper's nose for contrary winds proved once

more correct. Foul weather "somewhere between the Ausonian Mountains and the marshland," as he put it, created enough commotion seaward to push the *Felicitas* away from Astura, so that it had to keep off the troubled waters one more full day. The Severian Way, Laurentium, Ostia, and Portus seemed to flee on the right-hand side, villas and groves, breakwaters, harbors, and lighthouses disappointingly far. Other ships, too, tossed and listed northward in their search for safer moorings, while fishing boats took to the open waters. Expositus mumbled under his breath, but there was no helping the delay.

The morning of Wednesday, the last day of July, an oil slick on the sea could not have made it calmer. For all of the slate black sky above the iron hills farther north, perennially storm-ridden and lightning-charged—or so said the skipper—the weather over Alsium resembled a polished mirror, breezy and perfectly warm.

"You had better head to Rome from here," suggested Expositus. "It'll take you less time than if you continued with us."

Aelius was more than willing. The harbor facilities were modest but adequate; nonetheless, Alsium had seen better days. Now only a few of the great villas looked kempt from the shore; gates on the beach were locked, no sign of recent use around their seaside fish ponds; vines crowded walls and pathways. The imperial residence, whose works of art were mentioned in his travel guide, seemed to have been locked up since well before the Rebellion; servants at the gate said no official party had come to visit in nearly ten years. According to Harpocratio, Serenus Dio had managed to acquire a collection of books here from the guardian, two of which—a Latin-Etruscan dictionary and an Etruscan grammar—were rumored to have been kept there since the deified Claudius's days. Dio, his trafficking and his death seemed worlds away from this aging gentility, and even Antinous had tumbled back into Aelius's memory until he recognized a small statue of him at a flower-decked crossroads shrine. There he parted from his escort, sending it ahead to the *Castra Peregrina*, or Foreign Unit—now Special Agent Barracks on the Caelian Hill. He'd follow unencumbered by luggage, on horseback, to savor his first visit to the Italian mainland south of Bononia.

At the Aurelian Way roadside station of Towers, he stopped long enough to draft a note to Aviola Paratus. *I look forward to meeting you,* he wrote in conclusion, *but have some business to attend to beforehand. Please stand ready to hear from me some time after the first week in August.*

For himself, he noted:

Everything I read in the books about this area is true, from the villa where Julius Caesar was met by noblemen at his return from Africa to Marcus's maritimus et voluptuarius locus (as you read in Fronto). It is indeed a pleasurable spot by the sea, among ilex and olive trees, dark groves and shrub-lined streams, neglected mineral springs, ancient burial mounds of Etruscan chieftains (see Strabo) along the way. Caere and Artena were powerful once, but only ruined citadels mark their location today. I am proceeding ever in a southeastern direction, careful not to get off at the wrong turn, as side roads multiply hereabouts; the Aurelian Way is what I am to follow at least until the eighth milestone before Rome, where supposedly I'll join up with the Cornelian Way and see the City walls!

A curious incident upon my first entering the station at Towers: seeing me, and not even knowing who I was, the station master told me that an hour earlier, a couple of men had been asking his son for someone resembling me. A mistake, I should think. How was anyone to know of my coming, given that I was to touch land at Rome's harbor? Either that, or what ben Matthias said, that I should be watching my back even on board, is true. Sailors are easily bought off, and it is possible that through them someone learned of my arrival, and even of the change in landing place. If so, who are these men preceding me? Egyptians? Others who want to make sure I do not find

Antinous's grave, and the documents supposedly contained in it? The thought that a conspiracy against Rome might last through the ages curdles at the sides of my mind without taking a definite shape. I asked the station master for a description of the twosome, but he could give me none, since his son—who spoke to them—has meanwhile taken off for a supply trip to Volaterrae.

Now, however, thanks to this likely case of mistaken identity, the "dusty roadside" to Bebiana Martial spoke of, seems to me a little less welcoming, and I find myself staring searchingly at those I encounter on the way.

Near Bebiana, fifteen miles from Rome, Aelius could not resist making a diversion to see the property once belonging to Virginius Rufus, who'd twice refused the crown after Nero's death. Its porches were of stone rich in seashell inclusions, the quarries of which stood at a little distance. Less than one mile down from them, a reduced army post occupied the right-hand roadside. Manned by Pannonian soldiers, it was clean and spiffy, the perfect place to water his horse. Its commanding NCO was just done debriefing one of his men and stood to salute the visitor.

"He's back from chasing a poacher," he informed Aelius in the gravelly voice of one used to shouting. "But if the bastard was a poacher, Commander, I'm a son of a bitch myself."

"What makes you say so?"

"He was signaling to a confederate from up there, the quarry top."

"Don't poachers alert one another of the army's coming, in these parts?"

"Not if they use flags and do this. See what my boy wrote down." On a slate, hastily jotted down with chalk, Aelius read,

I left-I right; I left-V right; III left-I right; II left-II right; IV left-V right; IV left-III right; IV left-V right; I left-V right; III left-III right; II left-II right; IV left-IV right.

"It's army signaling, Commander."

"I see that." There had been haunted nights in Armenia when the only contact with the next unit in the enemy-infested land had been the semaphore system. Aelius stayed with his hand the NCO's offer of chalk and translation, having already deciphered the message himself. "Did your man catch the *poacher*?" he asked, giving back the slate.

"He lost time marking the sequence of signals, and then rushed back here to show it. His patrol companion is still searching for sender and receiver, and I ordered two more men to scour the hillside. Damn if I can figure out what it's all about, but poachers, they're not."

"It depends on the game they're after." Aelius was already out of the door, and soon mounted. "If the men are captured, keep them here and send immediate word to the *Selecti Alae Ursicianae*, my bodyguard at the Special Agent Barracks."

"Where's *that*?"

Updates in nomenclature found their way slowly through the ranks. "It's the old Foreign Unit Barracks," Aelius explained.

Midday was just past, and shadows had drawn back under trees and walls of stacked stones. Cicadas in the bushes fell silent when he regained the Aurelian Way, and then clamored again behind him. Ahead, the increasingly undulated land swallowed the road, showed it more distant, swallowed it once more with a donkey-back hump, and another. Villas up for sale sat mute amid drying gardens, their eaves garlanded with swallows' nests. Aelius rode on, halfway between disquiet and irritable curiosity: because, whether or not the inquirers at Towers were looking for him, there was no mistaking a semaphore message that read, AELIUS VENIT. So, they knew him by name, and that he was coming to Rome. Posing as travelers, being mistaken as poachers, two or more men were on to him. It thrilled him, in one way, as risk always had fascinated him. Memory of his evenings during the Rebellion came back, and how Anubina, in her shady bedroom, would help him take off his armor and say, "This piece of danger I remove from you. And this piece. And this," until he was naked in front of her. *I miss her,* he thought, *and knowing her married, happy, a mother of two children, makes me lonely and jealous.*

At Lorium (the local station master, busy waterproofing a sizeable cistern, pronounced it Laurium), another imperial villa stood with its principal building on a hillside, castlelike on the plain around it, about one mile from a small bridge. The travel guide read that it'd been abandoned after Commodus. Uninteresting market stands lined the road for a piece, and then the ups and downs began in earnest, in what Fronto had called "a bunch of steep and slippery stretches." No news of strangers looking for him, at least.

It was afternoon when Aelius crossed another bridge on the Arrone river, a place called, significatively in his mind, *Caput Serapi,* but no Egyptian landmark and no temple of Serapis was in sight. Even the massive round sepulcher watching the verge with its timeworn portrait statues was silent about any relation to Africa. Here the road forked, and the milestone read Via Portuensis newly written under the old nomenclature, Via Vitellia. Along the Aurelian Way, low meadows were more and more giving way to wooded dales full of birds. As long as the birds sang, it meant there were no men lying in wait; the old habit of watching himself underlay all he saw, and heard, without taking away from the beauty of the land. Soon, pouring out from under trees, tombs, and isolated farms like a liquid, shadows began to lengthen. On the fringe of hills, sheep and longhorns of Pannonian stock headed for their pens and stables.

Beyond a roadside trough where the ever-present mosquitoes clouded water-filled hoof prints, a wooded hamlet, otherwise unmarked, was listed in his guide as Buxus; boxwood abounded, in fact, a small fenced copse of those trees must be the *silva mesia* mentioned in passing. The station mistress nearby was talkative. She gave him an earful of useless information about Christians coming to celebrate two of their beheaded "martyrs" here ("Rufina and Secunda, have you ever heard commoner names for so-called saints?"), and four Christianized Jews at a place thereabouts, called Nympha ("The parents had common names, too, but the two sons' were unpronounceable!").

Asked whether anyone had inquired about an official's coming, she said no. "But then, with all that I keep a road station, it's not like I listen to gossip or anything." Counting the money Aelius had paid for fodder and a quick meal, she grumbled about high prices and bad business. "For all their foolishness, Christians brought some activity. Now there's little traffic aside from mule drovers, and they hardly spend anything. If it wasn't for the rose plantation down the road, I might as well close shop."

By this time, the summer day was winding down. Aelius decided to press on toward the hill that would allow him to look upon the city, and stop for the night. A dark pine forest crowded the road past the rose garden mentioned by the station mistress (it had been the property of one of Commodus's freedmen); beyond, from what he read, would begin a convulsed tract of land marked by deep sandstone valleys, canyons caused by hundreds of years of quarrying, cane groves extending for miles, brick kilns, army and navy burial yards between the Vatican and Janiculum hills. Ideal ambush country. Anyone waiting for him there could easily have the upper hand. Now the nomenclature on the road markers read Aurelia-Cornelia; knowing that soon the roads would split, and the second would lead to the very door of Hadrian's Tomb made him eager to get to the crossroads, but prudence dictated otherwise. Having taken a small room at the station called *in Colle Pino*, Aelius resolved to start again at sunup. Still, impatience made him leave the hall where a few travelers idled and ate: On foot, he wandered with the last light of day to the rim of the hill, where an opening among the trees, under a precipitous and limitless sky, showed him Rome beneath him.

Notes by Aelius Spartianus:

I have seen It! It would be too easy to write that words do not suffice, or there are no words altogether to describe the sight. Words are poor, but they do help to give an idea of what one witnesses. Imagine a balcony-like glorious hill, wild and solitary, whose flanks are thick with canes, and so deep that brooks and rivulets winding below are invisible and cannot be heard. Nightingales calling from one grove to the other, as I did not hear since the Armenian days. As I stood there, without any of the feared ambushes having materialized, the road followed from the ship to this point seemed to have disappeared altogether, as if swallowed into the lifetime of the man I was before seeing Rome.

There was a moment when I myself felt as though I had not lived before. My life and doings to this point seemed puny and wholly unimportant, and my daily concerns too petty to be listed. I saw why my father, in his thickheadedness and ignorance, wanted me to be educated and ready for an event such as this. He, who never has seen Rome and never will, but fought in its name for forty and more years. My grandfather, who had seen it once, and never tired of telling about it. My mother's folks, who taught here as freedmen in the emperor's house under three princes. All of these have brought me here: not my research, not the investigation, not the suspicious deaths behind me and the unexpected one that I am to find tomorrow. It seems to me tonight that all conjured to bring me to this point, including my survival at war and during the Rebellion, including the tenderness of my time with Anubina, my travels, my anger and fears. I understand the deified Hadrian's impulse to give shape, in stone, to the accumulation of sentiments that his wanderings and experiences must have heaped within his genial mind.

I, Aelius Spartianus, grew up in foreign barracks and am nobody. I will build no palace, but I am privileged to write the history of the men who did, and whose work this magnificent City is. Below me, torches and flickers of light marked the thousand streets and alleys of Rome; under a nearly full moon, the first thing I made out was a burial pyramid, which made me feel as though Egypt is not letting go. Soon I noticed the massive baths, temples, Hadrian's great tomb by the river, and

*the glorious bridge leading to it, white like milk; the Palace, a
city in itself, malls, sanctuaries. Distant and against the Alban
hills, hazy but unmistakable, the Flavian amphitheater, in the
neighborhood of which I am to travel tomorrow. From afar, I
knew shapes and rooftops never seen in person, recognized the
hollows where the Great Fire began and spread, the quarters
where aristocrats ruled in the republican days, the sacred
precincts and groves: Each dimly outlined building meant an
episode, birth or murder, plot or entire revolution. Gods inhabit
this place! I looked and asked myself, How can anyone ever en-
danger the capital of the world? Our enemies dared, through
the years, and always lost. We are those who teach the world
how to live: Any threat is—must be—doomed to fail.*

*The truth is that I could have made it easily to the City
gates and entered it tonight, but I couldn't bring myself to it.
I was afraid of its enormity, of its walls. Maybe ben Matthias
is right in reminding me that I am a barbarian, because just
like one I cowered inwardly before the power of this inhabited
head of the empire, and I couldn't even bring myself to find a
little bed in a little building within it.*

*Tomorrow it will be another matter. Another month, and
the beginning of the second leg of my search. Someone, within
the great City spread before my eyes, has been alerted of my
coming, and is waiting for me. Soldiers should never know-
ingly walk into traps, but I cannot for my life think of a more
magnificent place to do it than in Rome.*

SEVENTH CHAPTER

1 August, Kalends, Tuesday (8 Mesore)

On the first day of August—dedicated to Hope and the Two Victories—Aelius was an awestruck tourist in a haze of sites and monuments. Having approached the City by the Cornelian Way, across Nero's and Agrippina's Gardens, he left on one side the horse track where Tacitus placed the first Christian executions. Then, at the crossroads with the Via Triumphalis, he headed past the marble pyramid to the paved square around Hadrian's glorious mausoleum (which he circled twice swearing to pass hours admiring it). At the foot of the bridge built for it, he entered the walls through the Aurelian Gate, whose powerful jamb he kissed. Mindless of the heat that heralded rain, he took in all he could of the district right of the Flaminian Way, where so much had been built or renovated by the deified Hadrian. Temples, theaters, arches, stadiums, porches—ben Matthias had been right in calling him provincial, but dead wrong in assuming he couldn't or wouldn't like Rome. He arrived at the Special Agent Barracks at sundown, wholly enthused, having neither stopped to eat all day, nor paid more than passing heed to the crowds and noise of the City.

On Friday, thanks to a rain that veiled all things with sticky haze, he talked himself into getting back to research business. Through his bodyguard he had already gotten an unwelcome confirmation: Lucinus Soter's secretary had died of his burns a week prior, so it came down to hearing whether his brother had any information to give.

The man lived in a refitted farmhouse, not far from the crossroads immediately outside the Ostia gate, where a shady lane followed Aurelian's walls. Aelius was expected. The meeting took less than an hour, in a small reception hall where the scent of herbs under the rain and the pungency of cat spray came through the window.

"Philo died trying to save his master," the grieving brother said. "As it is, all he saved was the money bags. What embitters me most is that he could have spared himself jumping into the burning studio. Lucinus Soter was dead already, so the flames had only books and swatches of cloth to destroy."

"Breathing smoke kills more than fire, I'm told."

"But it isn't that, Commander. Ask the fire brigade—I told them what Philo managed to whisper to me, that his master had his throat cut."

His throat cut. Aelius mustered his ability not to show his alarm. "Are you sure you heard your brother correctly?" he asked, and, "How did it all start, anyway?"

"A fire rose from the wood pile for the furnace. This I heard from the slaves, who swear that burning rags must have been tossed in from the basement window. The fire brigade examined the place, and agrees that it was not accidental combustion. The whole household rushed around to put out the flames, and I think that's when the murderer got in. Lucinus Soter was a heavy man; he moved slowly, so Philo's first impulse was to ensure he was helped out of the studio, right above the furnace room. There's no mistaking what he told me, Commander. He found the master slumped back in his chair, at the desk, with that awful wound and blood all over. The time it took my brother to see the uselessness of his task cost him his life, as the burning ceiling came down on him. Why murder him? This is Rome, sir. Lucinus Soter kept money in the house, everyone knew. It was the fire brigade that found the money bags in the garden, where my poor brother had thrown them from the window. Silverware and jewelry, we found melted in their caskets. So, the thieves got nothing out of killing two good men. As for the rest, go there, see for yourself if anyone could escape that hell."

Soter's house was one of those that had been carved out of the small uphill space between the baths of Titus and the massive walls of those Trajan had later built. It had been an elegant city home, Aelius had heard, once a consul's residence. Small in plan but three-storied, with no land around it, and not much light, its door had opened about three hundred paces from the amphitheater, though one could not see it due to the house's recessed location. Aelius saw immediately what peril the fire had caused to the neighborhood, judging by the houses across from Copper Alley, whose wall had been visibly tongued by flames and smoke.

Under a clearing sky of swift clouds, very little remained of Soter's property. The bricks and concrete fallen into the street had been duly removed; collapsed beams, caved-in walls, and unrecognizable rubble cluttered the site of the house itself. The real estate agent happening to survey the site brightened up when Aelius walked up to him, and quickly came to business. "New to the district, Your Excellency? There's much you can do with the place, you know. Get some able crew out there, and—"

"I can see the state it's in."

"Ah. Well, then—you can see that it's the land you're buying, basically."

"Basically? I'd say. All the few square feet of it."

"Still, it's the location, you know. Close to everything."

"Stuffed between two public baths. I bet one couldn't hear oneself thinking most of the time. And the entrance to the Titian Baths looks ready to fall onto the street, which means half of the hill will go with it." For all that, Aelius saw the immediate advantage of appearing as a prospective buyer. He straddled a broken rafter to enter what had been the atrium. "I might want it as an investment, that's all, or decide to do nothing of the kind. I hear a man died in the fire, so I doubt that buyers are lining up to take it off your hands."

"Well, you are welcome to survey the place. In case you decide it suits you, you can send for me down at the corner."

Once alone, Aelius could hardly make out the space that had been Soter's studio. The ceiling and part of the roof had collapsed into it, and although the fire brigade had cleared a path through the rubble to recover the body, still beams, blackened tiles, charred stumps difficult to decipher—probably furniture—occupied most of the floor. The pavement itself was sooty, streaked; from it and from the rubble there rose the acidic odor of wetness on burned objects, a sour cindery smell. Here, as far as Aelius could tell, where the opening of a window was indicated by gnarled remnants of its grill, had sat the desk, along the south side of the ground floor. Aelius recognized the metal claws of desk and chair, knobs and tarnished hinges. Paper and parchment, wholly combusted, left no other trace than a flimsy veil-like layer, mixed with remnants of the shelves in the wide bookcase niche. Black fragments resembling bats' wings, stuck here and there, must be all that survived of textile samples.

Was this how a large man burned? The amount of grease marring the floor where the chair had been, marked presumably the spot of the body's consumption. A few steps from it, threshold stone gave away the door's position. The stairs to the second floor, surely made of wood, had also gone: Marks of each step on the still standing inner wall pointed to their location.

Given the window grill, entering the studio meant passing through the only door. Philo's brother described the house as having two exits, one facing south on Copper Alley, the other, a back passageway, looking due north. Crammed between the blind walls of the two bathing establishments, the house could not be easily entered from the second floor either, much less the third. There had been a watchdog, apparently lost three days before the fire. On the wall by the door, to which it had been chained, a broken iron ring showed that it had escaped or had been set free. The ring had resisted the flames, as had the piece of masonry to which it was cemented. Aelius was reasonably sure the iron had been weakened with a metal file, so that it would give way under the strain of pulling. In Soter's house only a low fence separated the atrium from the street, a negligible obstacle for a large dog intent on getting over it. A significative detail, given what had followed. In a city like Rome, a dog might not easily find its way back home; unless, of course, it'd been captured and wilfully segregated in order to set the fire undisturbed. Why go through all this trouble to commit a theft, why stop to kill an old man who can hardly move, why run off without the silver? It did not make sense, unless Soter had to be eliminated because he knew—what? Did this murder have to do with Hadrian's letter, with the deaths in Egypt, with a much vaster plot? Aelius's head swam with hypotheses. Philo's brother told him that Soter had posted ads on wooden tablets at the neighborhood crossroads for the dog's retrieval, offering a reward. Aelius found out more from the Titian Baths' doorman, who'd agreed to nail one of them on the advertisement board space on his wall.

"Was the dog ever found?" Aelius asked.

"Not as of the date of the fire. Afterward, who was paying mind to it?"

The dog had been found, after all. Aelius only had to inquire a bit down from Soter's place, in a shop at the end of Copper Alley, near the Dacian Training School. Yes, it had ben found and brought back, but—since the house had gone along with its master—the disappointed finder had taken it along, hoping to sell it. He was one of the *Ludus Magnus* attendants, known in the district. He'd probably disposed of the large dog as bait in one of the amphitheater's hunting shows.

Too bad, the shop owner added. "It was a good-looking, black monster of a dog, and I bet worth more money than they would give to see it get chewed up by a bear in the arena."

There had been a time when gladiatorial games had attracted him, before the teachers Aelius's father had chosen for him had put into his head—not without effort—a cultivated disgust for the mercenary waste of human and animal life. Not that he really minded watching men killing one another (given his army training, he hadn't philosophically progressed quite as far as that), but now it revolted him to see animals slaughtered, so that His Divinity's restriction of circus-related expenses found him wholly in agreement and grateful for it. With all this, Aelius found himself walking across the Via Labicana to the crowded gladiatorial schools quarter, knowing before he got there how he'd find the smell of men and aggression that, all things being equal, he knew from his army life as well. It had started raining again from clouds ragged and blue. On the way, only his sense of duty could pull him away from every fugue of buildings, famous street corner, or renowned spot around the amphitheater, enthused as he was with all that towered over and enchanted him.

The *Ludus* attendant was eating at one of the hot lunch counters kitty corner from his place of employment. Garlic figured so heavily in the dish that Aelius had to step back when he first carelessly turned with his mouth full. "Well, no, I haven't sold the dog yet. Who wants to know?"

Aelius's expensive uniform spoke for itself. At once the man showed deference, although swallowing did nothing to relieve the reek of his breath. "I'm kind of keeping it, Commander, until I find someone who'll pay what it's worth, or at least the reward. Actually," he added, making up his mind about the visitor's ability to pay, "the dog's full value is the only way I could part with it, as it's cost me more than the reward in food alone."

"It's hard to believe, since you must get your share of carcasses from the arena. So, how did you manage to capture and keep a watchdog trained to attack?"

"I raise dogs for the circus on the side. That's also how I could tell this one was too good to get mauled."

There was no seeing the animal at this time, since the man kept his kennel outside the walls, where he lived. "It's past Two Laurels, out of the way," he said. "But unless you're interested in buying it, Commander, what's the point in—"

"Did it have a collar and chain when you found it?"

"It had a collar, of course, else I couldn't know whose it was." The attendant scooped with two fingers what remained of his lunch from the bowl. "It read the usual things, name of the dog, of the owner, the home address. The chain—well, it had a piece of it dangling, so I figured it had gotten loose because of a broken link." There followed wiping of hands on a much-used cloth that lay on the counter. "I kept the thing, in case they'd accuse me of having cut it myself. Now I bet you can't even see where the chain was hooked to the wall, with the fire and everything."

Aelius did not say he had already checked. "I'm not interested in buying the dog, but there's money in it for you if you show it to me."

"Are you a breeder?"

Already Aelius was heading out. Bound for the climb that past the Dacian Training School led him back to Copper Alley. "There's money in it for you," he called back, "that's all."

Minutes later, the same real estate agent he met in Soter's burned-out house was the one Aelius approached to find lodgings in Rome. Money was not a factor, since he had ample credit for his living expenses through His Divinity; still, he was unwilling to pay an exorbitant price. His requirements were that the place be furnished, on a hillside or at least with a panoramic view of the City, not ostentatious, and away from overly loud streets.

"Anything else?" asked the real estate man a bit acidly, taking notes.

"Actually, yes. I'd like to be within reach of a good library or well-stocked bookstores. How long will it take you to find me a place?"

"Well, let's see." From a stack of papers, the real estate man took out a list of property to let, and buried his nose in it. "Ready to go, furnished and with servants, there's this small house on the heights overlooking the Altar of Peace. Lovely spot. You'd also have a good view of the temple of all the gods, the deified Augustus's tomb and sundial, the celebration columns—plus of course Domitia's Gardens and Hadrian's Tomb, across the river. Or you could take a two-story flat on the east side of the Caelian, close to the old Foreign Unit Barracks, across from the Guards' Barracks, old and new. It's not what you'd call a quiet neighborhood, but it's becoming fancy, and you can look out the upper windows onto the Antoninian Baths, the gardens near Old Hope, and be close to four of the principal roads out of Rome. Public libraries are everywhere, so take your pick."

The house across the river from Hadrian's monument was tempting, but there were practical advantages to the barracks district, in view of having to deploy his bodyguard sooner or later. Aelius made his choice site unseen, strong of his recollection that historical families lived on the Caelian, and three emperors had called it home.

That evening, *The place is perfect,* he wrote in his notes.

My quarters overlook the street leading from the Special Agent-Old Foreign Unit Barracks (westward) down to the valley. Immediately to my left is the V Cohort of Fire Police and Night Patrol, and farther to the center of the hill, the road splits under the arch of Dolabella and Silanus to reach the Temple of the Sun and that of the deified Claudius. Facing the entrance to the northeast lies the sprawling house of the Valerii, and behind this, the army brothels; these face the aqueduct, and the residences of Licinius, the Anicii, and Nicomachi. In the house, baths, bodyguard rooms, and service areas are on the ground floor, and studio, bedroom, and balcony with dining area upstairs. My studio window faces the front and valley side; off the dining room is a balcony on the valley side; the bedroom looks on the back; no windows upstairs on the cohort side.

*Not only do the great families have their fabulous town-
houses in this district named for Isis and Serapis; one of the
tyrants defeated by Aurelian (Tetricus) lived there, and so did
Philip, and Commodus, too: The bedroom where he was assassinated, I went to see already, availing myself of His Divinity's ever-useful letters of presentation. The guardian (but I
don't know how much one can believe these things) pointed
out an alcove with blood stains still visible on the wall, there
where the bedstead of the corrupt prince had once stood.*

The name Castra Peregrina—*Foreign Unit—has been
removed from the facade of the barracks, as by imperial order
(still affixed by the entry gate), although folks still refer to it as
such, by habit. For all the concentration of army units on this
hillside, still there is great order, and not much noise. The gardens of the wealthy buffer sounds. Regarding my research,
upon arrival I ensured the deified Hadrian's letter's safekeeping. The closest libraries to my quarters are those in the Titian
Baths, and especially the great one in Trajan's. Not far from
Tetricus's house is the temple popularly known as* Metellus's
Isis, *which I have admired from the outside. From its priests, I
am soon bound to ask whether someone else can supply me
with the information on Antinous, his death, and his burial
place that I so hoped to receive from the late Lucinus Soter.*

3 August, Supplicia Canum, Thursday (10 Mesore)

On the day when—in the past—watchdogs were crucified in memory of their silence during the Gauls' invasion of Rome, Aelius continued his intensive sightseeing. He strove to form a mental map of
the city within the City Hadrian had built, from the hillside of
marble dedicated to Venus and Rome to the temple of all the gods,
and from the completion of the brightly painted Dacian column to
restorations everywhere. No temple was dedicated to Antinous per
se, although a religious order in his name existed at the Iseum Campense. His portrait was also recognizable in the decorative rounds of

the triumphal arch on Broad Street, and in the occasional roadside altar. In his biography, Hadrian had never mentioned a shrine to the Boy within the walls, nor a burial place: As the list of his constructions seemed to go on forever, it'd take some time to sort out which ones he ought to investigate. Meanwhile, Aelius's books and papers were being arranged in the upper floor of his flat, where, having learned from him that his arrival in Italy had not gone unnoticed, the head of his bodyguard and two hand-picked men insisted on joining him.

Aelius resisted at first, and even after giving in, it seemed to him that there was no reason for such alarm, but his soldiers' concern had stuck, or else exhaustion from travel caught up with him, because he had nightmares. At one point, he dreamed to be facing a sky-high, gleaming tower that burst suddenly into flames as if struck by Greek fire. The place resembled neither Rome nor Nicomedia, but a city God knows where: All he knew was that he stood directly below it, and there was no escaping what seemed to crumble from heaven itself. Awake in the dark, he could not at first remember where he lay, and struggled for a while to control fear, but already the bed under him was real, Rome sprawled outside the window; Soter's burned-out house accounted for the rest.

4 AUGUST, FRIDAY, (11 MESORE)

In the morning he received an invitation, requesting his presence at Philo's banquet of the Lord Anubis on the following day. This, Aelius understood to be a memorial dinner, held in one of those religious institutions called Houses of Life by the secretary's brother. The address pointed to the neighborhood of the great Isiac shrine, Iseum Campense. As it might introduce him directly to the Egyptian community in Rome, he accepted, and then gave himself a three hours' pass of leisure and art in the deified Trajan's Baths.

Sunday afternoon he followed up on the matter of Soter's watch-dog. Taking the long way around, he made an excursion to the Sitting Hall and monumental apartments once belonging to the Varian family; nearby was the barracks arena, which Aurelian had embedded in the walls, bricking up part of its archways. The sight of this building once impressive and freestanding (as had been the old pyramid tomb by the Ostia Gate or the Praetorian Field) struck him negatively, bound as it was to hurried graceless bastions. For the first time after so many hours of numb admiration, Aelius was reminded that danger did exist, even for Rome. That bricks and mortar and added courses of cemented stones, blocked doorways and wall-encased buildings do mean something in the life of a City. National security—more and more of late celebrated on monuments and coinage—may be like other official phrases about eternity, peace, invincibility: an idea in need of reinforcing.

It was only an aging arena built for the army, gobbled by walls. Yet, Hadrian's ancient letter speaking of danger to the state didn't seem so remote in front of this place, built to entertain the army, then used by the army as an obstacle against aggression. Outside the City altogether now lay the rest of the Varian Gardens: their largest part, with the overgrown racetrack—the obelisk marking its middle fallen sometime over the past thirty years—fountains choked with weeds, paths invaded by grass. Nothing that a good cleaning couldn't make spiffy again, Aelius thought as he went past to rejoin the main road, but somehow the feeling was of abandonment planned for a long time, if not forever.

The kennel lay along the Via Labicana, at the IV mile out of the great travertine gate stacked with aqueducts, where the roads to Praeneste and Labicum parted. Aelius cantered by the garden wall and thickets that gave name to the vast imperial property of Two Laurels, lost behind bird-filled trees. Turrets and cupolas, tiled roofs showed here and there. Just beyond, he'd read, Hannibal had camped five hundred years earlier. Across the road—if the sources told the truth—that first casualty of the wars against Carthage, Attilius Regulus, had once worked his modest farm. Presently the Imperial Guard had its graves there.

History filled this land like a sponge, one could squeeze it forever and still not get it all. Now the imperial property aged perceptibly under each blanching summer, the laurels grew wild, and nothing remained of those frugal ancient habits. Mown fields, roadside shrines and tombs, still and without shadows, seemed enchanted. Aelius wondered what this stretch of land would look like in another five hundred years, whether the City would overtake it with its noise and pavement, or else walls and shrines would be left to decay more, as it had been for the great Egyptian cities the desert covered today. Surely no one would know or care that he had once taken this road, on this errand, nor whether his search had met with success.

Past the arches of Severus Alexander's aqueduct, at the foot of a narrow bridge, he slowed down, then halted his horse to look. His first impression was that the dogs had gotten loose from their cages and climbed a hillock to the right of the road, where their silhouettes could be seen crouching against the white sky, but he realized as he drew closer that the hillock was actually a funerary mound topped by a garden, and the dogs, statues of dogs. Hadn't he read that the deified Hadrian had built monuments to his favorite hounds? It seemed to him a sign, when he came near enough to read the inscription, and recognized it as one such memorial.

The live dogs, instead, could be heard from afar, ahead where the road dipped slightly among cane groves. A homemade sign marked a side track to the left as leading to Vivariolum. Less pitiless than the Egyptian skies, but so much more open than any he'd known in his fog-filled childhood and mountain soldiering, the horizon had no color whatever in the fullness of the early afternoon. Left and right of the track, aside from the occasional family tomb (most of them worn by rain and showing increasingly featureless marble portraits), sparse estates dotted the foothills, their gardens lost behind walls, the tracks leading to them lined by stumpy mulberry trees or unequal cypresses.

Disappointment awaited at the kennel. The *Ludus* attendant scratched his head as he spoke. "A widowed lady came yesterday with her maidservant, looking for a good watchdog, Commander, and as she offered what I wanted for it, I couldn't pass it up, but I did keep the collar and piece of chain for you, since she wanted to choose her own leash, and all that. Women have no business choosing dogs, I say, because they get all mushy and end up putting cloaks on them and other such nonsense, and give them names like Love and Trinket."

When he was handed the links of chain, Aelius *knew* it had been artificially weakened. A well-executed plan had permitted at least one killer to enter Soter's house undisturbed. Late at night, the household would be sleepy if not asleep; in the confusion of people following any fire, strangers going in and out might not be noticed. Why, then, had the money bags not been stolen at once, waiting for Philo to retrieve them? Why was the silver left untouched? Perhaps murdering Soter had been the sole aim all along.

Aelius put the chain link in his travel bag. "Any idea of who the lady was?"

"The way she spoke to the dog, I figured she had seen it before." From a kettle on the open fire, the attendant busied himself filling bowls with a mix of gruel and meat scraps for the dogs' supper. "Her face was covered, see. Maybe she was the dead man's wife or girlfriend. Well, yes, sir, I agree—it don't make sense that she ought to pay for what was hers: beyond the reward money, I mean. But she offered full price, so I wasn't about to argue."

Far from being married, according to Theo's concise gossip, Soter's sexual tastes had been wholly different. Aelius was intrigued at the idea that a mystery woman had come, veiled and in the sole company of a servant, ready to pay more than the dog was worth. Did she plan to get rid of the animal, in case the fire brigade should come looking? If she was an accomplice, why had she not demanded the broken chain, proof of foul play in connection to murder and fire?

There was no finding out more from the *Ludus* attendant, other than the lady seemed young, spoke in a low voice, and her woman servant was not Roman. "She had an accent, Syrian or thereabouts. Did most of the talking, too."

Aelius placed a coin on the table. "Could she be Egyptian?"

"Thank you, sir. Could very well be. If I was you, Commander, I'd ask in the III district. Them Egyptians all know each other over there." With a bowl in each hand, the man started for the back door, where the cages were. "Listen how they welcome a meal, the idiots—they don't know what's coming, on the next hunting show. Care to take a look, in case you want a dog that can bite a man's arm off?"

"No."

Riding back, Aelius struggled to shake the melancholy of hearing the caged dogs fight over the food. Overhead, the sun barely inclined westward. Pigeons circled isolated dovecotes, as they had when he had traveled to Pammychios's house and found him dead. Threats and dreams of threats seemed so far from this suspended peace. Yet, two of his guardsmen had followed at a distance, riding in the fields; they'd been completely out of sight, but now he caught a glimpse of them turning their horses and heading back even as he did.

Had he continued on to the XII milestone, along this same road he'd have reached the place where Aviola Paratus lived—the Pannonian-born collaborator Tralles suggested to him, the blind veteran hungry for action and unwilling to accept retirement. At first Aelius had toyed with the idea of having him summoned to his quarters on the Caelian, but given Paratus's infirmity and officer rank, he'd go visit him instead. He would do it now, unannounced, but he wanted to pass by the kennel again, and there would be time enough to see the veteran during the week. Before evening, instead, he hoped to speak to the head priest at Metellus's Isis, the temple Soter had attended and patronized ever since his arrival in Rome.

The grating calls of invisible crickets in the fields followed Aelius's return toward the Praenestine Gate; aqueducts crisscrossed, dissecting the pavement in a dazzle of alternate light and shadow, and like a wave of sounds there came over the wall the noise of the City.

After a stretch of well-kept gardens at the crossroads with Blackbird Street, the triple arch topped by the Egyptian goddess's statue came up, and then Metellus's Isis, across from Tetricus's porticoed house. Restricted by shops and stalls shaded by awnings, crowded with idlers, the Via Labicana continued beyond the temple's lovely façade, and at the end Aelius could barely make out the navy barracks and the square around the amphitheater. The Isiac sacred precinct, between what remained of two sacred woods, featured the decorations expected of its exotic quality, including the smiling heifer-face of Hathor that reminded him of Anubina.

Yet this was not *the* Egyptian district; Egyptian stores and concerns existed throughout the City—restaurants, community centers, shrines. Still, he heard the temple was well attended and comparatively wealthy. Given its nearness to the gymnasiums and blood sports arenas, it provided a meeting place not only for female believers (respectable ladies, one expected that), but of prostitutes as well, female and male. Up to the precinct's gate, in the sleepy sultriness of the afternoon, they occasionally called out from the shade of porches, but mostly sat fanning themselves.

"It's not a good thing," the priest told him, having heard the reason for Aelius's errand. "A terrible loss. You might already know that Lucinus Soter—we knew him by his Egyptian name, Nebos—came to Rome from Antinoopolis right after the Rebellion. As his birth name suggests (it means lord) he was well-to-do, educated, from a priestly family. One of the last to read fluently the ancient writings. His passion for textiles was a byproduct of his hailing from the world capital of fine cloth." Preceding the visitor, he reached a small room overlooking the inner court. Completely hairless, his tanned head resembled the gilded eggs whose shells Aelius had been shown in Letopolis, supposedly Antinous's last meal in life. Had he had eyebrows, the priest would have knitted them with his next words. "But what Soter really was, his enterprises in Rome tell loudly: He was an ambassador and a cultural representative, a support for all who came from Egypt and had difficulty becoming integrated. He was a scholar of all the Roman princes who ever furthered Egyptian religion and art. It was through his money that we restored temples and neighborhood shrines. No one in this community wants to believe he was murdered in cold blood by thieves, but we can't think of any other reason why such a life would be snuffed. Just imagine, he was awaiting a guest from Egypt, a historian who had been recommended to him by friends, and the opportunity to discuss matters so close to his heart thrilled him greatly."

"I am that guest."

"Then you've lost a never-to-be-repeated opportunity to gain information, Commander."

Aelius had not imagined Soter's knowledge to be so irreplaceable. If that weren't enough, the scent in these religious places was always heady, something between women's perfume and sweet pickle. The walls reeked with it. He took a step closer to the window, filling his lungs with the warm outside air. He said, showing none of his disappointment, "Is there anyone else who might direct me to the principal Egyptian buildings in Rome and provide translation if needed?"

The priest made a face, something between denial and hesitation— a curious play of features Aelius did not know what to make of, except that it seemed artificial, a layering of pretension over something else. It came to him, also, that Theo had never actually said he would send word about him to Soter—had he? How else could Soter be awaiting him?

"No one knows Egyptian Rome as well as Lucinus Soter did, Commander. Not even the priests."

Aelius chose not to insist, only because he wanted to see how long it would be before an alternative would be given to him. There was one, no doubt. Perhaps one already agreed upon, since he was after all the stranger and the soldier coming to ask about matters outside of his culture and belief. And business.

With the light of the court behind him, the priest's figure seemed narrower than it was, nearly a cutout of a man, with that gilded egg topping it. Without preceding the description by anything like, *Well, yes, there is somebody,* or, *I do have one more name in mind,* he said directly, "He goes by Onofrius—which is Latin for *unnophre,* Osiris the Resurrected. A former adept of ours who turned Christian during Aurelian's first years, when it was easy, and is now an ex-Christian."

"Ah," Aelius said, because he couldn't think of anything else to say.

"I'm sorry. Do you object to apostates?"

"Not particularly. I am not in the prosecution business."

"Then you won't mind." A smile opened in the priest's bald face, much like a thin crack on an egg.

"This Onofrius used to be a tourist guide for Egyptians on visit to Rome, and I expect he did the same for those who later wanted to see the Christians' execution and burial places. He was never officially associated with *our* temple, but naturally we knew of him. Lives by his wits, and I don't know how trustworthy he may be. They tell me he is a creditable guide, but I leave it to your judgment whether to hire him or not."

It's your responsibility if you choose him. Aelius took the hint. "Where do I send for him?"

"As of last report, he roomed near the Great Turtles."

"I don't know where that is."

"In Mars's Field, across the street from Severus Alexander's Baths. One must take a right without going as far as the marble deposit. It's a tenement area, you'll have to ask."

"Before or after Domitian's racetrack?"

"Before."

Making mental note of the instructions, Aelius asked details about Soter's image and role among urbanized Egyptians, but it all came down to goodness, culture, affection by all, surprise at his demise. He'd heard similar words from Harpocratio, and that was the way it seemed to be with these tight-lipped southerners. The apostate Onofrius, perhaps looser than his compatriots, was beginning to sound interesting.

Because the priest politely led him toward the door, "One last question," Aelius added. Was Soter married, or had he female relatives?"

"Why, he lost his mother and sisters during the Rebellion."

"That, I knew. But was he married or—?"

"Not he."

The little words. Amazing how people would use small dry phrases to refuse information. Aelius realized he had struck the immovable wall of what will not be said, so he stepped out of the scented room, not without relief.

On the wall as he left the sun-filled temple precinct, his eye caught rows of religious notices in the customary Greek. Memorial inscriptions, calendars of festivals and holy days passed before his incurious eyes. The last tablet before the doorway read, *In memory of our Lord Anubis's banquet for Lucinus Soter, celebrated by his friends in the Egyptian community nine days after his death.* The third tablet from the end, however, mentioned the funerary banquet held in June at Lucinus Soter's expense, in honor and remembrance of his late Antinoopolis friend, the *justified* Serenus Dio. After the Greek text, signs and figures of the ancient Egyptian script—presumably a translation of the words above in the language that so few knew by now.

It remained to be seen whether a connection with Serenus's death had caused Soter's murder by blood and fire. Doggedly, sundown being still far, Aelius found his way to the station of the II Cohort of the Fire Police and Night Patrol, in whose district Soter's house had stood. There, he easily pulled rank to secure information about the "lady in mourning" whom the dead man (or his watchdog) might have known. The police inspector showed him all deference, but seemed to think the question amusing in the context. Like many uniformed men he made much of masculinity and made an obscene gesture to indicate Soter.

"It's like this, Commander. The Egyptian cloth merchant was

one of those. He frequented free adult males, was private about it, so there was no reason for us to know much more. Just what we happened to observe on our beat. Of late, I can tell you he'd taken up with a youngster who lives on Blackbird Street. He's reportedly from somewhere around Naples. Lives off rich men. Discreet, soft-spoken, doesn't get in trouble. No one knows much about him, other than those who're intimate. And *they* don't say much."

"No women?"

"As far as I know, no women. The fire was definitely set, by the way. You might have heard what his secretary said, about his having been killed beforehand. It could be, but the place was a regular oven by the time we got there, and there was little left of Soter when we sieved through the house. About the other matter, would it help if I gave you the catamite's address?"

"Yes, it can't hurt."

"At this hour, he might not yet have started his business rounds." The inspector was like so many Aelius had known, bound to their jobs until routine didn't seem reason enough to get up in the morning. He made himself useful, but only because there could be some remote benefit in doing so. So he gave directions, offered an escort, all in a placid and unhurried manner, as it probably didn't matter to him either way if Aelius accepted. Aelius said he thought he could find the address, and would go on his own.

"Then, Commander, that's about what I can do for you. When you get back to Court, be so good as to remember that we were helpful, here at the II Cohort. My name is Procullus Vatia: not Proculus, eh? Pro-cull-us."

When Aelius left the police station, the long day drew close to sunset. Breathtaking green rays spread from an invisible point in the west, where buildings unknown to him—past the old Servian walls—hid from view the sinking sun, and what clouds under the horizon caused those shadow-rays to be cast. He did recognize Maecenas's Gardens ahead, and the tower from which they said Nero watched Rome burning. It was a good old tower, curly with caper bushes, full of pigeons at this time of day, under that crown of green rays. Not at all the frightful, gleaming tower of his nightmare, bursting through with fire and collapsing upon itself to crush him.

5 August, Nones, Saturday (12 Mesore)
The address Procullus had given to him led Aelius to a narrow brick house called Caesares Septem. There, languid-eyed under a cascade of tight black curls, Soter's companion stood on the threshold of the cozy second floor bedroom, in a thin gray tunic revealing torso and hips as through a fog. The face was a girl's, pouting and seductive. Aelius saw dark nipples pushing through the gauze at a pert, open angle, a neat trick on a man's body. Not girlish at all, the thighs were rather long and slender. What lay between these, under a belly unaccountably round and low, Aelius was at a loss to say.

Perhaps because he'd been stalled by that old bag of a servant until he'd just pushed his way in and upstairs, more likely because it irritated him to be here in the first place, Aelius rallied from surprise quickly enough to sum up his vexation. "Look here," he burst out, "it happened twice to me in my days to end up with prostitutes who turned out to be men, and in both cases I beat them within an inch of their lives. So, which one is it—man, woman, or what?"

"Hih! Always a big scene. That's why I stay away from soldiers."

"*Which one is it?*"

The prostitute shrugged, a bit intimidated and clearly irked to show it. Having heard the reason for the visit (Aelius described himself as a state official pursuing Soter's case), she snapped her fingers for the servant to fetch her a wrap. "All right," she squarely faced the visitor, "all right, so I'm a woman. You found me out. I don't think that's really much to His Divinity's envoy, and in any case, I'm not answering any questions. Unless you're ready to beat me within an inch of my life even in the state I'm in."

Whores and their reticence, how he despised the reaction. Suddenly, by association, Aelius was mortified to discover himself thinking of Anubina still as a whore, keeping silent as she did about her

daughter, but Anubina had never been so brazen. Like other im-
poverished girls, she'd been sold into prostitution by her widowed
mother and done the best of it. The first night he met her she sat on
his knees, and without making love they slept embracing in bed.

The recollection riled him even more. "This is ludicrous. Why on
earth—whatever your name is—would you sell yourself as a man to
those who are bent that way and would find you out at once?"

"The name is Cleopatra Minor, and that's a stupid question." She
snatched the proffered shawl from her servant's hands, morosely draping her shoulders and midriff with it. "How about because there are
men who are a little more complicated in their tastes?" She walked
into the bedroom and sat at the foot of the bed, one leg tucked under
her. "It may be hard for a soldier to understand, since you're happy to
compete for the loudest belch or the grossest curse word."

Aelius was not sure whether he should step forward or just leave.
"You really know little about soldiers," he grumbled from the doorstep,
"so let's leave it at that. I thought it was common knowledge that Soter
liked men."

"*And* women, I can tell you that." She looked over with that artful pout, an expression Aelius had known on women before, falling
for it occasionally. Helena, at Court, was a specialist that way, and in
other ways, too. Now Cleopatra Minor was saying, "He knew who I
was before renting me out, and keeping me for the past ten months.
I'm carrying his, so you understand his death is distressing to me at
least in three different ways."

Aelius was beginning to feel the unique foolishness of being in a
brothel, an uncomfortable precursor of excitement. Hadn't he, in his
career, come to such places, such rooms, and discovered that once his
body was satisfied, a small ache—like a thorn in the chest—had not
found solace? Hadn't Anubina been the only one to cure that aching
spot? At Court he'd had Helena, with the wiles of an old harlot and
the sheets of a queen. Not even then had he been given what Anubina
was able to create: a place of quiet and safety, as close to peace as a

soldier could get. This girl was pretty, would be beautiful once the pregnancy was through, but his task by her had nothing to do with beauty. Sticking to his reasons for being here, "I can guess two ways Soter's death troubles you," he said, "loss of upkeep by him, and the damage to your reputation as a transvestite." But he was losing anger already. "Unless you liked him, too, in which case I'm sorry for you. It's hard to lose someone."

"As if you knew." With an unexpected flourish, Cleopatra Minor grabbed her tumultuous head of curls and removed it, exposing a boyish scissor cut. At once she looked smaller, less threatening, and less attractive. She stood from the bed and Aelius stepped back to let her pass.

Outside the bedroom, a carpeted space was occupied by a table and armchairs; stepping toward them, the girl gestured for him to follow. She sat down, with a cynical look of weariness on her unpainted face. Twenty, Aelius judged, twenty-one at most. He'd known such girls in Asia and on the frontier, and somehow they seemed cut out of the same brittle substance, lacquered over with bitterness. "Anyway," she said, "I can't show myself in public for the next three months. Then there'll be the child's pension and nursing bills, so I must keep busy. Some of my old regulars are wondering what's wrong with me. The story of mourning Soter is wearing thin, so I'm off to Naples with the excuse of learning new tricks from the boys at Fortunatus's. You know, the male stew that originated in Pompeii, and was patronized by the deified Trajan, Hadrian, and so on."

Aelius came over from the bedroom door, but did not sit down. "It was a bad way to die, for Soter."

"Until a few weeks ago, I visited him often. I could have been there with him and been killed, too."

"Instead, you have his watchdog."

"How on earth—?" Her surprise was genuine, but no telling whether it concealed worry that he had found out. She fussed with the shaggy hair on her temples, sticky with the heat of day; all without looking at him directly, which was unusual for a prostitute. Aelius was not vain, but he wondered if she didn't like him, or—vice versa—felt unattractive to men at this time. Dressed as a youth, he wouldn't have noticed her in a crowd. As a girl, even "in the state she was in," she came close to arousing him; and he wasn't about to let her suspect it.

He said, roughly, "I know, and that's that. What about Soter? Did you notice him acting fearfully of late?"

"I can tell you that Soter was afraid, but that was nothing new." She used a hem of the shawl to blot her neck, with her eyes closed. "Like all the rich, he feared folks would rob him or worse. At least two nights a week he'd spend here. He would have servants deliver him to my doorstep and usually come to get him during daytime. When he stayed late and had business early in the morning, the retinue looked like a holy procession, there were so many torches and tapers."

"Did he say whether he feared anyone in particular?"

Her eyes were open again, and on him just the time to say the words. "If men were to tell whores what's going on in their affairs, we'd all get killed sooner or later. I wouldn't know, and frankly wouldn't tell you if I knew."

He wondered whether Anubina had those tired circles under her eyes while she carried her children; whether she, too, had continued to *work* until the growth of her belly displeased her clients. "You told me there's a stew in Naples that the deified Hadrian patronized. I'm interested. What about it?"

"It has nothing to do with Soter's death."

"Is it as historical a place as you said?"

Her mood rallied a little. She spoke looking at an imprecise place on his shoulder, a bit amused, avoiding his face. "Why, in certain circles it's legendary! The official version is that he met Antinous over in Asia Minor, but they tell you a different story in Naples. They say he was—Hadrian, that is—passing through the city on his way to some faraway land or other when he stopped for *refreshment* along the way. Antinous was a new arrival and had hardly had the time to get used to his little bed that he was snatched off. There's a tablet in verses inside the stew that gives you the story and how Antinous made out afterward."

"What about *that*?"

"Well, everyone knows: He fell into the Nile, was drowned, and they buried him. Nothing special, but the verses are pretty, and I liked them."

"Does the tablet say where he was buried?"

"I don't recall, exactly." A droplet of sweat came down her forehead, and she wiped it with her ring finger. "I think it says he was buried where the Emperor later died—something of the sort."

Her nails were bitten nearly to the quick. Aelius noticed it, and realized she'd caught his notice, by the way she put her hand under the shawl. He said, "You mean Baiae."

"I guess so. No one cares nowadays."

Far from it, he thought. This was a new one on him. He'd never heard of Antinous being at work in a Neapolitan bordello. "Are you literate?" he asked.

She stared at him this time, with some attention. "Whom do you take me for? Of course I'm literate. And I didn't take the name Cleopatra Minor without knowing who the Great Cleopatra was."

"What I mean is, did you read the tablet with your own eyes?"

"You must be used to cows in your army brothels! I write poetry myself. And, yes, I read the tablet and even wrote the verses down. I copy verses everywhere I go, but what does it have to do with Soter?"

"Do you have the text here?"

"Good God, yes." Amusement played on her face, briefly. "I wouldn't have guessed it, but I say you're queer after all."

"Don't get your hopes up, I'm just curious."

She was gone the time necessary—Aelius saw through the door—to take a rolled-up scroll from a shelf in her bedroom. "Here are the verses." She walked back, handing it to him. "Enjoy."

Written in Latin, and copied in a decent hand, the text of the tablet "set," she said, "in the stew's entrance hall," read,

> Born in the East, buried in the West,
> died in the South. Now the Bithynian,
> whom the imperial friend encountered here
> to their mutual delight,
> is naught but shadow and dust
> close by, where Hadrian took his flight from mortality,
> riding in Helios's chariot.

In fact, the verses were insignificant, and the information they conveyed close to useless, except for the tidbit about Antinous's permanence in a male brothel. Aelius could see why this detail would be omitted in the official story of the relationship, out of respect for the deified Hadrian. As for the emperor's autobiography, he'd never actually said where he'd met the Boy. Only that the encounter had taken place in Antinous's eleventh year, and Hadrian's forty-fifth.

"Here it doesn't say that the Boy was buried in Baiae," he commented.

"But that's where Hadrian died, isn't it?"

History said that while his tomb in Rome was being finished, Hadrian had actually been cremated and buried in Puteoli, near the resort city of Baiae. The poem opened the possibility that Antinous had found his resting place there as well, but somehow Aelius doubted it. Hadrian's heir Antoninus had not received the surname of Pious just out of filial piety: It was unlikely that he'd allowed a common grave to the emperor and to his commoner lover.

It all begged the question, also, of whether Antinous had been in the process of being groomed to look like a woman in addition to acting the part of one.

When he asked her, Cleopatra Minor said she didn't know. "Who can tell? Of Trajan, they say he liked grown men, including some of his married officers."

Aelius limited himself to muttering that things at court had been getting better since. Of Hadrian, well, he'd read that he liked married women, and young men. Did it mean that for Antinous he'd made a passionate exception, choosing him as a bedfellow when still a child, or did it imply something else? Could the Boy have been kept merely as a favorite page until late adolescence, when physical attraction would be acted upon? Was it even remotely possible that the relationship had never grown to be a carnal one? It would explain why historians who'd always heaped ignominy on imperial lovers were uncharacteristically silent about Antinous. Only the Christians seemed to have read into that constant companionship a licentious and possibly violent meaning. Well, a man who builds monuments for his hounds is not likely to lay his beloved lover (or friend) in a box somewhere, but what about the state papers supposed to be in the grave? Would Hadrian commit the imprudence of marking the tomb, when enemies of Rome (he could never be sure they had all been gotten rid of, whoever they were) could get into it and, while removing proof of their existence, desecrate the body? How sick, how mad, how mindless had Hadrian become before his death, that he wouldn't make sure his orders to defeat the enemy had been carried out?

"Are you still there?" Cleopatra Minor spoke up. "You look like you're off to Baiae yourself."

He glanced at her. More likely than not, Anubina had turned so ripe, so weary during her pregnancy. How the next words came to him was odd, because he said them with the freedom that place and woman allowed him, but meant them as more than a compliment, as a way to console her. "And frankly you look as though you could make a fortune in this City even as a girl."

"Thanks. You haven't seen the competition, I can tell."

"I have *seen* it, but not close up yet."

Looking over, she smiled, either at the implicit flattery or her distrust of it. "Life is hard, soldier. I'm sure you know. Back to Antinous: at Fortunatus's I learned he had his own house in Rome, but there's no way to see it now."

"Why, was it destroyed?"

"Buried. And unless you have the means to dig up the Antoninian Baths, there's nothing doing. See? Historians think they know everything, but the juicy tidbits about whores and male lovers are often disregarded by them. The boys at Fortunatus's said Antinous's house looked upon the Appian Way, and one got to it by a little side street near Drusus's Arch, the one they call Arch of Remembrance. Was supposed to have Egyptian pictures in it. I was told it was actually covered over well before the baths were built, on the orders of Antoninus Pius."

I n the steam bath of midmorning, Aelius left the house at Septem Caesares by the back gate, where the old servant had directed him. "If you're still in Rome after mid-October," Cleopatra Minor had told him as he started down the stairs, "I will be back from Naples by then." Crossing the well-tended little garden, he overheard barking from the guardian's room and looked in. A large black dog snarled at him, pulling the long chain that granted it movement back and forth across the floor. *It's unfortunate animals can't speak,* he thought. Of course, she was the one who had retrieved it, but too late to save Soter. As things were, Aelius had no clues about the men Soter feared during his last days, and whether his nemesis had anything in common with those who had first frightened and then killed Serenus Dio. The same, likely, who had started the fire in Theo's storeroom, and were forewarned that Caesar's envoy had come to Rome. Fire, blood, water: Of such components was made the nameless threat, capable of striking across provinces as it seemed, and remains unseen. The "poachers" who had signaled his coming to Rome had never been identified, much less caught. For all Aelius knew, they could be watching him right now from across the street.

Bound for the State Library by the stranger's roundabout way, Aelius had time to reason that perhaps the verses simply took poetic license with the facts. They could mean that Antinous's soul abided by the Emperor after death, not that he'd been buried inside

Hadrian's temporary tomb at Puteoli. According to tradition, the tomb had originally belonged to Cicero's family, and as far as Aelius knew it was still standing, empty after Antoninus Pius had removed his predecessor's remains to Rome. He'd have to see for himself, unless he found a precise description of it somewhere.

State correspondence was kept at the deified Trajan's Ulpian Library, and usually permission of the City Prefect's office was needed to consult it. As the registers were about to be packed for removal to the library in His Divinity's new Baths, Aelius impressed upon the staff the urgency to receive a reading pass. Scrutinizing the crates under the librarians' annoyed control, he pored over originals and copies, and kept at bay the constant temptation to get lost after unrelated historical leads. History, larger than any part of it, beckoned and tried to make him forget the anguishing urgency of his task. He had no time, no time; so he limited himself to making a note of what private letter, what official brief he'd have to go back to when working on the lives of other princes.

At sunset, when closing time interrupted his readings, Aelius had just enough time to follow directions from the library to the address Philo's brother had given him. There, in a religious school on the street that led from Vicus Pallacinae to the Iseum Campense, the banquet of Our Lord Anubis would begin shortly.

It was lucky that familiarity with Egypt had inured him to such sights, because the great shrine stood before him as a perfect delirium of statues and obelisks in a mixture of styles, ghostly in the halflight. Lions, sphinxes, baboons, dwarf gods, and dog-headed ones crowded around him as he sought the doorway—private, recessed, and unlit—of the House of Life.

L etter from Aelius Spartianus to Diocletian Caesar:

> *To Emperor Caesar Gaius Aurelius Valerius Diocletian Pius Felix Invictus Augustus, his Aelius Spartianus, greetings from the eternal head of the world, Rome.*

There might be significance, Lord, to the fact that I began my survey of the deified Hadrian's buildings on the recurrence of supplicia canum. *Owing to your clemency, the day no longer implies annual crucifixion of innocent animals, but it is a reminder of the vigilance ever needed to maintain the security of the state. As I reported in my first, hurried note from the capital, the organizational needs of my historical research and investigative task have been met through excellent lodgings, and the astonishing availability of information in the many libraries and archives. It thrills me beyond belief to walk into the Ulpian Library in particular, with the wealth of its collection, and also the place where my mother's ancestors were manumitted during the reign of the deified Hadrian and made free men.*

Tonight I have attended a funerary banquet near the Iseum Campense. where I learned a few interesting details on the fortunes of the Egyptian community in Rome, and also on the man whose death prevented me from gathering information. It seems that in the days before the fire, Lucinus Soter told friends that he felt watched; Philo's brother did not go as far as admitting that, but had mentioned to me how the police discounted his master's unease, to the point of convincing him not to replace his watchdog after it disappeared. What I hoped to gain from Soter directly I now will have to reconstruct piecemeal, but I am not discouraged.

Indeed, while preparing to meet Aviola Paratus, I trust that every step I take in this blessed City will bring me closer not only to clarifying matters relating to the deified Hadrian, but also to resolving what more and more appears to be an intentional chain of events initiated by Serenus Dio's discovery of the ancient brief. As for the latter, it was deposited in a safe place secretly, and by my own hands.

Regarding the physical state of Rome, about which you

*desire details, I can report that the labor on your monumental
baths continues apace, its surface to cover eventually just short
of twenty-nine acres. The Sodality of Felicitous Fortune has
been fully refunded for the razing of its premises to make room
for the monumental swimming pool. Twenty-five hundred of
the projected three thousand basins are in place. Official opening in less than two years' time is expected. The repaving of the
Great Forum is nearly completed, and that, eleven years after
the disastrous fire that raged from the foot of the capital to the
deified Hadrian's monumental temple of Venus and Rome (still
in need of repairs), all three of the major restoration works you
ordered are completed now. As for the Senate House (Curia),
rebuilt from the foundations, its bronze doors have just been
installed and the marble floor is all but laid out. The Marcian
Aqueduct, less than ten years from the earthquake so damag-
ing to its distribution castle, has been not only repaired (as you
saw in your visit last November), but the water volume is in
the process of being potentiated.*

*Still, many buildings await attention: Stadiums, amphi-
theaters and other public entertainment places carry the marks
of careless patching-up during previous administrations; I hear
that cracks open every other day, and that a heavy rain often results in the collapse of soffits and cornices, to the risk of Roman
lives. Decius's Baths on the Aventine are closed and structurally
unsound. If the tepid pool hall's ceiling gives way, I am told, the
whole thing may come down. A curiosity: Mons Testaceus,
made up of discarded wine and oil jugs by the river bank, has
reached the height of a hundred feet, and is facetiously nicknamed Drunk Hill.*

*You also inquired, Lord, of the prosecution of Christians
in the City. Coercion is applied according to the law, but the
trials are not as visible as elsewhere in the empire, perhaps because here citified habits moderate religious extremism and*

*the accused watch their steps. The cult places are closed, but their cemeteries (including the large underground ones and the ugly one grown like a barnacle on the side of Gaius's horse track in the Vatican Field) have not been disturbed. Of some interest among the trials presently being carried out is that of the soldier Cyriacus, because it pertains to both your clemency and your monumental baths. In fact, this is the same man who—from the nearby house granted by you to his sect in the past—has been ministering to (and probably agitating) the Christians condemned to hard labor on the construction site. Incidentally, the Christian head bishop (or "pope"), Marcellinus, has apparently abjured during his recent detention, an act which has earned him his fellow believers' charge of tra-*ditor, *but now is said to be retracting his abjuration.*

On a separate sheet, Lord, I will send a list of selected prices of goods and services as observed in Rome. Meanwhile, I continue to seek everywhere the burial place of the boy Antinous, keeping in mind the dictum, Si monumentum quaeris, circumspice!

With thankfulness and greetings, written by Aelius Spartianus in Rome on Saturday, 5 August, Nones of August, in the twenty-first year of Our Lord Caesar Diocletian's imperial acclamation, the seventh year of the consulship of Maximianus Augustus, and the eighth year of the consulship of Aurelius Valerius Maximianus Augustus, also the year 1057 since the foundation of the City.

EIGHTH CHAPTER

That night, Aelius swore to himself never to attend an Egyptian wake again. Not only had all the commonplaces about the people and their religion been confirmed but he'd felt out of place, estranged by the incomprehensible prayers, ritual drinks, and chants. It was the same cruel Egypt, he recognized it well, to which somehow he managed to return again and again. After finishing the letter to His Divinity he'd tried to sleep—without success. So he'd sat up and then paced the floor, and finally stood on the little balcony that looked upon the valley.

A waning moon like a tipped ladle poured a flushed light on things known and unknown. Below, the Antoninian Baths loomed on the Appian Way, rising out of their glossy piazza like a tall island; where the road split just ahead, a clot of deeper darkness indicated the arch Cleopatra Minor had spoken of—the Arch of Remembrance. There, under the farthest corner of the baths, had stood Antinous's house, before earth filled it and millions of bricks were heaped upon it. Aelius could envision the blind rooms stuffed with earth, and puzzle over the possibility that Hadrian's successor, having in his bigoted piety deleted *this* remembrance of the Boy, might have destroyed his tomb as well. Was it possible? Was it? Could he trust the possibility enough to relax, to let go of this anxious piece of his search at least, because in that case—whatever Hadrian's letter said—neither he, Aelius, nor anyone else could lay his hands on a proof of conspiracy against Rome.

Those he had met tonight (Nilus So-and-So, Lotus Something— the names taken by second and third generation Egyptians who had never even traveled to Egypt, but fiercely stuck to tradition) maintained that Antinous was buried in Hadrian's estate at Tibur. Had they been there? No, but their elders had, and had seen the obelisk marking the grave. The priest with the shiny egg head, talkative over the meal once all ceremonies had been attended to, disagreed. Of course he would: For him, Antinous was buried in Antinoopolis. Only an old man knew Cleopatra Minor's version, having years earlier been shown the Boy's tomb near Naples, but *near Naples* led nowhere.

Chants and recitations aside, there was no interrogating the dead, no embalming them into eternal life. For a moment Aelius was tempted to ask for help from—he couldn't imagine whom. Gods, the One God, his men's Mithras, Osiris, he believed in none of those. Only in the civic duty of devout observance, according to Roman custom, which for him was a sufficient object of faith.

Past the arch, graves clustered on both sides of the ancient road furrowing the valley. Soter had chosen to be buried at the fourth mile of it, while Philo had gone to his rest in Vatican Field. His brother knew nothing of the cloth merchant's recent correspondence, but he did confirm that Soter and Serenus Dio had been friends in Egypt before the Rebellion.

I'd give anything to know whether Serenus wrote about his find to Soter. And if so, what is it that Soter could tell me, that someone had to cut his throat for it? Was it because he spoke the old language, and could help me to read the monuments?

All seemed completely disjointed and unsolvable tonight, a

hopeless jumble. If he looked up, more confusion: crowds of stars shone but for those nearest the half moon, put out like wicks by its halo. Recognizable to him were only the Swan, spanning endless wings overhead, and the Eagle, tilted as if gathering energy to dive; in its talons, a cluster of dim lights, one of which bore the name of Antinous—the "new star" the wily Egyptian priests told a skeptical Hadrian to have appeared at the Boy's death.

Then, from somewhere on the hill, behind the house, there came to Aelius the call and stepping together of the night patrol, a familiar and comforting sound in the great strangeness of the Roman dark.

7 AUGUST, MONDAY (14 MESORE)
Reading pass in hand, he was back at the Ulpian Library well before the baths' opening time.

It took him until midday to discover, filed alongside real estate matters and bills personally paid by the deified Hadrian, a lengthy report by the constructor who had refitted the republican tomb for its temporary imperial guest. The report had been sent to the emperor's successor one hundred and sixty-six years earlier, one month after Hadrian's demise, and a full eight years after the Boy's.

The description of the monument was attentive, even tedious in its details. Aelius skipped measurements and finicky commentaries on the thickness and breadth of cornices and marble slabs, in order to find what he sought.

> The interior of the monument, excellent Lord, had been left untouched since its construction for Cicero's daughter two centuries ago. Because it has been a long time since anyone brought offerings to Tullia's Manes inside it, the door had been sealed by the city of Puteoli's administrators to ensure safekeeping of the urn. What I plan to do, following the orders that originate in your filial piety, is the following:

Since there is a simple niche in the chamber's wall, and this containing the aforementioned urn, I will remove the same, and entrust it to the fathers of the city until such time as Your Excellency will decide where to remove it to.

Other than Tullia's bronze statue, a libation table, altar, and a semicircular seat (all in excellent marble), there are no fittings in the chamber. This appears to me to be both a shame and an opportunity. A shame because I cannot imagine your father's ashes to rest in such unadorned surroundings, even miserly by modern standards, and inadequate for an emperor's role in life and death. An opportunity, because it will allow me—if and when I receive your command—to decorate it as it becomes the late Prince of Rome.

There followed a comprehensive description of the betterments the constructor planned to bring to the interior, which Aelius decided to have copied for possible future use, but was not important now. The second-last sentence, however, was intriguing and as far as this turn in the investigation, definitive:

Thus there will remain one body, one man ensconced in this chamber, and, given the exceptionality of the case, in order that an imperial tomb not be surrounded by other burials as if it were one of many, I will raze to the ground the monuments of family freedmen that through the centuries proliferated around it. All appropriate care will be taken that those still containing human remains be closed first by priests, the caskets removed and placed elsewhere according to law, piety, and tradition.

In this manner, your father's monument shall stand alone at the center of a cultivated area planted with laurel and oaks, as it is fitting, and become fully visible to

all passing along Cicero's estate on their way to and from
the city of Puteoli.

No other burials around the temporary grave. One body, one man
buried in it: the emperor himself. This seemed to confirm that Antinous lay elsewhere. It saved Aelius a trip to Campania, but also revealed another dead end in his pursuit of the Boy's resting place.

8 AUGUST, TUESDAY (15 MESORE)
Aelius had seen blind soldiers before. Of all injuries, loss of sight had
always seemed to him the hardest to bear, as it forces a man used to
doing for himself, going freely, and acting on his own, to depend on
someone else for the simple task of looking before crossing the street.
Of Aviola Paratus, he knew that infirmity had not come by accident
or in battle. It had been purposely inflicted on him while a prisoner,
after Numerian's unlucky Persian campaign twenty years earlier. The
Persians, Tralles had informed him, had massacred Paratus's unit,
executing the commanding officers who'd survived the slaughter, and
blinded the junior ranks, leaving them to die, or—by chance—grope
their miserable way back across God knows what hardships and endless roads. As such, Paratus, even before Aelius met him, was supposed to represent all that stoicism and old-fashioned hardihood
represented. What stores of bitterness must by necessity lie at the
bottom, it remained to be seen.

The man he actually encountered, by a shady al fresco table of
the well-appointed tavern at The Glory of our Lord Aurelian's, looked
the part perfectly, except for the complete lack of any apparent bitterness. Shorn but for the stubble army emperors had made popular,
with his hair nearly shaven and like a gray skullcap no longer than
the face stubble, he was lean and wiry but solidly connected, long-
limbed, sinewy, as if fashioned out of aged wood. The long, northern
skull was at once delicate and firm, with horizontal lines creasing the
brow, signs of thoughtfulness, it seemed, rather than of care, and a
firm mouth that seemed about to smile, ironic and sensitive. Behind

him, at the back of the tavern, rolling vineyards crowded with grapes all but covered the reddish earth. Whitewashed outbuildings, straight fences, absence of weeds—all bespoke familiar army discipline.

Paratus greeted him first, and as Aelius afterward sought his hand, Paratus clasped it hard and held it.

"You have no idea, Commander, of what it means for me to be considered once more of use to my country."

Aelius kept silent. Such words were expected. A bit rhetorical, perhaps, but then he recalled how at least twice, in Armenia and midway through the Rebellion, he had felt rather used by his country, and not so well reconciled to the idea of being little more than meat stacked against the enemy. Now this blind man's words shamed him.

"Your letter reached me in good time," he resolved to say, "so I thought we should meet."

How much he should add next, was for Aelius another reason for hesitation. As far as he knew, Tralles had only informed Paratus of his research on Antinous's death. A man who has served in intelligence-gathering might by habit keep abreast of what else there might be (Aelius's informal checking on the Christian trials, his looking into Serenus Dio's death), and draw conclusions from what he hears. Paratus stood unaffectedly, and even when Aelius invited him to sit down, he waited until he heard that his guest preceded him.

"I have taken the liberty," Paratus was telling him now, his hand groping for a scroll he had in front of him, "of drawing up a short list of sites you might wish to visit while in and around Rome, in connection with the deified Hadrian."

Aelius received the text. Scanning it, he saw how distances from Rome and between locations had been indicated, as had the roads along which the various places lay.

"I would have done a better job, had I been able to survey the sites myself," Paratus apologized, "and I fear there may exist useable shortcuts built lately, with which I am not familiar."

"I don't know what to say." Aelius shook his head. "This is as careful a survey of the deified Hadrian's works and properties as I

have laboriously managed to put together in weeks, and you listed
some buildings I would not have thought of."

"The sources being what they are, it's understandable." Self-
consciously Paratus smiled, lips tight. "It isn't much, but I realize that
if I am to convince you that I may be of use, I am to do the best I can
of my memory and my policeman's way with asking information." A
slight wind rose, and Paratus filled his lungs with it and said, "I remember your unit from the days of the Rebellion. You did wonders in
the courtyard of Thoth at Hermopolis."

"It cost us plenty."

"But it won the day. There was envy for that action, as it put you
in such good light with His Divinity. I believe ben Matthias swore to
do you in then. *You* were the one to eliminate. It gave us some worry
at headquarters. Luckily, it all went well."

"Pannonian luck." Aelius had not known there had been envy
among his colleagues for his military successes. He asked himself
now whether his old friend Tralles still felt that edge, and had refused
to help him because of it. For the sake of information, "Where in our
province were you born?" he asked.

"Brigetio."

"The army camp?"

"No, at the south side of the civilian city, by the glassworks. But
my uncle Breucus, after whom I was named, did serve in the I Legion
Adiutrix. Have you been to Brigetio lately?"

"No. I heard it's lost some of its population after the last trouble
on the frontier, and some of the estates are being abandoned."

"I heard the same, and I'm glad I can't see it." Paratus placed his
hands on the table, palms flat, thumbs touching. "Speaking of more
pleasant things, I am proud to inform you I began my career on the
city beat of the V Cohort, Night Patrol, in the Second District, with
4,600 tenement houses, 27 storehouses, and 85 baths in my day. I did
well, and was promoted to commissioner of the VI Cohort in the
Great Roman Forum District, with all that matters in Rome com-
pacted into some 14,000 square feet, plus nearly three times as many

roadside shrines as the previous assignment, nearly 3,500 blocks of tenements, and 86 baths. In those days they chose us because we were tall and handsome, and only the guard—with its expensive getup—made a better show than we did on parade."

Aelius smiled to himself, because his father, his sisters' husbands, all were likewise proud of their army garb to the point of vanity.

"I used to love working at night," Paratus added, "in the dark streets. Who would have said I'd walk in the dark ever after the Persian Campaign? But that's how it went. Now when I'm not traveling I take care of this place, which does well because it's the best stop out of Rome before Ad Quintanas—and my wine is better. The wife stays at Minturnae, with our two sons who are in business down there. They take after her and are settled—tame, I'd say, good at making money in their maternal grandpa's tile factory, which has turned out a handsome profit ever since they took it over. She's a good old girl, and knows I must be away for long stretches. Has grandchildren, now, so she doesn't miss me much, or so she says. What about you, Commander?"

By comparison, his life seemed quickly summarized. Aelius shrugged, relaxing in the breezy shade. "Well, I served in Armenia after Egypt, and was at Nicomedia until the spring. For the rest, as any soldier's son, my entire life has been reckoned by army events. I turned eight on the day Sarmatians and Quadi invaded Pannonia, and remember it well; my twin sisters were born a year later, when Carus entered Mesopotamia as a victor and was then found dead in his tent. At ten, my father was away a long time when Numerian's army rebelled after the death of Carus and eventually chose His Divinity."

"How about a glass of wine?"

"Don't mind if I do."

Cellar-cool wine was brought to the table. Sniffing the green breeze from the vineyard, Paratus rounded his shoulders as he drew the full glass to himself. "When your sisters were born I was with Numerian in Persia. The rumble of the Persian war horses I have in my

ears to this day—the chaos of thundering hoofs when they reared in
fright, as we clashed swords on shields; and then our line bulging
back, breaking, the unforgettable stench of horse and man sweat as
they crush against you at full speed. It took me a year to get back,
feeling my way through enemy country, before I finally heard the
cheers of the imperials calling out Diocletian's name. You remember
Siscia had fallen into rebel hands; it was murder trying to pass
through the region."

Aelius nodded, as if the man facing him could see that motion of
assent. It was always like this, in the army. Measuring time according
to campaigns, exchange of updates on frontier towns and camps,
stolid esprit de corps; no civilian ever fully understood how necessary these preliminaries were to all transactions. He took a sip of the
fruity, cool drink, letting it rest in the back of his mouth before swallowing. The deified Hadrian having been a soldier, such updates
might have been meaningful for him, too. How had Antinous, never
in a war, reckoned his short years?

Next, Aelius summarized the aims of his research in Italy, fram-
ing his interest in Antinous's burial as one element in his biographical reconstruction. Listening with shoulders straight, his head
slightly tilted back, Paratus was saying, *yes,* under his breath. "As a
former policeman," he spoke up then, "the question of the Boy's
death is intriguing for me. The leads you gathered in Egypt seem
promising. I can assist you in reconstructing the scenario of his
death. Have you already sought out the incident report, required by
Egyptian law?"

"Yes, but it was no use. The archives were damaged by flood
years ago. I only found the *nome* governor's reply to the report, and
that in bad shape. The lines supposed to give details on the state of
Antinous's body are washed out."

"That's too bad. It's worth looking into the State Archives here,
in case a copy was sent to Rome for safekeeping. In case it was not,
we'll go with what we have. Contemporary private correspondence of
the senatorial class might be useful, since the deified Hadrian had

critics in that quarter. None of it would be kept in the State Archives. However, His Divinity's letters of presentation would open private collections to you. I can prepare a list of still extant families whose holdings could shed light on those old events."

It was an idea he should have thought of. Aelius could kick himself for having to be told, but was grateful for the suggestion. Why had he not sought a research partner from the start? As he sat there, he felt the sting of having to keep secret *the rest:* the three deaths, the fear that an old conspiracy might yet (or continue to?) do damage to Rome unless its identity—hidden in Antinous's grave—was revealed. Prudence requested partial silence for now, although he felt an overbearing need to share information with a man whose suffering proved inner worth, and with whom he had so much in common.

Paratus was saying, half-apologetically, "The Boy's final resting place, I am afraid I cannot physically help you in finding, although I am not wholly without resources. I have a young manservant who accompanies me to the great libraries occasionally, to read texts for me. If you are prepared to do the legwork, I can supply indications. Which all comes down, as you perceive, to my entreating you to let me be of service again. I do not expect you to answer now, but kindly think things over and send me word."

Aelius had already made up his mind, but dropped a noncommittal, "I will," as he rose to his feet. Imitating him, Paratus felt around for Aelius's proffered hand. "That's good enough for me." Which could have been his farewell, saving a policeman's impeccable instinct for arguments left unsaid. "Is there anything else I should know, Commander?"

"Nothing else."

A rubicund, dumb-faced stable boy led the army horse from the stable. Nimbly Aelius mounted ("The rustle of cavalry leather"— Paratus half-smiled—"a beautiful sound.") and soon both men, one riding slowly to allow the other to walk along, came to the stony verge of the road.

Paratus sought and found with his foot the stubby column

marking the XII mile, and the end of his driveway. Again he sniffed the air, filling his lungs. The breeze had fallen. "It's one of those afternoons that look as still as wall paintings, isn't it? The wicker fences all tangled up with vines, and not a leaf stirring—I wager the colored ribbons hang from garden statues as if they were starched."

"It's true," Aelius said.

"Lovely?"

"Very."

"How I miss it—I'd lie if I said I didn't. You know, I used to wonder where the birds go, in days like this. None in the sky, and every blade of grass turned just so, or standing straight. I swear, we'd see such afternoons on the campaign trail and fall for that peace and quietude, until peace would explode and then it'd all look like the wild jumble of bodies sculpted on stone coffins, or the war columns in Rome. You, too?"

"More than once." When ben Matthias had wounded him in Egypt, the day had been much like this. Aelius recalled silence, then havoc, the thud of the arrow coming in, and blood frothing up his throat like sweet vomit.

Paratus lifted his seamed face to the sky, away from Aelius. "I have sat on guard in the mountains of Commagene, above the tree line, where the row of stone gods sits up high. I have sat nights by the toppled heads of those giants, on the mound the Great King built for himself. The stars rise at your right if you look at the statues, on your left side if you watch the valley, which was my duty after all. The wind is all that one hears in the night, and there is the great breath of the sky above where one by one the figures take shape above and then decline, until one sees them as a chart fixed in the heavens and yet about to be erased by the day. This is the Hunter, with his dogs rushing alongside him, all as though leaping into the great earth, with the Kinglet that marks the Lion coming after, the Little Goat above, and the bright eye of the Bull already grazing the earth. There are signs above, and signs below. To the *reader,* they are as clear in the dark as they are during the day hours. To the illiterate of the spirit, they are incomprehensible even as the ticking and whirring of insects is unintelligible and in the end meaningless. What do you say to that?"

Aelius thought of the constellations on the mosaics of Hadrian's barge, truly *a chart fixed in the heavens.* Paratus would be useful indeed. With a click of his tongue, he bade the horse start on the way back. "I say that I have kept watch nights also, and heard the wind, and that I, too, can *read.*"

A t his quarters, a letter from Diocletian awaited him, sent from Salonae on 12 July. It had been delivered by a courier shortly after Aelius had left in the morning and received as all correspondence by his head guardsman.

"It has never left my hands, Commander," the soldier told him. The formula was one agreed upon, and Aelius paid no special attention to it. A slip in the dark sealing wax made it appear as though the imperial signet ring had pressed it twice, but slippage was a fairly common occurrence. *Bodyguards will be bodyguards,* Aelius told himself, and with a terse nod of the head, walked into his studio to read the text.

It was a reply to the message he had sent on 28 June from Antinoopolis. Diocletian generally encouraged him to continue his research, without forgetting his additional duties to report on prices, and the state of the religious trials. Before the closing formula, it added, "In relation to the investigation you have by my permission undertaken, see to it that you apply yourself with zeal, since it is my will that the welfare of the state be watched over by all. Private and public crimes are an abomination against Roman order, and you are to make use of your authority as Caesar's envoy to get to the truth. Besides, this veteran you mention, Aviola Paratus, was in our early days one of the best acquisitions to our cause. During the Rebellion, he acquitted himself with distinction despite his infirmity. I recommend him to your attention, as his police experience cannot but be of use to you as you pursue possible enemies—old and new—of the greatest empire on earth."

Had he known a few hours earlier, his conversation at The Glory of Our Lord Aurelian's would have ranged well beyond historical details. Aelius was glad of the endorsement, and ready to forgive Tralles for his initial lack of support. In fact, he'd just begun a note to him when the coming of Onofrius—*tour guide to the selective*—was announced to him.

After Aviola Paratus, the apostate looked insignificant. Down on his heels, he wore a jaw beard, really a continuation of sideburns to circle the face; an unfashionable mustache drooped from under his nose to the sides of his mouth. Judging from his shabby clothes, guiding tourists did not ensure a profit. Because he vaguely resembled a scout who'd led his Armenia unit into what could have been a deadly ambush, Aelius found him distasteful at once. Army scouts, needed in mountainous no-man's-land, had been a lifeline to Roman units during the Persian campaign; strung out through barren passes, his regiment had been betrayed as it reached the next plateau; only because some of the army horses were not geldings and shied at the scent of female Persian mounts, was the hidden enemy revealed. The scout had been executed on the spot. As for this Onofrius, resembling the traitor in looks and clothing, he was likely not dangerous, merely unlikable.

He showed up carrying notes of introduction from the head priest at the Iseum Campense, and from two perfect unknowns who'd satisfactorily used his services. In the book-filled studio of Aelius's quarters, Onofrius listened to his prospective employer with hands clasped and head low, meaning perhaps to look pious, or thoughtful, or both. A window was open behind him on a sky of great sailing clouds, and only his outline was discernible. His voice, when he spoke, had just enough of a southern singsong to irk Aelius.

"You have to begin by looking for the obelisks, Commander. Where's there's an obelisk, there's a tomb."

Aelius stepped out from behind his desk to reach the window sill, and have the advantage of looking at the guide in the full light. "That's not true," he commented. "There are obelisks in the middle of racetracks and squares."

"Ah, but that is in Rome, you see. In Egypt—"

"In Egypt they are also found in front of temples."

"Well, you will just have to trust me. If we find Antinous's obelisk, we have found his tomb. Which in his case, owing to his divine state, may also be a temple."

"Well, that's consoling news! Rome is *full* of obelisks."

"Truth." Apparently resigned to being scrutinized, Onofrius kept his eyes obstinately on the floor. "But I know what most of them are, and where they come from. I say we begin with Rome's obelisks, and if we do not find what we want here, look outside the city, especially the imperial villa in Tibur, or Praeneste."

"I was hoping that, in your profession, you'd know where imperial friends and followers or the Caesars are buried."

Visible food stains, only faded by washing, might be the reason why Onofrius kept a hand on his chest. The gesture gave him a look of earnest protestation such as Aelius had seen in merchants swearing on the fairness of their prices. He said, with a quick look upward, "I have never heard of a directory of imperial favorites' tombs. For one, Commander, there would be too many entries—you'd need an encyclopedia. For another, some of them were knocked down when memory of their masters was officially condemned by the Senate—those of Commodus's infamous Saoterus, for example, or Helagabalus's fellow debaucher Gordius. I have myself seen His Divinity's soldiers using pickaxes on the mausoleum of one of Carinus's darlings, on the way to Portus."

"So?"

"So, Antinous's grave, since shrines to him are still open all over, I'd say is still standing, but where, that's another matter. That's why I say you must look for the obelisk."

The man might know his business after all. "I don't know what I thought before coming to Rome, but now it feels like searching for a needle in a haystack." Less irritably Aelius left the window sill, to which the Egyptian repaired again.

"Ha ha! 'Needle' meaning obelisk, that's good. That's very good. Except that you are looking for a needle in a sewing box. If I may say so, my familiarity with the provenance of most obelisks in Rome, makes the task less daunting."

"Go ahead, then."

Onofrius's left hand, fingers spread for the count, served him as an abacus. "To begin with, you may eliminate the one in the Circus Maximus, brought here from Egypt by Augustus Caesar, as was the one of his monumental sundial. That at the Vatican horse track came from Alexandria in Gaius's days; Domitian erected a couple of them by Augustus's Tomb, where they are still." The left hand closed into a fist. "You see, we're already down a few. Domitian filled the Iseum Campense with obelisks large and small, which you still see there today. The one they call 'of the Moon,' in the Gardens of Sallust, was inscribed in Rome, copying what it reads on the Circus Maximus's one."

"What about that on the Capitol?"

"I'm not sure about that one, though I think it's very, very old. There's also the obelisk of Hadrian's water theater, the naumachia, behind his tomb, but that bears no inscription, so it doesn't help us any." Pinching his fingertips again one by one, Onofrius pretended to reckon large numbers. "Little shafts are all over, on private grounds as in public places. Commodus built three fake ones to replace those lost in the great fire during his reign."

"There's the middle-sized one I saw in the Varian Gardens."

"The fallen one? Yes, there's that one. I never included it in my tour, since it's overgrown and broken to boot."

Aelius let out an impatient sigh. "This is all fine and good, but can you read the old Egyptian language?"

"Better than anyone in Rome, Commander."

By a rounding of shoulders in the halo of daylight, though Aelius couldn't see his features, Onofrius signified modesty. "When it comes to ancient letters, there was a man whose sandals I wasn't worth tying, but he's gone, so I'm your man."

"Is it Lucinus Soter, you speak of?"

"Yes, the one we called Nebos. What a loss! But then his death is my gain, so what can I say?"

Notes by Aelius Spartianus:

There being no time like the present, right after our initial interview I began the perusal of Rome's obelisks with the man Onofrius, and can tell already that—after so many false starts and wrong turns—I have stumbled upon a piece of good luck. Nearness and the heat of day brought us to start our rounds here on the Caelian (there are two midget obelisks in the inner court of a palace now state property, near the Special Agent Barracks), and it was only natural we'd then leave the City by the Porta Asinaria and follow the walls. So we headed to the Varian Gardens, straight for the racetrack, which is a good-sized one, a bit longer it seems to me than the Vatican one. It has no spina, or if it did have such a central obelisk, it was a wooden structure that left no trace.

Outside the curved end, there lay the obelisk I'd glimpsed on my way to the kennel when looking for Soter's watchdog. There's no accounting why, if it was ever used to mark the middle of the racetrack, it should now lie prostrate without. Perhaps it was brought here toward the end of Helagabalus's wicked reign, and never erected.

While Onofrius scampered about to see if he could free the shaft of the brambles and nettles covering it, I sat on the stands among the weeds sprung up in between the stone seats, having already invaded the dirt floor where chariots ran and games were played. Here Helagabalus uselessly plotted to murder his cousin Severus Alexander, and here the soldiers came looking for him and his meddlesome mother to cut their throats. Slightly turning my head, I beheld the powerful brick cascade

of Aurelian's wall incorporating the old aqueducts at odd an-
gles, and half of the arena. How it all spoke of things shrink-
ing! It has probably never been so extended, the city of Rome,
and yet these buildings dissected and mutilated, filled in and
made blind by bricking up windows and arches, already speak
another language. I couldn't guess the antiquity of the monu-
ments and fountains around the racetrack, but the gardens
themselves are so overgrown, so unkempt. I doubt it is because
Caesar resides elsewhere. The deified Hadrian hardly resided
in Rome during his long reign, yet everything points to things
running in perfect order in his absence, including the upkeep
of offices and public buildings.

Here's the spiritus loci, *I thought, when a small snake*
came slithering between the chinks of the stones, like a string of
green drops of water. I sat and looked at the silence of the
bushes and overgrown hedges, the dry fountains, the immobil-
ity of puffy clouds beyond the aqueducts. All seemed in bal-
ance and motionless, as Paratus said, and as happened to me
at other times: perfectly held together for the moment, yet not
particularly meaningful.

But the spirit of the place had come to greet me: soon I
heard Onofrius call out, making noises like a spitting camel.
He claimed to have discerned something interesting on the
obelisk, but there were too many creepers bound around it to
read further. On principle I carry flint on my person as well as
in my saddlebag, so it seemed handy and a good idea to burn
off the brambles and clear the stone. Well, I had not consid-
ered (and neither did he, who being from a warm climate
ought to know better) how dry the day was. The fire started
small, in a handful of dry grass, but then it caught on to the
rest of the bushes and got quite out of hand. You couldn't see
the flames because of the brightness of the sun, but smoke
belched upward worse than on the day they burned the old en-
gineer's books in Antinoopolis. It was regular arson, I'm

afraid. Had it not been for the fire brigade of the II Cohort and the stream nearby providing the patrolmen with water, matters would have gone badly.

It took them some time and much ado to put down the flames by heaping dirt on what patches of vegetation they could not douse with water. The brigade leader was enraged— I couldn't very well fault him for it—so I had to resort to a counterattack, charging him and his with endangering the City by not keeping such abandoned areas trimmed and safe, as law commands ever since Nero's days. We had a shouting match, but in the end he gave up on hauling me before a court of law. It'd have been a nuisance most of all, since I am Caesar's envoy. Still, I didn't want to miss a moment, now that Onofrius (the scum had taken to his heels as soon as the authorities showed up, and only crawled back after their departure) swore to be on to something. He even forgot himself and thanked Jesus Christ for the discovery.

So, what was it about? After the row with the patrolman and with acrid smoke still hanging over us, I was in no mood to dillydally. Onofrius—and I'll have him beaten if he's lying—indicated to me the pictographs on the broken obelisk where he reads the name of Antinous. "What else does it say?" I urged him, and he caught another word here and there, apparently a formula that commemorates the Boy's life.

Keen as the temptation was to whoop in triumph, I realized the unlikelihood that:

1. *The obelisk had been meant for this place;*
2. *Antinous's grave was anywhere around it;*
3. *The inscription did refer to burial rather than mere celebration.*

The granite being still hot from the fire, Onofrius could not scrape off the blackened roots and thorns enough to continue his interpretation. We did manage to free from dirt the top portion, half-sunk in silt, which he declared represents Antinous as

the Justified Dead, facing a god. Similar scenes are supposed to
be carved on the three other sides, but unless and until we set
the obelisk right again, I will not know whether this is the first
significant breakthrough of my many weeks of travel. Uncon-
vinced that the Egyptian is to be trusted, I have put two of my
men after him, with orders to watch him day and night for at
least two weeks. Meanwhile, as of this late-hour writing, I also
have my Pannonians discreetly keeping an eye on the Varian
racetrack.

9 AUGUST, SOL INDIGES, WEDNESDAY (16 MESORE)

In the morning, Aelius realized it was easier said than done. The
commissioner of the II Cohort called in early, and with firm courtesy
asked to see his paperwork, imperial presentation letters, in short to
identify himself and his reasons for being in the City.

Given the incident of the fire, Aelius kept a conciliatory attitude.
After providing the requested documents, he apologized for not in-
forming the Cohort of his research, and let the commissioner know
that in the next few days he'd send a crew to unearth the Varian
obelisk, and if possible restore it to its upright position.

The commissioner, a wall-eyed bulldog of a man, shook his
head. "I fear that will not be possible, Commander."

"What do you mean?"

"That it will not be possible for you to trespass into the Varian
Gardens again."

Trespassing was in fact what Aelius had done ever since carrying
out Diocletian's assignment, and he was not half done with it. He
kept cool, aware of how policemen will turn pigheaded with their
betters if a shred of law permits. "As you have read, His Divinity's
safe-conduct allows me to circulate unhampered through crown
properties."

"I read that, but I see nothing about setting fires."

"No fire would have been necessary had the grounds been kept
clear of weeds and refuse."

"Well, Commander, contravention of one law does not justify a second breach."

The argument was unimpeachable. Aelius stayed on this side of annoyance, choosing an apology as the lesser evil. "It was imprudent on my part, and I regret it. You may rest assured that there will be no more fires set, so I'd appreciate it if you would grant me and a work crew permission to visit the Varian Gardens again."

"Ah, that's not up to me, you see." Giving back the documents with a purposefully slow turn of the wrist, the commissioner pursed his lips as if about to spit. "That kind of permission is strict competence of the city prefect. You're in luck, because his office is down the road on Mother Earth Street, by Trajan's Baths. As soon as the city prefect returns from his travels, your application can be processed, and then it'll be a matter of a week or two before the permit is issued."

"Is there a vice prefect I may meet?"

"There is, but permits are exclusively granted by the prefect himself. He's off to Sardinia, but never stays away past the end of the month."

Aelius seethed. If he was enjoying the episode, the commissioner made instead a good show of self-control. He politely executed an about-face, and saw himself to the door. "Between now and then," he added looking back, as he stepped out with a toothy smile, "you will be so good as not to use your bodyguard to watch public property overnight. Pannonian cavalrymen, are they? I always had a soft spot for Pannonians, unlike those who think them a bit slow."

There was nothing to do for the moment. When Onofrius punctually showed up, Aelius had to content himself with being dragged across the City from one obelisk to the next, none nearly as interesting as the one interdicted to him. Worse, the guide's version of the fatal trip on the Nile was identical to the official one Aelius had heard at Antinous's temple. Nothing to be learned there. Only Onofrius's jaded views of the Christian controversy about apostasy made bearable—in these days of official prosecution—the sweaty pilgrimage to Egyptian relics and the occasional Christian site. From Isis of the Sea to Patrician Alley Isis, from the memorial reliefs of priests of her cult to the slim funerary pyramid of Gaius Cestius and its more impressive twin by the Cornelian Way, Onofrius spouted information. Aelius became convinced that Rome was more than a haystack when it came to Egyptian monuments, and its countryside a field of haystacks. Finding Antinous's burial seemed no easier a proposition than when he'd first set foot in Egypt.

I n the evening, having returned past the sunset closing time of the great thermal buildings, Aelius took His Divinity's advice—*When in doubt . . .* —and spent close to three leisurely hours in his lodgings' baths. Looking at the scars on his body under the veil of water, he let his mind wander to unrelated thoughts, private and often unattended to. Could it be that because he missed Anubina it meant more than nostalgia of those nights? How often had he dismissed the thought of her in the last two months, saying to himself, "She's married, happy," when he wanted to say, "I am sorry I lost her"? Soldiers get so used to buying their nights, that they forget how a woman makes your day, too, if you love her. But love was a big word: Aelius chased it off by swimming and thinking of other things. He then caught up with correspondence, jotting down to Aviola Paratus confirmation that his services would be welcome.

10 August, Thursday morning (17 Mesore)
Less than two hours after his courier left for Paratus's tavern, first thing in the morning, Aelius received a note from him. The courier must be reaching the XII mile about now, so it was hardly possible, even for a self-aware veteran, to anticipate matters enough to reply before being officially contacted. The note—a single line in the jumbled handwriting of the blind man—had nothing to do with thankful

acceptance. It gave Aelius the sick feeling that whatever it was that he found himself pursuing, elusive and large, had struck again, and missed only by chance.

There was no need of comments before the devastated vineyard. The work of years had been destroyed by slashing the vines close to the ground, so that it'd take just as long before hoping to produce wine from this lot of land again.

Paratus's female servants cried on the tavern's doorstep. His male slaves were at the far end of the vineyard, checking with the laborers whether any of the farthest vines had been spared or could be salvaged.

Paratus himself bore no external signs of anger or anxiety. Supreme pain might have long ago inured this face not to show reactions to lesser stimuli. His voice, however, signified a change in him that wasn't fear or resentment, but rather the expectation that certain things be made clear.

"Commander, I have served no differently from you. For longer time than yourself, I daresay, and can tell a threat carried out when I'm struck with it." Without giving Aelius a chance to ask what had happened (it'd be a rhetorical question, both men knew), he added, "It's no coincidence if I meet you on Thursday, and by Saturday not only do they do this to me, but go through my papers and correspondence. I am the first to admit the importance of history, but do not believe for a moment that it is to keep me from helping you gather information on an imperial biography that they wrecked my house and wine-making. There has to be *something else,* when I myself catch somebody rifling through my office and am slammed aside and harassed about 'Hadrian's letter,' as if I kept state papers. I'm alive only because I can still fight and fly at him and he goes off minus a finger (I'm sure of that, my head grower found it afterward on the floor), so I *need* to know what is going on. Since there was gossip before I left Egypt that not one, but two deaths seemed to be of special interest to you, I believe I do have a right to prepare myself to protect what's mine."

Aelius wondered if imagining the damage, feeling it by touch, was as heart-rending as seeing it. Odor of mashed grapes, too unripe to harvest, came from the ravaged vineyard like a green wave.

"Well." He took time. "What do *you* think?"

"With all respect, it's not my task to come up with hypotheses."

"It's—a complicated matter."

"Is it? I can tell you there are some odd clues lying around: mention of old imperial correspondence somehow desirable, although I ignore the reason for it; your task related to the deified Hadrian, which seems innocent except for those deaths in Egypt, pursued by you at the same time. How do I know? Policemen talk, in Egypt as everywhere else, if not more." Turning his back to the vineyard, without help Paratus groped toward the shady back lot of the tavern. "What am I supposed to *think*? The first victim was an antiquarian bookseller; the second, his servant. If they say the first died in a boating incident, the freedman was definitely done in. Maybe there was more mischief I don't know about, since I left Egypt before you did."

Aelius followed, with a grumpy need to curse. "Go on."

"Lead me inside, please, where we may talk." *Inside* was a small corner office, easily reachable through the main room, and stuffed with volumes. "I have to have them read to me," Paratus explained, "because reading is one habit I wouldn't give up. As for the door, it's never closed—I like to hear what happens in the tavern."

"Well, I'll close it now."

Paratus stood at his desk, which alone occupied one third of the space, and waited for Aelius to pull up his own chair to it before sitting down. "Apparently," he said, "you connected the two deaths in Egypt. So it could be that Serenus Dio was supposed to supply you with a document, just as he sold you history books during the Rebellion. Was it the letter they speak of? Maybe, and maybe his servant was the go-between, but who would kill for a piece of paper? Was it to keep you from receiving it, and if so, where did it go? Perhaps you are here to find it, for all I know."

In his teeth, "I'm not," Aelius said, which was true enough.

"Well, maybe someone thinks you do. Or—given what happened last night—that you had it and gave it to me, God knows why." From outside the window, came the voices of customers asking the servants about the ruckus—"Really?" and "When?" and "No one is safe nowadays"—and the grumble of the answers. "Now, Commander, there are only two likely reasons for men to commit murder over a document: its value in money, or in terms of power. Why would anyone ruin my vineyard over 'Hadrian's letter,' after so many years, when he must have written thousands? I say it's either a treasure map (we all recall the story of the capitalist Herodes Atticus finding Xerxes's gold trove), or some kind of still-standing power game. If I were still working in intelligence and it didn't sound fantastic, I'd venture to say it involves political threat. By whom?" Elbows on the desk, Paratus rested his chin on his fists. "Take your pick. Weren't our armies betrayed by a so-called Germanic ally three hundred years ago already? Do you think the slaughter in the Teutoburg forest was an isolated incident? And eastward, from Armenia to Egypt, across the Tigris and Euphrates corridor, the Persians took over Parthia and pressure us all along the border. Saracen clans, whole tribes are courted by them and by us at the same time, and meanwhile our garrisons fall to small units trained in guerrilla tactics. Look *outside* the empire's window, Aelius Spartianus, and you will see the many shapes of our enemy."

Aelius felt weary, for the first time since he'd started out from Aspalatum. These months of worry-free research he had received as such a gift from the court were turning into a race against time, except that he did not know the deadline. Clues at first wholly unrelated to his task revealed themselves as necessary pieces of a larger, more sinister puzzle, with higher stakes and faceless adversaries.

He laid out the matter in a few sentences, adding nothing of his speculations. Paratus listened without interrupting, and even at the end of the account he stayed dour, as policemen often do to allow a host of other sentiments to run undetected.

"So they know you're in Rome," he said after an interval, during which his sightless eyes—sunken back into the head beneath the lids—had seemed to Aelius two distant wells, never to give water or serve the passerby again. "Soter's killing and the fire aimed at destroying his library prove how well they knew of your coming. It satisfies me that there is power behind this rather than money. It also alerts me to the fact that you will be as much at risk as you were in Egypt, and worse. It does change my position by you considerably."

Aelius took a couple of deep breaths. "You may pull back if you wish."

"After receiving confirmation that you accept my services? No, you mistake my intentions here. What I meant is that before I was merely to assist your research. Now it is imperative that I also look out for you—as a figure of speech, of course."

"I need no looking after," Aelius began, but the pretension of his own words brought him to modify the sense of the phrase. "What I need is someone to use as a sounding board."

"But let us not forget that danger is real. I will not ask you if and where you have the letter. If you don't, you might paradoxically be better off. If you do, do not tell me or anyone else where or by whom it is kept. If its contents is unknown to your adversaries, it is the only thing that keeps you alive in this ugly business. If even just one other man knows the contents, even partially, he might be simply waiting to do you in, so that the Boy's grave may never be discovered."

"What about the man you surprised right in this room?"

A description was of course impossible to have. Paratus judged him a southerner, Greek-speaking, perhaps but not necessarily an Egyptian. "It could have been a soldier who served a long time in Egypt, like those in the river patrol. That's all I can say, and perhaps have gone too far with the hypotheses. The confusion of the vineyard had just been discovered, and my people were all paying mind to that. He escaped minus his ring finger, as I said, which—I regret to say—was not kept for further study. My grower, who was the first to join me, described it as tanned, with a worn and dirty nail, but couldn't give me enough details to try to understand the man's trade. Traces of blood indicate he went off across the road, where he probably was picked up by a companion: His soles left bits of mashed grape leaves on the floor where we scuffled, so it stands to reason he was one of those who cut the vines." Paratus reached for the few objects on his desk, inkwell, waxed tablet, blank paper, as if making sure they were in place. "We keep dogs and do have a guardian, and they all slept through the act. Put to sleep, literally. Finding out who might have doctored the water will be the next piece of investigation."

"Are you hopeful?"

"No."

Merchants came and went, not only at Paratus's tavern, but at every establishment along this trafficked tract of the road. Muleteers, soldiers, and idle voyagers made up the number. No special security beyond dogs and guardians was generally needed anywhere. In Paratus's estimation, given the extent of the damage, at least four men had been involved, and it would have taken them, with the right equipment, the better part of three hours to carry out the task.

"I am less angry about the loss than I am for having been caught unawares." Paratus spoke in a clear effort to control his temper, flaring now that he had to come to terms with his role as victim. "I am not one to let his guard down. This shames me most of all. Warnings have a way of making me intolerant. Did you speak to anyone about coming to see me the first time?"

"No. And I traveled alone to your place, then as now."

"That, too, may have to change, depending on what we find out. I doubt that I am the quarry, if not a possible collaborator of yours. You remain the target by definition. Tell me, have they already tried to attack you?"

"Not that I know of, exactly, but there have been a couple of episodes—"

"They tried to attack you, be sure. Give me details."

Restively Aelius did. As he spoke of the ambush on the Nile, of the bandits laying siege to his group on the way to Alexandria, Paratus's hands closed into fists, tighter and tighter. More questions followed, and the tension was unrelenting.

"This Onofrius, Commander, how much do you know about him?"

"Not much. I do know—he said so himself—that he's three times an apostate, by sacrifice, incense, and certificate. He wanted to make damn sure he'd escape punishment, at any rate."

"I had better check him out. Informers have been the lifeline of my first and second career, and several of them still owe me."

"Speaking of that, I will make sure there is an indemnity issued for the damage to your vineyard."

Paratus's fists opened a little. "Thank you, I appreciate it. It's a reminder for a soldier to see what violence does to a place and to someone's livelihood. I trampled through a few cultivated fields in my day, without giving it a thought."

NINTH CHAPTER

Despite his present difficulty, Aviola Paratus remembered to give Aelius a list containing a handful of names—aristocratic descendants from court-connected families in Hadrian's days. All were out of Rome for the summer, he added, which was to be expected. On his own, however, Aelius had already tracked down another promising prospect: a widow of senatorial rank, vacationing just beyond Praeneste. In the morning, by courier, he had dispatched to her address a note of introduction, requesting an interview.

By the ninth hour he was back from Paratus's devastated property.

Onofrius awaited at his doorstep. "Your bodyguard wouldn't let me in," he complained. "There isn't a shred of coolness or an awning here, and I'm half-baked."

"You could have gone to sit under the shady trees there, or there."

The guide glanced at the two directions indicated by Aelius, left and right of his lodgings.

"Not a chance, Commander. Barracks aren't any place I want to get close to, and down there—army brothels!"

"Well, what do you want?"

"I was told to show up every morning, and I'm wondering whether I'll get paid for the times you're not in, or choose not to use my services."

"You'll get paid."

Onofrius tapped his left chest to show gratitude. "Then, there's the matter of the obelisk. I'm not sure that I can translate what's written on it, even if we manage to clear it of dirt."

"And why not?"

"If it was carved by the deified Hadrian's order—I'm only supposing, mind you—it might have been done in Rome. That usually means shabby work. There are plenty of fake inscriptions around, only looking like Egyptian language. Ignorant stone-cutters copy a figure here, one there, but it's like throwing letters together pretending they are words."

"We don't know enough about the obelisk yet to tell who wrote it, and when. What is the matter with you, are you afraid of something?"

"Only of you, Commander. In case you shouldn't get what you want, whatever it is. The authorities have already gotten involved—I don't want trouble."

It could be the truth, coming from a worm who recanted his religious creed in every way he could. Or it could be another case of sudden weakness in the bowels, as he'd seen in Tralles. "What about Lucinus Soter's monument," Aelius asked, biding Onofrius to follow him in, and upstairs to his studio. "Is it written in old Egyptian script?"

"I haven't seen his monument."

"No matter, I have other work for you. I'm told there are several Egyptian statues and objects in the imperial villa at Tibur. You're going there with me."

"Tomorrow?"

"Never mind when, I'll let you know." From the window, with the voices from the baths below, and the afternoon bustle from the road, there came a shrill, rustic note of cicadas in the trees. Aelius poured himself water and vinegar—the army drink—from his canteen, and filled a cup for Onofrius as well. "You said Soter was the authority on things Egyptian. Did you ever meet him?"

Onofrius drained the cup. "I had the honor. When everyone else in the community gave me a hard time for flip-flopping on religion, he made sure I got a package on Egyptian New Year's. He even let me handle some of his correspondence while his secretary Philo traveled home to Alexandria for a death in the family." Unaware of Aelius's heightened interest, or ignoring it, he shuffled as if tired of standing, but was not offered a seat. "Not that there is much call for that kind of information, but when it came to old script, he was the one to go to. It's a small community, ours, and now they'll have to come to me, even those who wouldn't give me the time of day."

"Soter and I had common acquaintances in Antinoopolis."

"Most of his friends were from the Heptanomia. I'm from the Arsinoites, myself."

Aelius drank directly from the canteen, a long gulp. "So he must have known the army supplier, Serenus Dio."

"Truth. He got *packs* of letters from him. In the month and half I sat in for his secretary, I must have filed away a dozen. May I have some more water? Thank you. After Dio drowned, Soter quit attending community events. Even his boyfriend, the one they call Cleopatra Minor, had to go visit him at home. We'll see how the community fares now without his support."

"Hm. Would anyone in the *community* set him on fire?"

For a moment Onofrius quit shuffling, but he looked neither surprised at the question, so far from the reason for his hiring, nor troubled by it. "If he'd made a will that would benefit the Egyptian community, you bet. Temples want their cut from rich believers, and priests are not above curtailing payback times, whether they follow Isis or Christ."

It seemed all a little too neat, too cleanly falling together. A tall tale, that Soter had been so openly killed and burned to get his money. Aelius wondered whether he was being fed gossip or an artful tale, impatient for the report Paratus's informants were gathering on this rancorous little man.

"Am I to show up tomorrow morning, Commander?"

"No, come the day after." At about noon the following day, as they had agreed before parting, Aviola Paratus would arrive and take up lodgings in the old Foreign Unit Barracks, where a few rooms were kept for visiting or retired officers. Nearness would simplify their exchanges in view of the investigation, and afford the veteran the protection of sturdy walls.

Before nightfall, Aelius's courier returned from the estate of the noble lady Carminia Repentina, very much her own woman by the way she urged him to visit ("Here I'm bored silly"), and chose the day for him ("Early next week, Tuesday at the latest, and make sure you send word beforehand"). It was welcome news: entitled to the address of *clarissima foemina,* she was related through her late husband to Marcius Turbo, a friend of the deified Hadrian, and famous epistolary writer. In the country for the summer, she was the sort of well-introduced aristocrat whose library and acquaintances could come handy to a researcher: and, who knows, to an investigator as well. Visiting her was high on Aelius's list.

11 AUGUST, VIGIL OF THE IDES, FRIDAY (18 MESORE)

Biding his time until midday, Aelius went to inquire on the city prefect's expected return from Sardinia. A westerly wind carried masses of swift clouds over the City, without relieving the heat; if anything, churning it up in the valley where once Nero's round lake had lain, and now the Flavian amphitheater took its place. As Aelius rode across it, the height and size of the arena, skirted by a narrow ring of shade under the summer sun, dwarfed all; and yet everything around it was colossal—terraces, ramps, the 130 feet of bronze nakedness of what had been Nero's statue and was now the Sun's. Surely even in the days of the deified Hadrian, flower and garland sellers in the arena's archways had resembled bright ants under a handsomely turned-out

mound. People seemed small in Rome. Aelius's horse pranced when a
fine water spray whipped by the wind flew sideways from the marble
cone of the Sweaty Fountain and tried to drink from its basin.

At the city prefect's office on Mother Earth Street, they said that,
weather permitting, the magistrate was due back between the last day
of August and September 2. In the vice prefect's chambers, meanwhile, the trial of two relevant Christian deacons was taking place.
Following the hum of voices from the room, Aelius decided on the
spur of the moment to attend. Soon however, be it the heat or the oppressive repetitiveness of the process—where stolidity of questions
was matched by stolidity of answers, neither part having the least intention to change opinion—he developed a headache, which peaked
with the foregone sentence by the magistrate: immediate beheading
in the *usual place*. In this case, the legal formula for executions meant
a crossroads at the IV mile of the Via Labicana—the turn-off Aelius
himself had taken a few days earlier to reach the kennel, and twice
gone past to visit Paratus the day before, the place with a colorless
horizon, silent rows of stumpy mulberry trees, and unequal cypresses.
Asked by the court if he wished to go along in his role as an official
observer, he said yes, telling himself he was only doing it to clear his
head with a ride in the country.

Relatives and friends of the condemned, not allowed in the trial
room, waited outside the prefect's office. It surprised Aelius how,
contrary to the excitement of Egypt, here these matters seemed routine, and no anger whatever was exhibited by the judge or the accused.
Wholly composed, the deacons nodded in reply to the greetings of the
small crowd, bade them come along, and that was all for reactions.
The picket left shortly by the Via Labicana. Aelius rode well ahead of
the group, minding his sore head. When he neared the arch of Isis a
flight of pigeons caused him to look up at its cornice, where the mild
goddess against a racing sky held her inclined ewer in a charming,
eternal gesture of religious attention.

After the execution, Aelius was still idling by the turn-off when he recognized Aviola Paratus in the traveler approaching on a stout mare, led by a servant on foot, and followed by a boy with a pack mule.

"I smell blood," Paratus was observing. "An execution, was it? Are we at the IV mile?"

"We are."

"Commander Spartianus! Is that you? I didn't expect to meet you here."

Aelius explained briefly. Side by side, having sent the servants ahead for privacy, they continued toward Rome, now and then passing the mourners who returned on foot from the deacons' beheading. The wind was falling, swelter and clouds thickened as a result, but Aelius's headache was beginning to wane. He took a deep breath of warm air when Paratus asked, "How did it go?"

"Like every other execution. Quickly. It intrigues me that before the blow, their followers unfolded napkins in front of the two, to soak up the blood."

"Ah, yes. Then they'll cut them into strips and little squares, and keep them as relics. There was a flourishing commerce of them already when I served in the V Cohort."

"It seems rather idolatrous for people who swear to have a faceless god."

Paratus smirked. "We all need images, in love and in hate. If we don't have them before us, we tend to substitute others for them, or make them up, as they say the deified Hadrian did toward the end, seeing plots everywhere. A faceless enemy is the worst."

"I can't agree more."

"Take me: After so many years of darkness, I still need to make up the faces of those around me. My aging wife's, those of my sons, who have become men and I have to imagine how their childhood faces turned adult. I came up with a mental picture of your face, too, but as I have never seen you and never will, it is by necessity based only on the faces of people I knew before losing my sight." They had come less than half a mile since their meeting, and already one of the gates of the villa at Two Laurels was visible, like a rusted spider's web in the distance. All along the way, spots and streaks of blood on the lava stones of the road indicated that the deacons' bodies had been carried this way for disposal. "Time passes, and changes everything. Which brings me to wonder why should anything dating back to Hadrian be of consequence now. It's been more than a century and a half! I have been thinking about my first hypothesis: the northern enemies, the Persians, the desert tribes . . . All of them we dealt with through the centuries, and defeated or contained. Military prejudice spoke through me, and—I believe—might be speaking in you, too. We see enemies everywhere, connect events that have nothing to do with one another, in order to keep on the alert and justify our careers. The Empire is different these days, the very way we conceive of ourselves as Roman citizens is worlds away from those years. Do you really think a danger can last that long?"

It was the question Aelius had asked himself from the start. Had he been mistaking accidents along the way as related threats, to give importance to himself and his search? Why did he feel the imminence of great danger when none objectively revealed itself? As they neared the villa's grounds, he stared at the gravestones of the Imperial Guards crowding their square of land across the road. Soon he would be close enough to pick out the familiar Pannonian surnames from the many Germanic ones. "The emperor's letter doesn't specify, but three deaths over a long-forgotten political threat are three too many."

"*Four* deaths, unless you take Philo's demise to be accidental to the fire."

"Right. While still in Egypt, I began to examine the threats to the deified Hadrian's rule during his lifetime. There were conspiracies against him, after all."

"All of which were discovered in time and dealt with, from his brother-in-law's bad-talking him to Trajan when not even Trajan had been nominated emperor yet, on to the various plots that never saw the light of day. But you're the historian, you would know best."

Aelius stared at the soldiers' monuments. Neatly kept like all army cemeteries, this one was aging better than the glorious imperial gardens facing it. In a fallow stretch of land beside the graveyard, far from the road, the executioners were burying their victims under the blasting sun. "Palma and Celsus come to mind," he said, "and Neratius Priscus, but they were just ambitious men whose aims were personal, and surely not meant to overturn the state. Let's leave aside the tales of how Trajan's widow had an actor impersonate him from behind the deathbed curtain, and nominate Hadrian his successor. From all I have read, the presumed enmities by consuls, jurists, generals, and imperial hangers-on didn't amount to much. None of them had *real* power to do damage."

"There was a revolt late in Hadrian's reign."

"You mean the Jewish War? Yes. We know how *that* ended."

"Still, it was a threat to the empire, judging by the way it spread, and less than eight years ago we were both involved in settling the trouble in Egypt."

"The Rebellion in Egypt had nothing to do with the Jews."

Invisible blackbirds were whistling in the dense park of the imperial villa. Paratus turned his head toward the sound, and instinctively Aelius did the same. "I wouldn't be so hasty in counting them out, Commander. What about ben Matthias?"

It was a vexing point for Aelius. "If he's involved, he's too clever to get caught at his own game. I regret seeking him out, because I have somehow felt toyed with ever since. In Egypt I suspected him outright, and even considered the possibility of having him clapped into preventive custody. Now I'm not so sure. Paradoxically I even think that—with all his traffics and acquaintances—he might be of service, but can we trust him? If not, and he feels we're on to him, he would merely shift the focus of his activities to one of his lieutenants. He has friends and business partners all over."

"And fellow believers, do not forget." Paratus stroked the neck of his patient mare. "I consider myself a tolerant man, but I tell you, today we proclaim the Christians a peril to the state, as if Christians were anything other than secondhand Jews. And while from the start

Christians stupidly got themselves known by their mindless antiso-
cial habits, paying with their lives for it, Jews toed the line and remained free to weave their intrigue. But just because they pay taxes
and officially stay out of trouble, it doesn't mean they are not plotting
one of their revenges. They never forget, you know."

"Yes. Ben Matthias has an old score to settle with our army as
well."

"And you. Do not trust him, Aelius Spartianus. He'll try to contact you, you watch. Write you, or come to Rome 'on business,' and
just *happen* to run into you. We both know how he fought dirty during the Rebellion. People remember the names of Achilleus and
Domitius Domitianus, but tend to forget those of their advisers. *I*
know, because I was on Domitius's staff when he revolted. One was
ben Matthias's brother, and another, a hothead come directly from
Judea to run arms and stir up trouble."

Aelius's headache had passed. He could nearly enjoy the increased
traffic on the road as they approached the City gate. An appetizing
odor of fried fish came from taverns and food stands, crawling with
people at this hour. Paratus was right. Hadrian's contempt for the
Jews was proven by his restrictive measures and harsh military campaigns. Ben Matthias had not concealed that he knew Aelius was in
Egypt on imperial orders, but what else, how much else did he know?
His thugs kept him informed, and were everywhere. Egyptians and
Jews were difficult to tell apart, whatever ancestral enmity had
marked their common past. "Yes," he said, "Jews and Parthians are
the only peoples I can think of, dating back far enough, to have con-
stituted a threat to Rome. Since the deified Hadrian, some thirteen
emperors fought against the Parthians and their Persian rulers."

Paratus nodded. "I know all too well. Parthians are a very good
guess."

"But Hadrian never fought against them."

"No. He fought against the Jews."

"Well, God keep us from another Judaic War, and from Parthian
Armenia. What do you say if we stopped to have a bite?"

While they had lunch at The Roasted Donkey, sultriness turned to rain. Across the wide doorway, stable boys ran to shelter the horses and mule, passersby sought a doorway or picked up their step. Paratus ate slowly, nearing food to his mouth with care. Aelius lent an ear to the patter of water on the tile roof, its thickening and then braiding into a gurgle in the drains. He waited to speak until the customer at the next table—an army man—had paid and left. "What annoys me," he said, "is the *feeling*—I have nothing else to go by—that there are many involved in this matter. You know how a soldier's awareness of unseen threat is what he drinks and eats on campaign, what he sleeps on and is saved by. I waver between telling myself, 'There's nothing to this, you're making it up,' and knowing there is a clear and imminent threat, with old roots, whoever and wherever is its mastermind. They—yes, I know, 'they' is a vague term, but someone knew I was coming to Rome, after all—manage to stay ahead of me just enough to keep information from me."

"*Some* information, not all."

"Yes, but what I did gather, I stumbled upon by chance. Theo's tidbit about the storage room, even the broken obelisk here in Rome—if it ends up being genuine. They were unpredictable bonuses, and in any case, not enough for me to come to any conclusions yet."

Paratus put a piece of bread in his mouth, and chewed it through before passing his right hand near the plate in search of his wine cup. "Which means we are back to finding the Boy's grave, where it all began."

By the time they left the tavern, the spate had abated. Rain fell in a welcome, even way, and accompanied them up the Caelian Hill. By the angle of the climb, to Aelius's surprise, Paratus could tell how far they had proceeded toward the barracks. At one point, "We're not far now," he remarked. "I can smell the quince in the Valerii's gardens, and the army brothels, too. There's a scent of girls."

"I don't smell anything."

"You don't need to. You have eyes." Paratus lifted his face to the rain, smiling. "When you're blind, you even get in the habit of imagining yourself in a place so strongly that you feel you're there. Darkness cancels out whatever surrounds you in reality, so the mind is free to *see* as your eyes once did. That's how I can still see the nights in Commagene, down to the smallest star, or the game of light and shadow cast by the aqueduct along this road on sunny days. I believe we ought to imagine the night during which Antinous died, and reconstruct the movements of those on board. Ask yourself: What time of night was it? Where along the river did it happen, and is there a reason why it happened where it did? Never mind what it looks like now, as what remains of the Boy's cult has likely made the spot memorable. They sell souvenirs there now, there's no doubt, and all that. What did it look like nearly two centuries ago?"

Having presently reached Aelius's quarters, they went in to dry up and change, as there was no hurry for Paratus to claim his room at the Special Agent Barracks. "Well," Aelius spoke rubbing his head with a towel, "it's the old borderland between the Heptanomia and the Thebaid, which the army now scours for Christian hermits. Hadrian's Road had not been built yet—"

"Hadrian's Road. My God, I recall how it goes straight to the coast, and from there you can travel back by way of Porphyry Mountain where the quarries are, ending up south of Abydos. Have you been there?"

"I've been all the way down, or upriver—depending on how you consider it. To the First Cataract, to Ivory Island and its army post. Population: human, sixteen; crocodiles, three hundred at least." Aided by his servant, Paratus was changing into dry clothes. Scars on his forearms and legs showed what else the wars had left on his body. Aelius remembered how Anubina had studied the scars on his body with a seamstress's eye, critical of the surgeon's work, and told him not to come back with more. So now she had her farmer husband's callouses to look after, which had cost him nothing but a day in the dirt. "As for the location where Antinous fell in," he continued, "I read

all I could about it and went there myself, but there's nothing geographically remarkable about it. On the right bank, in those days
there must have at least existed fishermen's huts and moorings for
their boats. The river stretch runs between the inland ruins of a place
called Her-wer and mud walls of a shrine to Bes. Now it's all Antinoopolis. Across the river, as far as I could reconstruct, sand bars, ruins, and cliffs."

"Any historical or religious significance?"

"None in Antinous's day that I know of, but, of course, not far on
the left bank is Hermopolis with its shrine and courtyard of Thoth.
The locals say the old name of the place was Khnumu, which means
"eight," and stands for the eight great gods of Egypt. The place was fabled to be where the cosmos arose from chaos."

Now fully dressed, on his own Paratus was lacing his boots—an
operation Aelius could also do in the dark, by long habit of predawn
reveille. "Ah, yes. That is the place where *Ma'at* is brought about. Justice, cosmic order, the Right. A highly meaningful location for the
Emperor's favorite to die, I should say. Doesn't *that* suggest something about the significance of the place?"

"Only if one believes in it. If so, it might mean a place of generation—"

"Or *regeneration.*" Paratus clapped his hands, causing a sharp
echo in the changing room. "Stay with it, stay with it." He urged answers like a demanding teacher. "A place where order is made out of
confusion, where the world begins—or begins again. Did Hadrian
believe it? Did those traveling with him? Did the Boy? It might have
meant plenty for the Boy if he did away with himself, and for the deified Hadrian if he had any say in what happened. If you wish to solve
the riddle, Aelius Spartianus, you must familiarize yourself with the
stage, the players, the plot, and the deus ex machina."

Nothing but a drizzle remained of the rain when the two men left
the house. Swallows came and went from the dripping eaves, and already the sun struck distant roofs with a glint of arson. Top-heavy
clouds, livid at the lower hem, cruised the horizon past the temple of

the deified Claudius; colors stood out like stains. Aelius respected Paratus's wish not to be led by hand toward the barracks and limited himself to keep talking, so as to give a reference point to the blind man.

"I must say I tend to exclude the emperor from the list of suspects. Take the other incident that happened during the trip, the
episode Pancrates speaks of in his poem: the lion hunt. After all, on
that occasion the lion did attack Antinous's horse. The emperor need
do nothing had he wished for an accident."

"Well, Commander, he did do nothing, at first."

"But then he killed the lion, saving Antinous's life."

Paratus must have felt the sudden unevenness of the paving
stones, because he sought Aelius's elbow ever so lightly. "All right,
then. Did such an act make the Boy beholden to the emperor for his
existence?"

"Everyone is, to an extent."

"None of that court talk." Impatiently Paratus recovered from a
misstep in a puddle. "Did it? Did it mean Hadrian owned that life,
now, and could do as he pleased with it—even terminate it, if
needed?"

Aelius was struck by the words. The next puddle, he stepped into
without even noticing it. "Or did it mean that Antinous's life was in
any case forfeited through such a narrow escape, therefore, it was as
if he were dead already? He could then give himself up voluntarily to
the nether gods, or Fate, or whatever, in order to benefit the emperor."

"Exactly. Think of Alcestis, giving up her life for Admetus. Think
of Orpheus, attempting to rescue Eurydice. Think of Demeter seeking her daughter in hell, or Isis resurrecting her husband. The con-
ceptual world is full of these myths."

It was heady stuff. Aelius wished for the ever-nearer entrance to
the barracks to recede, not to interrupt the conversation. "Yes, and I
saw them illustrated on the floors of the imperial barge, but what do
they mean? Why would the emperor seek some kind of rebirth? No

one can be resurrected, especially if he isn't even dead yet. The deified Hadrian went on for another eight years."

"Yes. One year for each of the eight great gods of Egypt." Paratus
stopped, and Aelius with him. "Try to reason—if we can call it
reasoning—like those who believe in horoscopes. Would the emperor have lasted that long had the Boy not given himself up for him?
Even Cassius Dio suggests—" He waved to chase the thought. "No.
No. This is nonsensical esoteric talk, and we will never enter the
minds of men so long gone enough to understand their innermost
beliefs. Are we close to the barracks now?"

"Quite close, but not enough to be overheard by anyone."

"Good. Quickly, let's go back to motives that require no stretch of
the imagination. Envy, jealousy, despondency, grudge, vengeance—
those are the rules of engagement in most suicides and murders."

"What about the accident theory?"

"An accident is just that. What is there to say? After all, when natural death was concerned, the emperor did not go to such great
lengths to celebrate the defunct. A state funeral, a memorial temple
as due to ladies of the family, that's all. Even after his chosen heir
died, I'm not aware there were cities founded, shrines built or priest-
hoods endowed. Let's go." Mildly prompting Aelius by the elbow,
Paratus resumed his walk. "I'm anxious to try my hand at circum-
venting the prohibition to dig up the obelisk."

At the entrance of the barracks, they had to wait for the guard to
summon the officer of the day. The afternoon had cooled considerably
on the hillside, with a pleasant feeling of washed weariness in the air.

"Before I go," Aelius said, "I meant to tell you that tomorrow I
will collect Onofrius and travel to the deified Hadrian's villa in Tibur.
It is high time I visited it. Did you find out anything about him, by
the way?"

Paratus shrugged. "Not much, but enough. Onofrius is a nobody. No one wants him, neither the Egyptians nor the Christians.
He can only be trusted as far as he can be thrown. It's true that he sat

in for Soter's secretary, but that was last year. If he's on someone's payroll—other than yours—he'll betray himself by starting to spend money."

15 August, Tuesday (22 Mesore)
Notes by Aelius Spartianus:

> I have come to the great villa at last. The wall around the property, flanking the road that enters Tibur farther ahead, was designed to be fully manned once. One reads that up to one thousand soldiers were posted around it, though now the booths and stations are empty, except for those at the sides of the monumental entrance.
>
> The day was a near perfect day of sun and clouds, rapidly taking one another's place because of high winds. I came to this place as a long-sought island, although it makes no sense to me that I should feel this way. I cannot say that the site looks familiar to me, never having been here, and the authors' descriptions—first among all that of the deified Hadrian himself, who succinctly yet exhaustively described the construction and role of the villa—hardly prepare one for the chaotic order of this residence. Not being altogether certain of my ability to do justice to it through written words, I told Onofrius (whom I set loose to survey Egyptian inscriptions with the proviso that he doesn't get in my way) to go to the Tibur archives and secure a copy of the villa's plan.
>
> The ensemble, numbering hundreds of rooms, courts, and other spaces, is articulated upon three axes, so that the visitor finds himself changing direction nearly unbeknown to him, by following a colonnade that suddenly opens up into a long inner court, perpendicular to the colonnade through a fugue of small halls or marble pools. The effect is of being suddenly redirected, losing one's original path. Thus the effect is of a labyrinth, even though there is no objective center anywhere. It

is a constellation of palaces, baths, and service buildings on several stories, and terraced gardens alternate with artificial valleys in such a way that occasionally the sky is only visible above in narrow ribbons or squares.

Statues of Antinous are everywhere, one feels watched by him continuously, but in a friendly way. The scent of overgrown boxwood and myrtle under the midday sun is heady, especially around the theater. Sycamores, cypresses, and dwarf palms abound. Oleanders have become a forest; what were once grassy knolls are reduced to much depleted patches of weeds. Old rosebushes still thrive here and there along the promenades, and around the smaller shrines empty pots probably used to contain anemones, as in the Gardens of Adonis.

The hounds that freely roam the villa, I am told, descend from the many packs the deified Hadrian kept on these grounds once. They are a handsome lot of short-eared, long-headed, curly-tailed slender dogs, mostly black and white, which the locals call Gyptii, the name being—as I believe—a corruption of the original term "Aegyptii."

Most furniture has been long ago removed from the lofty halls and bedrooms; some of it is stored in Tibur in warehouses under lock and key, sealed by the providence of His Divinity's representatives here. Other pieces, including sculptures, were removed to the imperial villa at Praeneste (where I hope to go next), others were, according to accounting still kept on the premises, transported to the City in Palatio by the princes who followed the deified Hadrian, specifically Commodus, Caracalla, and Helagabalus.

The superintendent lives in the city, up the hillside, as I understand, in a small estate not far from the villa they call Quintiliolum, facing the Anio waterfalls. He had been informed of my arrival, so he came speedily enough, for a civilian. When I expanded on the reasons for my visit, and my intention to stop for a few days, at once he offered me quarters

*in his house, and when I thanked him but declined, he made
so bold as to insist by adding that he has four daughters. As if
soldiers of some rank were not used to being invited by parents
anxious to marry off their girls. It tickled me that he tried,
though, because it's really rather provincial.*

*In order not to offend (I will ask him for favors soon, so I
might as well gain his undivided interest), I finally agreed to
have dinner at his place at least twice during my stay. I re-
tained the right to choose the evenings, as there will be times
when I do not wish to interrupt my observations in order to
change and ride to his house. The girls might be pretty for all
that. Apparently he has educated them, and their mother was
one of the beauties of her day, and "of pure Sabine stock." The
sort of girls Romulus and his men cajoled into being kidnapped!*

*The residence ceremonial halls are all but empty. Not
only the furniture, but hangings, drapes, and, in some cases,
the doors have been taken away. One can tell from the way
some floors are laid out that carpets were meant to cover them,
and those have gone as well. Such is the height of the ceilings
that one's steps rumble and echo, back and forth sounding
from wall to wall. Niches that once held books are void, gathering dust. Fixtures such as lamps are still in place, and to all
appearances functioning. I aim to find out tonight. The windows are generally intact, and where one or two panes have
fallen out or been broken, parchment has been fitted neatly in
their place.*

*I was informed that the waterworks still function well, al-
though they only get turned on twice a year, in the summer to
give a thorough run-through to all the fountains, and in winter,
to make sure the pipes haven't burst somewhere along the complex system of underground conduits. Spigots and spouts must
number in the hundreds, and there are two large thermal baths.
All but the largest outdoor pools are kept empty and reasonably*

clean, although it must be a job to lift up leaves, topsoil, and twigs that rapidly accumulate in the basins.

The larger open pools are instead in a deplorable state, full as rain allows, for which I scolded the superintendent. My intention—really—is to force him to open up all the spigots again and allow water to run through the villa, although the seasonal opening has already taken place in early July. The water in the open pools is static and malodorous, given the vegetable deposit at the bottom, algaelike plants, and so on. They provide a breeding place for mosquitoes and water spiders as well, and I've seen frogs and water turtles jump in or lazily swim on the green surface.

Especially deplorable are the conditions of the most magnificent of the villa's sections, at least to my eyes and at this stage of my investigation. The area is the so-called Canopus, a narrow artificial valley lined with shrubs and flowers, in the middle of which lies a long pool (the superintendent calls it a "Euripus," but the term is erroneous, since such fountains have maneuverable sluices that create a flux and reflux, as in the natural body of water by that name. This is rather what is termed a "Nile" (see Pliny the Younger's description), and I can't imagine how anyone could mistake it. The whole valley reproduces a Nilotic landscape so clearly that I was stunned upon first looking at it, as though at once I had been transported again to Alexandria or had never left.

As I said, the state of the Canopus is sad, a fact all the more vexing since it is obviously the villa's monument meant by the deified Hadrian to celebrate the Boy. Portrait statues of him, gigantic, perfect copies of the one I saw in the temple at Antinoopolis, flank the large conchlike pavilion at the head of the long pool, set into the crotch of the hill. I will describe elsewhere the sparkling depths and marvelous architecture of the pavilion, but must first explain why this Nile must have once closely resembled its namesake.

Even with some of the ornamental statues pushed off their pedestals and into the marshy length of the pool, I could imme- diately "read" it geographically, recognizing how the images of Bes-like grotesque sileni on the right side of the onlooker stand for the ancient site of Besa, near which Antinous met his fate. Facing these figures stands a statue of Hermes, to signify Her- mopolis, across from Besa; a water-spouting crocodile marks down from Hermes the site of Crocodilopolis, below which a marble Apollo represents the city of Apollinopolis Magna, and so forth. Near the sileni, funerary-basket-bearing maiden fig- ures once held up a fragile and elegant marble entablature, per- haps meant for climbing vines. This has now all but collapsed due to the forcible knocking down of the statues.

I was so angry and insistent about hearing the reasons for such an outrage that the superintendent promised to fetch me a decrepit servant who claims to have been present when it was done. Tomorrow I plan to find out from him. Meanwhile, di- rectly confronted on why he has not set the statues right, the superintendent replied that an extant imperial order origi- nated their removal. By which Caesar? I asked, and was not surprised to hear the name of that monster, Helagabalus. I will follow up on the veracity of this pretended order in Rome, as it must be stored in the archives somewhere.

With a detailed plan of the villa in hand, Aelius decided to spend the night there. The superintendent did all he could to dissuade him, mostly because he'd have to supply the minimum necessary to fur- nish an appropriate bedroom. As for Onofrius, he would not hear of staying, blathering some tale—which of course he claimed not to be- lieve by faith—about demons hiding in the villa ever since "the widow and her sons were martyred here by Hadrian Caesar."

Aelius looked up from the plan. "What kind of nonsense is that?"

"It's not nonsense. The Acts specify she was the sister of Eugenius, a city employee in Tibur when Telesphorus was pope. She was drowned and her seven sons were killed here, in front of the temple of Hercules. I'm not a Christian, mind you, but I'm not spending the dark hours where there are demons."

"Balderdash!" Aelius laughed. "The temple of Hercules is in the city of Tibur, not here."

"Makes no difference, Commander. Remember while we were approaching from Rome, when I pointed out to you that place along the road called Septem Fratres? Remember I didn't want to look? That's where they're buried. The whole place is spooked."

"Well, I'm staying."

The shadows had begun to lengthen under the cypresses and sycamores when a bed, linen, and a few implements were brought to the building once meant for officers of the guard. The superintendent returned personally with dinner ready and a set of keys to the few buildings usually kept locked. He insisted on leaving servants ("There are only a few of the field slaves way out at the edges of the property, a mile off; they'd never hear you if you called"), and threw up his hands when Aelius said, "Why should I call?"

Water was turned on in the back latrine and bath at the end of the hall, on which ten doorless rooms opened, each with three alcoves. Separate water rooms and tanks were concealed throughout the complex, and when—unseen and unheard—a serf turned the spigot somewhere in the higher grounds, it was like a magic trick. With a rust-red surge, like blood from a wound, water gushed into the bathing pool and turned clear nearly at once. Cold to the touch, it swept up a few leaves from the pool's bottom and rapidly filled it; nearby fountains and drains awakened and sang. Aelius could only imagine the entire villa once plashing and rippling from its countless water mouths. He chose the tenth room in the officers' quarters, and had the servants move from the nearby residence a multiwick lantern so that he could sit up to study the villa's plan. Then he was finally left alone to work and think.

Well into the night, convinced to have the general layout of the villa well in mind, he took the keys and set off for the western belvedere tower. Moonlight and a starry sky would hardly suffice in the maze of dark buildings, and a hand lantern would do little to help. Starting out was easy, a left turn immediately out of his room and out of the officers' quarters onto a paved court. Here, the tall walls of the residence and a crowd of roofs created the first uncertainty; gaping to the side, a deeper darkness pointed to one of the fountain courts, likely the narrow one on which the libraries opened. It was best to venture under the residence's portico, and follow the shady row of columns along its west side. Confidently, Aelius turned left at the corner and took the short side, finding the door, and a third garden court. Here, he made the mistake of choosing a short flight of stairs down, finding himself inside the ring of walls of the island residence. A sealed miniature villa at the center of a round canal, surrounded by circular darkness where his steps awoke dull echoes. Water in the canal was low, but shone like a metal belt. Through a fugue of spaces on his right, the blackness was broken by moonlight through windows or raining checkered from trellises. From room to room Aelius went, out into a stadium-like garden of overgrown bushes, static pools. To his ears came plunks of frogs in the water, small sounds of animals furtively sharing his space. He recognized the arcaded dining hall by the black-red-white cross pattern of the marble floor. Then out again, briefly, through another archway, to the main vestibule with its niches and female statues gleaming like girls awakened on their doorsteps. Outside once more. Dogs called from distant farms; a rustle of leaves, creaking of doors at the slightest gust of wind; hundreds of rooms like a deserted city or an abandoned army camp. If the ghost of Antinous did not haunt this place, it was unlikely that Christians ever would.

The complexity of the plan, seeming at first random, or at best the result of many changes of mind, was beginning to make sense to Aelius. Not that he knew—yet—what the villa's design might signify; but his night wandering, born of a biographer's curiosity for

Hadrian's mind, already took another meaning. Why was he expecting a hallway here, and an isolated building there, finding both? It wasn't just the map as drawn on charts or the pattern. It could be— he could not tell, yet, but the villa was a labyrinth and a key.

Past the cupolas of the large baths, Aelius climbed with more assuredness beyond the little Egypt of Canopus, to the high ground. Oleanders, myrtle, and clumps of fat lilies strangled the foot of the ramp to the west belvedere tower, which was locked. Here, as if on cue, the wind blew out his lamp, and he had to finger and try key after key in the hole before finding the right one. Above him, as in his dream, the tower blocked out the stars and seemed to lean over. In his nightmare, the high structure fell burning onto itself. Aelius unlocked the door and hastened in, groping to find the stairs, up and up to a doorway that led outside to a solid, round colonnade and to a firm terrace higher yet, where the night sky ran at him from such immensity, he nearly stumbled back.

16 August, Friday (23 Mesore)
Notes by Aelius Spartianus, continued:

> I am becoming convinced that this enormous villa is not just a pleasure palace. If it survives spoliations and the ravages of time, historians and other experts, centuries from now, will be troubled by the same question I have been mulling ever since stepping through its gates. What does its convoluted plan mean? Why, even as I pursue (and am pursued by) an elusive adversary, does it matter to my knowledge of the deified Hadrian that I see the link between his mind and this villa, between this villa and his grief? Does mourning become stone in order to last? What does a conspiracy turn into in order to do the same?
>
> The old servant recommended to me is in his nineties. He's lost all his teeth, and his gums have hardened like a turtle's beak, so that despite the loss, he can speak clearly enough.

His hair by contrast is thick, cropped short, yellow-white in color. Although doubled over by age, he appears hale and lucid. After a long existence as a servus *villicus, he's been put out to pasture in a decent little house at the edge of this immense villa, on the highland behind the observatory tower. Not bad for a rural slave. Like many elders, he claims not to recall what he had for dinner the night before, but to bear perfectly in mind episodes that took place sixty, seventy, and eighty years ago. If anyone knows about Antinous's burial, it is he.*

According to him, the damage to the Canopus happened during a visit to the villa by Helagabalus the summer before the monster was gotten rid of, in March, eighty-two years ago. The slave, whose name is Opilianus, was then about twelve years of age, and a gardener's helper. As such, he had the task of repotting flowers that had overgrown their vases, and of sweeping the paths on the southwest side of the villa, where Canopus was and is.

Apparently this was the same imperial visit during which Helagabalus mocked the slaves by commanding them to gather one thousand pounds of spider webs. "Several of us crippled themselves on that day," Opilianus said to me, scowling, "and one broke his neck and died, falling from a ladder as he tried to wipe a spider web from the ceiling of the throne room."

I will not waste time repeating what other absurdities that madman thought up during his idle reign, all the more since I hear that my Nicomedia army lawyer friend, Aelius Lampridius, is working at a biography of his. I do not envy him, and thank my good star that it isn't my task to report on that beast.

Anyhow, Opilianus says that Helagabalus showed up with hundreds in his retinue, most of them mimes and buffoons, and that for two days and two nights the entire villa was prey to their license. I understood from hints (unless I am so blinded by my antipathy for that tyrant) that Opilianus's young age made him a target of unspeakable attentions by the charioteer Gordius; only because his mother intervened saying that the boy had the scrofula in his privates, was he spared, and even given wide berth.

"They were a colorful lot for all that," Opilianus continued, "so I was curious. Everything they did, ate, what they spoke of, was for me a great wonder. Your Excellency understands that by then the villa had been practically empty since the days of Antoninus Caracalla, more than ten years, and in all my young life I hadn't seen visitors of rank show up at the gate."

Here is the truly intriguing part, that made the slave's gossip into valuable narrative (I must recommend him to Lampridius before he kicks off, as he's a goldmine of detailed reports just from that visit). When asked whether he'd heard the reason for Helagabalus's coming, he replied without batting an eye, "He wanted to see the burial place of the deified Hadrian's favorite."

Suddenly, my inspiration to come to Tibur seemed to have paid off in a big way. Before I explain how it then turned out to be a piece of information rather less direct—shall we say—than I hoped for, I will report verbatim what conversation ensued between us.

AELIUS: *Do you mean that the blessed Antinous is buried on the villa's grounds?*

OPILIANUS: *What else? Everyone knows that in Tibur.*

A: *Can you point out to me the exact spot?*

O: *Well, it depends—it depends on which burial Your Excellency refers to.*

A: *Is there more than one?*

O: *Why, yes. The first was right here. (Note: We were standing with our faces to the pavilion, and at the foot of the pool; he indicated a spot on the right, where one remaining basket-bearing maiden, copied from those in Athens, holds up the remains of an arched-and-flat entablature. As I mentioned, originally other such statues, with those resembling Bes, formed a porticoed front on the west side of the pool). There used to be a needle (Opilianus meant an obelisk) behind the statues, you can still see the base of it. It pointed out where the Boy was buried.*

I rushed to the place indicated by the old man. Surely enough, here was a porphyry base bearing the marks of having had a square shaft cemented to it and held by an iron. Out of forethought or sheer military punctilio for details, I had noted the grain of the obelisk in the Varian Gardens, and was thrilled to discover that its description matches perfectly the base at Tibur. Still, for the sake of historical precision, I asked Opilianus whether the obelisk had been removed by Helagabalus.

"Removed? And how! It was in the course of a dinner party when they ran around and swam in the pool, threw off their clothes and sent their slippers sailing like toy boats in the drain around the pavilion's dining table. The emperor was dressed like a girl (here I omit the obscene details of his outfit; Lampridius can pick them up in his biography if he wishes). He was jumping around saying that he was Isis and was looking for the phallus (not the word Opilianus used) of her dead husband Osiris. My mother was Egyptian—God keep her memory—so I knew even then what it meant. I also knew that the blessed Antinous had become Osiris by drowning in the Nile, so I figured that he wanted to dig up the Boy's burial place to do God knows what. By this time you can be sure the superintendent (in those days it was Ingenuus Regalianus, put there by Clodius Albinus Caesar, after Commodus's death) was pulling his hair by the handful. You know that Commodus, too, was at one time looking for Antinous's body, and didn't find it in the Egyptian grave."

The last detail I had learned from Theo in Egypt. I an-

swered that I knew, yes, without adding that, having failed at
the same search, I could confirm that the Boy's corpse wasn't
there.

Opilianus was on a roll now. He seemed to be reporting
on scenes that he'd only witnessed hours earlier, with such precision of details that I have no doubt he has absolute recollection of that day so long ago.

It appears that the drunken Helagabalus ordered the
slaves to fetch him the gardener and his helpers. When these
promptly showed up, he bade them start digging around the
obelisk, which he said always indicates the burial of an important man or god. He also told Gordius that—should he die—
he promised him a similar monument on his grave. Gordius
didn't seem to appreciate the idea. Meanwhile, Opilianus dug
with the others, meeting soon with the difficulty of removing
paving stones set in a star pattern around the base of the
obelisk. By the time they had labored enough in Helagabalus's
disappointed eyes, it was clear that no burial was in that
ground. Then they were ordered to secure ropes and to pull
down the obelisk, since it was likely that the "casket with Antinous's ashes" (Opilianus's own words, I don't know whether
Helagabalus actually said them) was encased at the foot of the
obelisk itself.

"So we pulled and pulled, with all those damn dwarves
and stinky acrobats around us, until finally the shaft came
down and broke in two—here, just about here—knocking
down the sileni. No cavity at the base of the needle, and no
casket. Helagabalus grew furious—not at the damage, but for
not seeing Osiris's phallus—and shouted to tie ropes to the remaining statues and drag them into the pool, to punish them
for 'lying to Caesar,' as he put it. It was a shame to ruin that
beautiful pool garden, where I'd learned to tend flowers and
had my favorite bushes, but we had our orders. Down came
several other statues, on one side and then the other, with

*cheers going up each time one fell on its nose into the water
with a huge splash. By now Helagabalus had had enough of
the entertainment, and he retired with a chum deep into the
pavilion, where I couldn't have guessed what they were doing,
except that his cries and laughter gave us all an idea. My master put his hands on my ears at one point and led me away."*

I'd been taking furious notes all along, and was about to
scrap one more possible repository for the Boy's remains. Then
I recalled how Opilianus had spoken of more than one grave
site within the villa's confines, and asked him.

"Of course," he shot back, "it's the round memorial, up
the hill by Hades' Grotto, by the laurel thicket. It was built
over a burial chamber from the days of the first villa." By that,
I took him to mean the estate of Hadrian's in-laws, which pre-
dates the great villa and constitutes one of its cores. "But I
should tell Your Excellency that after the craziness of the imperial visit, the garden crew had its work cut out for it. We were
forbidden to right up the statues, but the needle was gone, and
the flowerbeds needed fixing and replanting. It seemed a fine
idea to arrange periwinkle around the empty porphyry base—
there where you're standing now. You see we put the star
pattern together again, and a good job we did of it." Here, although we were perfectly alone, the old man lowered his voice.
"Then master's spade scraped something white, a square slab
about a foot per side. He kept at it, until we realized there were
six of them, never cemented, but forming once a kind of loose
box. Inside, not even a pin, but we figured that's where the
Boy's ashes had been put by the deified Hadrian at some point.
Only because Helagabalus had gotten bored, had the box not
been discovered, but when it was emptied or who emptied it,
no one knows."

Having until now felt assured that Antinous had been
mummified, Opilianus's revelation comes to me as a double

blow. First, it seems clear that the Canopus was a burial place, but no longer is; second, I might be looking for a casket small enough to fit in a square foot box rather than a man-sized coffin. The old man being fatigued, I let him go. Onofrius showed up meanwhile, ready to give me an interpretive tour of the inscriptions on Egyptian statues and the larger objects still in place. I intend to start (and deposit in the State Archives) a list of the statues and reliefs that still populate the villa: They are a crowd and had better be censed before anything else happens.

In the afternoon came more unwelcome news. Onofrius reported that the Egyptian inscriptions scattered through the villa predated Hadrian by centuries, which made them useless to the present search. Already in a cross mood, Aelius lost his patience when he discovered evidence of badly repaired damage elsewhere in the Canopus area.

Opilianus, who was supposed to meet him by the round memorial, sat in the shade of the laurel thicket and philosophically shook his head. "No, the damage you speak of has got nothing to do with Helagabalus. That happened much later, some thirty years ago. It was the prisoner queen who did it when no one was watching, owing that Aurelian Caesar was busy fighting the barbarians."

"You mean Zenobia."

"The same. A fine piece of woman, too, but women should not be rulers. A regular harpy, commanding us around like we belonged to her or something. And me already an old man, with my own little house to look after. I am telling Your Excellency, it was a shameful thing, leaving her here to gallivant around and do as if it were her own house. We had to sweat it out, to make sure she didn't break things."

From where Aelius stood, only the scruffy eastern rim of the Canopus valley was visible, and he looked away from it. "*Break* things? Why would she do that?"

"Didn't I tell you?" Opilianus scratched his badly shaven chin. "Well, I guess I didn't. What remained of the marble trellis of the needle was knocked down by her. She was looking for the same thing—the Boy's grave. I know Your Excellency is not a blue blood, being a soldier, so I can say it: The nobility, they're crazy, the lot of them. Too much getting married in the family. The queen had taken to digging at night if we didn't keep an eye on her. I can show you the places where she grubbed by herself, if we kept her from paying laborers to do it."

"It doesn't make any sense. Why would a foreign queen care where the Boy was buried?"

"Beats me, Your Excellency. My son was head gardener in those days—the last one, by the way, since the position was not renewed after Aurelian's death, and all went downhill from there. My son, called Opilianus like me, had been taken into her confidence, and she told him she'd buy his freedom if he helped her find the Boy's grave."

"Well?"

"Well, number one: My son was happy with his lot, and not in a hurry to be a free beggar in those days when jobs were scarce—not that they are plentiful now. Number two: He was not likely to uproot imperial property flowerbeds and dig up monuments for anyone, much less a woman. He said no, that he was under imperial orders, and so on. So she did her own digging at night, especially toward the end of her life. It'd become a joke with all of us."

Aelius recalled ben Matthias mentioning Zenobia, how she'd been kept for years a prisoner at Tibur and he ought to visit "the old girl's grave." Never mind the visit. Why would an oriental queen, and an enemy of Rome, be interested in Antinous's burial? Jews, Parthians, Zenobia's Persian allies: There was possibly a dim sense in all this. "Did she find something?" he urged.

"She found nothing. We watched her, and made sure she didn't do too much damage. This memorial right here, she managed to get into, but we caught her at it, and nailed the door shut. The day she

died, we all breathed freely. Her sons never came to visit again, and I
believe they still live, if they weren't done in meanwhile. My own son
died a year ago, and to the last he worried that someone would come
digging in the gardens."

17 AUGUST, THURSDAY (24 MESORE)
Notes by Aelius Spartianus, continued:

> *They call it here* heroon, *in the Greek fashion. It is a marble
> building shaped like a round basket, with columns running
> about it, twenty-two in all. Such, some believe, was the age at-
> tained by Antinous at the time of his death and twice the years
> he spent with his friend and master. The door, the key to
> which is long lost, did not open—and wouldn't anyway, given
> the silt that has accumulated all around. The entire monu-
> ment appears, in fact, to have sunken somewhat through the
> years. The nails placed by Opilianus Jr. to impede entrance are
> rusted, and I was able to pull them out without much trouble
> today, the feast of Portunus, god of keys and openings. By
> looking through one of the nine slit windows, I discerned a sar-
> cophagus inside. From this, I gather that Antinous's body was
> at least for some time kept here, unless of course the monu-
> ment is a cenotaph, like the one in Egypt.*
>
> *Since no effort would avail me to force the door open, I
> engaged the help of Opilianus's great-grandchild, a boy of
> eight, who could slip through one of the openings and report to
> me what he saw. I held little confidence that he could open the
> door from inside and let me in, but the alert lad was able to
> accomplish it, as the lock could be easily worked. It is a marvel,
> if one considers the frost and rain and rust of those many
> years.*
>
> *I couldn't help but consider how long since the light of day
> shone inside the burial chamber. Rats' nests and dry leaves*

surrounded a perfectly plain porphyry sarcophagus, which—
resolved in my duty and notwithstanding Opilianus's grudge—
I instructed the servants to open. Not a mean feat given the
size of the lid and the cramped conditions of the interior. Inside (I cannot say if I expected it or not) we found one of those
alabaster vases called in Egypt "canopic jars." I recalled Theo
saying how, after the drowning, Hadrian traveled south to
Ptolemais and Thebes with the Boy's heart in a "jar, bearing
as a cover the human head of Imseti, which is under the protection of Isis." This jar has in fact a human head. Whether it
was supposed to be the sole contents of the grave, or the body
itself—ashes, mummy—had been there once, I was left wondering.

Inside this sealed, translucent container, I thought, was
the once beating heart of one so loved! Onofrius, trembling in
his superstition, told me that the ancient characters on the jar
read, if it is to be believed, "Antinous the Justified." On the
back of the jar, [Mu], three wavy lines; [khebs], a sun disk followed by a human leg and what seems to be a plough. Onofrius
says it is to be read as "water stealing," or "water thief," which
reminded me of Dio's dream of the Boy taking water from the
Nile with a ladle, and of the priest telling me in Egypt that
praying to Antinous protects one from water thieves. Does it
help me in the investigation? Not at all. The only consolation
for me was that the jar measured just under one foot in height,
hence might have been destined to be the contents of the marble box under the Canopus obelisk. Is there a mummy, then?
Was there ever one? With a heavy heart, I had the unopened
jar dutifully replaced in its sarcophagus.

Having finished this task, although there were no clouds
in front of the sun, daylight began to fail, Before I could realize
that an eclipse was in progress, the servants scattered like
the superstitious lot they are, and no explanations or threats
availed. I was left alone by the heroon, and remained there to

prove the foolishness of superstition until the sun disk was obliterated altogether, and the stars flickered again in the livid grayness of the sky. The coincidence struck me all the same, so that in the unnatural chill of the phenomenon I had to wonder what it may mean, if not portend.

TENTH CHAPTER

Draft by Aelius Spartianus for a letter to His Divinity:

The wanderings with Onofrius brought us today to the gardens of Nero's mother out in the Vatican Field, and to the neighboring Domitia's Gardens. We'd already scoured half the City for obscure Egyptian monuments, and now in the water theater called naumachia Hadriani *my noxious guide—endless purveyor of trivia—insisted that here the Christian patriarch named Cephas, which is Hebrew for "stone" (hence Peter, as he is known among them), was executed under Nero. This is at variance, I observed, with the tradition that wants him buried at a short distance from the place,* teste Tacito, *in the horse track built by Gaius Caligula just as Tacitus writes. Peter's modest burial, by the way, is in plain sight, a witness to the even-minded policy of all Caesars since the events that followed the Great Fire.*

Taking an opportunity to go off on my own, I gladly retraced my steps on the Via Triumphalis (the imperial ladies'

gardens are aged, but traces of topiary elegance survives).
At the crossroads with the Cornelia, which runs in front of
Hadrian's mausoleum, I passed again the marble pyramid
that impressed me upon arriving in the City. By this time I
have seen other large ones (including Cestius's one clear across
town), while miniature ones crop up here and there, and
though the peasants refer to all of them as metae, *they scarcely*
resemble the conical turning posts of a stadium.

By this time Onofrius joined me, and began telling me
tales of Christian trials where all kinds of miracles took place,
from thunderbolts striking the judge to rings of fire protecting
the virtue of women defendants. He even told me that whip-
ping left no trace on the martyrs' skin, that lions in the arena
refused to bite, etc. When I asked how is it then that none of
them survived the executioner's blade, he fell entirely silent. By
which I understood that he was either without an answer, or
afraid I might think him still a Christian. Leaving his non-
sense and the overheated City for a few days will be a pleasure.

20 August, Sunday (27 Mesore)

Carminia Repentina had been called Minula by her late husband Tuscus, elected to the consulship with that Annius Anullinus—now proconsul of Africa—who had his hands full with Christian trials. Aelius,
having survived two endless dinners in the company of the superintendent's daughters at Tibur, came to her estate on a day when the
wind seemed to have tucked itself under the rug of the world.

Slaves were splashing the porches' floors with pails of water,
causing steam to rise in the garden. Through this mist, like a middle-
aged nymph, Repentina came forward to meet him and at once asked
what was new in Rome. Expecting the question, Aelius had caught up
with city gossip as best he could; he dropped a few names in the appropriate slots, and made up for the rest by presenting his hostess
with a new edition of poems.

"Imagine," she uttered, "Sammonicus Junior! How did you know I liked philosophical poetry?"

"I didn't, but it was the latest edition available, and I thought you might not have acquired it yet."

There was no way of coming to business before agreeing to view the family tree, Tuscus's death mask, a dozen portrait busts of ancestors, and the many honorific diplomas hanging from tablets in the hallways. Placidly Aelius accepted indoctrination, with an eye to the promised library, but also with real interest for the views of an old school noblewoman.

"The great families have all but disappeared." Repentina spoke in a well-bred aristocratic whisper over her quickly flapping fan. "Soon there will be none of us left, and *then* Rome will realize what an irreparable loss it suffered. Why, there have never been so many blue eyes in public office! When I was a girl, you could go to a party and not see one set of blue eyes."

"It's a fact worth pondering," Aelius said, repressing a smirk. "I wonder what the eye color situation was in the days of the deified Hadrian."

"Well, you know, I do not mean to brag, but the late consul's family was well acquainted with imperial matters even then. On his mother's side—they are Anicii, as old as the hills and glorious for centuries—the ancestor in question is that Marcius Turbo who put down the uprising in Mauretania and was made prefect of the guard after his role in Dacia and Pannonia. It's his correspondence you want to see. Marcius's son Lucius traveled with the emperor." Once inside the summer dining room, crisscrossed by strategically opened windows, she sat in a wicker armchair and bade Aelius do the same. "He was a great mountain climber (all the men in the late consul's family have beautiful and sturdy legs), and accompanied Hadrian to the top of Mount Etna and up Mount Casius, where they were nearly struck by lightning while making a sacrifice. The priest was killed— he, too, was a relative, but by marriage, and I won't belabor the point—and Lucius had his hair singed by the thunderbolt." A grizzled pile of curls, outmoded not to say antique, gave Repentina the odd look of a stage mask, although sternness of features—unrelieved by carefully retouched beauty marks—revealed the formidable guardian of ancestral virtues. Minula was an impossibly charming nickname for her, and Aelius had the impression that no man ever, much less the late consul, had succeeded in changing her mind. With the flip of her forefinger she summoned a servant and told him to open up the library. "You see I prepared myself in view of your visit."

"I am most thankful." Aelius had villa-grown fruit forced on him, and was compelled to sample all of it even though he'd much rather start viewing the shelves. "Did Lucius also travel with the emperor to Egypt?" he managed to ask.

Repentina studied him, perhaps evaluating whether she'd do him the favor of answering. "Yes," she said then in her raspy whisper. "He was one of those golden boys, spoiled and curly, and it reportedly took his father the rod and three costly Greek girls to straighten him out afterward. You know Hadrian's boys always had curls. Well, Lucius went along, and made friends with the rest."

"The *rest*?"

"Yes, the others, Antinous's contemporaries. There were scads of them, and they did things boys do—hunting, riding, partying, along with some serious studying, because Hadrian liked his companions reasonably educated. At any one time there were eight or nine of them around, so the family story went. The nine idols, they called them— Pancrates called them so, actually, because he was a gossip, and it's a miracle he didn't get his head lopped, charlatan and poetaster that he was, as many did at that time for much less."

Aelius thought it prudent not to look overanxious and reached for a plum. "I have never read this in Pancrates."

"I'm surprised you read Pancrates at all. Hardly anyone does these days. Anyhow, it's not in his poetry, but in the letters of the imperial secretary, Suetonius. Suetonius maintained a correspondence with Marcius Turbo, who worried about his son Lucius frequenting the imperial crowd. The plums, I look after myself—I trust you can tell the difference."

"There's no comparison with market-bought, madam. Was Antinous one of the nine?"

"If Suetonius is to be believed, he was the tenth idol, and the most important. Just think, the saplings of these plum trees were brought from Sicily by the late consul. A veritable Cincinnatus—historians ought to rush to write his biography. Of course, I would prefer if a Roman did it."

Aelius caught the hint, and said something to the effect of knowing at least two City-born colleagues who would welcome the challenge. "Are any of Suetonius's letters to Marcius Turbo extant, by chance?"

"The late consul had several of them copied, and yes, they are right here, but you won't get to see them unless you stay until the end of the week."

"Madam, I am obliged."

"But do you accept?"

It meant four days out of his schedule. "I accept gladly," Aelius hastened to say. Private correspondence of this sort was hard to come by, and besides—plums and portrait gallery notwithstanding—he appreciated how a widow's summer in the country had to grow boring after a while. "Could you give me the sense of Pancrates's gossip?"

Repentina left her armchair and said, "Come," inviting him to follow with a curt wave of her hand. "It seems that by the time the imperial party left Arabia and headed for Egypt, there had been a heated argument between Hadrian and Antinous. It might have had to do with the fact that Hadrian took Lucius along on the mountain climb (Could he help it, I say, if he was a good mountaineer?), or the fact that Antinous had cut his hair short and was growing a beard. Both of them are presented in Marcius's letters as possibilities. The library is this way, mind your step. Oh, it's incredible what went on during those trips, apparently. Fussing and slamming of doors and spiteful hissy fits, worse than at the hairdresser's before a wedding.

The boys started taking sides, too, at least those who were in the imperial retinue during this leg of the journey."

"How many were there?"

"I don't recall, you'll have to see for yourself whether the information is spelled out in the letters. I know that Lucius and young Modestus and Alcibiades and of course Antinous were there. There might have been more." The library—also a reading room—was well-lit and impeccably dusted. From a low shelf, Repentina took a bound index and put it in Aelius's expecting hands. "The situation grew so intolerable that the empress asked to be put ashore with her girl friends and ladies-in-waiting. Even Hadrian had enough of it at the end and took the occasion of the lion hunt to get away from the barge."

Keeping from throwing the index open taxed his eagerness, but Aelius checked himself politely. "I thought the emperor took Antinous with him."

"Not according to Marcius Turbo. He says Lucius was supposed to go along, but that he, as his father, prevailed on him to stay on the pretext of a sore shoulder." With a critical forefinger, the lady ran the edge of the closest shelf. "Hadrian might have wanted to be alone (he loved to hunt, you know), because he didn't insist on anyone substituting Lucius."

"What about Antinous, then?"

"He followed of his own accord. It's a grotesque little episode Phlegon, Suetonius, and other contemporary chroniclers ignore, but it is fairly well described in one of the letters." Repentina bowed her head slightly, and left him alone.

The crossreferenced index, bright with rubrics, facilitated Aelius's search. Greek and Latin correspondence were listed separately, by writer and subject: Aemilius Papus, Attianus, Avidius Cassius—names ran under his eyes that he'd only read of in history books. Dusty names, forgotten glories: How likely was he to discover clues to a conspiracy? Through the open window, a dance of pollen from the garden sparkled around him when he lifted a midbook page to the sunlight, and knew even before viewing the document that he'd found what he was looking for.

It was in a letter from Marcius Turbo to Suetonius Tranquillus, *formerly director of imperial correspondence.* That the great historian had been dismissed from court for a supposed indiscretion, Aelius knew, but only the writing's date, days after Hadrian's death, justified the boldness of the exchange.

Do you remember, Tranquillus, what Cicero writes, that courage is a habit of the soul? The Boy took it into his head that he was not going to be left behind, and as soon as he could, he secured a guide, pack animals, and followed the emperor. Foolish youth! Had he not listened to the accounts made to the imperial party about the lion terrorizing the countryside? Or did he believe himself a match for the beast or the imperial marksman? Although it was then said (and the low-born Phlegon described the episode in his usual pompous tone) that Hadrian and Antinous went hunting together, such was not the case. Hadrian did not even know the Boy was in the neighborhood. He assumed him, and he told me so himself afterward, to be on the barge still, or at one of the many places where they stopped during the voyage.

The mischievous youth had been doing the same in Sicily and Syria—not wanting to be left behind, he'd gotten himself lost in the mountains the first time (there is a shrine still, halfway up the volcano, recalling the fortunate event of his being found by a search party long after the emperor had come down after seeing the rainbow of dawn), and the second time he'd risked being struck by lightning even as his master was with my Lucius on top of the mountain. This time Antinous advanced incautiously into the territory where the lion, unbeknown to him, lay in wait. His guide was thrown off the horse by the beast, and devoured under his eyes; pack animals and servants in the caravan scattered to the four winds, and the

*Boy was left by himself to confront the lion with a javelin more
apt to chase deer than for serious hunting.*

*It was a miracle that Hadrian, having drawn with his own
party close to the lion's den, and believing the racing animals
and escaped servants strangers running away from the beast,
decided to follow through. Imagine his surprise when he found
Antinous, whose horse had been clawed and lay dying, before
the lion already crouching for the fatal attack. It took that prince
an instant to send an unerring dart into the lion's heart, but I
leave it to your judgment what might have happened had he delayed, or—which would have been more likely—been altogether
elsewhere at that time. My Lucius, safe with me on the barge,
was not only spared that risky scene, but also what show of gross
recrimination is likely to have followed between the lovers.*

*Again you ask me whether I have sure information about
Antinous's death, but I told you in person all I know. You say
that* he was approached by obscure conspirators while in
Egypt, who—taking advantage of his present despondency—
tried to draw him to their side. *I ignore who your sources are,
for I never heard these rumors. Have you asked Caesernius
Quinctianus? What I do know is that the emperor set up a memorial obelisk for Antinous in his villa at Tibur, intending to
move it with the* mummified body *to Rome, but did not live
long enough to do it.*

Standing in the sunlight, Aelius stared at the sparkling motes around
him. This was the first oblique confirmation that a conspiracy did
exist in Hadrian's day, and had penetrated as far as the imperial en-
tourage during the Egyptian tour. By whom, for what reason, mattered less now than knowing he could postulate it. Did Suetonius
ever follow the advice to interrogate Caesernius, to whom Hadrian's
lost orders had been addressed?

Regarding Antinous's burial, the letter's closing sentence was
ambiguous. It could either mean that the body had been moved to

Rome without the obelisk, or that neither of them had made it to the City. One thing was established, though: Mummification had taken place, as Theo and his cohorts maintained. Should Onofrius be able to read a location (precise spot, district, city—anything would help) on the Varian Gardens' obelisk, the second-to-last step in finding the grave might be at hand.

To the lady Repentina, when he was collected by a servant for dinner, Aelius only said that he found the correspondence of great value and ample proof of the family's worth. In truth, the collection contained mostly accessory court gossip, and its one hundred or so letters would only take one more full day of reading. He was well content to play the conversationalist in exchange for the breakthrough. The names of Julius Capitolinus and the Right Honorable Vulcacius Gallicanus were dutifully made as possible authors of Tuscus's biography, and details furnished on the Court at Nicomedia, the Rebellion, and Egyptian fruit production.

"Close-up," she told him over a plate of villa-grown pheasant, and he thought she'd never shut up, "you rather resemble a youthful portrait of Agrippa, a bit frowning, but pleasant. The gray hair gives you a distinguished look, though your blue eyes, well, you can't help those. It's a good thing you like to chat, because—well, you may say, you have *urbem in rure,* and it's true that city comforts are not wanting here, thanks to the late consul. Still, in a rustic location, a visit is a treat not to be renounced. Indeed, I have a mind not to let you go off the grounds while you're here, because I can't see why you're determined to tramp to the old imperial properties at Sublaqueum and Praeneste, which are half-empty and the serfs have been stealing from them for centuries. There are no libraries left in either place. Perhaps it is good that Caesar's envoy be seen once in a while on the premises. As a military man, you'll be able to use the right terms, and curtail the abuses by nearby residents, such as running pipes from the imperial villas to their property—freedmen and parvenus do that, always did and always will, unless one watches them like hawks— cutting timber from state groves and copses and fruit orchards.

I have seen it myself and I screamed, you may believe it, so that the culprits stopped in their tracks and ran, though it was only a woman shouting from her sedan chair. Likewise, they've been lifting benches from the palace parks to reuse them in their paltry yards, and the like. The late consul was convinced that bad example set by princes who shall go unmentioned (you know who they are, dear Spartianus) and who consorted with serfs and freedmen, giving them the run of all these places, have brought us to this state of things. Blue eyes everywhere, it's an invasion in our public offices! I realize I'm bending your ear a little, but if it does take a little ear bending for you to remember to inform our Lord Diocletian, well, so be it. *Repetita juvant,* I say." Repentina kept encouraging the servants to fill Aelius's plate, and talked all the while. To his question, she stopped only enough to let the few words through the barrage of her own, and then lifted her eyebrows. "Do *I* think Antinous's burial is in Rome? Of course it is. Marcius Turbo used to stroll with his son in front of it, to remind him of what it means to be a favorite. Where in Rome? I have no idea, but I can tell you how to get to the Marcii's monument."

It took all of Aelius's tact to keep his promise to stay after receiving a note from Paratus on Thursday. It informed him that he had succeeded, through his old acquaintances in the ranks of the night patrol and fire police, in obtaining permission to "dig up, clean, and repair" the broken obelisk in the Varian Gardens. Replacement on its pedestal at his own cost was also a possibility, if it could be worked out, et cetera. Aelius chafed at the bit in the estate until Saturday. Then—taking advantage of the first of the three days of *Mundus Patet* celebrations, in memory of the dead—he left for the City against the promise to Repentina that he'd secure a Roman historian for the late consul's biography.

24 AUGUST, THURSDAY
(1ST OF 6 EGYPTIAN INTERCALARY DAYS, EPAGOMENAI)
A pale green midafternoon sky stretched waiting for stars when Aelius arrived at the Special Agent Barracks. He'd seen fine linen

dyed this color, hung across Egyptian doorways and gathered in lazy draperies; the severe army building, echoing with footsteps and shouted voices, gained from the lightness and gentle hue of that backdrop. *If,* he thought, *now and for two more days the dead wander the earth from the opening of the sacred well they call* mundus, *they must so much enjoy the beauty of this live sky.*

The few days Paratus had spent in his neat little quarters had sufficed him to "set up shop," as he said, with the help of his reading servant and the information he received from outside. True to his law enforcement past, he advised prudence about conspiracy hearsay, but the news had on him the effect it had worked on Aelius himself. "I could take excitement much better when I was young," he confessed. "It seems nearly too much to handle, now that we're so close to deciphering the obelisk, too. I do not dare ask what else you might have learned."

"It comes down to another version of Antinous's death, much less idealistic than the others. Jealousy and spite among favorites and his fear of being replaced. Since Marcius Turbo was the jaundiced father of one of the 'golden boys,' I must take his narrative for what it's worth. At the imperial villas of Praeneste and Sublaqueum I found nothing useful, although Praeneste's Nile mosaic in Fortuna's shrine is similar to those I saw at Antinoopolis, but the priesthood in the Boy's name no longer exists. There's also a family tradition that half-confirms a City location for Antinous's grave, no exact spot given. Presumably outside the walls, along one of the consular roads. Least believable of all is a piece of gossip from Suetonius to Marcius Turbo, alleging that—as he puts it—'Antinous was a natural son of that quasi defender of the Christians, Pliny the Younger', conceived while he was proconsul in Bithynia."

"That's preposterous!"

"It's more or less what I told my hostess. She is less skeptical, as in Trajan's days Suetonius was such a close friend of Pliny's, and there were rumors that the proconsul, being about fifty and having fathered no children from his wives, finally took up with a local girl, free-born. It seems unlikely that the Boy would then end up in a male brothel at Baiae. As for the conspiracy, in the lady's library I scoured the deified Hadrian's biographers for any word that might confirm it, but that hint privately reported by Suetonius is all I found. Still, I am thrilled."

"Suetonius was not above bending the truth," Paratus reminded him. "I thank you for sending me the account of your stay at Tibur—having never visited the great villa, I listened to the reading of it with great interest. Frankly, however, it was not prudent for you to spend the night there alone. Anyone could have followed you and waited for a chance to do you in."

Aelius felt too optimistic to care. "I dare most assassins to thread their way across that labyrinth, especially in the dark. Besides, I set my bodyguards at the entrances. Wait until I share a theory I developed during my visit there, and perfected in the lady's library. What about you, rather? News from your property?"

"Some. One of my sons is coming up from Minturnae to manage the tavern in my absence, and we're starting work in the vineyard again. The other son stays with my wife, just in case. I've given her enough worry through the years, and don't wish anything to happen to her." Turning his head to the barking of noncommissioned officers outside the window, Paratus seemed briefly lost after the sounds of drilling. "Don't you miss camp life?"

"No."

"I do. Being here does me good. By the way, in your absence I have also taken it upon myself to hire a crew, and pending your approval, the workers are ready to start on the obelisk even tomorrow. The II Cohort will have a couple of men watching, but it can only be to our advantage to have police cover. The only obstacle is that worm, Onofrius, who claims to have a group of Alexandria merchants coming to Rome for a guided tour, and made himself scarce. I had him swear that he'll show up regularly at your doorstep first thing in the morning."

"Excellent, thank you."

Paratus felt his way across the small room toward the window, and the echo of military calls reverberating from it. "Less than excellent. The II Cohort wouldn't agree to let your bodyguard join in. If I were you, I'd ask that your men stay in the neighborhood anyway."

"I'll think about it." But Aelius had no intention to display concern when physical threats against him seemed a thing of the past.

So, it was all coming together: he had a translator, a collaborator, everything was at his fingertips in the Great City. He left the Special Agent Barracks in great spirits, went home down the street to read his mail, and then allowed himself the luxury of relaxing in the public baths before closing time. Given the funerary flavor of the holiday, many stayed away from public places, so he chose Trajan's establishment, with a mind to browse afterward the nearby bookstores of Shoemakers Alley.

A elius would not be able to explain it afterward. One moment he was reaching across the packed bookstore for a volume on the counter, the next there was a thud, no, not quite a thud, rather a slicing plunk, like the sound of frogs jumping in Tibur's pools, the shush of one body fluidly penetrating another, and it would have remained a half-remembered impression had he not seen the glossy arc of blood scatter drops on the backs and faces of those around him. With that, pain like a blow in the collarbone, although his attention stayed on the motion of the blood arc, and how fishlike steel had threaded it in the air. A tumult around him, bodies jostling one another, by instinct his need to reach for the hand holding the weapon and stop it. A surprised face stood out in the bustle, over someone's shoulder, lips mouthing something like "Has-a-knife," and that slicing thud again, the brilliant scatter of drops, sick wetness under his arm, reaching for it before a new stretch toward the fishlike metal. His own hand spread blood around this time and missed the grip, folks coalesced and then floated apart. All the while he was perfectly conscious of the store, the wounds, blood spurting, his bodyguard like a bull charging him. Darkness lasted a moment, but in it, small animals sounds and flips in low water, the slow motion of Anubina's hand placing the plate before him, and the brightness of the copper jar in her room all had a place. The bodyguard was shouting, pushing a fistful of cloth against his collarbone and neck. From then on Aelius maintained full lucidity, although he remembered nothing of the time between the knifing and the moment a navy surgeon made a face and said, "Shit."

26 August, Saturday (Third intercalary day)

A slender line, thinner than a ribbon, separated deep sleep from a weird suspended state, during which—for the length of the night—Aelius perceived people coming and going, a murmur of voices, and pain, dull and wearisome. Mostly, anguish for being unable to intervene, as if cloth walls kept him separate from others, flat on his back, inert. It seemed impossible that such gauzy rags should suffice to hold him down. They floated above him at times, like a trembling, shimmery tangle of water plants, bending in the current, while he lay at the bottom half-aware, without strength. In and out of that feverish, submerged state Aelius sank and rose for hours well into the second morning. Then thirst and restlessness, irritation at the voices multiplying questions and explanations around him, brought him back in a weak spurt of energy.

"I *know* what happened, I was there." He dismissed all from the room except Paratus, who'd remained standing by the bed for the last three hours at least, and to whom Aelius said, "For God's sake, you, too, sit down."

"The bodyguard at the store's entrance had his throat cut," Paratus told him. "That, I don't think you know. The same would have happened to you had the crowding not impeded an attack from behind; even so, it's a miracle you didn't get your gullet slashed from the side." A look of angered frustration on the veteran's face revealed for once how much his impairment weighed on him. "Your head guardsman described the scene to me. How I wished I had my eyes—I'd never have permitted that the assassin be killed, because now we will never know who he was, or who sent him. As it was, the commotion drew the baths security to the place, and they cut him down."

Gloomily Aelius fingered his bandages, crisp with drying blood and whatever medication had been applied to the wounds. "Anything identifiable on him?"

"Not *on* him: about him. He was missing a finger of his left hand. We can assume he's the one from the band that struck at my place, but no more than that." Paratus's long gauntness seemed hunched with his present failure, to the point that Aelius—already grieving his guardsman's death—felt guilty for his imprudence. "Count your blessings that the Misenum Fleet headquarters were so close," Paratus continued, his elbows on the bedside table. "The navy surgeon seems to think the killer was a sailor, by the callouses on his palms. He also says the bleeding from your neck was so serious, he didn't think you'd pull through. This much, I know from my own experience: It'll be a few days before you can do anything about the obelisk or anything else."

"No." Trying to lift his head hurt too much, and Aelius had to desist. "No. There's no time. I want Onofrius in the Varian Gardens with the II Cohort, the bodyguard, whatever. I want the text read and translated within the day."

"That, too, is going to be impossible. Onofrius hasn't shown up. Contrary to what he said, there was no meeting with businessmen from Alexandria. Two of your men went to fetch him yesterday morning, and discovered he skipped town with his rags and latest pay. The police are looking for him in connection with the attack against you."

"He would not *dare*."

"No, but he probably indicated you to his accomplices, and then conveniently took to his heels."

Had he been sand, Aelius would have not felt his strength eroding more quickly than it did, as if water washed over him and made him shapeless when he desperately wanted to stay whole. "I should have had my men watch him well beyond the first two weeks," he said, but perhaps only to himself. "This would have never happened."

It was just as well that a rising fever kept him out of commission for the next twenty-four hours, giving him time to come to terms with his anger. Whispered voices returned in the bedroom, the surgeon's cool hands touched and tapped and caused pain. "Where is the letter?" he thought he heard someone ask. "Where is it?" But the room was empty, blue like Anubina's house, only dilated into a borderless space for him to sink into.

L ate in the morning of the third day, he was lucid enough to curse his forced immobility, and hear Paratus mildly steer the conversation toward what information they had.

"It's a fact, Aelius Spartianus. Consider it preparatory work to the reading of the obelisk; given Onofrius's betrayal, perhaps even a substitute to it. If your days in Hadrian's villa brought you to formulate a helpful hypothesis, let's hear it and judge where it leads us."

Propped up by pillows, Aelius stared at the ceiling. "Damn it, it's all I can do." The servant waiting by the door he ordered to fetch the villa's plan, and unfold it on the bedside table in front of Paratus. "My theory has less to do with the cause of Antinous's death than with its timing—maybe. I first had an inkling at the villa, but after studying it at length in Lady Repentina's library, I became convinced that the apparent jumble of buildings at Tibur had a purpose after all."

"A *purpose*?"

"I'm not sure—a meaning, at any rate."

"Well, it's general opinion that the emperor was mad toward the end." Paratus reached for the plan, feeling the edges of it with his fingertips. "There are those who say the villa was not completed by that time, and others that it merely represents his mutable humor."

Aelius lay back, impatiently shielding his eyes from what brightness of day came through the window. "And his passion for traveling, I know."

"It bordered on obsession, they say."

"But it was born out of necessity. I don't recall any historian ever remarking that the deified Hadrian traveled merely for sport."

"Even ruling is a sport, for some." Paratus smiled his undefinable smile devoid of anger, that expression just short of admitting, even to oneself, that one's been used in a huge game, but it's all right with him. Head averted from the bright window, Aelius observed that smile. He thought how only the stolid ones, like his father, never developed as far as that irony, doing their time and getting out still fully convinced that soldiering was the best opportunity for a man to get places. If he doesn't get himself killed in the process.

"I cannot *prove* that the villa is much more than a museum of sites visited around the world, Paratus. Scholars better trained than I seem to think that's all it is. What astonished me is how taking an abstract look at the plan itself shows that part of the grounds at least were laid out to represent the heavens."

Paratus's smile changed imperceptibly. "You're not serious."

"But I am. Place your hands on the sheet in front of you, and you'll notice I punctured the outlines of the buildings with a pin, from behind, so that you may follow them with your fingertips."

Amusement disappeared from the veteran's face as his index and middle finger lightly felt the plan.

"Keep talking."

"At the beginning, since different segments of the complex were built at different times, I was tricked into trying to make sense of those single elements. The residence and its service areas, the Canopus and Egyptian Quarter, the so-called Elysian Fields, and so on." Aelius found that if he closed his eyes and shut off the brightness of day, fever bothered him less, and he could think more clearly. It'd been the same thing in Egypt, when the wound had been much more serious, and he'd sworn to himself that if he lived, he'd find a girl and settle down. What he'd found was Anubina, no house other than her blue room, and wars elsewhere. Dry-mouthed with loss of blood, he reached for the canteen at his side. "Then I began to perceive that the final, or nearly final layout created a unitary pattern." The water and vinegar mix was just cool enough to freshen his tongue; savoring it, Aelius watched Paratus's hand move on the plan, tentative like his wandering the villa at night, swallowed by this or that corridor or portico that blacked out the stars. "It's a known fact that the deified Hadrian was an amateur astronomer. On the imperial barge at Antinoopolis, I had seen a mosaic representing Orion's corner of the sky, without understanding its significance until I realized that in the villa, too, thanks to connecting walls, pools, earthworks, the buildings combine to form a set of eight constellations."

"Go on, go on."

Aelius glanced over. "Where your fingers are touching now, that is the area of the residence. Reception halls, libraries, official and semiofficial quarters, which ought to be 'read' along their common perimeter, and recognized as Orion, with its main stars marked by the triclinium, external court, officers' quarters, and the island residence. Move slightly above the complex, and you will meet the audience hall, which I read as the Hare. To the right of Orion, the constellation astronomers call the Unicorn is represented by the great promenade porch, and close by, the two hounds accompanying Orion: the Greater Dog with Sirius, where the entrance vestibule leads into the villa, and the lesser one, with Procyon matching the spot of the observatory tower."

"What about this straight line?"

Aelius swallowed a thirsty gulp before answering. "That is the garden path leading from the vestibule to the Nile's pavilion. It matches the direct line between Sirius and the star called—not coincidentally—Canopus, after the hero by that name. The Keel of the Ship Argus is represented by the wall of the academy terrace. There, if you pay attention, a fourfold portico occupies the space that in the sky is taken up by the cross-shaped mast above the Keel."

"And Argus is the constellation Manilus connected with drowning." Paratus's delicate fingering ran the perforated sheet. "If it's true, it's absolutely stunning."

"It *is* absolutely stunning, and if it isn't true, or meant, it's a miracle of coincidences."

"Didn't the legendary mariner Canopus drown?"

"Some say that not only did he drown off the Egyptian shore, but gave his name to the Delta resort near Alexandria, and—we all know—to the southern navigational star for everyone traveling by land or sea. Any sailor can confirm it, or any of us who have soldiered far enough south to see Canopus." Talking was beginning to weary him. Aelius's impatience struggled against a torpid need to sleep, or lie still. "That scum, Onofrius, told me that for the Egyptians it is also the star of the dead, representing Horus-on-the-Horizon."

"And Horus is Osiris's son."

"Yes. Of course, Orion is identified with Osiris in Egypt."

Paratus's fingers continued to seek and follow, making sense of the design laid out before him. "And Sirius the Egyptians call Sothis, Isis's star of the Nile, identified with Anubis who watches over the dead. So this pinprick here—"

"The round memorial?" Aelius drained the canteen. "It marks the Dove, flying ahead of the Ship."

"But there's an important star missing from your map: Antinous's namesake."

"The emperor's memoirs deny that it appeared at the Boy's death—in fact, he had already observed the star years earlier. The Canopus represents Antinous at the villa."

"Still, everything feels upside down to me." Without prompting, Paratus turned the map around.

"Of course, I understand—this map is oriented not to the North Star but to the South, the direction from which for the Egyptians all life and all death come."

"That's not all. At the edges of the sheet, you'll also find the constellations Eridanus and Sea Serpent. Those are the two brooks bordering the spur on which the villa was built."

The surgeon's arrival interrupted the conversation for the time being. Paratus offered to leave the room but Aelius—still unwilling to

give away his fatigue—said it was all right, it wouldn't take long because he felt better anyway, and so on. Circumscribed by light from
the window like an apparition, the surgeon seemed singularly unim-
pressed by the patient's opinion: He replied curtly it didn't matter
how he felt, and he'd have to stay in bed until allowed to do otherwise.

"You know," Paratus cheered him up when they were alone again,
"I do believe you wasted your abilities choosing to lead a crack regiment, Aelius Spartianus. Analysis, theory-building, deduction—there
are better uses in the world for soldiers who can think."

Had Paratus smiled while he said the words, Aelius would have
felt less embarrassed by praise. Despite his protestations, his energy
was waning after the long exchange, and even embarrassment fatigued him. "I'm not even sure these considerations matter to my
original task. They seem to offer me a key, even though I still don't
know how and why the Boy died, not to speak of his grave's location.
The layout of the villa appears to reflect the most significant sight one
would observe in late October in a southern climate, *at the time of Antinous's drowning.* The imperial architect left no clues, no hints, but
that instant in time, whatever it really meant for the deified Hadrian,
was perpetuated in stone: Is it a murderer's confession, built for the
ages? I rather think he was not responsible for the Boy's death, that he
lived in the villa and walked through it like on a processional route."

"Future historians will break their heads before figuring it out,
but I am not sure your theory of the villa's plan exonerates Hadrian.
You're jumping to conclusions. The pattern might constitute a route
for atonement and forgiveness, who knows."

"Maybe."

Paratus's fingers left the map. "In any case, it is odd that no one
understood the villa before. You are clever and astute."

"Yes, and no doubt meant for better things than the army." Flattered by the words, Aelius smirked.

"Damn, is it my impression, or is it too bright in this room? My
eyes ache. I am not that clever. Probably, no one before me had reason to search for sense in an imperial whim. The deified Hadrian did

not intend for a private interpretation of his *house of grief* to be obvious to all. The astronomical pattern suggests that the villa should rather be understood as *a house of life,* as the Egyptians intend it, connected to spiritual learning and mummification rites."

"It brings us back to the Canopus as a grave site."

"It may very well have been, but not for long, as Helagabalus found out, having made a mess of the place."

Pulling of a drape across the window dimmed the light, but did not relieve Aelius's discomfort. The truth was that fever and pain were rising again. If Paratus understood his effort to keep up from the tone of his voice, he spared him by making a good show of not noticing. However, with the excuse of returning to his quarters and "checking on Onofrius's whereabouts with his informants," he took leave shortly thereafter.

It was a courtesy Aelius appreciated. Drinking did little to relieve his thirst, and if he moved his head from side to side, the medicine-smelling room seemed to oscillate like a ship's cabin. He lay covering his eyes with his forearm. Still, as he'd done at night in the great, solitary villa, under a sky so perfectly black and star-studded that his admiration had turned to disquiet, and then to fear. The darkness he'd felt around him then—once brightly lit to be sure, even in the late hours—and the obscurity of Tibur's mountain, had conjured to make him feel small and lost. Not insignificant, no, but minute in comparison to great lives and to the greatness, the tragedy of Life itself.

He slept through the rest of the day. That evening, when mail and a lamp were placed at his bedside, Aelius had to admit he was still too unwell to pore over the usual booksellers' lists and copyists' bills. Only a small note on papyrus among the rest caught his attention, and after looking at it without making up his mind, he reached for it in the end. Pain ran across his shoulder with the simple motion, and even unsealing it hurt.

Addressed to him care of the city prefect's office, it was miraculous that the note had reached him at all. There was no elegant heading and the handwriting was a beginner's: small, uncertain; but every word had been spelled with great care.

> *Anubina to Spartianus, very many greetings. To begin with, I pray that you are in good health, every morning and evening. My daughter Thaësis and my son Sabourion send you thanks for the gifts you gave them, and beg you to know that they also pray that you fare well. The most sacred Nile has reached 16 cubits in its flood, and vintage will begin soon, which is the same time of year of your first coming to this Nome. Wishing you to remain in the benevolence of all the gods, written by her own hand in the Philadelphia district, metropolis of Antinoopolis, 15 Epiphi (10 July).*

No affectionate whisper heard in the last eight years, no sign of physical love given or received since, had struck him like the words *"the same time of year of your first coming,"* sealed between guileless formulas of greeting and farewell. How simple could things be, and why did he always look for complication? Why had he feared homecoming so much, while longing for it? Aelius thought himself hard, not easily moved. Surely it was the fever's doing, but he found himself on the point of weeping over Anubina's letter, and what it really meant for both of them. No point in answering it, either. Night came and went, and so the pain, and so the fever. What stayed—and there was no remedy, there never had been—was the once more unbearable sadness for leaving her behind.

30 August, Wednesday (1 Thoth, Egyptian New Year's)
The first day Aelius left the house after the accident, on a morning when sparrows clamored heralding rain, Baruch ben Matthias ran into him in front of the State Cadastre.

"Fancy the coincidence, Commander! I no sooner set foot in Rome, and here you are. The world is smaller than a chicken yard." He'd cut his hair and trimmed his beard, looking every bit the seasoned traveler at ease with his surroundings. "Is that your northern complexion, or are you looking a little green around the gills?"

It was the old, crude banter. Much as Aelius sought a disquieting edge in ben Matthias's voice, he recognized only that ambiguous pretense of friendliness, so difficult to trust. The usual complement of young toughs was not missing, busy mingling with the locals at both ends of the Sacred Climb. "I thought you were planning to travel here in the fall."

"Plans change."

"So, let me guess what brings you to Rome: is it business, or business?"

"You are absolutely correct. Business, at least two ways: a deal with the Iseum Campense's *house of life* that will make me rich, and a wedding. My daughter's, you know. You remember her, the one who makes sweet cakes like your mother used to."

"Congratulations." Because Aelius was walking toward the back of the Cadastre building, ben Matthias followed him there. "And how did you leave Egypt?"

"As I always left Egypt. Like a trollop who's short on clients and long on bills. Prices keep rising, the trials of the Christians are proceeding apace, but we're both alive, so why don't we go for a cool drink?"

"No, thanks."

Under the great marble plan of the City, affixed for public viewing to the rear wall, the Jew cynically watched while Aelius took notes. "I thought you'd be interested in knowing that no one else got killed in the circle you were investigating, the queer merchants and their acolytes."

"Really? That's a relief."

"But there are two pieces of sad news: your war buddy Gavius

Tralles was killed in a riding accident alongside the Nile—we had nothing to do with it, if you're even remotely thinking that—and there's talk of an epidemic due to the flood. People upriver were starting to drop off by the time I sailed, so I'm not in a particular hurry to go back."

Aelius looked over. "I have known Gavius a long time: I'm sorry to hear it."

"I thought so."

"As for the epidemic, you don't live anywhere near upriver."

"No. But already in Hermopolis there were a few deaths among the river crews. I sent my family to the hills of the Arsinoites, where the desert wind takes care of vermin."

"What about Antinoopolis, any contagion in the Philadelphia district?"

Disturbed by the men's coming, sparrows had at first taken wing, but now came back to argue over crumbs from the surrounding market stalls. "No," ben Matthias answered. "But I never took chances beyond my ability to rise above them, so I'm here with my girl. She's marrying a local Jew."

"I see you're extending your horizons, Baruch."

The Jew looked smug. "You could say that, in more ways than one. But there isn't just me traveling. At Alexandria I heard the *Pietas Augustorum Nostrorum* would sail a few days after my ship, and Theo the spice merchant planned to be on it. No, no, I don't know him personally, but I understand you do."

"None of your business, is it."

"None whatsoever. It's just that you seem to have bad luck with acquaintances—or, rather, they run into bad luck as soon as they meet you." Pointing his thumb at the intricate map of Rome, "What about yourself?" he asked. "Have you taken up city-planning, or are they still after you?"

The impudence of the man. Aelius felt blood go to his head, neck and shoulder aching sharply. It was so obvious that he struggled not to answer angrily, ben Matthias burst out laughing. "I take it they're still after you—not that I should care. And the Butcher: Are you still pursuing his latrine-wall life? Let me tell you about *our* revolt during his reign—"

That afternoon, with a westerly wind picking up and sending clouds scudding from the mountains, Onofrius's body was fished out of the river near the marble wharf under the Aventine. He'd been dead a while, six or seven days at least, but there was no telling when exactly he had been thrown in the water. It was a matter of murder, since he'd been stabbed several times in the back. Paratus heard it through former colleagues of the V Cohort, who'd been called on the scene.

"He's only been identified because there are Egyptians working at the wharf, and they recognized him by his beard and clothes. Amazing any of them were on the job, too, as it's their New Year's holiday."

"I don't know what to think." Back from a useless day at the Cadastre, but having found archival proof of Helagabalus's order to leave Canopus in disrepair, Aelius was too surprised to elaborate. "This is really unexpected."

"Is it?" By contrast, Paratus had the coldness of a policeman on his martyred face. "I told you he'd betray himself by starting to spend money. However much he charged to sell your skin, he didn't get to enjoy it."

They stood at the gate of the Special Agent Barracks, in the wind that brought drops of distant rain. A setting sun knifed the clouds only enough to slap a blinding gold dash on the roofs of temples and shrines, but it would soon go under. Aelius felt revulsion at the thought of the miserable waterlogged corpse polluting stone meant for temples. So, death had violently met at last one who'd tried to avoid it in every way. It was nearly cold on the windy hillside, a first strange omen of fall.

"It reminds me," he said without explaining how he'd come to the subject, "Baruch ben Matthias just arrived in Rome."

Paratus shook his head. Framed by the gate, in the shade of sunset, he resembled a soldier's headstone more than a living man. "He did not, Aelius Spartianus. Ben Matthias has been in Rome for the past week."

ELEVENTH CHAPTER

Notes by Aelius Spartianus:

I have come to a dead end. All I did until now led me merely to a place in which I could have just as easily stood at the beginning. Antinous either killed himself (by will or accident), or was killed. As it is said that Isis built a shrine in every place where she found a limb of Osiris, so the deified Hadrian built memorials to the Boy everywhere he went. I counted four thus far: two in Egypt (along the Nile and in the shrine at Antinoopolis), and two at Tibur (the Canopus and round memorial). Other locations are pure legend, like the supposed one in Cicero's monument at Puteoli. Antinous's final resting place still eludes me, although I am reasonably convinced it is somewhere among the thousands of monuments outside Rome's walls. It seems hopeless. My research in the State Archives and Cadastre revealed nothing about the building or registering of such burial. The sources, from Suetonius to Marius Maximus, Cassius Dio, and the deified Hadrian himself, are silent about it.

Caesernius Quinctianus, consul in Hadrian's last year,
he who never received the letter that started my investigation,
has seemingly vanished from history. His deeds are scarcely
known. No autographed letter of his is extant, and his family
died out long ago. It intrigues me that Marcius Turbo advised
Suetonius to ask him about a possible conspiracy, but I have
nothing to go on.

Even the discovery that celestial patterns were repeated on
the imperial barge and in the villa's plan tells me little, other
than the time of Antinous's death was either anticipated by his
master—who cast his own accurate horoscope each January—
or memorialized after the fact. Aviola Paratus urges me to
concentrate on the Boy's grave, and he's right. But, including
my guardsman, there are now at least six corpses in the way.
By simple chance I am not one of them.

Today I plan to return to the deified Hadrian's monument,
and look once more among the burials scattered throughout
Agrippina's and Domitia's Gardens, and Nero's ones nearby
(the Egyptian burial ground in this area complicates things, as
sphinxes and small obelisks abound). Tomorrow I will scout
the suburban tract of the Via Tiburtina, leading to the em-
peror's great villa, and the day after, the Via Labicana again,
near which I found Antinous's obelisk.

With Onofrius gone, and ben Matthias unexpectedly in
the City, things are not looking good. His Divinity may soon
tire of granting me time to do one research, and hear me report
about other matters. Also, I worry about Anubina and her
children in plague-ridden Egypt.

Nothing but state property lay beyond the bridge that carried the deified Hadrian's first name—and Aelius's own. There, the sloping
ground once the suburban estate owned by Nero's mother met the
contiguous gardens inherited by Domitian's wife. The old pleasure

parks had through the years given way to a variety of uses: the horse track built by Gaius Caligula, long out of function, stables, sheep pens, and private cemeteries. Nero's bridge downstream, cutting across the river's curve where the Via Triumphalis led north, had lost part of its parapet, and was blocked to traffic by a trellis of beams. In the middle of the horse track, the tall Egyptian obelisk stood gray-pink in the green of copses and overgrown rows of trees, set against the Vatican hills thick with pines and summer-yellow bushes. At the foot of Aelius Hadrian's bridge, a large piazza of Tibur stone kept the gardens at bay around the sky-high mausoleum. Square at the bottom, like a fortress, it supported a wide marble tower rich in statues, topped by a gilded triumphal chariot.

Aelius had often walked these grounds, pacing the Cornelian Way to its crossroads with the Via Triumphalis, along the serpentine paths dissecting the cemetery grown on the side of the horse track, using its very wall. Christians (including the patriarch Peter) and followers of Isis were buried here. A small human-headed sphinx marked a girl's tomb, a leaning dwarf obelisk, devoid of inscription, celebrated the memory of God knows whom. Names scratched on bricks and badly incised on stone revealed the dead's origin: Soknopaios, Nilus, Ammon. In fact, the entire area was called "Egypt," and the theme was repeated in the nameless pyramid at the crossroads, on the palm-and-ewer frieze of a travertine burial tower nearby, and especially in that powerful pink and gray shaft Onofrius said had come from Alexandria.

Aelius sat in the shade of an acacia tree, thinking for the first time that perhaps he had wrongly pursued the Egyptian theme. Antinous was Greek, Hadrian had been in love with Greek culture. Why shouldn't the Boy have been buried in Bithynia, where his mother— whoever she'd been, whoever had been his father—was certainly still living at that time? *One becomes taken with clues, conditioned by them. What if the truth lies elsewhere altogether, and I have built upon mistaken assumptions from the start?*

East of Hadrian's mausoleum, sounds and voices rose from the raised causeway of the "new" marble wharf, sticking out like a massive cement and beams tongue into the stream. Aelius could imagine the scene downriver at the other wharf, where Onofrius had come bobbing up in front of the stonecutters. At the foot of the bridge, two of his guardsmen stood watch, as—at Paratus's insistent request—they never again would let him out of their sight, but that safety, too, was an illusion, as the accident at the bookstore went to prove.

Aelius left the Vatican district by the straight road on the right side of the river, leading down to Caesar's Gardens, where he'd cross over into the City over the bridge faithful Agrippa had built in Augustus's day.

The following morning, he rode out of the Tibur Gate past Veranus's Field and across the Anio river, nearly to the place called Septem Fratres that had so unnerved Onofrius. It was an itinerary of gravel pits and occasional estates, with Christian burials and oratories (barred and sealed by the state) built into the hillsides. Insects blackened the air along this or that marshy spot, even at the verges of the road. Two rich sepulchers called Aelius's attention because of their past beauty and ruined state. One of them, marked by a dog-headed sphinx, remembered a freedman of Hadrian's household, born in Hermopolis Magna. Its roof had caved in, while its companion to the side had lost part of the pediment. On this, if one lifted the ivy draping over it, the mutilated name of one ANT . . . was readable, and nothing else. There was a pedestal, too, but if it had once held a portrait statue, only the imprints of its bronze feet remained.

As every evening, at his return he stopped by the barracks to meet Paratus and discuss the day. The news awaiting him was that Onofrius had been seen alive for the last time by a neighbor on Saturday afternoon, as he headed for the Iseum Campense. "That would likely be the place where merchants from Alexandria would congregate," the veteran added, "so we cannot draw necessary conclusions from it."

"Never mind that." Aelius was ready to catch at straws, and Paratus's prudence irked him. "Did you have anyone ask about him at the Iseum?"

"I did. My informants were told Onofrius never made it on that day."

"But were there merchants from Egypt visiting the shrine?"

"As always. If it is as it was in my times, the compound serves as an exchange, a meeting place, and I'm sure prostitutes still hang out around it. Egyptian merchants make the Iseum their home away from home."

Aelius kept his suspicions about the Jewish merchant in mind. "Was Baruch ben Matthias one of them, do we know?"

Paratus wagged his head, a motion midway between assent and incredulity. "Yes, but he is not from Alexandria."

"Damn it, Paratus, he *sailed* from there!"

"You need proofs, Aelius Spartianus. All we can say for now is that someone surprised Onofrius while he walked to the shrine. It probably happened in an alley or doorway, else someone would have reported the attack. We can't even be sure whether they directly stabbed him from behind, or he tried to escape, and was killed as he fled." Again that temperate head-shaking, and collegial tolerance. "I appreciate how tempted you are to connect his death to the others— even to the attempt against you. But if matters stand as we think, *even if they stand as we think*, and he betrayed you to persons unknown, he could have attracted attention to himself by flashing money. Poverty and desperation aren't just an Egyptian reality these days. If ben Matthias is behind any of this, he will show his hand again. Against you, if he's given the chance, or me, or the spice merchant he cleverly told you of. But don't forget that my vineyard was ruined well before his coming."

"Well, that *consoles* me." Aelius was already on the door when he turned back. "Ah, I nearly forgot. The city prefect is back. He'd already heard of the fire that got out of hand at the Varian racetrack, and gave me a hard time about it. Claims I'm using Caesar's name to violate the law, which is an exaggeration, and wants to be kept abreast of any future *break-ins* on my part, as he called them."

2 SEPTEMBER, SATURDAY (4 THOTH)

Discouraging as it was to view the incomprehensible characters on the toppled obelisk, Aelius rode to the Varian Gardens on Monday. Afterward he followed the lofty arcades of the aqueduct to the Via Labicana, to reexamine the first suburban miles as far as the turnoff to the kennel. There was a remote possibility that Antinous had been buried on the grounds of the imperial estate of Two Laurels, so he negotiated with the guardian a guided tour of its vast park. Mausoleums of flint and white marble, the latest dating from Aurelian's reign, had been built without any order across the expanse of meadows and groves. Several dated back to the deified Hadrian's years, three of them—their inscriptions carved in soft stone and washed out by rain—shaped like small pyramids on square plinths.

"But I don't know why you look for him here, Excellency," the puzzled guardian told him as he escorted him out of the gate. "My wife's folks are from that province, and they can tell you the deified Antinous is buried in Egypt."

It was more or less coming full circle. Aelius returned to his flat on the Caelian Hill wanting to see no one, not even Paratus. He dismissed his bodyguard. For two days he secluded himself, neither answering letters nor reading or writing. Even on the day of the Great Games, when the entire City celebrated with processions and horse races, he stayed indoors. With his feet in the water he sat at the small poolside of the ground-floor baths, where outside light and sounds came damped through the narrow windows and thick walls. If he closed his eyes, he felt the ache on his neck and saw Egypt. The windswept Antinoan ledge and Hadrian's road, marked by soldiers' tombs. The tree shading Anubina's blue house. Crocodiles sunning themselves with their mouths open, ready to slash across the lazy broth of river water to feed. Between that place and the rest of the world lay buried Antinous, and the warning of danger against Rome.

On the third day, without telling anybody, he left by the Ostia Gate.

5 SEPTEMBER, NONES, THURSDAY (7 THOTH)

The *Pietas Augustorum Nostrorum* had made port near the salt ware-houses only a few minutes earlier. It was a stocky vessel, lying to in the dirty water of Trajan's harbor under a crown of seagulls. All passengers were still on board, and even merchandise had not yet begun to emerge from the hold. Aelius met the master of the ship at the foot of the gang-way, and after exchanging a few words, walked up to the bulwarks.

Resplendent in an embroidered white tunic, Theo recognized him first, and made a dainty gesture of greeting. Soon—the required thanksgiving prayer having been disposed of by the efficient captain—they stood side by side on the oscillating deck.

"What a gloriously sunny day to arrive." Theo beamed, his eyes on the bustling activity ashore. "We had a fabulous voyage, good weather all the way. I find you well, and am glad to see you: Are you here for someone?"

"I am here for you."

"Well, I *am* flattered. I wasn't aware you knew of my arrival. Boys, my luggage is on top, and be careful with it—yes, that way. At any rate, since I planned to look you up in Rome, Thermuthis told me to bring you her greetings. Oh, yes. Yes, contagion has reached Antinoopolis. That is partly the reason why I am here. We're all in God's hands, Commander."

Aelius nodded distractedly. "Are measures being taken against the disease?"

"*Measures* may be too strong a word, because there's nothing of-ficial about them. Anyone with an ounce of brain took to the high ground three weeks ago."

"I see. Do you know anything about the seamstress at the south gate?"

"The one who used to be Thermuthis's whore?" Theo inhaled the brackish air full force, blinking in the sun. "On the day I left she de-livered the two pairs of tunics I'd ordered from her. Nice, uh? This is one of them. She then closed shop, probably headed inland."

It was the best news Aelius could hope for at this time. When Theo added, smiling, "But you're not here to ask about a seamstress." Aelius only answered, "More in a moment. You heard about Soter's death."

The merchant's jovial face took on a look of compunction. "Poor fellow. Yes, I have. The hands of God, as I was saying. In fact, I know he would want me to, so—since I have come this far—I plan to look after his boy."

"Cleopatra Minor? He's off to Naples. And I don't think he's your type."

"Why not? How would *you* know?"

Aelius would add nothing. If Theo drew whatever conclusion from his silence, he chose to pass it under silence. After his luggage, sailors had begun lifting packets and jars of spices from the hold, so he stepped closer to keep a wary eye on their work. "Speaking of boys, have you found the grave yet?"

"No. And I don't expect to have much luck at it, since I lost the man who was to translate the text of Antinous's obelisk."

"Oh, right. Did you find out more about the unfortunate Egyptian tour?"

Aelius's mention of Marcius Turbo started off the spice merchant. "What stupid nonsense! None of it is true. Antinous would have never disregarded the emperor's orders, and this is pure fabrication. Turbo was hugely disappointed that his son Lucius was not the favorite he hoped him to become. Why do you think the other hangers-on had brought their young sons on the barge? Failure on their part to understand how things stood between the emperor and Antinous doomed their attempts from the start. Half of them had been Trajan's big boys, and as for Suetonius, he saw muck everywhere. Put no trust in these letters of disgruntled courtiers. Propriety was the rule of the game in that imperial household, as it is these days. Antinous would have never been referred to as *beloved* by the empress had his behavior been embarrassing or offensive to her through licentiousness or overt display of physical intimacy with her husband."

The outburst was unexpected, and Aelius found it curious. "But the texts—"

"The texts be damned. They all derive from a nontext, which is gossip. Boys, you just will *have* to be careful with my things! Look, Commander, do you really think Hadrian just 'happened' to meet Antinous during his travels?"

"Well, there's a story about the male brothel at—"

"Balderdash! The Boy had been selected since birth, the horoscopes pointed him out clearly; the Boy knew from the start what his role by the emperor was going to be, and how it would not be mere ill luck that should pluck him off at a young age, but the culmination of a long-determined set of events, in which he participated with full consciousness."

"Such as?"

"How should I know? Fate, the stars! The story is much more beautiful than what envious tattletales make of it, even if I may have been wrong about his long hair at the time of death. But—wait a minute—do you mean you have Antinous's obelisk, and his grave is not thereabouts?"

After two days of pondering it, Aelius was sick of revisiting the question. "It's a long story. The short answer is yes."

"At least I hope it's small."

"The obelisk? It's broken, but it does seem much smaller than those set up in racetracks. Why?"

"Well, funerary obelisks are small, usually two at the sides of a tomb's entrance, and inscribed on one side only with the name and titles of the defunct."

"I don't even want to start thinking about a twin of the obelisk I have. It's small and inscribed at least on three sides, the fourth being still buried."

"But is it readable?" Now and then reprehending the sailors, Theo watched them unload like a hawk.

"If it's simply a matter of reading it, I can do it myself."

Aelius was speechless. He remembered Theo being introduced to him as "widely read in the classics and in religion," but the unaffected offer caught him totally unawares. Even asking, "You can decipher the ancient characters?" struggled to come out of him.

"Serenus Dio and I were about the last of a breed, that way."

Theo's knowledge of ancient Egyptian writing was known in Antinoopolis, and perhaps outside of it. Any intention Aelius had had of protecting him from danger—out of humanity, gratitude for past advice, or just for Thermuthis's sake—paled before the renewed hope of reading Antinous's epitaph. "The obelisk carvings seem in good state," he hastened to say, "and the reason for my wanting to meet you here—let's keep it simple. Let's say that before I leave, I will tell you where to set up household ashore for the time being."

Theo threw up his hands in astonishment. "Whatever do you mean, Commander? I have lodgings already picked and paid for near the Iseum Campense!"

"That is precisely where you are not to go. Trust me, and if you don't, think about the way Soter ended, and see if business matters more than life. Yes, there *is* danger. I will have the obelisk cleaned and copies of the inscriptions delivered to you. Tell no one here or along the way where you'll be staying. Take the minimum necessary, no servants, and wait to hear from me."

Theo's happiness at having safely landed seemed gone from him altogether. He visibly lost interest in the beauty of the day, the sailors' tanned backs, and heard Aelius's instructions with a listless downturned face, like a big scolded pupil.

I suggested that he not come directly to the City. The place I chose is not far from the road, but secluded enough. It's the Isis's Knot at Puilia Saxa, just inland from Ostia. I'd rather if ben Matthias did not hear where Theo quarters, at least until the obelisk is translated."

Paratus said he fully approved. "If every time we do not meet for a few days you return with such momentous news, by all means let's meet only once a week." Despite the warmth of the officers' quarters, the veteran's window was closed, perhaps to keep him from growing nostalgic at the sound of army calls. "It is afternoon, I know, but— there being no time like the present—do we have enough daylight left to summon the crew?"

"Yes, it's becoming hazy with the heat, but there's plenty of time to get to the Varian Gardens."

By the third hour, with patrolmen from the II Cohort shielding their eyes in the sun to observe the proceedings, a crew of carpenters under Aelius's guardsmen engineers began operations outside the Varian racetrack. Blades of new grass, already sprouted amid the brambles burned weeks earlier, were chewed up by hoes and spades. In what little shade oleanders supplied, Aviola Paratus sat on a stone bench some ten paces off, while Aelius kept out of the way only enough not to impede digging. Soon, notwithstanding the soil around it had been hardened by the dry summer and fire, all three pieces of the shaft were exposed, and cleared of dirt. Lying on a wooden pallet, the obelisk appeared now nearly thirty feet long, of rose-colored granite, each face intricately carved from top to bottom on two parallel registers. Splashing from pails and wet-brushing followed, and then a couple of army stenographers began the laborious task of reproducing the pictographs.

This, Aelius thought, *or that set of signs must signify Antinous's name, or the emperor's; titles, kind words, the story of his life, prayers. If no location is given for the grave, it all stops here. If even the obelisk keeps the secret, the Boy is forever safe from men's hands. And Rome? What makes it safer, finding or not finding the grave? All I know is that I'm hungry to know.*

Gregarious swifts made noisy rounds overhead as shadows began to lengthen. The angle of light helped the copy work by making hollow lines and figures more evident, but at the broken edges pictographs remained difficult to identify, so it was tedious going. Sunset arrived before the stenographers were half-done.

Although Paratus offered to stay the night, Aelius would not hear of it. Everyone was dismissed from the place except two Cohort patrolmen and a picket of his own guards. During the day, the curious had been kept away by the police. Now the night patrol took their place, and there was no telling what the occasional traveler might think of armed men guarding an abandoned racetrack outside the walls.

As he'd done many times out on campaign, Aelius laid an army blanket on the ground and took his watch turn like the others. In-between, he sat up and counted the stars.

6 SEPTEMBER, FRIDAY (8 THOTH)
On Friday, between sunup and midday, the copying was completed. Only now, with the rolls of precious material in hand, did Aelius let go enough to inform Paratus he was going home to sleep for a few hours.

"Excited as I was, I haven't been able to close an eye all night. Do me the favor of staying here while they fill in the hole and haul the shaft closer to the wall," he said. "There are clouds gathering, and it might rain before long. Anyway, it is not advisable to try to patch the obelisk up without expert help, and before we know whether the text was copied correctly."

Bareheaded in the glare that precedes a summer storm, Paratus smiled his angerless smile. "I trust you call on a blind man's ability to command respect. Of course I will stay, and make sure none of us comes knocking on your bedroom door."

Theo had taken Aelius's advice to heart, and had scarcely moved from his destined room. At the soldier's arrival, though, he came downstairs and joined him in the reception hall, where a striped cat was the only other guest. A surprisingly fine rain had been falling for the past hour, so that the scent of revived herbs and flowers filled the garden window.

"There is much to read," the spice merchant commented after viewing the copy work. "But not all of it will be immediately relevant to your goals, if finding the grave is paramount. It was carved by non-Egyptians, too. So, give me an hour to search the inscription for geographic hints, and then come back to see what I found out."

Aelius had no intention of leaving the premises. He walked to the next room, where he paced for a while and then found the couch along the wall irresistible in the soothing patter of rain. He was soundly asleep with the cat in the hollow of his arm when Theo came to shake him some time later.

"Yes, yes. I have your translation," he said, chewing on a sprig of fresh mint. "There's also one of your strapping guardsmen to see you. Do they ever take their eyes off you?"

Alone, Aelius had been many times, despite the close quarters of a soldier's life. He'd always made sure there was a chance for him to walk away from others, and spend what time was possible on his own. To gather his thoughts, or—as he said—to *air his own differences*. It had helped him during the Armenian campaign, even though leaving the group increased risk, in order to think things over and make decisions. It had served him well often, being alone.

This afternoon, heading out into the countryside after leaving Theo, he had the sensation of being detached from everyone, adrift and without the practical means of reaching out for support. The structure he'd been building during the past weeks (no, for the past several months, since he'd set foot in cruel Egypt again), had collapsed under him not piecemeal but all at once, and with no hope of being caught by a safety net below. His *mistake,* like an unbearable light let into a room believed orderly, showed not only dust here and there, or small imperfections: The room itself had caved in, and nothing inside seemed at the moment salvageable.

It may be significant, too, that it should all hit him at a crossroads, a haunted place if ever there was one. His own predicament mirrored that unmarked intersection, creating four different directions, each one as likely or unlikely as the next. In his outer reality, he faced one of those lesser roads, well-built but not paved, of white dirt beaten down so thoroughly as to resemble cement. Only rain or a windstorm would prove it not to be such, and the washed sky gaped pitilessly clear just now. Distant graves marked the road farther ahead; it led to some village no doubt, where people he'd never met or would never meet spent their entire lives, in ignorance of what his error meant, hence caring nothing about it. Or him.

Behind, the same road—but it was not the same, as the intersection ended it and made it new. Other graves, farms, and farther back the sprawl of estates and houses proliferating like a live belt outside Rome's walls. Crowded Rome itself was for him the symbol of his loneliness.

To the sides, well, he could hardly bring himself to pay mind. Toward the sea, invisible but for the deeper sky hung above it, a low growth of trees and shrubs, a wayside shrine overgrown until it lost its shape, like a hairy wart on the land. In the direction of the mountains, fingers of ancient lava flows extended like talons, made friendlier by the vineyards dressing them. People living that way, too, each in his place and with his hard or lazy day half-behind him already.

Aelius Spartianus, who was so careful with his notes and took pride in his memory, had mistaken things and men completely. It was as if he'd unglued himself from the world, from history. Had he not felt so bitterly rooted to where he stood, he'd say it would feel like falling, falling. For an instant he understood Antinous in the act of leaving the edge of the imperial barge, before striking the treacherous water below. Vaguely sensing the mortal peril ahead, but already completely avulsed from the living. *You must do something,* his mind was telling him. *Quickly, something.* But he stood there with his useless notes and useless memory, between the edge and nothingness, precisely as Antinous had, who however, unlike him, *had understood.*

A t their evening meeting, perceiving Aelius's frame of mind, Paratus showed a friend's concern. What he could not see—the knitting of one's brow, an anxious expression—he surely detected from quick breathing, or the small rustle of nervous motions, cloth on leather or cloth on cloth. "Is anything amiss?" he asked.

"No."

Aelius couldn't say how things stood. Not yet. Until today both of them had been careful to function, each in his blindness. His own lack of sight had come to an end, and now he envied Paratus's dark world of remembered light.

"All I can tell you is that we have this much: a fragmentary sentence."

"Favorable or unfavorable?"

"Judge for yourself. '. . . Antinous the Justified, who is here, and here rests *within the garden bounds of the great lord of Rome.*' And nowhere does it say that the monument actually stood in the City."

"So. The burial could be anywhere."

Aelius read disappointment on Paratus's seamed face, as if his sedateness had received an unexpected blow he was at this time incapable or unwilling to accept. "Unless we read 'garden bounds' as a specific reference to the villa at Tibur. I'm sure I don't know where else to look for it in that jumble of buildings."

"Is it the end of the road, then? Do you *give up?*"

Aelius breathed in. On the threshold of his colleague's room, he faced gloom unrelieved by the window, through which only the mortified grayness of evening filtered. Lamps were scarcely needed in a blind man's space, but that murkiness was physically intolerable for him just now. He said something to the effect of having to go, and turned on his heel.

"Do you give up, Aelius Spartianus?" Paratus's voice followed him as he walked down the vaulted corridor of the barracks. "You'll have to stick by your decision, if you do."

Aelius gave himself time to reach the top of the stairs leading to the vestibule before answering.

"Yes. I give up." And his half-shouted words slapped the hallway like an order to himself.

N otes by Aelius Spartianus:

*Night, they say, brings counsel. But a night marked by anger
may bring more than that. I returned to my flat not even trying to keep my emotions at bay. Theo's written translation of
the funerary text kept rolling in my mind, squeezed of all possible meaning. I could neither eat nor go to bed, so I went outside on the balcony and sat there. I told myself that, having
gathered more than enough information to write the imperial
biography, I could very well list all possible causes of the Boy's
death, all burials and cenotaphs known and fabled. Better historians than I have been more vague on details than that. I
couldn't accept having failed at the other search, but uncover-
ing conspiracy (there is one) and murder (it has everything to
do with it) are not the historian's task. I told myself, too, that
I'm just a soldier who has bitten more than he can chew, and
not for the first time.*

*But I kept digging into my memory like a dog, lifting dirt,
coming up over and again with Theo's written words. How he
handed me the scrap of papyrus, how he accompanied me to
the door chewing on mint, how he stood admiring my young
guardsman. Then I remembered that between this moment
and the moment I took my man aside to hear his report, Theo
added a few more words. Namely: the Boy's obelisk was a very
late work in terms of Egyptian history; it had been carved in
Italy besides; the sign for "lord" was in later tradition identical
to the pictograph for "lady," and it might just as well mean*
one or the other.

*Aelius Spartianus, how can you have taken so many wrong
turns and made so many mistakes?*

*Fate itself held in front of your face the answer, by pushing
your ship north of the City, and forcing you to approach Rome*

from the Aurelian Way. The first sight you beheld looking down from the hill the evening of your arrival was the one you should have at once recognized! Not the garden bounds of the great lord, but of the great *lady* of Rome. *None but the gardens by the Vatican Field, named for the imperial ladies: specifically, the Gardens of Empress Domitia, whose very name contains the root of dominion!*

That area by the river, now a public park where the rich and poor—even the Christian elder called Peter—were buried, welcomed me to Rome, and I ignored the clues. One of its graves is what I began searching months and months ago. It all makes sense now: The verses Cleopatra saw in the male brothel, saying that Antinous is naught but shadow and dust / close by, where Hadrian took his flight from mortality/riding in Helios's chariot. *Why didn't I think of it? Hadrian's majestic tomb in the Vatican, in the Gardens of Empress Domitia, the bronze chariot of Sun-Helios crowning its roof, signify the emperor's name and role. The chariot at the top of the mausoleum indicates that flight into eternity, and isn't the whole Vatican area called 'Egypt'? Maybe that's what the guardian at Two Laurels meant, when he made the same objection. Antinous's grave—the* memoria Antinoi—*if it still stands, stands near Hadrian's tomb. And there's no stopping me from leaving the house at this time to make sure.*

7 SEPTEMBER, THURSDAY (9 THOTH)

The city prefect had pillow marks on his face, and mumbled, half-dressed from his bedroom's door, "This had better be of great importance, Commander Spartianus," which was less overt than the "Who in fucking hell is asking for me at this hour?" he'd been shouting a moment earlier to his secretary.

Having heard Aelius's request, he seemed briefly fought between apoplexy and a yawn, but all he actually added was, "Do what you want—you do anyway. I'm going back to bed."

Outside the City gate, the ramp of Hadrian's bridge gleamed over the musty depth of the riverbed. A gurgle of water binding the piers below, and the remote call of nightingales from the imperial gardens—a complex series of trills and chirps, prolonged and repeated—were the sounds that came to Aelius's ears once he and a few guardsmen stopped at the head of the bridge. At the opposite end, in the late night air a luminescence like corposant glared from the vast mausoleum at the foot of the bridge, and similarly white stood the two nameless tombs near it, seen so many times: the burial tower, a miniature copy of the imperial grave, and the marble pyramid at the crossroads by Nero's decaying bridge. It came down to deciding which one would be opened first, and Aelius chose the pyramid only on the strength of its perfect alignment with the Via Cornelia, built by Hadrian to connect his mausoleum to the Vatican Field. On such a clear night, an ideal line could be drawn from the pyramid's tip, nearly one hundred feet high, to the gilded chariot, higher yet, and as if lost against the stars.

No doors opened on the pyramid's sides, but midway up its south face, overlooking the road, what seemed like a deep window had probably served the crew to exit after sealing the ground entrance. A ladder was leaned against the marble wall so that a carpenter could climb. Soon he was calling down that it was actually a square door, the size of one of the outside marble blocks, closed by a bronze shutter. More than half an hour elapsed before the lock could be forced, at which time Aelius impatiently took the man's place atop the ladder. The flame of his tin lantern held to the hole trembled and was nearly snuffed out by the gush of dank cold air that flowed from within. Leaning in, Aelius saw a shaft inclining downward, apparently toward the center of the pyramid, barely wide enough for a man to squeeze through—unless of course it narrowed even more at the lower end. Sliding in head first might mean becoming lodged into a deadly funnel, or breaking one's skull against whatever floor (at what depth?) might lie within. With a rope tied to his waist and lantern extinguished, Aelius opted for lowering himself down feet first, to leave his arms free in case others should pull him out.

The shaft angled sharply. Despite the fact that, once past the marble sill, the building's cement core slightly retarded his fall, he slipped down faster than planned. The hole did narrow toward the center of the pyramid, too, and became distinctly uncomfortable, but Aelius was never restricted enough to stop sliding, and in the end he fell into a void mercifully short, onto a stone floor that did nothing to absorb the shock. Due to the angle of the shaft, darkness was unrelieved and perfect. Unhurt, Aelius stood, groping for flint in the pouch at his belt. The damp odor that had first met his nostrils must derive from water seepage through the outside marble lining, because down here—and Aelius assumed he was in the burial chamber—there was cool dryness, and if anything, a faint, old scent of balm and perfume.

After lighting the lantern again, he did in fact recognize a burial chamber, about twenty by fifteen feet across, barrel-vaulted. Two of its walls spangled with brightly painted Egyptian themes, while the other two stood blank but for the red tracing of unfinished frescoes, and the faint outline of the sealed doorway. In the middle of the floor, laid directly on the pavement without a stone coffin, was a gilded wood or cartonnage sarcophagus roughly shaped like a human body, not unlike the one Aelius had seen in Antinous's temple. Absence of grave goods testified the haste of the translation, perhaps the furtive nature of it, with an old man sick unto death witnessing the last act of mercy. The coffin's brown reddish ground danced under the flickering light. Here were the gold leaf images of dog-headed Anubis holding a vessel over a corpse, of Ma'at lifting in her hand the feather of justice and cosmic order, and the sign of Horus-on-the-Horizon; above and below, resplendent rows of lotus and lilies, and on the chest a narrow band with Greek gilded characters that read the farewell words, *Antinoe, eupsychi.*

Aelius had to wait until his breathing slowed down enough for him to continue his work. Ignoring the muffled calls from above, asking if all was well, he drew near the sarcophagus's head, where a window in the lid revealed the dead man's wooden portrait. Of exquisite making, it showed a young man of about twenty, with a gold-leaf crown in his hair. A face freshly shaven, paler where the beard had been sheared off, and lovely in a manly way; gray-eyed and tranquil, which no astonishment or pain seemed ever to have marred, a serious and thoughtful face that—Aelius, deeply moved, wanted to believe—had waited until now to exchange glances with him.

How sacrilegious any of this might be, or contrary to the deified Hadrian's will, he had no time to consider now. His hands fumbled with the seals of the lid, which in spite of his emotion came open easily enough. Beneath it, an intricate crisscrossed binding of bright red linen strips, purple-dyed, formed a complex multilayered pattern that resembled coffering, each hollow square dotted with a gold button at the center. At the feet of the mummy, for a moment so brief that later Aelius doubted having seen it at all, lay a fresh garland of roses and lotus buds, tightly bound, scented, which withered and turned black at once. On the body's chest, set at an angle, rested a flattish wood cylinder such as letters and documents are entrusted to.

The muffled calls from above had ceased. Silence returned to this space sealed and suspended above the ground, save for a low rustle as of wind seeking the shaft and burrowing down its length. Kneeling against one of the blank walls with his lantern on the floor, Aelius opened the cylinder and took the first of two rolled-up documents out of it.

There flowed the graceful letters, so like those he had with similar thrill read in Egypt, but distorted by age or infirmity, or great physical pain.

> I, Publius Aelius Hadrianus, feeling close to death and wishing to ensure our Antinous's presence close to my tomb, have hurriedly and in secret laid him in this place without the funerary gifts I planned for him to

have. In the document attached to this, I commit to
eternity how by his act he saved Caesar's life and Rome,
he who seemed mildness itself and at no time gave me
reason for reproach. He, who is ours and not mine
alone, as he belongs to the City. In the same document,
I also trace for posterity the sequel of events caused by
the occult, age-old enemy of Rome I have come to call
with the collective name of Water Thief. Such among
the Greeks is the term that indicates a water clock, hence
Time itself, devourer of all the empires of the earth . . .

Words crowded and faltered before Aelius's eyes. The *Water Thief,*
hidden in plain sight through memory, ritual, like the villa's plan, like
this most visible and nameless of sepulchers—a hint from the start of
his investigation, to which he'd been both blind and deaf. Even now
his ears, at first as if stopped by the utter silence around him, perceived that rustle as of coming wind again, but paid no attention.

. . . For more than two hundred years the conspiracy has
attempted against the expansion and well-being of the
greatest empire man has known. Its aims, decked in
anti-Roman ideology but in fact dictated by the most
ravenous greed, united a multiform and divided lot of
haters of the state. Beheading the empire, toppling the
tower of its might, bringing down the magnificence of
its structure . . .

The cloth suddenly gagging his mouth had the strength of a vise.
Right off, even before astonishment, an animal reaction hunched
him forward. Pulled back hard in a stranglehold, a knee rammed on
his spine, Aelius fully expected his neck to be broken by a twist, or a
blade to come gouging his throat, but the cloth kept cramming,
steadily cutting his breath. The lantern overturned or was kicked,
flickered out, and darkness like a taste of death ate the room around

him. He tried to heave off the attacker and the pressure around his neck grew so that he blacked out. Force left him like water. Aelius vaguely felt himself collapsing on his side, and as if another were struggling like a bound calf in his place, heart, lungs on fire. The attacker's crushing weight bore down on him, and Aelius came to only enough to know he was flat on his back being smothered, head forced against the floor. Then consciousness sank again. *Water, water, I'm under water, like in the river with the mud and herons, like my drowned dog, like everyone who drowned and drowned without hope. I'll let the bound calf labor and fight, buckle while I go down. There's sand at the bottom.* At the bottom, however, Aelius would not go down. Not after all this, not now—not yet! A rush of pain spewed him up into awareness that he was alive, straining free for a moment, thrashing about and choking again, furious at the proximity of his own death. Air jetted into his lungs only enough for him to suck it up with a gasp. *I'm sinking, I'm sinking. If I weren't, I'd reach for the knife in my boot, and strike with it as hard as I can.* The muscle spasm in reaching for the knife made him cry out. Unless water had long ago closed over him, and he was already dead.

A burnished edge looked like a wound in the eastern sky upriver, where trees from the imperial gardens crowded the banks at the bend. Seeing ben Matthias's face upon emerging from the shaft was less surprising to him than Aelius expected. "I should have known it was you," he said, breathing hard. Perched on the ladder, the Jew shrugged, extending his hand to help him crawl out. Below, his guardsmen's anxious faces looked pale while they slackened the rope, and a second ladder was leaned against the pyramid for Aelius to climb down.

"It's amazing what nose I have for knowing when a Roman gets himself in trouble," ben Matthias sneered. "I was just passing by, back from my real estate, and couldn't resist the commotion. Is he dead?"

"No, but I gave him a good stab, and he's hog-tied down there."

Ashamed of seeing the sun rise from a doubly profaned monument, Aelius was anxious to get down, and touch the earth.

"Not that the dark should make a difference to a blind man," commented ben Matthias.

Once at the foot of the pyramid, Aelius asked for a canteen, drank from it, and used the rest of the vinegary water to wash his face. He should ache after the struggle, but did not; the exhilaration of having succeeded wearied him and made him numb. It took him this long to wonder what ben Matthias, arms crossed with his back to Hadrian's monument, might be doing here.

Amused, the Jew prevented the question. "I really was passing through the Vatican Field, and the only reasons your pork-fed guards let me get close were the ladder and coils of rope my mule was carrying. When I found out it was you inside the grave, I thought it too hilarious. My rope, I said, my ladder—I get to lead the pulling. None of my business, but how did things sour between you and Paratus?"

Aelius watched two of his men going up the ladder, to carry out the veteran's arrest and the laborious feat of hauling him out afterward. He said, "You're right."

"About what?"

"It's none of your business."

Before noon, a Praetorian unit was dispatched to The Glory of Our Lord Aurelian's, where it took into custody Paratus's son and his servants. Orders were issued that the same be done with the veteran's family at Minturnae. With Rome's gates closed to keep accomplices from escaping, and interrogations of suspects underway at the city prefect's, there was really no one Aelius wanted to speak to but the man who had tried to kill him.

Behind bars in the brig of the Special Agent Barracks, Paratus sat on a bench. He showed no pain for the knife wound under the bandage on his side. Even his lack of anger abided, and the curl in the lips that seemed about to smile was ironic and sensitive. "So. The sweet rustle and smell of army leather. I expected you couldn't resist coming here, Aelius Spartianus."

"Yes, I imagined you would."

Without as much as moving from his position, legs crossed and back to the wall, Paratus let the smile dance on his mouth. "We're even, then."

"Not exactly. I won."

"Ah, that's where you're mistaken. *Not quite.* If you hope to find out anything from me, you have committed your biggest error to date."

What little light filtered down from the slit windows of the brig gave no sign of the brilliant afternoon outside. *There's so much more to this, too,* Aelius thought. Having read what Hadrian had entrusted to the Boy's burial, he found it hard to brag. "You won't talk, but yours will."

"Mine? They know *nothing.*" In his composure, Paratus did not give away whether he felt the other's insecurity. "How can you think such an organization functions? No cell, no individual knows more than he needs to act when commanded, and only when commanded. You'll find out nothing, and that is more than consolation enough for me."

The state flounders in dimness, it always did. Clumsy and arrogant, it mistakes the slits in the wall for the fiery reality outside. It does not even know its collective name, thinks all enemies and all incidents single and unrelated. Aelius himself saw little more than the fissure, and was dazed by it. Paratus read his mind. "The dark grows on you after a while." He smirked. "Have you ever thought that ignorance is preferable to terror? Be content with your little victory, Aelius Spartianus, and don't presume to ask me anything."

"I won't. But at least your personal reasons you gave me yourself."

"Did I?"

" 'There are better uses in the world for soldiers who can think,' you said. And, 'Power rather than money.' For a pensioned-off veteran too brilliant for his lot, the opportunity to serve in a big way, no matter whom he serves. Smile all you want, Paratus. Maneuvering, working for your private goals, seeking personal power—history is full of men like you, too cynical for idealism, *but on the market*. It's true, I have no idea of who owns you, outside or inside Rome: We have a choice of enemies. Always had. That you betrayed yourself in the end makes me hope for the future."

Paratus's quiescence had not appreciably changed, although there were small signs of muscular tension that even in this half-light alerted Aelius of the effort it cost him. "Don't forget I nearly killed you, so my hand must have shown less than you say, but you're bursting to tell, I'm sure."

A prison guard peeped in from the top of the stairs. "As soon as you're done, Commander—"

"I'm not done."

Paratus's detachment seemed more and more painted on his face, by long exercise in hiding his true self. "Well, then—let's hear it. Let's hear if your clues stand up to critique."

How reductive it seemed to speak of clues. Aelius took his time, thinking of the oracle he'd scoffed at, while it told the truth—that Antinous had died even as Serenus Dio had; of the Sicilian tales and the old tract, revealing that the Boy had met his end like Patroclus, never taken seriously by him. Paratus spoke of clues, but everything in this story was as firmly set beforehand as Ma'at's own inscrutable judgment, light and terrible like a feather.

"Clues?" he said in the end, "here they are. My first doubt arose when you and I first passed the V Cohort's gate on the way to this barracks. Along the road, you'd asked to stop by this and that landmark, but did not inquire about your beloved old headquarters. It made me think that perhaps—contrary to what you said—you'd recently been in the neighborhood, and I wondered why you lied."

"Weak. Not a clue. Nostalgia is not so omnivorous."

"Especially when it's not justified." In his uneasiness, Aelius had difficulty standing in one place, and began pacing slowly the floor facing the unoccupied cells. "True, it seemed a small, worthless doubt at the time. Then there was the curious 'slippage' of the seal on the

letter from court that recommended you to me—surely you had it
intercepted, read, approved in its contents, and resealed. Also, when
you gave me the list of aristocrats who possessed important archives,
they were all coincidentally out of town. It's summer, I thought, but
Lady Repentina's name, which should have been first on the list, was
absent. For good reason, too, because—and she'd have a stroke if she
knew—the late consul's ancestor Marcius Turbo was in on the conspiracy. Suetonius might have known, or not. Turbo's name is on a
list we found in one of your hiding places. A friend of the emperor,
and a conspirator! He was fortunate the deified Hadrian discovered
it too late to issue orders against him."

Paratus sneered, a mean expression that distorted his fine face.
"Circumstantial evidence, Spartianus. Seals slip, and the wealthy go
on vacation."

From every slit window, a short ribbon of sunlight parted the
dark floor ahead of him. Aelius took his time between bright spots. "I
also wager it was you who contrived the system of semaphores to be
informed of my coming even before I reached Rome."

"But you can't prove it. Ha! You can prove none of it."

"I have not finished. There's also the coincidence of your departure from Egypt after Dio's and his freedman's deaths, and the fact
that in your absence no murders or fires took place in that circle.
However, they began in Italy shortly after your arrival. You must have
raced quickly from Antium to Rome, to direct Soter's assassination as
only one who'd served in the night patrol and knew about arson
could. Then back to the XII mile of the Via Labicana, where you
made me find you under the grapevine by your tavern." Halting in
the strip of light cast by the window above him, Aelius let brightness
beguile him. "I admit, the self-inflicted damage to the vineyard was
genial, down to the cutting of an accomplice's finger. The attack
against me, instead, I'm not sure whether it meant to kill—you don't
seem to fail when you set your mind to it. Since you'd probably understood I would never share the imperial letter, you had to follow
me until I discovered the *other* document, and even help me do it! Of

course, there's Onofrius's opportune death, on the eve of translating the obelisk."

From his place in the glare, the bars dividing Aelius from the prisoner seemed reddish and hazy when Paratus's contemptuous voice came from the shade. "Average detective work."

"Except that I'm an amateur." Tempted to remain in the light, Aelius left it instead, and returned to face Paratus's cell. "By this time, it was my turn to guide the events. So I purposely gave you Isis's Knot as Theo's address, although I'd sent him elsewhere. Thinking me asleep at home, you stayed to supervise the removal of the obelisk while I actually brought the Egyptian text to him. It was there that one of my guardsmen watching the Knot reported how ruffians had come looking for the spice merchant at the tavern. Only you knew that information, so only your men could have gone there."

"Marginally clever."

"I'll take it as a compliment. Now, you did one of two things: Either you assumed Theo didn't listen to me and boarded at another place, or you realized I was on to you. In both cases you had to keep playing the game, because it was highly probable I'd get to the grave now. Which I did. Had I not been in such a beastly hurry to do it, I'd have instructed my bodyguard not to let you through, should you show up. As it was, they had no reason to suspect you, as we'd worked together until then. That was my mistake. When I didn't answer the guardsmen's calls from above, you had the perfect excuse to be lowered into the shaft. After all, night and darkness made no difference to you, and so on. Had you succeeded in smothering me, you could say I'd taken ill with the stifling air of the tomb, or broken my neck, or God knows what."

"But I disappointed you, and bitterly, too."

"That, you did." Aelius nodded to the prison guard, who had never moved from his place at the top of the stairs. "I'm only wondering if it was you who had Tralles killed."

Paratus laughed, and there could not be a more cruel sound than laughter without any joy, or amusement. "Why should I? The idiot was useful to us. You see, Aelius Spartianus—*Caesar's friend*—the advantage is in bringing the enemy to the point of fearing everyone, always, never knowing whom to trust. It was I who first spoke to you of Rome's enemies outside the frontiers. I simply did not add one detail: They are inside already. After a while, one needn't do much else before the tower comes toppling down."

From the letter by the deified Hadrian, contained in Antinous's burial, continued:

> . . . Beheading the empire, bringing down the magnificence of its structure, has been their aim ever since the Caesars's rule began. Wars were fought by princes before me without an understanding of how peoples and cities opposed to us were nothing but pawns of another power, and that not kings or lords, but fanatics maneuvered by mercantile ruthlessness hid behind raids and murderous actions so widespread and diverse as to conceal their common matrix.
>
> I learned to beware of those who came back from fighting abroad, whether it be the countries of Egypt, Parthia, Persia, or Armenia, especially if held prisoners for a time. This is because often, conquered by torture or blandishments, they became minions of the great enemy. Not trusting our own veterans! It seems like a heresy, but, as the attached document details, their armed hand occasionally penetrated Caesar's chamber itself, felling whenever it could those princes who would expand or safeguard Rome. It is fitting that as of this writing, thanks to political purges and secret military measures I was compelled to undertake during my reign, the peril seems abated. Historians will wonder at the cruelty of my late years, but I know all too well what actions are required of me in order to safeguard the state. Thus even these accounts are committed to the grave, as I prefer nothing to be made public, that may possibly incite others against Rome.

It was on the ill-fated Egyptian voyage that conspiracy came as close as the imperial barge on which we traveled. It sickens me unto death to write the names of Septicius Clarus, of Gentianus—who served in the Parthian war and was consul under me—of Mettius Modestus and even Marcius Turbo, all men I would discover too late to have directly or indirectly fed the beast. Another prince was voted to destruction, and the conspirators would have succeeded had not our Antinous placed himself between his friend and death. Now he abides with the gods, and forever grieving, I pray that his sacrifice may not have been in vain.

Newly arrived with the body of the beloved from my Tiburtine villa—where the month of October remains fixed in every building as in the very stars—I write this in Rome as I ready to leave for Baiae, from which I despair to return. The ninth day of May, the feast of Lemuria, dedicated to those who died before their time, in the twenty-second sad year of my reign.

PART III

Final Report

TWELFTH CHAPTER

Ben Matthias sailed on the same ship Aelius took to leave Italy. The *Felicitas Annonae,* under its skipper and Expositus as master of the ship, was heading back to Alexandria with a load of German glassware destined to Sicily, and a ballast of Campanian lentils.

"Whatever is going on," he said joining Aelius on deck, "there's a rash of arrests throughout Italy, have you heard?"

They were already in sight of the island's east coast, where the *Felicitas* would stop three full days. Aelius glanced over at the Jew without replying. He'd in fact striven to avoid him, but ben Matthias was not one to be discouraged. "I'm only telling you, Commander, so that you don't think I'm following you. I'd have stopped longer in Rome, but wholesale arrests always made Jews uncomfortable. Excellent arrests: aristocrats, merchants, high-ranking officers. It surprises me how many of them are confessing, but I know Roman methods of interrogation well enough. Even Aviola Paratus's sons are talking. The gossip is that authorities are holding Paratus himself for more than trying to kill you—and anyway I can't understand his motive, unless he was behind the murders in Egypt, too."

Aelius lowered his eyes to the green froth lacing the side of the ship, where twigs and leaves from the shore were churned by a braid of deep water. Carrying imperial orders for the Province's magistrates to initiate trials and arrests, he knew all too well what work expected him in Egypt. "Do not forget you recommended him to me when I asked you. 'Quiet man, pays his bills'—"

"Is it my fault if everyone spoke well of him? And to think that I gave you a hand when bandits surprised you south of Herakleopolis, even though you'd turned down my company." Aelius's expression must have spoken for him, because ben Matthias frowned in mock outrage. "You thought it was *my* men who assaulted you! Didn't I tell you that if I wanted to brain you, I'd do it looking you in the eye?"

Then it was Paratus's men who attacked us on the way to Alexandria, and nearly did me in along the Nile. What else, who else is involved in this? Snapping sounds came from above, where the wind-filled mainsail rode the Etesian gale. Toward the open sea, fish jumped in gleeful blue schools, like blades merging and descending on shimmering cloth. Aelius kept his eyes on the merry fish, breathing in the pungent, brackish air. "Baruch, do you remember when we met by the Cadastre, and out of nowhere—just as I was leaving—you mentioned the Jewish revolt?"

"I often mention Jewish revolts."

"You said that time after time, your leaders were approached by this or that conspirator asking to join forces, but always refused."

"Not out of virtue, be sure. Only because our fight must be our own. Had you asked, I could have told you some time back. Parthians, Armenian generals, even the occasional Roman grabby politician came knocking through the centuries. Why, does it make a difference? I don't see what it has to do with Paratus." Ben Matthias turned his back to the bulwarks, and looked up at the great horn of plenty on the red-trimmed canvas. "You know how I feel about Rome and Romans, but I bet money you're thinking that execution is too good for him."

"He's a veteran, and he'll get it. A clean one, too."

At Catania some of the passengers disembarked for good. Ben

Matthias, who had business at the local synagogue, was among those who would later return on board. Seeing Aelius leave the pier on horseback, he called after him, "Going a distance, are you? If you miss the boat when we set sail again, may I have your berth?"

CATANIA, SICILY, 22 SEPTEMBER, FRIDAY (24 THOTH)
Whether ben Matthias had been prophetic, on the third day, under Expositus's controlling eye, all travelers and merchandise meant for Egypt were accounted for, except for Aelius Spartianus. True to his motto of waiting for no man, the master of the ship punctually ordered the gangplank withdrawn, and already the *Felicitas*'s anchor was aweigh when the harbor police stepped in, halting the maneuver, on account of "Caesar's envoy being about to arrive from the military road." Expositus grew purple with the need to curse, but it'd never do on board and about to set sail again. So he limited himself to pacing the deck with hands twined behind his back, scowling landward.

Aelius's arrival necessitated the lowering of the gangplank again, an operation that the master of the ship—the taciturn Expositus—directed in reproachful silence.

Ben Matthias watched horse, soldier, and hound come on board. "Well, for crying out loud," he commented. "You don't mean to tell me you went all the way inland to find that horror!"

Aelius shrugged. "No. I *bought* it on my way up from Egypt."

"It has to be the ugliest creature that ever trod the earth."

"The name is Sirius. And it bit me before I bought it, too."

"I should have recognized your hand in the rescript forbidding possession and sale of dogs for the arena!" Ben Matthias shooed the hound from his bare legs, stomping on deck. "You annoyed several breeders in the Heptanomia, Commander."

"Not nearly as much as *one* breeder on the Via Labicana. Anyhow, laws are made at court—they can take it up with the imperial counsels."

Final Report to the emperor by Aelius Spartianus, in Five Parts:

1. The time has finally come, Domine, to sum up what I was privileged to discover regarding the vast conspiracy that ever since the days of Julius Caesar has lain in wait to threaten the Roman state. My information derives from the deified Hadrian's account, found in the blessed Antinous's tomb, and from interrogations and searches in Rome and elsewhere.

It begins in Egypt over three centuries ago, as a form of resistance against Rome's intervention, when Queen Cleopatra decides to ally herself with the deified Julius; indeed, her own demise, as that of the dictator himself, is in part made possible by the conspiracy. It is not political at first, or not strictly so. Vital commercial interests dominate at the start, especially as regards the spice trade, but also that of copper, gold, tin, and what other resources make the wealth of a nation. The conspiracy's goal, naturally, is to snatch control over those lucrative traffics from the legitimate authority of Rome. It is a high stake that will represent a risky game one generation after the other, causing a superficially invisible conflict where no quarter is given, between the magnates of commerce—foreign and Roman—and legal power. The means used are typical of all conspiracies: the organization in secret cells, infiltration, corruption of officials, and homicide. A mortal game that has not come to an end yet, because its final prize is never really achieved: control over commerce above all laws, all rules, all limits fixed in the common interest of the people. But the process aspires to even more—absolute power, global hegemony over men, wealth, and destinies.

Now, Domine, allow me to return to my account, there where I left it: spices and precious metals. As I believe, merchants from nations long involved in the exchange of those necessary goods fear Rome's growing power in the Mediterranean and Asia. Soon they see that—owing to Julius's rise to domination—more and more the City is likely to be governed by one man. Those who conjure against the dictator from within Rome are not without friends among these merchants: Crassus's wealth, and his own death in Parthia derive from his early success and later failure in dealing with them. Caesar's closeness to Egypt threatens the supremacy of the group. Stirring up those aristocrats who wish to keep power in their hands with the excuse of saving the republic is a means to an end: Caesar's elimination. After the Ides of March, the enemies of Rome draw a sigh of relief, seeing in the ensuing confusion the possible signs of political (hence economic) disintegration. But Marc Anthony soon strikes a new and more dangerous alliance with Cleopatra, and he, too, poses a risk, until the glorious victory of Augustus Caesar over him restores the state.

During his well-advised reign, the conspiracy seems dormant, but it is not so. In fact, one after the other, all heirs to the throne fall away, sudden fevers and accidents cutting their lives short. Agrippa, too, the possible strongman to follow Augustus, never returns from his last campaign. Afterward, the enemies' hand is recognizable in plots and assassinations of strong rulers who threaten their interests by military expansion or alliances. Among the noble victims are to be numbered the emperors Claudius and Titus. Nearly every excellent cadaver in Rome—so states Hadrian's letter—was a result of the conspirators' plan. To think that historians wondered why the Caesars died childless, and why so many of them perished in their prime! After the Flavian dynasty dies off, Rome is weakened. Coincidentally, once more the conspiracy appears to wane, but it is only gone underground, accruing small successes any time the Roman state's reach on the South and the East frontiers seems to waver.

Antinoopolis, Heptanomia Province, Egypt, 8 Phaophi,
(7 October, Nones, Saturday)

Aelius's rented quarters by the mall were ready for his arrival in Antinoopolis. Everyone but three of his guardsmen having preceded him,
all flats in the building had been requisitioned for security reasons, and
stalls across the road cleared to keep an open view of the marketplace.

Following the Nile southward had been for Aelius an exercise in
recent memory. Yet every time the flood receded, changes came to the
banks: islets sank or came to the surface, meanders once choked with
papyrus and marsh plants were swept clean, villages dissolved in water or survived, filthy and stuck in the mud. Deep odor of decay rose
from the wide fertilized band of the riverside, where one advanced
over planks or took long detours around it. Nearly back in its bed, the
Nile—wide as a lake until the third week of September—had filled
dikes and canals, which corvees painstakingly walked and repaired. It
was probably these conscripted masses that carried disease from one
region to the other, and farmers like Anubina's husband were the
most exposed to infection.

This was not exactly coming home, yet stepping into his room
and seeing a small, transparent scorpion scuttle under the bed made
him feel that for every change, some things stayed the same. Aelius
held back Sirius, knelt to pick the insect up with a cloth, and without
harming it, put it outside.

In the afternoon, what amazed him was finding the consumptive
judge from Turris Parva not only alive, but ensconced in the office of
the Heptanomia *epistrategos* Rabirius Saxa.

"*Legatos* Spartianus," he greeted him, "it's an honor *and* a pleasure! Oh, I am better. It's an odd thing, but whenever there's an epidemic I seem to get better. The trials against the Christians have been
put on hold, I'm sure you have heard, both within the army and
among civilians." With a bow of his head he received the sealed
orders. "We now have bigger fish to spear. They say Parthia is behind
it, but who knows. Parthia can't be behind everything that happens
to the empire."

"Did you receive the list from Alexandria?"

"Oh, yes. I know you had a hand in filling it out, congratulations, really. Names you'd never suspect: city administrators, army officers, businessmen. That Aviola Paratus should be a conspirator, *legatos*—scandal! Scandal, I say. One doesn't know whom to trust anymore, if veterans prove unfaithful. It's a bonafide purge. Treason, of course. All accused of treason. We'll get many of them—executed, I mean. Others will escape through the dragnet, because they are too connected to trade, foreign money, and mostly because we don't know exactly how they fit within the structure." When Aelius showed the names of guests at Dio's party, handed him by Harpocratio during his last permanence, the judge hunched his shoulders with glee. "One of them is already in jail!"

Aelius felt less sanguine. That some of Paratus's informants had spoken, there was no denying. Collaborators had been named. Documents had turned out at the veteran's Minturnae house and in the trade exchange at Antium, but it all remained elusive. Contacts among members, their charges—it seemed largely a matter of foreign intrusion in decision-making, a laborious insectlike work of undermining by appointing some magistrates, removing others, buying off others yet. Occasionally the conspiracy resorted to murder, most of the murders having been regicides. Whatever the judge said about the scandal of known names, no foreign potentates or leaders had emerged from the investigation, and these were the ones to go after. Mercifully, it would not be his task.

"Maximian Caesar's party at Court sees the Christians' hand in it," the judge was saying, staring at him bright-eyed with interest. "What do you think?"

Aelius shook his head. "It's difficult to tell how much religion has to do with it, and how much power-hungry churchmen might be pursuing their own interests through a secret society's structure." "They say that even now two generals at court, Licinius and Constantius's son Constantine—but I digress, *legatos,* I digress. What an intriguing vortex," the judge said, escorting him to the door.

Aelius thought, *Yes,* and recalled the day when he'd been talking to Tralles, and suddenly had felt how around the command post, the army compound, the city, and beyond, all seemed an ever-enlarging incomprehensible spiral, at the center of which lay the misery of human words and affairs.

Yes. What about Licinius, Maxentius, and even young Constantine, as ambitious as his mother Helena was keen on young officers of the Court? It was out of his hands now.

As he left, "What's the latest news on the contagion?" he asked the judge.

"The metropolis proper has been little affected, but the working-class districts outside the gates were hard hit. We no longer have a quarantine, and that's the best I can say."

I n the neighborhood of Anubina's shop, by the amphitheater, warmth and an uncomfortable damp wind stuck clothes to one's body. Few people were walking the streets. Her doorway was still locked, and asking merchants nearby, Aelius heard that two thirds of the businesses in town had reopened, but many owners still kept at a distance for health's sake, "unless they've died already."

Outside the south gate, the Philadelphia district had its usual sleepy air, and someone had even hung a garland on the door of the old chapel to the deified Trajan and his sister. Anubina's blue house under the acacia tree showed no sign of life, and no one answered Aelius's knocking. Shuffling barefooted, one of her young apprentices came out from next door to see who it was. She kept an eye on the place, she said, but had no idea when mistress might be back, in fact she knew nothing except that she was to keep an eye on things.

"I understand she was building. Could she have gone to her new house?"

"No, 'cause it isn't finished yet."

"Who would know where she is?"

The girl squinted in the sun, shrugging.

Next, Aelius went to visit Tralles's widow—the expected dues to be paid to an army colleague. She was a fat blonde who had gotten over her grief in the excitement of her daughter's approaching delivery. She thanked him for his attention while the girl, who looked about thirteen and thoroughly exhausted, sat by the wall trying to cover the bulge of her belly.

And so ended the first day of Aelius's return to Antinoopolis. A three-quarter moon struggled to appear from a sky that lingered bright when he rode back toward the mall. There he inquired of a bookseller about Harpocratio, who was reportedly due back from a business trip to Pelusium, and adding a wing to his villa. Theo was still in Rome, and—Aelius could imagine—disappointed to find out that Cleopatra Minor was really not his type. The stalls were closing for the night. How women had walked among them in June, ankles showing from their gauzy skirts, and how the sand-bearing wind had come down like sparkling rain.

Final Report, continued:

> 2. We come now to the deified Trajan's reign, shortly before Hadrian's rule. An accidental discovery (thanks to the fortunate arrest of an enemy agent during the Parthian campaign) alerts intelligence of a new Roman cell within the conspiracy. Danger comes close to the throne. The delicate inquiry is entrusted to the emperor's nephew, the future deified Hadrian, who chooses to conceal his investigation out in the provinces, under the guise of a libertine and bibulous life (see the historical commentary of Marius Maximus's). At Trajan's death, Hadrian inherits an empire never so far-reaching, so rich, or so threatened. This is why nearly his entire rule is spent in ceaseless travel and vigilance at all levels. The state's enemies make inroads in the City's power structure as well. History remembers (without citing their belonging to the conspiracy),

Quietus and Nigrinus, and others as well. The Great Jewish Revolt, so bloody and dangerous, is unrelated, but comes at a most critical time for Rome. The emperor will eventually settle it with the utmost severity, but between his successes against the conspiracy in Asia, there comes news of more intense activity threatening the Berenice and Myos Hormos trade routes in Egypt. He who wields the greatest economic power, he who controls the spice routes, will rule the world. The conspirators' names and their nationalities change with the ages; but they all agree that in order to rule the world they must crush the Roman empire. They are not faceless; they have too many faces. Thus, in the fourteenth year of his reign, despite insistent talk of possible attempts against his person, Hadrian sets off for the Province of Egypt. With him are the empress and members of the court, including Antinous. Security is high, although Roman intelligence is aware that infiltration in the army and even the imperial bodyguard is a likelihood. Incidents (see Cassius Dio for historical details) mar the trip from the start.

When the fateful trip on the Nile begins, there is near certainty that an attempt will be made at some point along the route. The deified Hadrian's account leaves no doubt about it. To make things worse, an informer is unwisely (or on purpose?) killed by a guard before he can give any particulars. Particularly perilous, in the river trip, seem the ancient sites of Her-wer and Besa. By the time the imperial barge approaches the area, the ladies and the more infirm or elderly of the distinguished guests have been left at Cynopolis. Antinous, invited to remain on land as well, succeeds by insistence to convince the deified Hadrian to let him follow. By this time of his life—and the portraits prove it—the Boy has turned into a tall and well-formed young man. As he is represented on Hadrian's triumphal arch, he has of late also let his sideburns grow into a beard. Is it mere imitation of his master and

friend, as Cassius Dio surmises? I believe Antinous has an-
other aim in mind.

It surprises me that no historical source mentions what
Antinous wore on the night he met his end. True, Marius
Maximus wrote that "his remains were gathered in purple
silk," but this was dismissed as a critique of Hadrian's exces-
sive regard for his favorite—allowing that his body be bound
in cloth meant for kings. In fact, as the account tells us, Anti-
nous donned the emperor's own outfit after he had retired
early, weary with the trip and feverish. Following Hadrian's
custom, he then paced the deck, precisely as the barge plied the
river between Her-wer and Besa.

I submit that at some point during the Egyptian tour, as
his insistence to follow Hadrian everywhere proves, the Boy is
approached by the conspirators. Hadrian makes no mention of
it, but the letters I read in Repentina's library make me suspect
it. Perhaps the Boy was tempted by Marcius Turbo himself,
who then, of course, denies knowledge of any conspiracy in his
correspondence with Suetonius. Taking advantage of Anti-
nous's closeness to the emperor, and perhaps of his jealousy af-
ter young Lucius is thrown in Hadrian's path, they try to
convince the Boy to join them, trusting in his youth and rela-
tive inexperience, and promising God knows what. Power?
Money? At any rate, the Boy realizes Hadrian is in mortal
danger. He cannot presume to accuse important men, but can
at least try to protect his master. Does he see himself as predes-
tined to do this? Do horoscopes and heavenly charts play a
role? We may never know.

ANTINOOPOLIS, 9 PHAOPHI (8 OCTOBER, SUNDAY)

Thermuthis pinned the flat braid of her red hair on top of her head.
She always got up late. Full daylight flooded her bedroom window,
showing the flank of Heqet's temple and a row of sunny façades
across the street. She slept alone, and rarely anymore received men.

Aelius, she'd invited herself when he'd last come to Egypt, for old times' sake. Which was why she let him visit her in her private apartment at the brothel.

"Yes, I know she left," she said.

"But whereto?"

"Ombi, on Hadrian's Way."

"Is she all right?"

Thermuthis looked over her shoulder from her dressing table. Her eyes searched him, then slowly returned to the array of makeup before her. From a paunchy little pot she scooped up white salve and dabbed it on her face, smoothing it upward with her fingertips, toward cheekbones and temples. "I've never seen you like this, Aelius." Massaging her neck came next, in meticulous half-circles. "Is this for real?"

"For God's sake, Thermuthis, I have to know if she's well."

"You *can't* be in love, and anyway, her family was infected shortly after she left the city. She headed for the interior like many others, but contagion was already rampant among the travelers. Her son was dead when one of my girls met her west of Ombi, while fleeing on her own right." Glancing into a drawer, Thermuthis distractedly pulled out a pair of earrings, put them back, and chose a twisted gold chain instead. "She said Anubina held the boy in her arms and wouldn't let the gravediggers take him, that she tried to crawl down into the common pit when dirt was shoveled over him." Watching him sit on her undone bed with his head in his hands, she decided not to ask him to clasp the jewel. "I know it's hard, Aelius—I'm sorry."

"Her daughter?"

"Both she and Anubina were very ill when I last heard, and her husband dead also."

"You have to tell me where she is, I have to go there."

Sharply Thermuthis turned around on her lion-footed stool. "You know she lost her other one, too."

"Her *other one*?"

"She was expecting a third child when you came in June, and lost it. I think it was because she saw you again, and it made her ill."

"She never told me!"

"She never would. She started bleeding here, while she was visiting. I had been teaching her to write, you know how ambitious and intelligent she always was. We couldn't help her, even though our in-house doctor was immediately on hand. She'd had her daughter here at the house, too. With her old woman making herself scarce after selling her, and you gone, she had no one else. A hard birth, eight months after you left." The gold chain in Thermuthis's hands glinted as she let it fall into her lap. "I believe she is dead, Aelius. Spare yourself and do not go looking."

F inal Report, continued:

3. I quote directly from the emperor's own words to convey the drama of what followed:

"The enemies of Rome, then headed by Artemidoros, merchant and gymnasiarch from Hermopolis, having origi- nally planned to assassinate Caesar in the morning during the ceremony in the city, saw an unhoped-for opportunity when they beheld what they assumed to be Caesar himself on deck, facing the water. Disguised as sailors, they brutally pushed Antinous from behind, and caused him to fall into the river. This in itself would not have sufficed to kill him, as he was a champion swimmer, but the assassins jumped in with him, and held him under water in turn until life was taken from him. By now, despite the darkness, they realized their error, and the gravity of having committed it. So, having killed Anti- nous, they at once began crying out 'Man overboard!' as is done on ships. It appeared as if, having witnessed the accident (or suicide, as evil mouths at once began to insinuate), they

leaped in immediately to try to save the victim, to no avail. Caesar was awakened by the cries, etc . . . "

Historians confirm that Antinous's body lay miraculously intact in the Nile for two days, by which time the purple clothes he had been wearing were loosened and torn off by the violent current of the Nile. Found later in one of the papyrus groves along the river, it was in these that the deified Hadrian commanded his Patroclus to be clothed after mummification, as a grieving token of gratitude for his sacrifice. Still, days passed before the emperor realized the true nature of the incident, and not at once did he identify the conspirators among his travel companions. Some, like Marcius Turbo, he suspected until the end of his life, when he finally had proofs against him, and accused him of treason—a charge that his chosen successor, in his goodness and desire to protect the senate lately so imperiled, was quick to overturn.

Indeed, well into the last years of his reign, having realized the pervasive nature of the conspiracy, the deified Hadrian's proscriptions and executions struck one by one all the Roman conspirators his agents were able to discover. Even men by the once glorious names such as Servianus were found guilty, and brought to justice (as we read in Marius Maximus). Unsure about the extent of the conspiracy in Italy and abroad, Caesar chose not to make it public; hence the imputation of unwonted cruelty by many historians against the aging and infirm emperor. No doubt toward the end his long and never quite won struggle against the enemies of Rome caused him to see himself under siege at all times. Illness, ever more serious eventually, enfeebled him to the extent that Antoninus Pius forced him against his will—though for his own good—to remove to Baiae, where, however, the emperor died.

Beforehand, however, he ensured that Antinous's body, which had always been at his side (first in his namesake temple, as long as Hadrian was in Egypt, then at his Tiburtine

villa) be translated to the nameless pyramid at the crossroads
of the Cornelia and Triumphal roads, enough progress having
been made on his own monument in Domitia's Gardens. I
read the choice not to inscribe Antinous's tomb not as an at-
tempt to conceal the identity of the beloved out of shame for
their relationship, but as a sign that the deified Hadrian on his
deathbed still feared the existence of the conspiracy, and its
possible attempts to desecrate the Boy's resting place. I hereby
ask you, Domine, to keep this wish for secrecy and the tomb's
location unrevealed.

OMBI, HERAKLEIDES SUBDIVISION, 10 PHAOPHI
(9 OCTOBER, MONDAY)

The hamlet of Ombi swarmed with those who had escaped the infected riverbanks, only to bring illness here. Housing did not suffice
the refugees, so a camp of tents and makeshift shelters had cropped
up in the windy, dry expanse around the single well. On this side of
the camp, the stench of death pointed out well before one arrived to
it, the place where victims were lined up in linen sacks for a hasty
burial. Closer in, barrows like raised scars in the sand indicated the
mass graves. Hadrian's Way ran alongside the barrows, straight as a
spear pointing east, marked by neatly carved milestones and swept by
veils of pale silt.

No one knew anything about anybody, and not even the rich
uniform, not even the offer of money made a difference. All they
could say was that contagion was at an end, but the survivors who
had weakened too much were still dying off, and no girls here, no
young women—only feverish old people. The village itself, a few flat-
roofed buildings on a nearby bare rise of the land, was occupied by
those who could afford to pay. Aelius left the horse with his guardsman and walked alone toward the scattering of houses.

As he'd so often done during a campaign, he had until this moment shut off all thoughts except those connected to the immediate
present, the next step, the next direction to take, in a void lack of

expectations. Now, however, he was too close to finding out the truth to ignore the difference it would make—the historian's hard challenge. Boots sinking in the crunch and collapse of sand, he understood Hadrian's agony during those interminable hours of searching, and how utterly useless people had been even around an emperor. From the doorsteps, wasted faces turned to him, the sick and convalescent squatted or moved about slowly.

"Where are you from, soldier?"

Aelius didn't even turn to see the man addressing him, and kept going. "Antinoopolis."

"If you know Hierax, head councilman, tell him his wife has just died."

"I don't know him."

The first three houses, crowded with women and children, had been taken over by wealthy farmers from upriver, none of them city-dwellers. The fourth was filled with bundles of clothes. In the next two houses, little more than huts, men sat on pallets playing dice. Higher than the surrounding terrain, the hamlet took in the north wind; scorching gusts between the houses created funnels that rose and collapsed depositing sand.

A corpse tightly bound in linen was being carried out of a door on the right-hand side; the two men hauling it kept their heads low in the wind, each heavy step a small eruption of silk in their wake.

Aelius would not come close. "Man or woman?" he asked.

"Woman."

"And whose house is that?"

The first man, unshaven, narrow-eyed, did not know. The second mumbled in his beard, "The seamstress Anubina's."

Aelius stopped breathing. For an instant, he had a strange split sense of reaching out for the body in front of him, and yet of running to the house to look inside, but he stood rooted where he was, half-turned to the place from which death had just been brought out. Unbearable to him like a mouth about to scream, the empty door gaped on a dark interior, and to that darkness he'd have to walk whether he wanted or not. Then, like a wavering pale flame, Anubina appeared on the shadow of the threshold, her head shaven in mourning.

She saw him first, and began sinking. Like a dream image, veiled by haze or silt or tears, ever so slowly she crumpled on her knees, folded down as a bird does, even as he clasped her to keep her from it.

He spoke with his mouth on the careworn side of her face. "Anubina, is she—?"

"My mother—I couldn't leave her behind, Aelius. Thaësis is well."

F inal Report, continued:

4. Of course, as I have known since reading the letter given me by Serenus Dio, he had also placed an account of the conspiracy and his successes against it in the grave. It was to remain a memory for the ages, since he had also given orders to destroy what remained of the conspirators. Alas, his orders were intercepted and never reached Quinctianus. To the best of my reconstruction, the army courier was killed between Baiae and Rome. As the head of the conspiracy—the Water Thief, in the emperor's words—resided in Egypt, the letter was then brought to that province. I suggest the port of entry was probably Cyrenae, from where departs the caravan route of Ammoneum-Lake Moeris-Hermopolis. How the letter was lost even to the conspirators, I can only speculate. It was July, the sandstorms beleaguered the Western Wilderness—Cambises's own great army had been swallowed by the desert! Anyway, the conspirators might have surmised orders had been issued, but when no prosecution followed, they assumed the worst had passed. They not only rallied, but even grew in influence during Antoninus's mild reign. Marcus Aurelius, who came after, probably had his end hastened by the conspirators through the introduction of plague-ridden coverlets in his quarters at

Vindobona. As for his dishonorable son Commodus, he went as far as collaborating with the conspirators, and uselessly sought Antinous's body at his Egyptian temple, to ensure there were no references inside the coffin to the circumstances of his death. It should be noted that as of this time the conspirators, ever renewed, but always powerful, ignored the existence of the account in the Boy's tomb, else they'd have savaged every temporary or possible grave site to make sure the document disappeared.

After Commodus, other Caesars were surely done in by the conspirators: I submit that among these are Pertinax (who committed the imprudence of not replacing Commodus's hangers-on after the tyrant's death, and of not executing Falco after he threatened his reign); Severus Alexander (murdered by Maximinus, whose son I suspect to have been a member of the conspiracy); Philip (unless he really died in battle) and his son; the glorious Aurelian, nicknamed "Sword-in-hand," whose assassin, the Thracian Mucapor, was listed in the rolls of the conspirators recently found in Rome. In other words, every prince who showed promise to reconstitute the glory of the empire (a task which you have at last accomplished by our good fortune, Domine) had his life attempted against and in many cases destroyed. The most recent self-styled usurpers, not by coincidence based in Egypt, were those Achilleus and Domitius Domitianus put down in the early years of your reign. And who soldiered in Achilleus's and Domitius Domitianus's ranks at the start of the Rebellion? Aviola Paratus, at the service of the conspiracy ever since his Persian days, when after being blinded he was given a chance to live by returning to threaten the Roman state. His change of heart during the Rebellion, resulting in the desertion of his old allies and enrollment in your army, was nothing but a ruse to allow him to come closer to the power structure in his quality as an

intelligence officer. Given the vigilance of your rule, he could
only look forward to being one of those agents who lie dormant
if and until a chink of weakness opens in the government. So it
was in the days of Augustus, Vespasian, Trajan, and, partly,
Hadrian himself.

21 PHAOPHI (20 OCTOBER, FRIDAY)

Baruch ben Matthias pretended to have heard nothing about the arrests in the Heptanomia and elsewhere. He and Aelius met by chance
at Theo's store, where the Jew was arguing over the quality to price
ratio of ginger roots, and Aelius had entered with his dog to ask
whether the spice merchant was back.

"He's not." Ben Matthias brandished the woody root against the
dog, to keep him away. "Why should he mind his business when he
charges enough to spend months abroad? Never mind asking these
shop boys, Commander, they don't even know the color of first-rate
mustard, much less where Rome is. I met the highway robber himself, shortly before leaving the city—happy as a fat rabbit in clover,
and saying he might stay through the winter. It surprised me seeing
him come out of a little house by the Ostia Gate, when I thought he'd
room at a fancy place."

So, he stayed at Philo's brother's even after danger passed, Aelius
told himself. The little house outside the walls had been where he'd
realized the immediate need to deposit Hadrian's letter in a safe
place, out of his hands during his stay in Rome. Two days later, filing
it at the Ulpian Library had been private and easy: one of the crates
packed for transfer to His Divinity's baths protected it now, invisible
and out of reach to everyone for a few years at least. "Well, never
mind," he said out loud, "I just wanted to say hello."

"The one who is back is Harpocratio. Shoo, dog, shoo—there's
nothing for you to eat, here." Having chosen two large ginger roots,
ben Matthias placed them in a basket, and paid. "The price is not
high, Commander. I just like giving shop owners a hard time. So,

yes—Harpocratio is back and looking for you. He's thrilled at the news that those who killed Serenus Dio will be brought to justice. None of my business, but how did you ever—?" Interrupting himself, the Jew began to laugh. "No, I'm not going to ask. I know what you'll answer, and I don't care, either. Roman justice is not my favorite subject."

Aelius smiled back, bending to pet his dog. "Roman justice is all there is, Baruch. You found that out. Roman peace is all there is."

"That's where you're quite mistaken, Commander." Already on the doorstep, ben Matthias stepped back to let Aelius pass first. "Please, you go ahead, dog and all—I insist, please. It may sound odd to your Romanized ears, but the world *is* larger than Rome. Older, too. There's talk that even now the spice routes, the wealth of the eastern provinces are actually controlled by men who may talk, walk, and act like Romans, yet are planning disaster with Rome's foreign enemies. *They say Helena's son Constantine is a favorite with them, and they're betting on his imperial bid.* But, as you would say, it is none of my business, is it?"

F inal Report, continued:

> *5. Serenus Dio's discovery of Hadrian's written orders to wipe out the conspiracy, mentioning the account kept in Antinous's grave, changed everything. Suddenly the evil work of three hundred years, perhaps more, stood to be exposed. Had the conspiracy been a thing of the past, nothing would have happened. A proof that Rome's enemies were still at work as late as the past summer is that Serenus Dio, incautiously dropping hints about his find at a house party, became at once a marked man. But those who pushed him to his drowning death (much as they had Antinous) could not find Hadrian's letter on him. Fearing for their secrecy, they killed Serenus's freedman Pammychios; in vain, as the letter was not found*

with him either. By this time I arrived on the scene. As you know, Domine, I cannot claim to have been aware of anything at first but my desire to investigate Antinous's drowning death. After reading Serenus Dio's letter, however, the shift in my research corresponded on the enemy side (for I was being watched even then, in my unofficial role as Caesar's envoy) to a change of plans, too. Suddenly, like Soter and Philo, I became the one to eliminate in hopes of securing the deified Hadrian's letter.

Once it became apparent that I had secured the letter, either by absconding it, or, as I did, by entrusting it to safe hands, the conspirators' task changed once more. They would have to follow my steps, leaving me unhurt though not unthreatened, until I led them to Antinous's grave. Through the unknowing help of my former colleague Gavius Tralles, they also placed on my path none else than Paratus himself, that seemingly unimpeachable veteran and war hero. To say that I fell for it is not a justification, but all spoke in his favor, and so it was that our collaboration began—even if it took the destruction of his vineyard (a cleverly conceived ruse) to convince me that he was pursued by the same enemies of the state. Believing that he was supplying me with helpful support, I was in fact the one keeping him abreast of my search for the Boy's grave and the hidden account.

Once the tomb was found, and the document secured, Paratus would only have to eliminate me to obtain and destroy it. Your awareness through our correspondence of the letter's existence, Domine, would have been kept incomplete without full knowledge of its content, and the conspiracy could have continued its hidden and pernicious life.

Now at last we can breathe a sigh of relief. The real Water Thief—Time—is on Rome's side again, and we are blessed among nations.

25 Phaophi (24 October, Tuesday), 304.

174th anniversary of Antinous's death

Harpocratio showed him around the new wing, among the buckets of paint, ladders, and drop cloths. "The truth is, Commander, that I am not redecorating. I am selling the place. All these months I tried to keep living here, but I can't take the thought that all his things are still here while Serenus is gone forever." Because Aelius felt embarrassed for supposing otherwise, and it likely showed, Harpocratio made a fussy waving gesture in the air. "I must shake myself from it; buy myself something. Buy myself something; go on vacation." His voice had taken once again the vapid tone, high-pitched and effete, that was as much protection as a cultural habit. Aelius was touched by his grief, much as the first time he'd met him, and like the first time, he went out of his way not to show it. Or so he thought.

"You have been very good," Dio's lover—Dio's *pal,* as Tralles used to say—was adding now. "As soldiers go, and as we've learned to know them in this province, you proved yourself a most unusual one. It makes me hope well for the future."

So it was, Aelius thought. His nature, God-given, was taken like everything else with him, for a professional trait. He didn't fit the mold others expected, so he must be an unusual soldier. Because he was a soldier, and not to be thought of outside that context. Passing from one room to the other, smelling the chalky freshness of paint, he wished there were a way to paint over the preconceived ideas others had of him or of anyone. A room is a room, like a man is a man, but soldiers and Caesars and homosexuals and murderers and whores, all were seen exclusively for what they did, or appeared to do. It was a historian's job to make sure of that—minding the *deeds.*

Hadrian, so long ago, had by far exceeded the mold in all aspects of his life, and his biographers had not been able to accept that slippery, mercurial self. They'd only been able to describe him by paradoxes and opposites, losing himself after the disquiet reality of a troubled imperial life. As for the Boy, in death he managed to be all that everyone wanted, whatever and whoever he had been in life. So much so that in the end it mattered little what the real individual had represented. It was all a question of interpretation.

And so with history. Perhaps there was no objective getting beyond the gossip, and the historian was relegated to the butler's role, an eye to the crack in the door, ear strained in the cupped hand. A door stood always between him and the past, him and the truth.

"Are you going back to Rome after this?" Harpocratio asked.

"No."

"Nicomedia?"

"Probably. I have to finish the biography, and have more to begin."

"And then?"

Then, who knows. Aelius had no idea, no other plans. He would wait. Even Anubina needed time to heal from her suffering, before agreeing to join him with their daughter. She had accepted no arrangement between them, had not moved in, had wanted nothing but transportation back to her blue house in the Philadelphia district. He'd known she still loved him as far back as the day he'd sat at her table, and she'd given him food. Things were so simple and so in plain view, when one did not complicate them. Give me time, she'd said, I can take no happiness before I let go of grief.

Opening a door onto the garden, Harpocratio asked, "So, are you satisfied with your research?" and stepped outside.

"No."

"Why not? You even made us all safe again."

"Let's say it's the historian's curse."

"There's a nice view from here, Commander. Come see."

Walking out on the terrazzo, where his host waited for him, Aelius considered it a strange metaphor of his task, that he should emerge from shadow to sun (Death, the beyond) in order to escape rooms and hallways redone, repainted, always only half-seen. Because, contrary to what biographers would like to think, history ends with its protagonist's life. The rest is—in one way or another— always conceit, and legend.

Harpocratio leaned over the banister, his golden little curls sitting like salad on his head. "Why can't you be satisfied, and just enjoy this lovely view?"

"Ask me in ten years."

"Why? We're Romans! Ten years from now the view will not have changed."

EPILOGUE

Shortly after Diocletian's abdication in 305, Licinius murdered the emperor's wife and daughter; Maxentius and Constantine separately usurped the throne, and fought it out with Roman armies at the Milvian Bridge, where Constantius's and Helena's ambitious son won the bloody day. Constantine's first official act in Rome was to visit Diocletian's great baths, alone, and requisition—from the lot brought in crates from the Ulpian Library—the file under the rubric of the deified Hadrian.

GLOSSARY

The Names

CAMBYSES—ancient Persian ruler, whose rich army vanished without a trace in the Egyptian desert

CASSIUS DIO—Roman historian

CICERO—Roman orator, whose daughter Tullia died young

DIODORUS SICULUS—Greek historian

HERODOTUS—Greek historian

MARIUS MAXIMUS—Roman historian

PLINY THE YOUNGER—Roman governor and writer, friend of Emperor Trajan

ROMULUS—legendary founder of Rome; he kidnapped women from the nearby Sabine tribe as wives for his men

TRANQUILLUS SUETONIUS—Roman historian

XERXES—ancient Persian king, believed to have buried an immense treasure

ZENOBIA—Middle-Eastern warrior queen, first an ally, then an enemy of Rome

The Ranks

DOMINE—imperial form of address, from Dominus = Lord

EPISTRATEGOS—governor general (of Egypt)

LEGATOS—a Greek term with many meanings: envoy, commander, lieutenant-general, ambassador

PRINCEPS—Latin for army leader, head of a specific unit, but also prince, and nobleman

STRATEGOS—Greek for commander, general; in Roman Egypt, also
   an administrator

TRIBUNE—Roman army colonel, regimental commander

COMES—Roman generalissimo; precursor of the medieval "count"

The Places

ANTINOOPOLIS/ANTINOE—vanished city along the Nile, named after Hadrian's favorite

ASPALATUM—today's Split, city in Croatia

BAIAE—resort town near Naples, where Hadrian died

BITHYNIA—a Roman province in what today is northern Turkey

BRIGETIO—Szony, a city in today's Hungary

COMMAGENE—ancient province in today's southern Turkey, toward
   Syria

CROCODILOPOLIS—Egyptian town, named after the sacred crocodiles

CYNOPOLIS—Egyptian town, named for sacred hounds

DACIA MALVENSIS—Roman province, covering parts of today's
   Romania and Hungary

DALMATIA—Roman province, today's Croatian coast

HEPTANOMIA—"the seven provinces," a Roman subdivision of Egypt

LEONTOPOLIS—Egyptian town, named after the lion

MOESIA—Roman province, occupying part of today's eastern Romania

NICOMEDIA—Diocletian's eastern capital, in today's Turkey

OXYRHYNCHUS—Egyptian town, named after a bony fish of the
   Nile

PANNONIA—Roman province, more or less covering the area of today's Hungary

PARTHIA—Land south of the Caspian Sea, due east of today's Iraq

PRAENESTE—today's Plaestrina, historical town near Rome

TIBUR—today's Tivoli, near Rome, where are the much-visited ruins
   of Hadrian's great villa

ZEUGMA—a city in Commagene

The Ships' Names

FORTUNA ISIACA—Isis's Luck

FELICITAS ANNONAE—Prosperity of Provisions

FELICITAS AUGUSTORUM NOSTRORUM—Our Emperors' Welfare

PENTHESILEA—Queen of the Amazons

PIETAS AUGUSTORUM NOSTRORUM—Our Emperors' Mercy

LAMPROTATE—The Shining One

THETIS—A sea nymph

TYCHE—Fortune

The Measures

ARTABA—Egyptian dry measure unit, about 1 1/6 bushels

DENARIUS—in Roman Egypt, a coin worth 4 drachmas

DRACHMA—a Greek silver coin, 3.5 grams in weight, used in Roman Egypt

MODIUS—grain measure, equivalent to a peck

Greek and Roman Expressions

ANAMNESIS—Greek for "recollection"

CHIOS—a high quality Greek wine

GRAVITAS—severity

LOUSORION—midsized cargo ship

LUDUS MAGNUS—principal gladiators' training school in Rome

MUNDUS PATET, SUPPLICIA CANUM—holidays: Opening of the Afterworld; Execution of the Hounds

NOME—one of thirty Egyptian administrative divisions, each headed by a *strategos*

PLINTHEION—brick house or city block

RESTITUTOR EXERCITI—imperial title, "He who rebuilt the army"

SACRIFICATUS, THURIFICATUS, LIBELLATICUS—terms indicating those who recanted Christianity during persecution: by offering a sacrifice to the gods, by burning incense to them, and by recanting in writing

SELECTI ALAE URSICIANAE—Chosen Unit of the Bear-Standard Regiment, Aelius's bodyguard

SALUS IMPERII—safety and well-being of the empire

SERVUS VILLICUS—a slave employed in a country estate

SI MONUMENTUM QUAERIS, CIRCUMSPICE—saying, "If you seek something large, look around"

TRANQUILLITAS NOSTRA—Diocletian's definition of his reign, as "our age of tranquility"

PRINCIPAL ROMAN EMPERORS

B.C.E. – before common era   C.E. – common era
(The dates indicate years of reign)

AUGUSTUS 31 B.C.E.–14 C.E.

TIBERIUS 14–37 C.E.

CALIGULA 37–41 C.E.

CLAUDIUS 41–54 C.E.

NERO 54–68 C.E.

VESPASIAN 69–79 C.E.

TITUS 79–81 C.E.

DOMITIAN 81–96 C.E.

TRAJAN 98–117 C.E.

AELIUS HADRIAN 117–138 C.E.

ANTONINUS PIUS 138–161 C.E.

MARCUS AURELIUS 161–180 C.E.

COMMODUS 180–192 C.E.

SEPTIMIUS SEVERUS 193–211 C.E.

CARACALLA 211–217 C.E.

HELAGABALUS 218–222 C.E.

SEVERUS ALEXANDER 222–235

GORDIAN I, II, III 238–244 C.E.

VALERIAN 253–260 C.E.

AURELIAN 270–275 C.E.

CARUS, CARINUS, NUMERIANUS 282–285 C.E.

DIOCLETIAN 284–305 C.E.

MAXENTIUS 306–312 C.E.

CONSTANTINE 306–337 C.E.